British Summertime

BRITISH SUMMERTIME

PAUL CORNELL

A MonkeyBrain Books Publication
www.monkeybrainbooks.com

MonkeyBrain Books
11204 Crossland Drive
Austin, TX 78726
info@monkeybrainbooks.com

ISBN: 1-932265-23-6
ISBN: 978-1-932265-23-1

Printed in the United States of America
10 9 8 7 6 5 4 3 2 1

Acknowledgements

Thanks for help, research, support, inspiration and critical comments to: Caroline Symcox (for love, always); David Bailey; Sue Bamford; Clayton Hickman; Steven Moffat; Jonathan Morris; Stephen O'Brien; Nick Pegg; Justin Richards; Cavan Scott; Nick Setchfield; Viv Turner; Mark Wright; Lucy Zinkiewicz and the Goodfellows. To my wonderful editor, Jo Fletcher, and literary agents, John McLaughlin, Bethan Evans and Don Maass. To my brother Terry for introducing me to science fiction, and to Mum and Dad, for bread and butter and honey.

Finished on May Day, Beltane, the feast of the Apostle James.

For Lisa Gledhill

I know that he is guilty of having the pictures on his computer, but he is not a paedophile. He never abused kids. Paul thinks paedophiles should be strung up.

The wife of one of the members of the
Wonderland internet child pornography ring,
quoted in the *Independent*, 15 February 2001

Know ye not that we shall judge angels?

Corinthians 6:3

There's probably something in *Revelations* about shit like this.

Nick Hasted, review of *Pokemon 2000:
The Movie* in *Uncut* issue 45.

Prologue One: Chipshopness

Fran finished casting the circle. "You can step inside it now," she said to Alison.

Alison had been getting cold waiting. It had taken them ages to light the candles. And for what? They were standing on the hummocky side of Bathford Hill, with a wet forest above them and the rain-lashed lights of the city of Bath down below. They'd walked up here through the woods from the car park. Alison's coat had holes in it.

"I'm only doing this because it's you," she said, and stepped inside.

Fran had started reading books about Wicca because she worked in that shop. Her latest craze lasted a week. Alison hated anything that required her to sign up for anything. "God," she'd said to Fran, when she proposed this, "is sleep." And, she thought now, the Devil is depression. She could feel the edges of it making this whole wet night dull. Only Fran's smile was alight. Alison took something not requiring prescription every morning, and that was working out. But still sometimes, particularly in the evenings, she felt everything was meaningless, and rather than curl up in a ball on the sofa and sweat and make little noises, she would go to bed and sleep.

Fran was about to do the incantation, or whatever it was she was going to do. But then she stopped.

Alison looked and sighed. There was a torch light in the trees down the path.

They waited some more. The rain fell on Alison's head.

Her dad would have disapproved of her doing this, if he were still alive. Alison felt a weird moment of fondness. It made her feel close to him, even if it was the him just before the end. Alison's mum was Jewish, which meant, she'd once said, that she "didn't have to put up with all that religious shit." Dad had probably been speaking in tongues on the night before they'd both died.

The light vanished into the trees.

"Probably just a homeless person," said Fran. "They come up here to shelter in the caves. That's how I found this place. I came here at Christmas on the food and blanket run."

"So some pissed crustie is gonna come and join in the ooga booga?"

"If they do, then that's the will of the Lord and Lady."

Alison snorted snot into her hankie.

Fran took a deep breath and addressed the darkness. "This is Imbolc,"

1

she said. "The arrival of Spring, and happiness and new things. We're here
to celebrate that, and to bring in to this circle the Lord and the Lady." She
looked at Alison. "Is there anything you want to say? To wish for as the
seasons turn?"

Alison thought for a second, and found, as she wiped her nose, that she
did have something to say after all. "Make the future safe."

"That is so Alison Parmeter. Here." Fran used her knife to cut an apple
and gave half to Alison. "We don't know what the future will bring, but
that's a good thing to ask for. We'll bury what we don't eat, so it can
grow."

Alison forced a smile. There were things about her which her mate
could never know. She bit into the apple.

August, 2000

Alison had muttered that maybe she'd like to go up to the Edinburgh
Festival.

Fran had jumped up and down and made herself a tartan hairband. The
Common Tartan, so as not to offend anyone.

She had been preparing for a working holiday in the Peak District, an
environmental charity sort of thing, down some caves. But she'd saved up
enough to do both.

They drove up from Bath in Fran's Fiat Panda.

They got pissed in the Pleasance Courtyard every night. Alison found
all the best productions to go to, picking and choosing from the kids with
leaflets on Prince's Street, until Fran started to say that all these plays and
comedy shows must be fantastic.

Alison made a little gruff sound in the back of her throat.

Two nights before the end of their stay, they left an unfamiliar pub in
an unknown street, a long way from their guest house, and went in search
of a chip shop.

Fran led the way. "There'll be one somewhere along here," she said.

She led them up all the wrong streets.

Alison let her. She tried to keep her frustration hidden.

They went down side streets which were obviously going to be lined
with small tourist and gift shops. Then main streets which had things like
W.H. Smiths.

They didn't go down any chipshoppy streets at all. Instead they passed
junctions to streets that were distinctly more chipshoppy.

Alison made herself keep walking, following Fran's bouncy steps.

After half an hour and a big circular path right round a big mountain
of chipshop potential, Alison finally stopped.

The look on Fran's face made her laugh. "It's probably just down here," she began.

Alison pointed in the other direction. "*This* way," she said.

She led Fran out of the non-chipshoppy area, and followed the gradient of increasing chipshopness. The chipshopness became more and more intense until eventually, beside a nightclub, a 'bab van and two pubs that were turning out loud students, the potential became reality and a chip shop manifested.

"Bargain," said Fran. "How'd you do that?"

Alison looked at her for a long moment, wishing she could tell her. "Lucky guess," she said.

Prologue Two: Seventh Heaven

Fran weighed the big rock in her hands and then heaved it to one side. It landed with a satisfying clunk that echoed away down the wet caverns. She peered forward, letting her helmet lamp illuminate the rock pile in front of her. No dark space. No gap as yet. No change in temperature.

It couldn't be long now. She turned to smile at Mick and Jules. "Can we bring the drill today?"

"And piss off the bats?" said Jules.

"No, you're right. The poor bats."

"I thought we had it, there," said Mick. "We're never gonna get through to the bugger." His face was white with rock dust.

Fifteen hundred feet above the three of them, it was teatime on a wet Sunday. The workers of Poole's Cavern had grown used to the thought of Grinlow Hill, the rump that the caves wound through, lying atop them, bringing the rain down into the valley. On top of the hill, Fran knew, was Grinlow Wood, with the lime workings and the humus that was absorbed through centuries down into the caves. That mixture of chemicals created the "poached eggs," stalagmites that grew fast, grew in human time. One of them had even started to form on the metal rail that ran alongside the tourist trail. The workers and guides didn't call them that privately, of course. Red and round on the top, tall and knobbled on the shaft. The cavern where they grew in their hundreds was Cocks Cave. Fran said to the others, when she'd had a couple of beers, that naming things like that was to let folk get a handle on things. She couldn't actually imagine the distance of rock above her head, understand that they were really under a forest. Intellectually, yeah, but not inside. Giving names to rock forms and stalactites—the Swan, the Mary Queen of Scots—was to make people think they were in control of what was going on down here. The seam that ran along the roof of the caves spoke of an ancient stream that had once come through here. Then it had made its way through a rock pipe as wide as itself. But the water, over millions of years, had broadened its course to create the caverns. That new space had given it room to become a rushing river. Fran would try and communicate her continuing wonder at these things to the others when they were at last orders in the Oak Leaf up near the treeline of the town. They'd laugh at her, because she'd only been here two weeks. But that was because they felt the same way about the place, though they'd been here years. She was just the only one who'd tried to find the words for it.

She stood straight and rubbed her lower back. She wasn't getting paid for this. This was fun. She'd been interested in caves since she was tiny, and the drippy dark forests and gullies of this bit of the world were way different from Bath. Her mouth was dry like it only ever got in the caves. She had hay fever, and that was another reason she liked to be down here, even losing her Bank Holiday Weekend, which she was allowed to have off. You didn't get pollen down in the sixth cavern.

She could hear the river rushing now. It was just getting its strength together. The loudness of that, the colour of the trees at the prim little entrance way, these were the signs that made Fran look forward to the coming of autumn. She looked forward to it because then there were fewer tourists in Bath, and the little hippie bookshop where she worked for Mrs Skipper got a bit full up, but not too full, and everyone squashed into the pubs and was noisy. Summer in the caves, autumn in Bath. Fantastic. She could do this every year. She ought to bring Ally up here next time. Something to get her out of herself. Fran had said in a postcard that she wanted her to come and see this place. Ally would see so many things in here, in that way she had of finding the little details other people missed. Maybe even find something buried in a corner somewhere. If she could get her away from that tosser with the Porsche for five minutes.

Ancient Britons had only come into the very first of the caverns to live. They would have liked the way the caves stayed at the same temperature throughout the winter. That was part of the commentary. (An archaeologist must have told one of the directors that many years back. Soon Jules or someone would have to write to people again to check that what they were saying was still thought to be true.) And if they'd lit a fire, then they'd have been very snug—like Fran hoped the homeless people in the caves above Bath could get snug. The Romans had stayed just that far in too, though there were five more empty caverns beyond that entrance, and they'd have been obvious, even back then. Fran thought it was because of the river, the way it roared and echoed like it was the angry god of the hillside. But that couldn't have been true in high summer, when the roar would be silenced. Maybe in summer the ancients forgot the cave and went and lived out in the valley. Or maybe they respected the god even when it was silent. The Romans had practised religion here, all right. They'd had their god of the springs, to whom they'd sacrificed jewellery and coins. They broke the pieces before dropping them into the waters and leaving them, so no earthly thief could spirit them away.

That was something else Fran talked about more than the others did. The way the Caverns were about broken trinkets. The Britons had left behind ruined and broken jewellery too, because they'd had a metalworking shop in here. They'd stamped their failures into the mud. And then the bandits of the fifteenth century, like the mythical Poole himself, who was both a robber and a giant, had come down here to scrape the edges off the pennies they'd nicked. Enough scrapings and you got a bar of gold, and you could still use the pennies.

The six caverns, to Fran, were the place where gold was broken and left. Early on in her employment here, she'd taken a pound and carefully squished it down into the mud, then caked it over. One for the future archaeologists. Not that they wouldn't have enough from the pool where the tourists threw their coins in. Jules harvested those for charity boxes, but she wouldn't have got all of them.

The man called Mick had proposed to his Helen down here, nearly a decade ago now. The engagement ring and the rock, and the shiny cathedral atmosphere of the sparkling lights on the wet surfaces... Fran could see it reflected in his eyes when he talked about it. At the time, he said, they'd just been trying to be alone, allowed in by Mick's key late on a Saturday night. They'd made love against the rocks in Cocks Cave, and Mick had touched one of the stalagmites accidentally. He'd watched the acid of his hands turn the angry prick a sooty black over the next few weeks. Whenever he passed the place he saw it, and thought of Helen, he told Fran. Though he couldn't ring her from so far underground. He'd often trudged back to the entrance and used the office phone on a whim. I were just thinking, love, how about we go out tonight? Or stay in. Mick had enough, he often said. He had his calling, the caves, and he was paid enough to keep going with it and keep a house and take his wife out to eat every now and then. His attitude made Fran smile and think of Marty, back in Bath. Marty was always saying, "yeah, okay," and grinning. He never had any money, because he'd buy rounds and pot with his Giro cheques as soon as he got them. She missed him, but he was on the phone, and he liked the sun, so he wouldn't have wanted to be down here with her.

It was Mick who'd set about the seventh cave, years ago. They'd known it had been there since the eighties. A radar scan of the rockface had revealed a vast space, with bizarre, angular features that didn't reflect like they should. Lots of mineral deposits down there. They'd had an expert come up from London and sketch out the sides of the huge emptiness with a marker atop a lighted table. So Mick had arranged for a geological survey team to stake out an area in the woods and send drills down to find the top of this new cave.

"Treasure in heaven," he kept saying. And if there were giant poached eggs or undamaged stalactites in there he'd be right, in terms both of the geology and the tourist trade. The drill had broken through and a tiny spy camera had been sent down the tube, and Mick had gathered Jules and the other workers in his office to look at the pictures he'd had e-mailed to him. He'd shown Fran the photos in the little museum by the entrance. They weren't the best images, because you couldn't light them properly, but what was there looked grand: a cathedral space, with the river running through at the bottom. Interestingly murky graduations below, like stepped volcanic rocks or some such. Something angular. You could throw a bridge across it and have the first cavern space in Britain that really rivalled what they had in France and Germany.

So Mick had got permission to dig through to what he'd christened Seventh Heaven. Jules had written up some new site posters for the museum, saying they'd be through to Seventh Heaven within the year. But it wasn't going to be as easy as that, they'd soon discovered. The bloody bats had been the problem. Two species of rare bat lived in Poole's Cavern, a tourist attraction rarely glimpsed by any tourist. Fran liked to sit on the bench by the entrance and see them fluttering out into the twilight, like agitated little leaves, their cries sometimes audible when they reflected off the rocks in the valley.

You couldn't disturb rare bats like that with digging machines and drills. Or so the woman from the Department of the Environment had said. So Mick got the gang together and they walked to the end of the sixth cavern, where the Sculpture, or the Brain as they called it, sat in front of the Rockfall. They talked about how deep that rockfall was, and how long it would take to move it, working only with their hands and picks, moving the rocks back along the Cavern like in *The Great Escape*, doing it only on closed days. They'd decided on three years. Which was all right. They were all lifers. Once you got into the Cavern, it got into you. They'd all courted down here, except Jules, who probably had, only she'd never say that to anybody. They'd all sat alone right at the back and switched the lights off and found their breathing getting slow and calm in the odd warmth for someplace so cold, and the odd dryness for someplace so wet. And now Fran was one of them, because she'd done these things too. People like Mick died in the job. He could reel off everything there was to know about stalagmites, and he could make little kids shut up and gasp by turning off a switch.

Fran's aim in life was to meet people like that and smile with them.

Those three years had sneaked past them. Mick had gone grey around the temples, but still had the pony tail. Two years ago, Jules' young man had been killed in a motorcycle crash on one of the bends through the valley. She'd become even more quiet; had started to keep everything inside her, Mick had said. She was smiling in all the old photos, Fran thought, looking at the pile of rocks. You put any of this crew back to back with what they'd been like when they started this... And they hadn't done it for money, but for the sheer joy of finding stuff out.

They didn't know if it'd be today, or tomorrow, that they'd break through. They had a set of hydraulic supports standing by, and a bottle of champagne waiting in the stream, secured in a net. They'd stopped moving the rocks right out of the Cavern and into a skip a week ago. Now a large mound of them sat there by the Brain. They had last dragged the radar in here two years ago, to check the rate of progress. Now they were just following Jules' maths. It was possible that the champagne would wait in the stream for another week or two.

By then, Fran would have gone home. She was half thinking about chucking her job back there, just to see them get through here. She wanted to be here for the ending of the story. But that would upset dear old Mrs Skipper, and Fran couldn't do that.

"Y'all right there, Fran?" asked Mick.

Fran realised she'd been staring at the pile of rocks, her hands on her hips. "Stupid rocks," she said.

Mick laughed and wiped his moustache on the back of his hand.

She bent to her task again, braced her legs and lifted another large rock.

She saw it at the same time as she heard the whistle and cry from the other two.

Darkness.

There was nothing in the gap beyond the rock.

As she was putting the stone aside, the gap gave way some more, the rocks falling inwards.

"Seventh Heaven," whispered Mick. He grabbed Jules and lifted her off her feet, and she whooped like she was the Jules from the photos. "There we are, my girl!"

But Fran felt she couldn't join them just yet. She'd have felt stupid. She knew she had a big smile plastered all over her face because she'd pulled open the door, she'd done it! A smell of something like Guy Fawkes' night, of gunpowder, was settling from out of the gap. But this felt weird, and not quite right yet, a bit of a fairy-tale. Because there was something else.

"Look, there's a light in there," she said.

It was coming and going, like something was moving inside the new cave. It reminded her, for a moment, of the light that had moved amongst the trees on the night she and Ally had done Imbolc. The same mystery. A bat, something inside her said. It'd be catching the edge of the light from the cave bulbs and their own helmet lamps. A bat meant there was an entrance none of them knew about.

But it wasn't moving like a bat.

She leaned closer to the hole to shine her helmet lamp through it. The other two were clustering behind her, Mick putting a hand urgently on her shoulder.

It was like a coin, flashing in the hands of a magician, catching the light at different angles. Fran leaned in further, nearly putting her head through the gap. There was just that glittering light, that falling leaf of gold, with brown darkness behind it.

And then the leaf turned, and the light wrapped around the object, and it was looking straight at her.

The face.

It looked satisfied. Certain and determined. *It's a statue*, she thought, stamping on her fear in a second. *We've found a statue.*

And then the face opened its mouth.

It was looking straight at her.

There was a flash. Fran leapt back from the hole, yelling.

She fell to the floor of the cave and scrabbled backwards, her legs trying to push her up so they could propel her away and out of the Caverns, into the light. There was something in her eye.

Jules and Mick were yelling, getting to their feet, turning to look at her.

Look at it! she wanted to yell. Look at it!

But something seized inside her.

She felt her arms and legs slowly halt, like they were buried in the tar of a nightmare. She was tugging against a great weight in her limbs. Something slow made her veins pulse and ache for a moment, like something was being shoved through her, something heavy on her heart. She felt like crying.

She saw Jules and Mick moving towards her, looking down over her, concerned.

Behind them was gold.

The face rose over their shoulders. It was standing behind them.

She couldn't be quite sure now that it was a face. Her eyes were telling her that it was more complicated than that, that each plane of the thing was catching the light at different angles. That it was catching light from no source of light. That it was casting shadows of its own on its own face. That parts of it were near, and parts were far, and parts were hidden by other parts.

But there was something more basic that told her it was a face. A sense of three interlinked circles, leaning over her. The Trinity, the three rings. With her arms and legs as stumps, she struggled, moving from her shoulders and knees, reacting to it.

The head rose higher above Jules' and Mick's shoulders. Fran knew she was crying now. Her face was wet. Her bladder had emptied. She could hear her own voice, because she could still hear! She could hear the urgent words of her mates, the clatter of them grabbing her. Jules was saying get her mouth open. Her own sounds were grunts, urges, primitive woman sounds.

The gold face was silent.

It stood high above them all now, looking down from the cave wall.

Fran knew that there both was and was not a body beneath it. It was a giant. Or it was a bathead. A golden, twisting leaf. Blowing in the no-wind.

It was still looking right into her.

It was beautiful.

For a moment Fran was on an aircraft.

She and Marty had flown to Prague on a cheap weekend break she'd saved up for. To surprise him on his birthday. She was humming silently as she sat beside him, his hands happily clasped in her lap. Her eyes rested on the clouds below them. The smooth hum of the plane. The brown and golden fields of people's lives. Moving by. Underneath.

Now. Absolute now. No past or future.

This had been her most still moment. She knew that like you know things in dreams. She knew she was in pain elsewhere. She wondered, lightly, if she'd been brought here to get away from that. Then she realised she wanted things. She wanted a drink. Her mouth was dry. She wanted to watch the in-flight movie. She knew that her headphones were missing from the net seat pocket in front of her.

She turned to Marty, wanting. Uncomfortable. She'd suddenly become very anxious.

"How long are we here for?" she insisted. "How long? I need to distract myself from that. I need to pass stuff on. I need meanings! What's to be done?!"

He looked fearfully at her. "What are you talking about?"

There was a flash. An impact of something in her.

She tasted blood in her mouth. She was biting Jules' hand.

She opened her mouth in shock and yelled a proper yell.

Her body collapsed onto the rock floor.

"Fran!" Mick was saying. "Can you speak?"

"Yeah..." Fran closed her eyes and let her head flop back. "Yeah, oh no, Jules, I'm sorry! Your hand..."

"Don't worry about my hand!"

She opened her eyes again, and saw that Jules was wrapping her hand in her coat, her eyes still fixed on her.

Mick got to his feet. "I'll call for a doctor." He ran off back down the caves.

Fran listened to the distant crunchings of his feet as he ran across the gravel. Familiar sounds. She licked the blood off her lips.

Then she remembered.

She jerked again, urgently, looking round for the face. But there was no sign of it. She made herself look at the gap in the rock again, but now there was just comforting blackness inside. The face, she thought to herself, hadn't been there.

Jules was looking at her, worried, caring, holding her right hand hard with her left. Her coat was covered in blood.

"I'm sorry," Fran said. There was still something inside her. She was different now. Fran was gone. The dream wasn't over. It was only just beginning.

Prologue Three: The Dream

Judas Iscariot stood on the Mount of Olives, looking west, over the Cedron Valley, down onto the city at night. There were lamps here and there, around the huge block of light that was the Temple and at the Governor's palace, but the sleeping city lay mostly in darkness. The smell of the anemones was heavy in the air. They were what made this place into a garden, rather than just one of the scattered groves of olive trees that gave the ridge its name. The master seemed to like this place. They'd stopped here often on the way to and from their lodgings in Bethany. Maybe it was the view. Or maybe it was that this place stood exactly between the city and the desert, the resting space between one thing and another.

"The things concerning me have an end," he'd said that evening, at the meal. He'd said that one of them would betray him, and had told Simon Peter to take the money he'd kept for food, and to buy a sword with it. So Simon would be forced to use it. So Jesus would be able to demonstrate his mercy to the victim of that attack. That had all been obvious to Judas immediately.

He had read the Scriptures in detail. Since his youth, he'd been expecting the fulfilment of these stories. Why was it that the others were surprised when such fulfilment came about?

And now the master had said those things to bring their fellowship to an end. There'd been no other subject of discussion ever since he'd declared that one of them would become a traitor. Or maybe that someone had always been one, a mole within the group who'd been running back and forth to the government with information.

Judas hadn't been able to help himself. He'd asked if it was him. If the master knew that... But, of course, he'd said nothing. He'd just looked at Judas with that beautiful smile. And Judas had known then that he really was going to do the terrible things he was going to do. Jesus had caught his eye a little later. "Go and do what you must," he'd said. His tone of voice was even, as if the instruction were to go and distribute money and the remains of the food to the poor, as was the custom. Or that he had to go and pay their Temple Tax to the office of the High Priest, Caiaphas, as had always been his duty. The others had taken it one of those two ways. But Judas knew. Judas always knew. And in his heart he'd thanked his Lord for making it clear.

Before Jesus had spoken, they'd been discussing which of them was the greatest, the most loyal. Who would be with the master to the last, and who would be the first to leave. Judas had had Peter's vote for the greatest of their number. Because, he supposed, he arranged everything, took care of the details, allowed the master to do his business in the world without having to be concerned with worldly matters himself.

The master was going to be brought down by trivialities. By the handyman.

Judas wondered how many of them thought that Peter was the traitor. The one who tried too hard. The one who was always looking over his shoulder. Peter was utterly terrified of what the next few days were going to bring. Judas could tell.

Judas had been walking to try and keep himself awake. A little while to go yet. He had returned from his errand and followed the route to the lodgings, up the hill and out of the city. He had not been surprised to see the fires lit in the grove. He had advised the Decurion of the possibility. From the pattern of the fires, the master, as was his habit, had taken Peter, James and John a little way off to pray on their own by the little river. Judas supposed that, as a result, calculations were being made amongst the group. Did separating them like that mean that Peter and the other two were above suspicion, or exactly the opposite?

He had started the end of things. He was actually going to do it. The bravery of the man, as always, astounded Judas.

Judas felt awkward about returning early. He could understand everything but his own actions, read everything but the choices of his own heart. It was all written. He had no choice in the matter. But because it was written, he was not sure why it should be written in him. He decided that he wanted to see some of them again. One last time. He wanted to hear friendly words while they were still to be heard.

He walked back into the grove and saw that some of the others were still awake, sitting in a group, talking in low voices. He went to join them. Bartholomew was trying to light a fire. Thomas and Simon were with him.

They looked up at Judas with some suspicion. "Where have you been?" asked Thomas. "It's been hours."

Judas sighed and sat down with them. "Thinking about the future," he said. "Looking at Jerusalem on the way up."

"Don't worry," said Thomas. "I don't think you're the traitor." He glanced at Simon. "But I've heard some of us saying it's you, Simon. You're the Zealot. You want to overthrow the Romans. The master doesn't seem interested in that, so—"

"Doesn't he?" said Simon, doing his best not to bridle at this oldest of disagreements, judging by the expression on his face. "It seems to me that's exactly what he's about."

"So who do you think it is?" asked Judas, looking around all of them.

He knew, or had a good guess, of course, what each of them thought, but it was the one topic that would prolong conversation and, freezing as he was tonight, he needed the warmth of his friends. Just this one last time, please, Lord. Let me enjoy them for who they are a while yet, before they hate me.

Bartholomew stopped trying to light his sticks and considered for a moment. "The tax collector," he decided. "The one that's worth the least to the master, that's closest to money, to sin."

"Don't be ridiculous," said Thomas. "I very much doubt that—"

"Have you thought that it could be Andrew?" asked Simon.

A noise came from behind them. It was Simon Peter, walking to the fire. His face said that he'd overheard them, but he kept the smile of the disciples in place, and his voice was gentle. But he gave no greeting. "I do not suspect my brother," he said.

Judas had started this little round of the sport, but now he hated it. It was like one of those games of latrunculi that the guards at the palace played endlessly. Now he just wanted it to be over, for the two glass Thieves to catch the King between them.

"Since you are *all* my brothers," he said loudly, "I do not see how I can suspect any of you! We are casting our stones without looking into our own hearts! This whole discussion is foolish!"

Peter put his hand on Judas' shoulder. "Well said."

Bartholomew had resumed his efforts. "I think the master has chosen this topic of conversation to test us. To see if we remain brothers."

"Or," Peter said, "to make an end."

They were all silent for a moment. Judas wanted to meet Peter's gaze, but couldn't. He hoped too much that there was someone else to share his burden. He got to his feet. He could waste his time elsewhere. It was selfish of him to stay here. "I'm going to get some water. I'll go round the back, so as not to disturb the master."

Peter smiled at his concern. He got to his feet too. "I should go back to the brothers and wait for him."

Judas couldn't help but stoop to take the hands of Bartholomew and Simon before he went. They managed to smile and acknowledge him, and Simon apologised for what he'd said about Andrew, though Peter assured him there was no need.

The two men walked silently for a while until they got near the river. "Will you come to wait for the master?" Peter asked.

"No," Judas said. "He didn't ask me to. I have to obey his commands."

"As you wish," said Peter, and went on his way.

Judas watched him go, carefully continuing on his own way for a few paces. Peter was the one who looked down on them all from his gentle position on high. Even down on the master, sometimes, when he had a love for him like a sibling. He was their big brother. And Judas loved him too, as he loved them all, as he loved Jesus enough to betray him to the exact death that was prophesied in the Scriptures and prepared every day in the city below.

To truly become what he was, God's Son, Jesus would have to die. Judas had seen from the first that none of the others, not even Simon, had the will to sing this last verse of the song, had not even thought of what life would be like without the master.

It was Judas' curse that he was always thinking. He had known the man was the Son from the first time he'd heard him speak. Not the *Messiah* that would free the land of the Jews with a thousand swords. But a different sort of Messiah. Judas had been a messenger boy and hand servant for the Governor's office. He had met Pilate twice. He had been responsible, in that service, for gathering together a mob and nearly killing one would-be Messiah, kicking him down the street. So Jesus might have been worried to see the lean, sharp face at the back of the crowd when he was walking down the street, allowing his hands to touch any who wanted to touch him. He had stopped and turned back and pointed straight at Judas. "It's you," he'd said.

"It's me," said Judas. Jesus had moved through the crowd, and had taken both his hands. And from that moment, his life had changed. He had never paid much attention to anything before, though he had always been able to hear lies for lies and follow a running man through a crowd. But as soon as he'd given up his job, and faced down the laughter of his friends with a shrug, and started wandering in and out of the city with Jesus, he realised that he'd started to see things differently. He saw the way the water ran, the way the birds flew, like some Roman with his auguries. He had known Jesus was what his life was headed for and created for the moment that he had met him, moments before, even as he'd heard his voice in the street and felt the world shift under him.

He had thought, for a while, that the others had this gift of reading. That they were predicting, moment by moment, which way the flock of birds would wheel. But then he won all games against them, and knew they did not.

He had wanted the others to see the path this had put him on, to take Judas aside and stop him from his pre-ordained course, to even put a sword through him rather than this.

But no. His course was obvious as soon as the world became obvious. Jesus had to fulfil the prophecies to be Christ. Therefore that, along with lodgings and food and ways in and out, had to be arranged.

He had gone to one of Pilate's men this very day, a Decurion in the auxiliaries. Someone he'd known, vaguely, in his old life. He had offered lies to Pilate about Jesus' recent activities, said that he wanted money in return, that he shared everybody's desire to have this done with before the Sabbath. He had insisted that he would give his information only to Pilate himself. A spy's request to make himself bigger than he was. But Judas just hadn't wanted lies about his master to spread outside of Pilate's palace. He supposed they would in the end. When the charges were read. That would be the hardest thing of all. All the more reason to make sure that, for a while more at least, his master's reputation would equate to his character. That outside, for a while, would remain the same as in, and intention would match action before those two separate designs meshed in a death that would need all intent to be the best action of the world.

Judas wondered how long it would be before the Kingdom. His eyes looked into the darkness between the trees. It might be forever. Or it might be immediate upon the sacrifice.

Pilate had been exactly the same as when Judas had been his servant. Rushed, hardly understanding anything about these strange locals and their foreign customs, and covering that up with a stumbling imperiousness. He didn't recognise Judas' face. He had his part to play too, of course. Only he had been chosen because he was the wrong man in the wrong place. Because that made him a fool.

Judas had been chosen because he was wiser than his peers. Something had picked him up as a baby, by the scruff of his neck, tossed him forward into history, and declared: "Judas Iscariot, I choose you!"

He went to the nearest tree and held it, holding his face against the bark.

There came a noise from nearby and he flinched, jerked around, thinking that the end had come too soon.

It was John, wandering back from being with the master. He was staring at Judas. His eyes were as big as the moon. As always. John talked oddly, every now and then. He would start coming out with rhymes, and declare things that felt like pieces of ill-made furniture, sentences with words that jutted and wobbled. Judas and his master both liked John. Judas found restful the times when the man made no sense. There was nothing to find in John's words, then. Although there would be, one day, when all the pieces flew together and miraculously there would stand a chair. It was like rolling the dice, every time, and sawing on the basis of what you'd rolled. One day the dice would be right and John's eyes would behold something more apt than anyone had ever seen.

Jesus called John a battleground, an abode of demons in which the Holy Spirit nevertheless moved. He would throw back his head and laugh when John made no sense, which made those around them uneasy, sometimes. Jesus had once said to Judas that he didn't mean that demons made John come out with his strange fancies. It was John's character when he was not drunk on whatever stars made him that way that was the battleground. Judas had understood that straight away. John would step away from women in the street, complain that they were unclean. Jesus had had to admonish him, gently, over the presence of Mary with the group. John had kissed his master's feet then, and had taken Mary by the hands and knelt before her too.

Now he opened his mouth, and Judas waited for what he had to say.

"You will never eat the scroll," he said. "Though it be forced on you seven times, or seven times seven."

"Yes," said Judas, feeling his usual sense of relief. He gave John a quick squeeze round the shoulder and sent him back towards the fire. "You go and get some sleep, brother."

John wandered off into the grove, still muttering to himself. In the morning he would be fine, as he often was. He could debate philosophy in the most profound way when he wasn't afflicted.

How wonderful it must be to be mad and free like that.

He had an hour or so yet. For a moment, he prayed. Please, Lord, let there be another way. Change the world. Intervene. See to it that he and I do not have to die.

Because Judas would have to die if his master did. By his own hand, or by Simon's sword. Not by Peter's. Big brother would never believe the truth in time. Judas could make Simon do it, the words would come to him, as the words had come to him to persuade a houseowner to give up his upstairs room for the meal that afternoon, as the words had come to him to arrange everything for life, and everything for death.

He could, he was sure, find the words to save himself, even. To persuade the others that he was not to blame for what was to come. Jesus would go along with that, would allow him to lie so that there would only be one death instead of two. Or he might order the disciples that no harm should come to his betrayer.

But that could not be. It was obvious.

There was no answer to his prayers, and every answer, in one.

Judas raised his head. He had sworn to himself that he would not go to his master and ask that he be spared this. Not when his master would not spare himself.

So they both would die. That was read now.

For it was not right that Jesus should die and Judas Iscariot should live.

He knew what his name would become. He knew that the other Judas of the disciples, the fair-haired boy who hardly had a beard, would be renamed by those who repeated this story and wrote it down. All *so* obvious.

He was the weakest link.

"Goodbye," he said, and with a last glance back over his shoulder, he slipped off through the trees to find the soldiers.

Alison hit the floor.

She woke up. She had her duvet wrapped around her.

She was lodged into the gap between her bed and the wall.

She turned her head and managed to get a hand onto her mattress. She levered herself up and hauled herself to fall back onto the bed.

Again. She'd had one of those dreams again.

What was it about her life that made her dream about Judas?

One: Is the Light on Inside her Fridge?

September, 2000

There were two things about Alison that Fran didn't know.

One: chipshopness. Alison had often demonstrated her skill in front of her mate. But Fran had never really got that there was something that went much further than intelligence and judgement going on in Alison's head.

And two: since she was little, Alison had had a morbid fear of the End of the World. Maybe it was growing up in the eighties that had done that, with the prospect of nuclear war on telly all the time.

The two things went together, Alison thought. One produced the other.

This autumn morning, Alison was walking in to work from her flat on the Upper Bristol Road, and her head was more than usually full of shit. The only thing that kept her walking was the idea that things would be better tonight.

Normally, Alison quite liked autumn. It was hard not to, when you'd lived all your life in Bath. The city seemed to relax when the sun was low and the golds and reds of nature matched the buildings. In autumn, even when it was raining, it was usually like the rain in a black and white movie on a Sunday afternoon. Lights would come on in unexpected places, and the little covered streets near the library would become full of people. The pubs would get crowded and the beer would go down well. Bath was designed by the old and the drunk and the Luftwaffe, and their combined efforts resulted in a city of autumn.

Normally, Alison quite liked Bath too. She didn't know why. Because she didn't know why was probably why she loved it. It was a continual relief. Just for once, just in this one case, she couldn't see the wood for the trees. Bath was just a bunch of great things set up and down a slope in a lovely valley. Wa-hey! Who could think about that?

But today it was raining in great sheets, like it had been for days. It made the hills above the city look dull green, and the buildings look dull brown. Today the autumn held no promise of anything but winter. It had been like this for two weeks.

Today, her thoughts were full of death. Like they had been for two weeks.

Ever since she'd got back from Edinburgh.

Fran had gone home to see her folks and had packed for Staffordshire that night and had been gone in the morning. Just two weeks ago. But in those two weeks Alison had wilted.

As she slopped along through the puddles, past the kebab shop, heading towards the bottom of town where she worked, she thought about last night's dream. Jesus and his Disciples in the Garden of Gethsemane. Where had all those details come from? Something her Dad had told her. She'd wanted to talk to him about other stuff, but he'd just go on and on. Dreaming about Judas. At least it hadn't been as dark as some of her dreams lately.

Dreams used to be good too. Like another life where stuff happened that she couldn't explain and didn't have to. But since Fran had left... Everything seemed to be since Fran had left.

She stepped over last night's chicken cartons and stomped chips and a thrown-up something, which she knew instantly before she looked away was Chicken Chop Suey. This was the little square with the tree, where the crusties hung about in the evening.

Patrick would say—

Patrick. Chuck or not chuck?

As always.

But it had got to a point this time. The arguments for and against reared up in her head again, and she shoved them back down. It was just a boyfriend, just one tiny relationship.

It wasn't the End of the World.

But it felt like it.

Just like this autumn felt like an autumn for the world.

She stopped to look into a shop window and saw an assistant drop a school cap onto the head of a tiny mannequin.

She turned and went on her way.

Tonight, all this shit was going to come to a halt, because tonight Fran would be back in Bath. Seeing her again would make everything okay. And maybe the two of them could laugh about the thing which had appeared in Ally's future in the last two weeks, which, like some childhood ogre, was now haunting her every thought.

"The End of the World," she said to Ted.

He unlocked the door of Linley's Racing and let her in with a grunt. There were times when you could say anything to him and he wouldn't notice.

"I can't get it out of my head," she said. "The End of the World is coming."

"Oh ah? You'd better go and change your board, then."

Ted was an independent bookmaker, a pouch-cheeked master of racing, with the face of someone who spent his time exactly divided between the windy downs of the stable runs and the smoky interior of the shop. He'd done well with Linley's Racing and had decided to branch into football, cricket and, to some extent, spread betting. You could pick a figure as to how many runs Nasser Hussain would make in the Test Match, and bet on him getting less or more than that, losing or winning money with every run that took you away from your target.

To risk getting into that business, you needed carefully selected limits (£10 per run) and good sources about your sports, people who lived and breathed football and cricket and could tell who was likely to do what. Such people could formulate tempting-looking baits for the window that were actually much worse value than they looked. Newcastle win 2-0 over Bradford, Alan Shearer scores first. You'd put a tenner on that. But someone who knew that there were six guys in the Newcastle squad more likely to score than Shearer, that he got his goals these days through lurking around the goalmouth, rather than in that initial fifteen-minute adrenalin rush when goals were usually scored in Newcastle's game, that the Newcastle defence usually let one through even when they won bigtime... add that to Bradford, who might let five or six in... it wasn't really worth a pound, let alone a tenner.

Alison hadn't paid any attention to sport before she'd seen the advert in the *Guardian*. But she'd instantly seen that this job, based in Bath, was the one she was best suited for in the world. She'd been in her last year at the uni then. She'd sent off the letter of application, carefully weighted with all the local reassurance that someone from Bath who advertised nationally would be after, and spent the week between sending it off and getting the answer watching and listening to sport all day.

That had been enough to get her past Ted's audition, although she'd made a couple of blunders. The Sunderland striker Kevin Phillips had been injured during her week of research, so she'd been unaware of his existence. But two weeks later, during which she'd kept up with her homework, Ted called back and offered her the job.

Only then had she told him that she still had three weeks of university to go. But he'd been willing to wait. And so, to Fran's amusement, Alison had gone from mathematician to oddsmaker in one move.

The twenty thou a year was a side issue. She could have made five times that playing the odds of the other bookmakers. Being in a shop doing something mathematical, meeting people, using her talent... This, Alison had thought, was one of the few jobs where she could have fun. Where chipshopness could be good.

For the first few weeks it had been. Until she'd learnt everything. Until she started to do it automatically. Until she'd met all the people, and they were mostly old men, that were ever going to come through the frosted, nicotine-plastered door.

Out of that moment of frustration had come her big idea. The Long'uns. Big chain betting shops, like Ladbrokes, took on huge, stupid bets with very long odds. Life on Mars; Elvis still Alive; Aliens Land. An independent like Linley's couldn't afford the huge whacks that'd result if any of these came true. But Alison had persuaded Ted that some of these mad things attracted bets and just weren't going to happen. The Elvis one, for instance, went on her slate. She called around the chains and got their sample odds on the Alien ones, and cut them in half. Ted spent a Sunday morning in the backroom talking it through with her, and finally he'd nodded and said they'd give it a go. Alison got her own wipeboard in the corner for her Long'uns, and a display board in the window.

The board did what Alison wanted. It brought in new trade. But that didn't keep her head up for very long. The guys who came in to make stupid bets on these things weren't the intellectual bandits she'd hoped for, the guys with the hotline to NASA and the subscription to *New Scientist* who'd run in to grab those odds as the saucer hovered above the White House lawn. They were, instead, men who didn't care about keeping their money. They were usually there with a gang of other blokes, and they'd put some normal bets on the horses, or more often on one of Alison's spreads, and then they'd look up and smile at the board and slap down their money and say "and a pony on Elvis!" like they were proud to be chucking it away.

These were the sort of men that Alison stayed away from. She could read all of what was on their faces. She peered out from the backroom where she was bent over the sports pages, and would wince at the sounds of the board going into action again.

When she asked him to take it down, Ted said she was mad. They were making money they'd never have to pay back. These lads wanted to give it to them. If Alison didn't want to call odds that were never going to be used, he'd do it himself.

So the board stayed put.

She had met Patrick in the betting shop.

He was a big black block of overcoat with a blob of golden hair on top.

"And a pony on the aliens!" he'd said. "And you are?"

"We're going to have dinner twice," she'd said to him. "Then go for a ride in your... Jaguar. Shag at your place."

He'd blinked and kept his mouth shut.

"And then fall into a relationship that will last a long time." She'd taken care not to say "slump." "So why do you want to throw your money away?"

"Christ, dear one!" he'd laughed, looking at her like she was a tasty morsel. "It's only money!"

As Ted bent now to pick up the letters from the mat, she went to the board and looked long and hard at her most tasty Long'un.

The End of the World: 5000/1.

It was tasty for Ted because of how it was defined. The extinction of all human life, by any means. The ultimate bookmaker's bet: one that could never be collected.

They told them that, and they still put money on it.

That was one of the reasons she'd started to become convinced it was about to happen.

She grabbed the cloth and worked the marker pen off the board. Then she wrote the new odds, the odds she felt this morning, into the fuzz of old felt tip where they kept changing.

3000/1.

Ted looked up. "Summat going on, Alison?"

"Not," said Alison, throwing down the cloth, "for very much longer."

The End of the World.

Alison stared into her glass of Bellringer.

The day had been grey, rain, smoky men, racing noise, newspaper print on her hands. Now she was in the Garricks, waiting for Fran.

Why did she think the world was going to end? What did that mean?

It wasn't three thousand to one. It felt like a dead certainty. She would have bet on it, but for what Fran meant in her life. Fran would never bet on anything.

Alison had no idea how it was going to happen. She didn't consciously work out what was chipshoppy and what wasn't. She didn't know how reading about a football player in Hello! gave her information about how he was performing on the pitch. She fed match statistics, interviews and profiles into her head, and out came what she needed. She asked the thing questions, without really knowing she was doing that, and it gave her answers. Only in the most simple cases could she walk back through the process and say, that's why I thought that. She could train herself, like she'd done for the oddsmaking job, by exercising the skill in a particular way. She'd heard that tennis players reached for balls before they could see them coming, that cricketers at the highest level had their eyes closed when they hit a six. It was a samurai thing, a performance beyond herself.

She'd often hated it. It was what made her dark to Fran's light.

But never before, in her whole life, had it led her here.

The End of the World. It felt like a folding-in, like an equation that defined a certain set of things that could happen and no more, with the parameters getting smaller and smaller. The image in her head was of origami going the wrong way, of paper vanishing into her hand.

Every new detail of Britain now seemed to turn back on itself. The News of the World, "naming and shaming" paedophiles. The fuel protestors and their pickets and convoys. The World Climate Summit breaking down.

Fran also thought these things were awful. But she didn't see them as steps. Slippings. The way the world would crumple into itself and die.

Alison told herself that it was just the rain, just her moping at how the dream job had turned out.

But no: she wasn't depressed right now. She was right.

She drained her pint in one long swallow.

She was always right.

Which was bad news for the world.

She heard Fran walking up to her from behind as she lowered the glass and found that she had a great big smile of relief on her face at the familiar footsteps. Thank God. "Hiya," she said, getting to her feet to give her a hug.

Fran smiled back at her. "Hi," she said.

But Alison felt it then. Felt it in the hug.

She stepped back from her. "What's wrong?" she asked.

"Nothing," said Fran. "Why?"

Alison looked her up and down.

There was something. Alison knew as her friend looked at her that Fran returning to Bath wasn't going to bring the relief she needed.

Because now there was something of the End of the World about Fran, too.

Two: No Logos

They were the legion.

They were from the future.

There were two steps to membership: baptism and confirmation. The words are Christian, but they were beyond that. They were the answer to Christianity's question.

Fran was one of them now. She was them.

But she was still aware of herself.

She was sitting down in the pub, in her body, saying hi to Alison.

It wasn't like she *wanted* to tell her. She didn't really *know* this stuff. She was speaking, telling Alison about the journey home and how this dull old woman started talking to her on the train.

Which didn't sound like her at all.

It was important, Fran knew, to keep the I. *We* had *no* ideology. That was very important. *We* had only the mission of the Four. *We* could do *anything* to complete the mission. But there was a feeling in the *we* that it was important that they were still many individuals. But that wasn't an ideology. If they had had an ideology they wouldn't have been able to enter the Underlying Ideology and infest it.

That was as much as she understood. She, not *we*. But she'd only been baptised. She hadn't been confirmed. She might know more then.

It distracted her from Alison for a moment. She wondered, in that moment, what these strange thoughts meant.

Fran wished she could get this thing out of her eye.

Time is ours, she thought.

A sign on the way down south saying the time was sponsored by Accurist had made her laugh, because it chimed between what she and *we* were thinking.

> *The human body is ours because food is ours. Anorexics have to die to escape us.*
> *Reproduction is so us. This is the horniest state I've ever been in.*
> *Because I can see the camera angles.*

She could imagine the sudden techno swoop around the table as Alison got up to get her a pint. She could imagine herself, sitting there, the hero of this story. Being part of *we* made you the protagonist. She looked great. Zoom in to her eye to see the gold gleam there for a moment. She was CGIed now. Full of power.

She could see the values in the pint Alison brought her. Tradition, genuine, quality, organic, history.

Tradition is ours. And the future is ours.
Genuine is ours. And lies are ours.
Quality is ours. And waste is ours.
Organic is ours. And artificial is ours.
History is ours. And history is our best, biggest lie.

"Why are you laughing?" Alison asked her.
"I don't know," said Fran. "It's good to be back."

It's good to be the Prince of the World.
Woo woo.

Alison was starting to panic inside. It was like talking to a shop window dummy.

"Let's just have the one here," she said. "Then we'll go on to some other places."

Alison and Fran walked through Bath at night, the rain pissing down on them. Everywhere there were people: groups of kids walking, sitting on benches, swinging around the white poles with the floral displays on top, drinking in the street and tripping over.

Alison looked at Fran. "So tell me about the caves."

"Oh, you know, I dunno if I'll go back. It was all..." She shrugged.

"How was... what was her name, Jules?"

"Fine. How about All Bar One, do you want to do All Bar One?"

Alison inclined her head a little.

At All Bar One, in the lights of the Abbey which boomed in through the big windows, Alison stared at Fran while she talked happily about getting back to the shop, and how Mrs Skipper was thinking about doing the place up for Christmas, and how her Mum was taking driving lessons. But not about the huge worry that was sitting there in the back of her head. The question was, was it something that Fran was finding the right moment to tell Alison, or something that she was never going to tell her? Questions like this came up for Alison all the time. They defined her relationships with her friends. Human faces were full of cues, languages of thousands of shouted, whispered and spoken syllables, gushing all at once. Alison could only get the gist, thank goodness. But the gist, and this had been hammered home during a first year at university of bleak loneliness, duty on Nightline, six boyfriends, election to Welfare Chair and three suicide attempts, two of them serious, was that sometimes people genuinely hated, feared, lusted after, wanted to kill, were jealous of, wished harm to and loathed those people whom they also loved without question.

Once she'd understood that, somewhere between the haze of the wrist bandages and chairing her first Welfare Committee meeting, she'd been fine.

Ish.

But much more careful.

"Are you pregnant?" she asked.

"Oh no, why, do I look fat? No, I'm not pregnant! Cheeky mare!"

"Very Northern."

"No, come on, why do you ask?"

Had she got involved with someone up north? If it was something like that, why didn't she want to tell her about it? She wouldn't tell Marty. Though she would feel very sorry for him. No, Fran would never do that. She would have gone straight to him, done the right things. "You just look really tired," she said. "Like you're a bit down. On the inside."

These days, when she saw one of those big opera feelings sweep over a friend's face like the shadow of a cloud on a wheatfield, Alison could usually say just the right thing. It was concealment, these days, that really got to her. Holding back. Lying. Because she could see the wall, but usually not what was behind it.

Patrick said everything that crossed his mind.

Concealment coming from Fran right now was doubly painful, because Alison really wanted to open up to her, to say something about the End of the World. She'd kind of planned the conversation in her head. She'd lead to it from talking about TV shows like *The Weakest Link* and *Survivor*. They were the shows that would have been made in the last days of the Weimar Republic if they'd had television: the nasty laughter, the heckling of human sadness.

Life is a cabaret, old chum.

She knew that Fran agreed with her about stuff like that.

Fran sighed, her eyes meeting Alison's over the rim of her glass. "Yeah, well, I am. A bit. I need to get pissed, come on."

So they did.

They drank at the Hobgoblin and the Assembly and the Rummer until chucking-out time, and they talked about stuff like how shit *Big Brother* was, although Fran seemed to be agreeing with Alison just because she was her mate.

At last orders, they went to the 'bab shop on Great Pulteney Street and got some chips, and then sat on a bench by the bus stop, their backs to the great weir behind them. The rain now had dried to a few splatters in a wind that ripped around the corner. Kids were standing around the 'bab shop, queuing, about to go clubbing, eating their chips. The last few punters were leaving the Rummer. Above the parade of shops was the Parade Hotel. A few lights were on here and there in the guest bedrooms. There were a few lights in the bridge too, where people lived over their shops. Alison could hear the rush of the weir behind her, and the cries of seagulls circling for dropped chips.

Alison finished her 'bab first. She turned to look over the railing to where the river was rushing down the weir, getting bigger and fiercer every day now, carrying with it whole branches.

There was a duck there.

It stepped up onto the highest shelf of the weir and was washed back down again.

It tried again, and was swept once more back to where it had been.

It tried again. And failed. But it looked like it was going to keep on trying.

Alison wondered why a duck was doing that. She could only see it because of the pale soak of white light that illuminated the weir. She couldn't figure it out. Which was great.

She looked back to where Fran was carefully munching her way through her veggieburger. "Good?"

"Mmm." She was looking off into the distance, still troubled by the huge weight that spoke to Alison of the End of the World.

It was time for the big guns. "I think I'm going to chuck Patrick," she said.

"No!" Fran turned to look at her, her mouth satisfyingly open.

And the next thing she was going to say was: "Fantastic! He's such a rich wanker."

But what she actually said was: "That's terrible!"

Alison almost carried on speaking. The realisation of it stopped her short.

Then there was a little bit of pleasure. Looking at Fran's smile. A surprise.

And then it troubled her. Through the drink. For a moment.

Fran suddenly just continued, "No, no! You're my best mate, right? You want to chuck him—fine. I'll kick his arse!" And she kicked the air. "You want to marry him—fine. That'd be better. As long as I'm the best bridesmaid. I am gonna be the best bridesmaid, aren't I?"

The *we* was getting very good at letting the I run in the right way, Fran was thinking. They were agreeing with Alison. They were letting Alison's ideology do all the running.

That seemed to be a natural state for the *we*. A default mode. To be part of that was such a relief.

Alison seemed to be reacting to Fran just like she would if it was still just Fran she was talking to.

She made one mistake, talking about the conditions of being fat and thin. That wasn't something Fran would say.

Fran knew she could reject the thing in her eye. The *we* allowed free will. That was the whole deal. But then how would she live?

The thing she was part of ran everything. They had for thousands of years. They were going to be in charge into the far future. If she wasn't part of it, she'd be against it, and that would be terrifying and, worse, she'd be powerless. She so didn't want to be powerless now.

To get out of what the *we* had made, you'd need to do something inconceivable. Something terrible.

Fran was thinking about how little cash she'd got while she was talking to Alison. It was easier to think in the two ways while she was pissed. She wanted so many things. A really nice car, one which had a CD player. Wanting felt good. She worked in a very stupid place. Mrs Skipper was a complacent, fluffy little woman who'd boxed Fran into going along with all the things she believed.

God, how sad had she been?

The look on her face when Fran told her she was quitting was going to be so wonderful.

Alison had been boring tonight.

The contrast between her life and Fran's now was stark.

It was like the moment in the movie trailer where the narrator says "now." Now they're on the run. Now she's breaking loose. And the music goes all *Jump Around*.

Now Fran is finally free to have the time of her life.

"Of course you are." Alison was now watching every muscle in Fran's face.

"So it's like when... you know Alex thought I shagged Marty that night, upstairs at that party, while I was going out with Alex, and I only talked with Marty?"

"Yeah. This is Schro—"

"And Alex chucked me for it, and told everybody that I'd done that—"

"Yeah. This is Schro—"

"And then Alex got all mates with Marty again, and agreed with him that he'd never done that with me, but kept on hating me for doing that with Marty. And I'm like, what is this—?" She pointed vehemently at her crotch. "Schroedigger's pussy?"

"That. Yeah." Alison threw her head back and laughed at the line she'd heard so many times. Relieved. This was still Fran. "How is this like that?"

Fran frowned. "Like what?"

Alison leaned her head on Fran's shoulder for a second. "Fran. What is it you want to tell me?"

"Nothing."

"There is. Go on. I've been waiting for it all night."

"Mine's nothing at all. It's really nothing, Alison." She paused and thought for a long moment. "Something happened in the caves. I will tell you, okay? Just not now."

"Okay."

"I've got to sort it out in my head."

"All right."

"But it's not about you. You know that? It's not about you."

They held hands for a moment, and Alison felt really hugely better about this. "I know. I do now."

"So what about yours? What is it you're worrying about? That's not Patrick."

"How did you notice that?"

"Well I notice things too. I'm very sensitive."

"You are."

"So tell me."

Alison made herself look steadily at Fran. "It's the End of the World, Fran. An ending like a book has an ending. Everything's getting knotted up. Caught up in itself. Turning in on itself. Like the umbilical cord's got tangled. Like something's got inside it. I don't think there's any way to stop it. I can think of Christmas, but not far beyond it. I can't imagine another February. And it terrifies me, Fran. And there's nobody I can tell."

But she didn't say those words at all.

She'd just imagined saying them. In drunken precision. In some world where what was inside her could be let out, where she could communicate, and all her reading of the world would be put to some use in making her way through it.

Alison bit her lip. When she was seven, a girl in her class had asked her how she could always guess what they were going to have for lunch, and Alison had told her it was because she was very clever. The girl had bullied her for the next three years, and got everybody else in the class to bully her too.

One big wall between Alison and the world. Even between her and her best mate. And she'd only think of that reason when she got home.

"I'll tell you mine when you tell me yours, okay?" she said.

"But it's nothing about me?"

"It's nothing about you."

"Okay."

"Okay."

"So—" Fran dropped her wrapper onto the pavement. "Let's go to the pub with the glass door."

"Okay," said Alison. She turned back to the weir. The duck was still trying to take that step upwards, still falling back.

She turned back to Fran. She wanted to say that Fran would normally have carried that until she found a bin.

But she couldn't find a way to say that either.

A few streets away, in the Green Tree, a middle-aged man in a really good wig and excellent prosthetic make-up was laughing his head off.

His name was Douglas. He was tucked in at a tiny table in the corner with three big lads from a builder's merchants in Walcot. It was drinking-up time. They were laughing at the looks they were getting from a table of office girls across the bar. The looks were, Oh God, keep them away, but the builder's merchants had taken that for encouragement and were muttering growly one-liners to each other.

Douglas loved it. Good old rough cheer. He'd only met these lads tonight, but they were the absolute salt of the earth. What Britain was all about. Douglas liked nothing more than to meet some people he liked in a pub and talk to them for a while and then go on his way again. He loved the bottom end of Bath. The lowest point of the slope.

To him, the city was like a cunt. There were the springs, that went deep down into the ground. There were the folds of complicated and messy stuff, leading from the sink at the bottom to the rarefied heights at the top. There was the ragged line of several linked streets that ran right down the middle, connecting everything. And there were the churches and high buildings, phalluses, pins that were placed in the thing to stretch it out like a butterfly on a board. He'd seen some images like that. They always reminded him of his home town.

This lot knew him as Tony, a photographer from Box.

He slapped his hands on his knees in a theatrical sigh. "Oh, I don't know. Women!"

The leader of the gang, a big man with a ginger beard, guffawed. "You treat 'em rough—"

"And she'll be eating out of your hand!" another broke in. The youngest one. He had a goatee and a tanned neck around which he had a little loop of beads.

How old was he? Seventeen? Still a virgin. If he'd been gay, Douglas thought fleetingly, he might have fancied a boy like that. But there was no way he could be gay. Not if he wanted to get along. He was a man of the world, he'd had a few girlfriends, just missed National Service, nearly got married once, but her dad didn't approve. That was what he'd told them. That was his role as Tony.

He'd really enjoyed playing that role tonight. He'd winked when they asked what sort of photographs he took, and had then sobered up and said, no, you know, babies lying on their front on rugs, that sort of thing.

In his time, he'd been a plasterer, an ice-cream man, a lollipop man, a football commentator on local radio. Many other things. Now he'd met this lot, he had enough to be a builder's merchant to the next crowd he drank with.

He did this professionally, as well as for fun. And for protection. From the very people he was one of.

He let his eyes drift over the girls across the bar, closed tight in their circle, in their suits. One of them tossed her hair to glance back at him, then looked away. The others already looked beaten down by the world. Shaped. Fitted in their places. But she looked awkward, the new girl, not yet certain what she had to be to get on.

Not knowing was always the most lovely thing in the world. He was half the misogynist he pretended to be.

No, that was a dangerous thought. He looked back to his mates.

They were good lads. He was like them. He was not some maniac. He was like all of the ordinary, decent, straightforward people who made their lives in this city.

He closed his eyes for a moment as they thumped the table with their glasses. He was getting tired. Too tired to laugh along any more.

He got to his feet and took a long look at the girl across the way. He'd been wrong. She looked up at him. All that worry about her eyes. All that make-up. Already. It was a shame. "Gentlemen," he said. "It's been a real pleasure."

The men got up too, shook his hand, slapped him on the back.

"Women, eh?" said the youngest of them.

Douglas headed for the door.

Alison and Fran ended up at the pub with the glass door. It was at the top of the town, beyond all other pubs. It stayed open late, way past opening hours, but locked up. You went and knocked on the door and, if the old Goths behind the bar liked the look of you, they'd let you in.

Fran tripped over, landed with her palms on the door and kissed the glass, leaving a lipstick mark.

They let them in.

They ordered red Breezers.

"And big..." Fran held her arms wide. "Big gold bracelets. Broke up into pieces. It's all about broken gold. The caves."

"Terrible. Breaking gold. I had a necklace when I was little. This girl broke it.'"

"Grrr. I would have punched her. I would have kicked her." Fran kicked under the table. "Ow."

"Met a bear. Late at night."

That wasn't Fran. That was a voice from across the pub that made Alison's brain switch on. Like something lunging at you in the street made you sober, just for a second. Her mind had caught what he'd said. Passed it on up. 'Cos it was important.

The voice had come from the booth across the way. A boy with a tight green T-shirt and a frizz of bleached hair was waving his pint about, his mouth open in a sort of daring half-grin. He was talking about something forbidden, Alison instantly understood. A drugs conversation? He was talking too loudly.

About *bears*?

She didn't understand. She could feel the crap bit of her brain twisting around it. How could you *meet* a wrap or a tab?

That was why her brain had picked it out. It wasn't often it found something it couldn't read.

She raised the bottle to her lips and slid the drink down her throat in one smooth motion. It rocked her insides.

She'd found something else that was a mystery to her. Hooray.

Fran was talking about something slowly, many times, going over it again and again.

The trailers, Fran knew, were usually better than the movie, because the trailers told you what was absolutely the hottest thing, and the movie, even the hottest movie, was what was hot yesterday.

We, the Golden Men, were like trailers. *We* were a rumour, *we* were like the best bit of gossip. *We* were what was coming. But *we* had always been here.

Well, *we* had arrived sometime before history, anyway. The Four had split up when they arrived, and went in different directions, doing different things. *We* lived in people's heads. *We* were an idea. And sometimes, when necessary, that idea would leap out of brains into what human beings saw as the real world. Then the Four have bodies, and can be hurt. They once were individual mortals. They stored their bodies in the idea those bodies interfaced with.

Fran realised she was repeating individual words from this stuff, over and over.

The Four had been trapped, just for a few years. For a tiny span of time. Before and after *we* were free to do what *we* had to do for the mission. There was ritual and there was purpose, but there was no ideology, only what *we* set up for the rubes, the ticket-buying public.

We were gentlemen. And, Fran thought, therefore she was a lady in the gentlemen. There wasn't a lot of female feeling. She was one of the boys. *We* were showmen. *We* were the snake wrapped round the tree of human history. *We* brought people fire. *We* put the desire in their bellies so that they'd develop and move on and want things.

Fran had freed them. Freed *we*. She had moved aside the last stone. As *we* knew someone would, because *we* had written the story in which that happened.

We are so money. *We* are so phwoaarr. *We* are so everything.

And I let we *escape.*

I'm so proud.

Why was there something sad about *us*? Why do *we* feel like *we*'ve already lost when *we*'ve already won? Is that what's necessary to make *us* keep *we* going? Is that what keeps *us* mad and angry? Do *we* need to have desire too, when *we* fulfil all desire?

What was this angst when *we* were the world-dominating masters of creation? God, *we* were in charge of these insects, so what else was there? What was there for *us* to envy and feel jealous of?

Maybe it was because *we* were the authors. *We*'d come up with this story. *We* knew how it turned out.

Fran looked at the boy across the room and her body shivered. She kept the words coming out of her mouth. Alison had noticed him. There was something about the way he and his friends were moving, strutting, so big in this little place.

Oh fuck.

Confirmation was coming for Fran.

Alison looked back to the kids, who were talking in whispers now about their secret thing. "Hey," she whispered to Fran. "What are they talking about?"

"Who?"

"Them. They said bears."

They turned to look at the kids around the table.

A few moments later they realised that the kids had stopped talking and were looking straight back at them. The boy with the golden hair was grinning.

He came over and sat down and started to talk to them. They were being chatted up! Alison shared a smile with Fran. She burped on the Breezer and asked the boy to get them both another.

And from then on, everything got complicated.

Three: There's No Truth in the Rumour

April, 2129

They had been talking about the music, Leyton would remember later.

Ralph Vaughan Williams, "The Lark Ascending." Jocelyn had been complaining, wanting something more modern.

The *Crimson Dragon* was arching up the wall of Earth's gravity well, its wings shining as it slipped out of the planet's shadow into the sun. The music reached a peak just as the *Dragon* did, sliding over onto its back and rotating to even out the heat distribution on its surfaces.

Leyton found that he was humming along— until Jocelyn started humming along too, but in a mocking way. He looked back over his shoulder and frowned at her. "Corks, Joss, do you have to harp on so?"

"I'm a captive audience, Squadron Leader." Her casing turned a notch so she could look him in the eye. One of her immaculate eyebrows was raised. "You're going to have to choose. Allow me my foibles or put something on the jolly old deck that I can dance to."

"Dance?" He thought his eyebrow probably matched hers.

"Yes, dance! Didn't your last head dance?"

"No. Bit of a wallflower, old Toby." Toby had taken the brunt of a shot that had filled the cockpit of the *Crimson Dragon* with molten metal: a parting gesture from a wing of rock bombers, some of the last of their kind, caught as far out as Pluto orbit. Toby's instinctive last thought had taken the ship back to the emergency dream bay at Borneo. Leyton had ejected without knowing where he was and had been caught in the nets. There hadn't been enough left of Toby to hold a proper second funeral. The Padre had said the benedictions over the flag, and that had been cast out into space from one of Borneo's locks the following evening.

The next morning, when the *Crimson Dragon* had rotated through the station's engineering section, Leyton dropped into his seat to find Jocelyn waiting for him. That had been three days ago. Despite all his protests that he should return to action as fast as his ship had, Wingco had made Leyton take his five days' combat leave, a luxury the Fleet could afford these days. Besides, he'd decided at length, it was only good sense to get to know your new head out of combat.

They'd gone on a series of proving flights: suborbital hops; station-to-station runs; dreaming out to Europa and back. Leyton had found that he wanted to talk to Jocelyn about Toby. But he didn't. Bad form, to talk of the twice dead to the ones who'd come to take their place. He'd made it to Squadron Leader through that silent lottery. Since he'd joined Dragon

Squadron, six of the pilots and eight heads, including Toby, had fallen in combat.

So today they'd been aiming to dream all the way out to the Oort Cloud, to visit the cometary garrisons, a major test of precise navigation that held the distant possibility, if one of the garrisons went to alert status, of joining a combat patrol. The Wingco had carefully ignored that possibility and offered no orders against, surely aware that after three days Leyton was starting to feel rather useless. Being back in freefall was one thing, but it was the terror of combat that he really craved... as long as his chums were out there in terror also.

In Earth orbit was the last place Leyton expected to hear an alert signal. He'd been reaching out to adjust the volume of the music, a compromise that he guessed Jocelyn wasn't going to accept with good grace—

—when suddenly the cockpit was awash with red light, coming from starboard to indicate the direction of the threat, and the bass throb of the proximity alarm was booming from under his seat. The music cut out.

Without thought, he grabbed the joystick and rolled.

The *Dragon* spun her armoured belly between him and the threat. "What is it?" he shouted.

"A dreaming," Jocelyn was calling back. "A big one."

Leyton thumbed the fuselage camera in the same moment as he looked skywards to activate the dreamlink to base. "Borneo, this is *Crimson Dragon*, we have encountered a dreaming—" He blinked to send his right ascension, declination, distance and telemetry. "Investigating, over."

Borneo Tower murmured urgently in his ear in confirmation as the images sprang up onto the cockpit in front of him: a gravitational lensing of the stellar background, a round target of distorted stars. He'd learnt in simulations to see such roses blooming and fire into their hearts as something appeared there.

Which was why his thumb had flicked the covering off the trigger on the joystick. But he wasn't going to fire now. This close to Earth, the incoming dreamer had to be a Fleet ship with a wounded head.

Leyton waited.

But nothing came through the dreaming.

The *Crimson Dragon* gave a sudden lurch. "What the blazes was that?" he shouted, automatically compensating for the course change. But the pressure on the joystick was continuing.

"The dreaming," called Jocelyn. "It's pulling us towards it."

"How?!"

"Don't ask me, I've only been doing this for a week."

"All right." Leyton lit the main stack for the first time since they'd left Earth's atmosphere, spinning the *Dragon* to point the engines straight at the dreaming. The distance between them was rapidly decreasing, he could see, the fuselage cameras turning to find the shape in space and feeding directional information onto the cockpit display.

The numbers flicked around. The distance to the dreaming stabilised as the blazing engine stack made the *Dragon* shudder, held at one thousand two hundred feet, began for a few seconds to increase, and then started to slowly tick backwards again.

"Flaming meteors!" whispered Leyton. "We don't have the power. Joss, dream us out of here!"

"I can't."

"*Damn* the regulations!" he said, then chided himself. "'Scuse my French, but could you—"

"I'm doing my damnedest! That thing is taking up all of the imaginative territory. I don't think it is a dreaming. Not exactly. It's something we haven't encountered before. I can't see a way through."

Leyton let go of the controls, aware with a quiet coldness in his stomach that there was now nothing he could do. He turned back to look at Jocelyn, who had her eyes closed, her mouth a line of concentration. "Come on, old girl," he whispered.

Her eyes opened. She looked afraid. "Squadron Leader," she said, "there's no way through. We're going in."

Leyton met her eyes and knew that there was nothing left to be done. "Thanks for letting me know," he said. He turned back to his instruments, and saw through the cameras the fluttering of space racing straight at them. "Hold onto your hairpins. This could get a bit rough."

The *Crimson Dragon* hit the dreaming at orbital speed.

Moments like a dream. Photographs that seem to have happened to someone else.

Golden statues. They were in the dreaming with them. A bronzed eye that looked implacable, uncommunicative. It was deep red outside. Like blood.

Uncommunicative was fearsome. The enemy was uncommunicative.

They passed through the palm of a hand. A classical image. The boat in the hands of the God. Being turned. The laughter. The plan. The capriciousness? No. This was deliberate. They were to be placed amongst the stars like Andromeda and Perseus.

This was enemy action. Things were being changed by the enemy.

This was not supposed to be. And yet—

Elea Jacta Est.

And that was the last clear snapshot.

The ship spun and exploded into the sky.

Into the stratosphere. Leyton shouted at the sudden dislocation. He could see the curve of the Earth below. His heart raced with the joy of it. They hadn't gone anywhere!

But they were still in trouble.

Heat flared along the *Dragon*'s wings. Caught at the wrong angle, the green surfaces reddened and the tips glowed in many colours as metallic elements flared off into the void and splattered onto the cockpit monitors. The red, white and blue circles on the wings vaporised.

Leyton grabbed the joystick and hauled. Heaved with all his strength. He roared with the effort of it. Falling into a rogue dreaming and then burning up in the atmosphere—not on his nelly!

"Get tower on the dreamlink!" he shouted.

"Can't," Jocelyn called back. "Can't find them."

The nose pulled up, just a little. The blueness of the Earth filled the windows in front of Leyton. A familiar green shape was sliding lazily into view. At least they were heading for Britain.

Leyton felt the first shocks of deep atmospheric entry, a distant thunder that was going to get louder every second. He pulled off one boot with the other, stamped on the toe of his Spacefleet-issue sock and hauled it off as well, then grabbed the dial of the radio between his toes. It was a back-up system. He'd never had cause to use it before. "Borneo Tower, come in. This is the *Crimson Dragon*, Squadron Leader Leyton. I have an emergency, over." He hit the receive button with his big toe.

A babble of sound burst into the cockpit. Leyton frowned. It sounded like news broadcasts in English, music stations... "Is that music?"

"Couldn't dance to it."

Leyton tried to look at the dial from where he was still matching his muscles against the roaring atmosphere outside. That was the spot on the Spacefleet frequency, he was sure of it.

"You ought to get out of here," Jocelyn said. "We're rather beyond regulations on that matter now."

"And leave you in the lurch?" Leyton grunted. "I wouldn't dream of it."

"But I insist." There was something unusual in Joss's voice now, something suddenly desperate. "Death was a bore, and I'd rather one of us were bored than both."

The roaring in the cabin had now become a scream of disintegrating air and metal. "Not just you, though, is it, old girl? We can't contact the fleet, so the missile crews are going to get caught on the hop. We're coming at it at rather a low angle. And that's jolly old England right in front of us." The sweat was soaking through his shirt now. He wished he could free a hand to pull off the knot of his tie. Inside, his stomach was cramped by the fear. The muscles of his face wanted to scream. But if he hit the tag that would send him spinning off safely into an orbital descent suit, the ship would destroy a village, a factory.

A school playground.

"Hope you don't mind, Joss," he said. "But we're going to pop in to Farnborough for a spot of tea."

"Gracious," Jocelyn murmured. "If I'd known, I'd have worn my pearls."

That brought a smile to Leyton's parched lips.

The *Crimson Dragon* became a blustering white comet in the sky over Southern England.

It made a high, keening sound as it fell, the sound of something trying to fly.

It burst the sound barrier as soon as there was air enough. The booms echoed across a patchwork land below, where roads were jammed with traffic. There was a landscape of green rain beneath them.

Leyton roared at his craft as the picture below became clearer and clearer. He hauled back on the joystick with all his weight. The radio blazed snatches of life from below into his face.

"A paediatrician in Wales has had her house attacked by a gang who apparently mistook her for a paedophile..."

He was getting some lift from the wings now. He just hoped they weren't too damaged to take her up, if he got them back to the right angle.

"Petrol protestors have threatened to block access to fuel depots once more if the government continue to ignore..."

Clouds burst over the nose. Thin and wispy. Then gone. Leyton could see details on the ground now. Scattered houses. Farms. Roads. He would not be responsible for killing hundreds of innocent people. Not for one!

"... campaign in the election as a candidate for a party representing a multinational car company..."

Leyton could feel the heat through the armour now. But the *Dragon* was built far too well to disintegrate. Would that it could. Leyton would gladly have met his maker, would have tipped his cap to him and said he'd had a good innings and asked the way to the cricket ground.

"Countryside Alliance protestors insisting that the right to hunt lies at the heart of..."

That entrance into heaven might yet come to pass.

The stubby mass of metal that had once been a ship plummeted through more layers of cloud, dark and stormy. And then they were falling free, a burning coal, sliding down above a rainlashed stretch of English downland.

Leyton had said Farnborough. But he had no idea, at this height, where Farnborough was.

He set the joystick controls for atmospheric flight and opened the jets. Not much left of them. Or the wings. He was pleased, when he heaved on the joystick again, to find a little lift. "Come on old girl," he whispered. "We'll find somewhere."

"Can't see Wimbourne Mast," said Jocelyn. "Can't see the Purbeck Range. The maps say this is Dorset, but they seem to have got muddled."

"If we can't find a spaceport, then an airport."

"We're way past Bristol, unless you can turn her. We're not going to make Reading."

"I've flown here, Joss. I see the lie of the land, the hills are all accurate, it's just... Well never mind that now. We have to find somewhere." The landscape was racing up at a dizzying speed now. Leyton felt the gravity in his stomach, felt the green hills below coming at him like they were a punch aimed at his face.

He switched to the belly camera, and was relieved to find it still working. Individual fields were starting to flash by beneath the *Dragon*. The angle under the nose was getting smaller and smaller. He could turn to the left or the right. He could hold them up just moments longer. He had to decide.

The ground rose to meet them.

And then fell away again. The huge valley opened up before them.

Fields and fields. A few roads. A few cars.

Leyton saw the blaze of blue battered crops along the horizon. Linseed, wasn't it? He realised at once this was going to be the *Crimson Dragon*'s last home. Depth. Length. The right distance.

He cut the jets.

The ship dipped like they'd dropped over the edge of the roller-coaster.

"Here we go, Joss!" Leyton shouted. "Sorry about your hairdo."

"I'll see you in the Fitzroy Hotel," said Jocelyn.

Leyton smiled, his eyes locked on the blue blur speeding towards him. He had nothing to do now but hold her level. He knew he and Jocelyn weren't going to survive this crash. That didn't matter. What mattered was that he had done his duty to the utmost of his ability. Nobody else was going to be hurt because of them. "What does that mean?" he asked, the thought about the hotel suddenly striking him. "I've never heard—"

He was flying through the air just as his mouth was forming the next words.

He yelled.

The scream of the small rockets underneath him was lost in the roar.

He twisted in his seat, his legs kicking free. He saw pieces of the canopy splintering against the high blue.

The seat collapsed into a mobile mass at his back. The rockets gave a bang and fell away.

Dark sky above.

Blue beneath.

He saw the *Crimson Dragon* hit the ground.

One moment it was skimming across the surface of the flowers, sending clouds of plant and mud up into the air in two great swathes of light blue.

Then it hit.

It buckled.

Tripped over its nose.

The blackened lump bounced spinning.

Once. Twice. Three times.

Then it flew high in the air and fell flat. Skidded to a halt, sloughing across the field, pulling streaks of black and blue with it as it ploughed the soil into a half moon.

All in silence.

And then the rumble of it reached him high in the sky like thunder from below.

"Joss," he said.

Something thumped him in the back.

The chute cracked open above him and his body stretched at the end of it.

Unwillingly, instinctively, his ankles came together, his knees braced and his fists closed over the control straps.

A plume of black smoke from the corpse of the *Crimson Dragon* rolled up to meet him. It levitated him back into the air, the heat stinging his hands.

He opened his mouth, wanting to let himself cry out. But the taste of the smoke made him close it again.

The smoke was everywhere.

And then he was out of it.

The ground swung up to meet him at a much more friendly rate: a little dirt path at the side of the field. A wooden fence topped with wire. There were flints on the paths.

He hit and curled his knees, daring the ground to push back harder.

He fell off his feet and rolled.

The chute tried to drag him into the crops.

He hit the catch and let it go. It spun off, plucked this way and that, a big white canopy under the dark sky, blooming out over the light blue.

He collapsed into the crop. The hard stalks gave beneath his back.

He lay there, staring up at the sky. Rain fell into his eyes.

And then the wind changed direction and the blackness swept across his vision.

Leyton wanted to scream, though he was uninjured. He wanted to yell out in bloody anger at Jocelyn for having done that, for having conjured up some head heaven of the Fitzroy Hotel and promising to meet him there. He wanted to rant at the black smoke that was making him cough and choke. He wanted to open his throat and let the sobs that had crowded there out into the world.

He did not.

He put his right palm flat down into the blades of the plants and heaved himself to his feet.

The gravity felt strange after so long in freefall. He pulled the remains of the parachute harness off his back. He looked around quickly to find where the remains of the *Crimson Dragon* lay at the base of the column of smoke. He ran in that direction.

The heat drove him back a hundred yards from the wreck, in the trail of debris and hot earth thrown up by the impact. He could feel the intensity of the fire on his face. He couldn't make himself go further. That was the electrics and the cooling oils going up. Had they used up all the rocket and jet fuel in the descent? He could see, in the blackened shell in front of him, the shape of the cockpit assembly. The black shine of the canopy was still intact. Jocelyn might still be in there, might still be alive—

The rescue jetcopters would be here in minutes. But she might not have that long. If he could get to a road, find some farmer with cutting tools—

He turned on his heel and ran back along the dirt track, suddenly becoming aware that his shirt was browned from the heat and smoke, that maybe he was burned too.

He ran in the heat, under the bloom of the smoke.

The fence had a gate in it, which led to another field. He clambered over it. Another field beyond. It led down a shallow hill to a road at the bottom, a farm looking like a toy a way along. He was in one of the big Dorset farming valleys. They'd say he'd abandoned her. But he couldn't just stand there. He started to run, his feet tumbling over each other, down the cracked stubble of the hill. They'd harvested. But not the linseed. Surely an engineered linseed crop would be ready by now? His parents had a farm. The war. He hadn't kept up. Hadn't called home for months.

His thoughts were a blur as he burst out of the field at the bottom of the hill and threw himself up onto a gate. He stood for a moment on top of it, looking at the farm in the distance, shimmering in the smoke haze. He aimed his thoughts at it. He would make himself run to it.

He would.

He started to heave his leg over the gate.

And then he fell, into darkness.

Four: England's Dreaming

Leyton woke up in a ditch.

He was aware of a nearby noise. He didn't know why he'd been asleep. He felt for, and found, a bruise on his forehead.

The sky above was getting dark with night. He could see it through gaps in a mass of ferns and nettles that had fallen on top of him.

The noise in his head was a jetcopter.

He sat up. The rescue choppers! The *Crimson Dragon*! Jocelyn!

He got to his feet and looked up the slope. The first thought that struck him was that the smoke had gone. There were vehicles up there on the hill. He could identify a couple of fire engines and an ambulance, standing by the black shape of the *Dragon*. They'd find Joss was dead. He could see that now. Heads didn't survive prangs like that. She'd got him out while she could, the brave old thing. People were standing round, walking back and forth. He couldn't see very much, just the light from torches and vehicle headlights. It was still raining.

It struck him that the shape of the vehicles was odd. It was like they'd deflated their skirts. Did they do that when attending an accident? He'd been in several prangs and he'd never seen the like. The 'copter was buzzing around overhead, sweeping its own lights over the fields. They hadn't found him in all that time he'd been asleep. The chopper was sweeping as if looking for approaching people, not staying long enough to watch for a man on the ground.

Bit odd, that.

He looked more closely at the chopper. Those weren't Fleet roundels on its fuselage. The red, white and blue rings were too thick. And there was no eagle in the centre. And... the sound of the engine wasn't right, there was no whine of the jet engine. It was some ancient crate they'd pressed into service. In the heart of Britain? It wasn't as if the rescue services lost many of their birds.

The chopper was heading in his direction. The searchlight was moving across the field towards him.

He looked again towards the wreck.

Leyton realised that he had his hand raised, ready to wave to the chopper.

He lowered it.

Was it possible? Could some sort of enemy force really be here in such numbers in the middle of England? They were going to say he was crazy, that the bump on the head had knocked him silly.

But—

The helicopter roared towards him. The light swept up the gate beside the ditch.

With not another thought, Leyton rolled back into his hiding place and threw the mass of undergrowth over his back once more.

He waited as the noise and light passed overhead.

Then he stuck his head out and watched the lights on the chopper receding into the twilight for a moment.

He slid out of the ditch, ducked his head and started to jog along the track.

Little tracks led to little roads, farm roads. Leyton took his cap and greatcoat from out of his seat pack and put them on against the rain. He actually broke into a sweat, despite the chill.

His plan, such as it was, was to find a main road and then make his way to a city, London, if possible. He'd hidden from a couple of police cars and ambulances rushing past, and noted each time that they weren't carrying the insignia of the World Emergency Services. They were also very primitive. They looked like early electric runabouts. Local reserves? Maybe. He didn't understand it at all. But he did know that he wanted to report to someone from the Fleet. There was a horrible feeling in his stomach, telling him that things were wrong. He didn't know what. The English air tasted beautiful as always, full of the smell of distant bonfires. But there was something gritty underneath that taste. An oily smell in the rain. There were piles of leaves at his feet as he marched down the lane. But they were blanched, discoloured somehow.

All should be right with the good earth in autumn. But it wasn't.

Maybe this was the bang on the head taking hold. When he got to a major road, he'd flag down a hovercruiser and get some cove to call ahead to Fleet HQ. The boys could all have a good laugh at him running off and laying low. Squadron Leader Leyton, secret agent! Undercover in Dorset.

If this was Dorset.

He realised when the lights washed over him that he'd drifted off as he walked, that he hadn't been listening.

A tractor roared round the corner from behind him and carried on up the muddy track. There was something wrong with its engine. It was chugging. It came to a halt and the driver, a silhouette in his cabin, turned round to look at him.

"This is private property," he called.

Leyton couldn't help smiling. He jogged up to the vehicle and doffed his cap to the man. "Terribly sorry," he said. "I've misplaced the road."

The driver, who, up close, was a chubby man in a rough green jumper, looked bemused at him. "I'll show you then. Come on."

Leyton sat back in the worn plush seat with relief as the farmer opened up the engine again and the tractor moved on. "Your fuel cell sounds like she's in a pickle," he observed, making conversation.

"Sounds all right. Just filled her up."

"Filled her up? With what?"

"Diesel, what d'you think?"

Leyton wondered if the man was joking. "Can you still get that?"

"Hah!" The man laughed and nodded vigorously. "Can you! You're right there!"

Leyton nervously joined in the laughter. He saw that there was a printout newspaper stuffed in a canvas pocket bolted to the door of the tractor. He pulled it out and unrolled it, though the inkiness of the print made him want to drop it.

He held it by the corners and found that, as he looked at it, he was suddenly unaware of anything else. It wasn't the headline. His eye had gone to the date, like it always did, but he'd only now realised that he did that: because this time his gaze held there. On the date he was now living in. Inhabiting.

A date that was a hundred and twenty-eight years ago. The start of the twenty-first century.

He dropped the paper.

He struggled to try and pick it from the floor, did so, looked at the date again.

He was on a high tower, looking down at nothingness below. He wanted to run back to the wreck, to see Jocelyn. To see what remained of Jocelyn.

He was lost.

He turned to look at the man again. "How far is it to Bath?" he said.

Leyton found his spirits sinking more the further the farmer drove him. He wished he'd paid more attention in his history lessons, instead of gazing out of the window, waiting for the afternoons when he would play jet cricket. All he knew about this era were the books and articles he'd read about his heroine. At least he was going to the right city for that! So he'd know the territory a little. But how useful as history were books that wanted to romantically focus on one particular person?

The farmer began to talk, following Leyton's question, in a long, slow voice, for some reason taking Leyton as someone who obviously shared his point of view. Britain in this age was ruled by a despot, it turned out, a tyrant who had taken power for himself and his cronies and had subjected the countryside to a campaign of terror designed to crush his enemies. Leyton just nodded. That made sense: the many conflicts he'd read about.

He didn't feel part of this civil war. Did he have to be? Yes. If people were being abused, he couldn't stand by. Not the sort of thing a chap did.

But to be taken from his own cause, the war to which so many of his friends had given their lives... to which he'd given his life...

The dreaming space must have done this. To cross interstellar distances there had to be an element of crossing time. And this one had been different, pulling them in like that. But dashed if he knew anything about it. He was a combat pilot. He knew how to kick out of a dreaming if the head told you it wasn't doing the business, but as to how it all worked...

The darkness outside of the cab of the tractor had become absolute.

He waved goodbye to the farmer at the crossroads of a smaller road with a bigger one. Cars were speeding by. He held his arm high and let it sway back and forth. The rain had become a muddy spray, illuminated by the headlights of the cars.

He'd had an urge to stay with the man, to ask where he called home, where he was going for the night. But from the man's demeanour, friendly as he'd become, it was obvious that he wasn't going to invite a stranger to share his hearth. Security, Leyton supposed. The tyrant hadn't many friends in the rural communities, but there would still come a point where the farmer wouldn't want to speak openly in company he didn't trust. He'd hinted darkly that he'd be part of some action against the régime shortly.

Leyton was only thankful that his uniform hadn't counted against him. He really should hide it, before he came to the attention of this tyrant's security forces. But it was his only comfort against the rain and the cold as he trudged along the thin strip of grass by the roadside.

The air tasted foul here. In this backwater they were still using fossil fuels. The farmer had commented on how much they cost. So they must be using some form of money as well. That went along with the books he'd read too. There were several songs about that. The tyrant must have starved these areas of technology as well as resources and instituted his own system of coinage. So the countryside was polluted, and the whole area suffered. As he walked, Leyton racked his brains for big, obvious historical reference points from this era. The early twenty-first century. They'd just have had the millennium celebrations at the end of 2000. They must be right at the start of one of the Rebellions. Yes, he was sure of that, that was the blessing of a round number that one could remember for exams. In which case, this tyrant was about to get a nasty surprise at the hands of the Empire and the President in exile. As it said in "Invasion Song," there'd be an army forming in the Hague at the moment. What were the names of the eight Rebels? Craven the first and second... and that was as far as he could get. He thought of reference books, and the thought made him realise that those books hadn't been written yet. All those things which, until today, he could have reached out and put his hand on... they were all gone.

He was walking north, towards Warminster and then Bath. Silly, really. But it was the only place he could be guaranteed to see familiar things. It wasn't at all about Elsie, or their shared tastes in music. Or perhaps it was.

He was walking along the grass verge of a sort of bay where cargo-carrying diesel transporters were sitting, lights on in their cabin, when a car pulled in opposite him, its engine idling.

"Hey!" shouted a man. "Do you need a lift?"

Leyton found, to his horror, that something inside him wanted to laugh or cry. He forced his jaw shut and just nodded, and trudged over to the welcoming warmth and light of the car as the man opened the opposite door.

Two hours later, Leyton stood at the end of the Royal Crescent, looking across the curve of Georgian buildings, over the grass and the ha-ha that rose a level from the park beyond. In the darkness, through the rain, if he kept his head at a particular angle, he was in the city he knew.

Elsie and he had taken a picnic out onto the grass three Summers ago, at the end of his matrimony leave. What would she say to him now? She was there if he closed his eyes. Always. He could hear her voice.

She would say to stop moping around and do something. To jolly well accentuate the positive. She would be mock-stern, and fix him with her blue eyes, daring him to tickle her. She'd brush the curl of brown hair back from her brow and attempt, for just a while, to be serious.

"I don't know where to start, Elsie," he whispered.

The man who had given him a lift was a pilot in what he called a Royal Air Force, so presumably the tyrant was one of the ones who'd claimed a royal lineage. But the pilot had seemed decent enough. He'd stopped for Leyton because of the military silhouette of his coat and cap, but didn't object when Leyton, hating the lie, had said that he was on his way to a party, that he'd got the uniform from a shop. He was in an age, he realised, thankful for the Mozart on the car's audio system, where he had to deny his rank and uniform. He and his fellow flier hadn't talked much.

Leyton had met Elsie outside his Wing Commander's office on Borneo. She was a tracking officer, brought over from Cambridge to help with the great arrays of interception equipment that were now being set up all across the solar system and unified into one system through the dreamlink. She'd been walking in as he'd been walking out. With an hour clear for lunch, he'd stayed on the wheel, doing gravity exercises, pushing his legs against the walls, until she'd come out again. Then he'd run into her accidentally, and asked her for a technical rundown of the equipment which, earlier that day, had led his squadron out to Chiron after what had looked like a trio of enemy scouts, but had turned out to be a previously unmapped asteroid.

She'd defended the system, as he knew she would, and they'd ended up discussing it that evening over a pint in the mess.

She came from Newcastle. Her family had an algae farm in Walker. It was always sunny there. She'd said that then, and Leyton had later seen it: the flat, gentle sun on the acres of green, the waves on the water the only sound.

He'd told her he loved her the third time he'd met her. He'd just got back from a combat sortie, and Jimmy Clark had bought it. The *Silver Dragon* had been shot up by an enemy fighter as it swept past, liquid metal shells bursting through the cockpit at short range. Leyton saw the glittering cloud of particles hanging around the crate as he'd pulled his own ship alongside, matching Jimmy spin for spin. Jimmy had survived the attack, but his cabin was leaking. Dragon Squadron had formed up around him and headed for a nearby support ship. His head was dead, so they weren't about to dream out of there and leave him behind.

They'd talked to him all the way. About the cricket. About how it looked like the Saudis were going to win the Test Cup this year. "Terribly dull in here," Jimmy had said. His cabin was leaking air and he had a hole in his suit. The safety systems had been cut away and Leyton could see sealant spilling uselessly down the side of the ship. "If I were you chaps I'd pop on ahead and get the beers in."

Leyton had laughed. "We're astounded by the elegant spin, Jim. Were you thinking of correcting it at all?"

"Absolutely not. I'm enjoying it. Ah. Sorry. I think my com's going to go down soon."

This was how things went. So they should just hurry up and get there. "Are you absolutely sure about that, Jimmy?"

"Yes, definitely on its way out. You wait and see about the Saudis, chaps. And tell..." A long pause. "Definitely about to cut out. Definitely."

That was why Leyton had pulled close to the other ship. As Squadron Leader, this was his responsibility—unofficially, of course. He could see Jimmy through the cockpit. His helmet looked to be all that was holding his head together, as the bloody things were designed to do. He didn't have much in the way of a face any more. "Don't worry, Jimmy," he said. "You're off on leave."

"Thanks, skip."

Leyton carefully switched off his com and pushed together the two exposed wires that switched off his flight recorder. He knew the others would be doing the same: he couldn't order them to do so. He thumbed open the trigger for the belly cannon. "Godspeed, Jimbo," he said. And then he'd fired a single burst at point blank range into the patchwork of Jimmy's cockpit.

Then, a moment later, when he'd seen, he fired another one.

When he walked into Borneo that night he'd gone straight to the mess, found where Elsie was talking to the other girls, pulled her to her feet and stared into her scared, intelligent eyes. "I love you," he said.

"Oh," she'd said. "Good."

"Will you marry me?"

"Not yet." And she'd taken his hands and led him off to her quarters.

She'd produced a bottle of whisky and drank one glass while he had two. He was called away then for the debriefing, and came back afterwards to find her in civvies.

They'd had a row that night. A brief one, when he'd got to a point of drunkenness and realised they were talking about nothing, but couldn't find it in himself to talk about anything else. He'd said the tracking system was futile, had suddenly bellowed at her that it was her fault, and had grabbed her shoulders. She'd shouted at him and he'd let go, got control of himself again, excused himself.

She hadn't seen him for a week after that. But in the end she did.

They always rowed on the first night of his leave. He knew that she was going to sit there and listen and let all the cramped and curled-up things inside him unfold.

He didn't like the feeling. He liked being with her in the days that followed, being somewhere different, seeing different things, having her thoughts infiltrate his, her voice and his presence a music that made time run past, until the final night together, when he'd be faced with having to fit all the huge things back inside.

They wouldn't row on that last night. He'd just be silent, and so would she.

She suggested, a year after they met, that perhaps they should get married after all, because on those last nights the most sensible thing was to make love.

They'd both been fond of the City of Bath. He'd discovered it during his student years, on trips to see Somerset play outside the County Ground. It was easier to get a ticket at the outgrounds. And that was when his musical tastes had been developing too, and he'd started to become interested in the music of the previous century and the place of Bath in that history. He'd walked the sites, squatted to touch the pavement. She'd known the city as a child. Her parents had lived on the outskirts of Bristol and for her Bath was Christmas and shopping sprees. She hadn't known about the musical connections like he did, but liked listening to him tell her.

They had taken boat trips down the river. They had sat under the trees in the Circus. They had been to the movies in the Baths complex. This Bath of 2000 was flat in the valley, while theirs had been tall, with slender spires that reached up to match the hills. This Bath was dirty, while theirs had been polished pebble brown and white. This Bath was infested with people and fuel-burning cars, while theirs had been open, airy, disturbed only by the hum of motors in the sky.

He could hold their Bath in his eyes, so long as he didn't move his head.

He wanted to collapse here, all at once, to make himself die by switching off some inaccessible internal switch. To not lose consciousness, but to forcibly give it away. For a moment or two, he tried.

He could not.

The rain was still falling on his shoulders. In his memories it had always been sunny here.

Go on, she would have said. Start walking. Find something. You're never happy when you haven't got at least three things to do.

It had been two years now since she had died. And she'd been his only joy.

Leyton found that he understood the horror of what had happened to him now. For the first time in those two years, he'd been left alone with his thoughts. And it was possible that that was how he was going to remain.

"This is hell," he said to a tree with black, polluted bark.

But start walking.

"I don't know where to begin."

Start walking.

"I'll go mad. You'll have to put up with me foaming at the mouth."

They might be able to use the ship's technology, use it to oppress the people even more. If the tyrant is planning to do that, you have to stop him. The remains of the ship are your responsibility, and that is your duty.

He swallowed hard, feeling the pressure of the tie around his neck. Then he made his face hard once more, managed to approximate a look of bright, interested hope. His eyebrows were ragged from old burns. He raised one at the cockeyed angle that had always made Elsie laugh.

So. He had something to do here after all.

He turned to take in the rest of his view of the park, the crescent and the terrible low houses beyond. He took a deep breath. And started walking.

Five: One Eye of a Different Colour

Alison stared into the bathroom mirror.

The mirror was grubby. The bathroom was grubby. Alison lived on the Lower Bristol Road in a Victorian house that had been divided into six flats. The frontage was baked black by decades of grime from cars. The pavement by the front door was too narrow to fit a pushchair on without one wheel sticking out over the double yellow lines. Alison's flat was tiny, a kitchen/lounge area and a bedroom only just wider than her bed. She shared this bathroom with three lads and two couples.

These were the facts.

She'd woken up that morning fully dressed, lying across the bottom corner of her bed, with her head, arms and legs dangling. She'd woken up, raised her head and immediately thrown up.

Over her CD collection.

Throwing up while lying down really hurt.

After lying there for a while thinking about that, Alison got to her feet. She thought about heading into the bathroom to get something to clean up her CDs. Then she smelt the previous vomit and vommed again, this time over her pile of paperbacks.

She stumbled straight into the bathroom then, fell to her knees and spent the next half-hour getting rid of everything that was in her stomach. Which, from the taste of it, was mostly beer. Red Bull. Vodka. And, bloody hell, Pernod.

She didn't remember the Pernod.

Christ. Where had she ended up?

After making sure there was absolutely nothing left inside by dint of putting her finger down the back of her throat and waggling it, she slowly, carefully, got to her feet again. She leaned on the basin.

She looked at herself in the mirror.

There was something in her eye. Not in her reflection, but in her vision. Like she'd been looking at a bright light.

Last night. The smell of Pernod. A bright light.

She rubbed each eye in turn. Then closed each one. It was just in the left one. A little cluster of green against the browny-black of her eyelid.

How was that possible? It was light outside. It felt like it was around nine o'clock. She'd been asleep for at least a couple of hours. So how could the flash from any sort of light still be on her retina?

Oh Christ. It must have been damaged.

No. Just her being over the top. It couldn't be. She'd think about that later.

Pernod.

She *hated* Pernod. Where had she been drinking that? Where had she seen the bright light?

She washed her mouth out, cleaned her teeth, washed her face and then turned from the mirror. She headed out into the hallway and then back into her bedroom, suddenly exhausted again. With a little *ow* of realisation, she did what she should have done first time. She found a relatively clean mug, went back into the bathroom and swallowed a few cupfuls of water. Then she took one back into the bedroom with her.

She closed the door, arranged the pillows and lay back.

Shit. She'd done nothing about the vomit.

Later for that.

When she closed her eyes, she could see the green shape again. It was like a bunch of grapes. No... a cluster of coins. Like they were falling out of a hand.

Gold coins. A golden hand. Where had she seen the golden hands?

She opened her eyes again.

"Oh Christ," she said.

She'd dreamt that. She must have dreamt that.

She had an image in her head, another of her snapshots. She was looking straight into the eyes of a golden statue. And the statue had a hand on either side of her face. A moving statue.

At least she didn't have to go to work on Saturday. Too many people. Too much money. All grey.

Before she could think any more, she was asleep.

She woke around three in the afternoon and immediately guzzled down her mug of water.

Her dreams had been full of gold. And... yes... there was still this sodding thing in her eye. She rubbed it a couple more times. It wasn't going to go away. And she wasn't going to be able to stand it much longer.

She wasn't in any pain or anything, it was just... she hoped she wasn't going to have to put up with this thing for the rest of her life.

The smell made her look around the room.

She had never seen old vomit before.

Alison put her hands over her face and slid slowly off the bed in the direction of the bathroom. Again.

It was while she was wiping her CDS individually that the first links started to come together in her head.

The smell of Pernod.

She was running her hands under water from a tap in a kitchen sink.

Not her kitchen.

That golden man. Someone painted gold?

"Chris." The kid with the yellow hair. No, bleached. Fran was smiling at them both. He'd smiled a very simple, non-sexual smile, and that had sent her head round in circles. She'd seen that exact smile only on some very particular Christian men who were spooky in an entirely different way, and gay men, and not all of those. Even the girlfriended men had a smile that was a notch different.

The CD slipped out of her hand.

The Bears.

That had all come back in a rush. What were Bears? She could see Chris saying the word. Not from a distance, in the bar, as she'd overheard him. Up close. Later. A whisper to her. Like a kid in church.

Bears. She'd thought it was drugs.

Drugs. She'd said to him, later in the night, "Have you got any Bears, then?" And the others in his gang had all jumped and looked at each other and at her and Fran. And she'd known that this was what she'd thought it was, a big mystery.

But this was all from the early part, while they'd still been in the pub with the glass door. They'd left together. She could remember the colder air on her face, two lots of arms holding her up. The same for Fran, beside her.

Christ. She could have been raped.

Where had they gone? She remembered a kitchen. But that was all. Solid wood. She just had bits. The golden face. The water. The word on his lips.

She went and sat on her bed. Oh God. She searched for experiences like this, for things she couldn't understand. And now she'd found one. And it was horrible.

She was going to have to have a bath.

Alison loved baths.

She made sure that everyone else was out and then carefully used every last drop of hot water to fill the tub. She didn't have the energy to scrub it first.

She lowered herself into the water, to which she'd added a capful of Fran's aromatherapy stuff.

The door was closed. There was just the gentle whirr of the extractor fan and the lap of the water. Often, when she could negotiate a bath from the other inhabitants of the house, Alison would fall asleep in it.

Today she was going to use it to do the exact opposite of what she usually did.

She focused on the fragments of memory she had from last night.

She used to do this when she was a kid, when she was lying in bed on the edge of sleep, way before she'd learnt what a terrible burden this thing in her head was. Before she'd started to do everything so quickly that it was awful, she would focus on something that had happened at school that day. On how, maybe, she'd learnt long division after three problems and finished off the rest of the book in that class. She would remember the smile on the face of Miss Dodd, and then work out all the things that Miss Dodd had been thinking. On those nights, she decided that Miss Dodd was sad about something, and one breaktime, because she loved her dearly, she'd asked her. And Miss Dodd had just said that no, she wasn't sad about anything, and had looked at her with a look of complete, complicated, awfulness that had made Alison never want to ask anyone about anything ever again.

Before the end of term, Miss Dodd had left the school.

Now Alison would probably have decided that Miss Dodd was a manic depressive within thirty seconds of meeting her, and would have crossed the street to avoid her.

Little things like that made her life into a box.

She was going to sleep after all. She added some cold water to the mix. She *was* going to do this.

She concentrated on Chris's face. He was about seventeen, with a little monkey mouth and high cheekbones and that fluff of bleached hair. Big brown eyes. And that brotherly, drugged smile. But he obviously wasn't on anything that night apart from a couple of pints of Bellringer.

He wanted her to see something, because he was showing everyone the same thing. The zeal in his eyes. Like it would convert her.

That had told her it wasn't drugs. So she would have said... she *did* say, out loud, "What do you want to show to everyone, but you have to hide it?"

She was so direct when she got drunk.

So they must have answered her. Chris was so eager to tell, he must have answered.

Maybe not then. They wouldn't have gone immediately. They'd have had another drink, got to know the two of them a little. The girl with dark hair didn't want to tell them anything, so she'd have held them back. She could make Chris do that. Had they had more than the one drink in the pub? Close call. Chris would have wanted them to see whatever it was while as sober as possible. No, they looked like students, they wouldn't have the cash to buy her more than one, and she and Fran had been down to small change, had been going to go to the cashpoint on the way home. But they must have sat there talking for the one drink.

She couldn't remember much about that.

Then the cold air, being supported by Chris and one of the other lads. The dark-haired girl walked beside Chris. Not jealous. So they had a real boyfriendness going. Fran nearby, also propped up. Saying something over and over again. Probably about caves.

One of us, they'd said to her. You know where we're going. That was a big laugh from all of them.

There were no clues as to where they'd taken them. Just a big dark hole in her memory with no obvious way in. The University... No. They hadn't walked. That big hill she'd got so used to. She would have felt it in her calves this morning. They'd have had to have taken a taxi, and this lot didn't have the cash for that, and there were six in the group, too many for one cab. Alison and Fran made them six, and the others hadn't minded, so they were going to where they'd already arranged to go, or lived, not to a mate's who'd let them crash. Not to Fran's. Fran lived with her Mum and Dad. No drunken people going back there.

She'd been happy with Fran by then, even though Fran hadn't told her her big thing. There had been trouble ahead, a great weight, but drunk, Alison had thought they could maybe face it together. That after Fran had told her, they would be able to sort something and the End of the World would fade away.

She didn't know if that could still be true. Why was that?

There was a kitchen. A big kitchen. That sink was huge. One of these kids must be rich and local. Or... or many other possibilities. A bottle of Pernod. Which was an expensive drink, too. Had she seen it? Maybe. It was hard to tell with products, you saw them so often. There was a big wooden table. She remembered the feel of her elbows on it.

The moon. A full moon, through the window. So... Alison twisted in the bath and got a sense of which direction she'd been facing last night. She had that because she'd seen the moon earlier that night, and it would have moved... she didn't know how far it would have moved. She needed to read a book about that. There'd been nothing between the window and the moon, no line of trees, or buildings. So they must have been quite high. But no hills in the way. Well, the pub with the glass door was quite near the top of the town. They might have just gone a little way, to one of the buildings on those hills.

What had happened in that kitchen?

She looked at her palms, turned white and wrinkly by the water. Tiny indentations, a little tender... She'd fallen on the road, caught herself on her palms. She remembered the others hauling her to her feet. That's why she'd wanted to wash her hands.

She hadn't *finished* washing her hands. She'd have the whole moment, and she didn't. She got very focused when she was pissed. So she wouldn't have just wandered away from it.

So they must have called her away. Perhaps Chris or Fran had put a hand on her shoulder and said look.

And the only thing allowed to interrupt such a small, vital thing would be something really important that wasn't going to hang around forever. Look! A rare bird!

Or a Bear.

So she would have turned... and what had she seen?

It must have been the man with the golden face.

There was something odd about the mental picture she had of that moment. There were his hands, on either side of her face... He couldn't have kissed her, she always remembered when that had happened... There was his face. But she had the weird feeling she was in a theatre. Because... blacked-out limbs. Like a magician or a mime artist. There didn't seem to be anything in between his hands and his face. Like it was just a head and hands.

And the bright light had been almost immediately afterwards.

The thing in her eye hadn't been there before that. She couldn't remember anything since.

Oh Christ. Fran. Fran screaming.

Fran had screamed. And everybody had laughed at her for doing that, and somehow that had made Alison feel okay.

Fran was screaming like she'd turned a corner and run into something that she thought she'd got away from. She was screaming like she was in a horror movie.

That was the last thing she could remember.

What the fuck was this?

Alison leapt out of the bath and towelled herself down, then ran back into her room and grabbed the phone. Fran's Dad answered the call. Fran was out. Yes, she had come back last night, there was a note. She'd gone to work early. The note said she was going to stay out tonight and would be back tomorrow, Sunday. It didn't say where she was going after work.

Yes, he was certain it was Fran's handwriting. Was anything wrong?

Alison assured him that there wasn't.

She put down the phone, her hand shaking.

A note. Fran must be alive to have written a note. Mustn't she?

She needed to know what this was about. She needed to know right now.

By the time she got to Bilbo's Books, it was five-thirty. Alison could see Mrs Skipper moving around in the dark in the shop, switching things off. The window was full of crystals and incense and a little fountain, the continuous trickle of which Fran had said did wonders for your bladder. A few people walked quickly past in the narrow roofed streets of the Colonnades.

Alison knocked hopefully, smiled through the window, and a moment later Mrs Skipper opened the door.

She'd been crying. Her face didn't like to admit that, but it was red at the cheeks. "Oh," she said. "Alison dear. If you're looking for Fran—"

"Yes."

"She doesn't work here any more."

"What?"

"She came in this morning, but only in order to give me her resignation. She said she'd work out her notice, but I got... well, I got a little tearful. She's such a nice girl. It took me by surprise. I said no, you want to go, you go when you like. You don't know... she isn't in some sort of trouble, is she? You know... drugs? Because she's always been close with me, she's been like a daughter to me, and now she wouldn't tell..." Mrs Skipper's mouth pinched up, trying not to cry again. "If you see her, you tell her—"

"I will," said Alison.

She tried all Fran's favourite pubs. Nobody there had seen her. She called Marty.

"You mean she's got back?" he said.

"Yeah." Alison hated to let him know. Fran had called her before she'd called him? "So you haven't seen her at all?"

She didn't want to give him the details. Not while they sounded so mad.

Because obviously nothing had happened to Fran last night. She'd got home and come in to work quite safely. She was alive and well. She'd come home tomorrow and Alison could ask her what had happened and get a clear explanation about everything. Even about the golden man.

But the screaming. And she was *laughing* at the screaming.

She couldn't understand how she could have done that, even while very drunk. The thought of her friend being hurt was panicking her now. Why hadn't it made her frightened then?

Maybe that was it? Maybe Fran hadn't called her because of that?

And had left her folks a note. And hadn't come home for her boyfriend.

The Saturday night of Bath started to build up around her. There was one more thing she could do. It was desperate, but she was desperate already. Far more desperate than anyone else would be.

The pieces didn't fit. They didn't fit like they wouldn't start to fit in the last days. She knew what it would look like to an outsider: that she had needed Fran to be there, to hold off her own collapse. That she hadn't got what she needed from her that night. That she was equating whatever scary thing had happened in their little world to the end of the whole thing.

As above, so below. As inside, so outside. She was at the start of a frightening ride now. She knew it as she headed off for the top of town, her head bowed against the rain as the darkness drew on.

She was going to try and find that kitchen.

Douglas picked the envelope off his doormat and opened it. It was stuffed with cash. No writing on the front, no band around the notes, as always. He took it into his kitchen and counted it out on the tablecloth. Five hundred exactly. Not like that time when they had underpaid him by ten pounds. He had nobody to call to complain.

He was trusted and relied upon by those in power. And he had to trust them in return. He was an excellent citizen, in his place. An excellent feeling, one that kept a smile on his face. When he wanted it to be there.

He wondered why he had opened the envelope so fast. Why he had counted. He didn't always do this. He had been reading, recently, about a new theory of mind, one that appealed greatly to him. His reading was almost entirely about psychology and consciousness, about why one did what one did. This version had it that consciousness was only a monitor, that one's actions were controlled by unconscious processes that only reported their actions to consciousness after they had been decided upon. He had not thought, just then, I will open that envelope, though I know what is inside it. He had not thought to count the money. He had just done so, and then thought that he had thought those things before the fact.

Douglas had an entire library about the workings of the mind. He read on the subject as enthusiastically as a psychology graduate. And every now and then he looked up at his bookshelves and thought that it was all piffle.

His head itched. He took off the wig and found the latest three plasters. The itching was coming from underneath the one on the very top of his head.

He couldn't quite remember if he was wearing facial hair. Something about his sideburns. He pulled gently at them and found that one was real and one wasn't. Same colour, thank goodness. He made a note to himself to shave the other one and stuck the note to the corner of his desk.

He went into the bathroom and peeled the wig back. Some pain there. He was going to have to shave his head again soon as well. He picked up the smaller mirror he kept for this purpose and held it and his head at the right angle so that he could see the trepanation in the bathroom mirror. It didn't look infected. The wound looked clean. This had been his first penetration of his own skull, simply to allow more oxygen into his brain, several years ago. He selected a new plaster from the bathroom cabinet and replaced it over the hole. Should he check the others, the ones that had gone further? Each of them was a hole that went deep into his brain, a couple of inches down, placed according to a detailed map of the lobes that he had created himself, pieced together from his decades of reading. He had used a power drill, with a bit specially selected for just the right length. There had been remarkably little pain. Remarkably little blood. He had felt different after each penetration. Much more the normal, everyday man he was seeking to be. Which was ironic. Each step seemed to take him a little in the wrong direction, as well as the right one. Two steps forward, one step back.

No, he decided, he would surely feel more than a little itching if any of them got infected. But that would be interesting too. To live in a relationship with another kind of life. That would make him a more whole person again. He closed the cabinet door.

That had not been a real question and a real answer, either. There had been no "decision." He had already "decided" not to interfere with the bores into his brain before his thoughts had circled round the matter.

All this was good. Reassuring. It meant that, left to itself, whatever his conscious desires were, his brain, his body, his self, altered by itself, was steadily on the road to improvement, to being exactly who he and it both happily wanted to be. By accident. Except that it was also by design. Nothing to be done, anyway. It would all work out in the end.

He went into the front room and booted up the computer, because this, obviously, was what he, whoever he was, wanted to do at this time. He didn't want to go out. Not tonight. Not the right sort of crowd on a Saturday night. Drunken oafs who might abuse him. Though it was always good to see the shock when he turned and injured one of them. He didn't know why the possibility was in his head. He had already decided, that was why he had started the computer. He had nothing to contribute to that "decision." The phantoms of will were obviously necessary to people. That was still how people talked, how advertising worked. You want this. You want that. No you don't. You just needed to be told about it and you would go and get it. Want didn't come into it. Not unless it was the basics: food and sex. And how many people actually *needed* the food they ate every night?

He chided himself. To think deeply about such things was to be not one of the normal people. He had used meditation and prayer of various denominations and fasting, all in an effort to be normal. And all of them had complicated the nature of that normality. At least, he thought that was why he had started out on this path. That was what made most sense.

He should get a regular job. But there was great risk in that. His disguises might not stand regular contact. He came and went, doing the little interventions that he did. He would need references and a fixed identity, which would show him up for what he was. Whatever that was.

He sat down at the computer and slipped the picture CD into the hard drive. He wondered which of the images he would prefer tonight? So good to have pictures. No moral decision with pictures. No problem. If he still felt this need, then buying the disc had been a bad thing to do, because it gave the creator of the disc money for making it, money that would filter down to an urge for new creation, to make new photos. But using it once he had bought it, and he had bought it a long time ago, was not a bad thing at all.

That oft-repeated loop was gone from his head in an instant. He had never said those words to anybody. He'd liked to have said them to the therapist he sometimes paid, to have someone to talk to, but he knew she wouldn't understand the difference between buying and owning. She'd want to take the disc off him. And it was one of the things that kept him on the straight and narrow, kept him walking towards being an upright, wholesome, normal man. That and serving his country, and the company of good, normal folk.

He found that he had selected the image labelled "Running Woman" from the Vietnam conflict. The woman was naked, burned by napalm. Faces in the photo looked bored; they did not comment.

He unzipped himself and took his cock out and started to toy with himself.

He loved historical photos. They meant so many things, depending on who he was. But at least half of those things were going to make him come.

Alison made herself keep walking uphill. It was quieter up here, especially as night fell on a Saturday. You could hear the sounds of the city below, and the murmurs of televisions from the front rooms of the Georgian houses. There were upper bedrooms illuminated and bicycles chained against railings outside cellar kitchens.

She had kept calling her answerphone, to see if Fran had left a message.

She should have called Patrick by now. He could have come round, reassured her that the thing in her eye wasn't permanent, told her that Fran would show up. Marty would have called him straight off.

Maybe the fact that she hadn't called Patrick was a sign of something. He would take over the situation, ask her for all the details. See if he could use his money to bash away at everything until it gave up the truth. And he'd be pissed off, without saying so, that she'd been out late at night with men.

It was like he expected her to be a wife already.

She'd returned to the pub with the glass door first, and had waited, drinking water, until Kath, the barwoman from the night before, had arrived for her evening shift. Alison had told the landlord the truth, that she wanted to find out who the two of them had left with. When Kath came in, the landlord pointed Alison out and the woman with the big scarf and glasses had come over, half a laugh and half a frown on her face. She was wondering, Alison saw, if this was going to be the sort of complication she could shrug aside. She'd just arrived from shagging someone and was fulfilled and happy and felt that she could just walk away if Alison had any shit to offer.

So Alison became a bit pitiful, took the woman into her confidence, hinted that she'd got involved with one of the boys and was filled with romance and needed to see him again desperately.

Kath had gushed. She told Alison everything, and started making extra bits up out of romantic speculation until Alison asked a few hard, precise questions to stop her. She didn't know who the four kids had been, hadn't seen them before. There were two boys and two girls, who appeared to be in two couples, but she wasn't sure. And the blonde girl who looked like she was out of a Hitchcock movie!

Alison carefully kept the smile straight on her face. Fran would have loved that. But it made her sound just like the missing person she was.

They'd all left together, and they'd headed uphill, round the corner, towards the Circus. No sign of them looking for a taxi. Alison asked if the look of the start of their walk had indicated that they were walking very far, and Kath said that they looked as if they were only going a little way, but from the look on her face Alison knew that the woman was just guessing and had no way to tell, and was wondering what kind of question that was.

Alison was going to ask if the pub sold Pernod, but then a sudden thought came into Kath's face, and she said, "Mind out for the dog. The boy told you. He was going to bark when you got in unless you were quiet."

Alison's thoughts collapsed into a line of facts. A dog. So that would also be a reason for her to wash her hands, apart from the fall. She didn't like the feeling of dog on her fingers. And noisy dog meant someone who could be woken by a noisy dog: a parent. So Chris lived at home, probably just up the hill, in a house with the attribute of doggishness.

She had thanked Kath and left straight away.

Her hangover had started to weigh down her thoughts as she climbed. She didn't recognise any of these houses. From here you could look down on the city in the twilight, and it looked sleepy. Not busy. A gentle drizzle. There was a bonfire somewhere nearby. The leaves of the forests that rounded the horizon were still green. Not enough brown. Autumn was holding off.

Holding off the End of the World.

Alison had been playing the *Cabaret* soundtrack all week. Lyrics and rhythms kept coming back into her head as she walked, looking for doggishness, one line going over and over: "When I go, I'm going like Elsie." She couldn't get it out of her head. She'd analysed it out of existence, crunched it up until there was no life or nourishment left in it. It hadn't been a very deep text to start with—Alison devoured huge old novels from the library that carefully had nothing to say about now—but it was like the last track on a vinyl record, just playing over and over in her head, with no meaning left to it. A worm in her brain. It matched the useless march of her boots uphill. When. I. Go. I'm. Going. Like. Elsie. She knew very well that it was about a wasted life, but also about a sacrifice to joy in the face of the end of civilisation in pre-war Germany. And there was defiance in it too. And many other trace cultural things that she'd understood in moments, hours, days. And sidelights that were just about her: how could the word Elsie contain any pathos when it was now an old woman's name? When it was just there to rhyme with "Chelsea" anyway?

But now it was a mantra, or the opposite of a mantra. Something Alison's brain played emptily as it walked because it wanted noise inside it. This dead lyric was like a sentence being read out over her, over and over. She got associations from it. The West End. The bright lights. The big opening night. Glamour.

She was thinking it because she didn't want to think of the other thing. Of what might have happened to Fran.

Her eye was starting to hurt. The something in it still wavered at the edge of her vision, got in the way of the streetlights.

She found no doggishness for several streets, turning this way and that randomly. She found birdishness, cattishness, even small doggishness, but it would need a big dog's barking to wake up a house, and up here so far there were just flats, student houses, divided houses, not the big family homes with gardens that brought big dogs into being.

There was no gradient of doggishness, not up here. There would be little islands of it, without any sort of attraction to get her there. This would take days—if this was where they'd gone at all.

Alison stopped and leant heavily on a lamp post. The light had come on, pale pink. She was very tired. She felt like she was going to throw up again.

She had met something magical. Something that had touched her. Something that she had failed to understand. And it had given her this bloody thing in her eye.

And it had made Fran scream, long and hard.

And it had made Fran absent herself from the world, when Alison needed her most.

There was nowhere left to look tonight. Tomorrow. Tomorrow everything would be okay and Fran would be back. She turned on her heel and headed downhill, home.

"When I go I'm going like..."

Shut up, Alison said to her brain. Shut up, shut up, shut up.

Six: The World Set Free

Frederick Cleves walked slowly up to the gate and gazed at what lay beyond.

The field had been covered in tarpaulins. They extended all the way along the track of the crash. There was no sign of the public or the press, or even the farmer who owned the land. Military vehicles stood about. Sappers were going to and fro with metal detectors. It didn't look like anybody was digging or taking anything apart yet. So the protocols were being observed, and everyone knew what they were dealing with.

Thank God for that.

He carefully hauled himself over the gate, feeling the ache in his joints. Someone soon was going to say something to him about retirement.

At least he'd lived to see this.

He had expected it for so long. Wanted it. A new threat to the security of the British Isles.

And it had had to arrive now. And here. The irony was very bitter.

A couple of times previously during Cleves' time as Joint Intelligence Committee Chair there had been possibilities. Something from the murky and impenetrable amateur world of Unidentified Flying Objects would rear up into the murky and impenetrable professional world of intelligence, and Cleves would become interested for a moment, ask for something to be put in tomorrow's Red Book on the matter. These reports had always turned out to be dull and bereft of meaning, dried-out legends drained of the human fantasies that had created them, a slight to the cool cream pages on which they were set. There never had been a moment when he could, in all honesty, do what he had always wished to do, which was to set up a working committee on the subject. He had always kept in the back of his head, along with the hundreds of other things that were kept there and nowhere on paper, a rolling list of which members of the four security services he would recruit for such a committee. But, through the decades, those people had never even been aware that they were on such a list, let alone met. Cleves was master of all British intelligence and had to show restraint.

Last night he had called them.

The news had taken slightly less than two hours to reach him. Two RAF bases in the West Country had tracked an anomalous object, not, as a call to Jodrell Bank had revealed, recorded on any of the space debris logs, entering the atmosphere and exhibiting the characteristics of controlled flight. At the same time, GCHQ had detected anomalous signals and had trained a satellite antenna on the flightpath of the object. Cleves

63

remembered a time when there would have been aircraft standing by to scramble at any incursion into British airspace, but that hadn't been so for a decade. The base commander at RAF Lyneham had got two C-130s into the air as soon as he could and diverted another, but by the time they flew over the scene, the bird was already on the ground.

Cleves had seen the photographs over his dinner, smudging them with the sauce from the duck, and had arranged a service car for early the next morning. He'd immediately made a few calls to Five, from the Director downwards, and then to GCHQ and the Chief Constable of Dorset Constabulary. The protocols were services only, so the Chief Constable had to be brought into the circle on that, and made aware of his responsibilities. By the end of the conversation, the man had cancelled all police leave in his county. The last step was to check the depth of the press fix. Cleves spent ten minutes writing a cover about an experimental aircraft, forwarded it to all parties and then, once they'd all signed up to it, dipped back down into Five and had them launch what Cleves still called D Notices based on that. Apparently two local reporters had got to the scene of the crash within an hour. They were forcibly taken away by the police, and the Chief Constable had made them remain in the office as their editor was read the D Notice.

Cleves had hardly slept that night, and had been up to meet the car, his suitcase packed, at dawn.

Dorset. This had to be in Dorset. Perhaps there *was* a God, and he had a wry sense of humour.

Yesterday morning, at his home, Cleves had received a letter on old-fashioned rice paper, a long chatty yarn from an old friend who these days worked for a multinational oil company in Canada. The letter was about cricket, the chances for Yorkshire in the coming county season now that they had hired Wayne Clark, an Australian, as their coach, and the potential for an exciting meeting between them and the touring Pakistani team, possibly to be coached by Yorkshire's great icon, Geoff Boycott.

The only important thing about the letter had been the last couple of paragraphs, quoting the batting averages of various Yorkshire players over the last two seasons. The sixth average gave a code that unlocked the rest of the letter.

The letter concerned matters in Dorset and nearby counties: matters that gave Cleves bad dreams.

And Dorset was also where this had happened: where heaven had touched the Earth. Where the game might suddenly have begun again: a game which might unite the world against something bigger than itself.

Cleves knew from a lifetime of service that there were such things as coincidences.

He'd left his driver at the bottom of the lane and had walked the last mile himself. He wanted to smell the new scents that the craft from another place had brought to the British countryside. He wanted to anticipate the moment as he walked the ground. He had had to sluice his feet, on the way in, in the solution designed to stop the spread of Foot and Mouth.

Now he hopped delicately onto the very field where the connection had been made. That's one small step for an elderly man.

He heard a shout. A police constable was approaching him at speed, waving his arms as though Cleves was in danger. The JIC Chairman smiled. A nice touch, that. The cover had spoken of danger to the public, beyond the danger they associated with the disease and farming areas. This young man had bought the lie. The Chief Constable had kept the truth confined to his most senior men and those who had arrived first at the site. Some effort had been made to divert that car, but a policeman is not easily turned back from a shout. The men involved had been made to sign the Act, promoted, and given responsibility within the clearance effort. The Chief Constable had wanted to send them on leave, but Cleves had murmured that policemen take their holidays where there are bars, and the strangest stories are the ones which we feel most able to tell.

The paramedics and fire crews who had also been scrambled by local 999 calls had been given minor explanations. Being driven back by the heat of the hull, they'd been hosing it from a distance to cool it down; there was nothing that didn't fit with the cover. They'd been assured that the craft was remote-controlled, and sent home. They, unlike coppers, were always glad to be let off when there were no lives to save.

"You can't enter here, sir," called the policeman. "There's the possibility of explosion."

Cleves smiled at him and didn't move. How wonderful that we are here together, he thought. You may even know, one day, of the great events upon which you attended.

"Come on, sir. You don't want to get arrested for something like this. What's your name?"

Cleves chuckled. That was one of those questions that he was often asked and had never answered, and, even though his name and rank were a matter of public record, he wasn't going to start now.

"Don't you laugh at me, sir," said the constable. "What do you want here?"

"The truth," said Cleves.

A call came from behind them. It was the Chief Constable, marching over at speed, his cap held under his arm. "Let go of him, for Christ's sake! Don't you know who that is?"

Cleves smiled at the policeman. "No, he doesn't. And he won't, Chief Constable, if you don't mind. Now then, would you be so kind as to show me everything?"

The Chief Constable led him off towards the sheeting. He looked back over his shoulder at the young policeman. The boy was staring after them, red-cheeked, wondering. A perfect innocent.

They lifted the tarpaulin for him so he could look at the wreckage.

He didn't know what he expected to see. His grandchildren provided him with views of the alien these days. That had changed so much since the war, when a kind of terror of what men had done had brought down godlike beings in silver ships. These days, everything was tentacled and muscular, a mixture of biology and machine. The alien was the other, always, and now that other was what we were afraid of becoming.

Perhaps he was expecting the angelic, or the demonic, but he was disappointed by what he saw: in the darkness a mangled cockpit, a crumpled mass of controls. That was surely a joystick. So they had hands, and sat in seats. All very familiar. A familiar design aesthetic. "No bodies?" he asked.

A sapper, a Major, walked beside him and the Chief Inspector. "No, sir. Not so far. We're waiting for the teams to come together before we open it up, or remove it, under the protocols, sir. But I really think we could make a start, sir—"

"No, you could not. We want experts on hand when—"

"Sir! Sir!" It was another sapper, mashing his way through what remained of the linseed at speed. "Sir, we've found a parachute!"

The chute had drifted a couple of fields away, down into the next valley, and had got caught and hidden in a copse of trees. It had been seen by one of the sappers who'd walked to the fence for a cigarette.

They brought it, and the mechanism it had been dragging, back to the crash site on a jeep. Cleves stared at it.

"An ejection device," said the sapper. "More advanced than anything we've got. That looks like it would fold out into a seat."

"My God," said the Chief Inspector. "So we're looking for—" He stopped, as if unable to say the word in serious company.

But something had caught Cleves' eye. He reached out and moved aside a black tag that hung from the ejection unit, a label near where explosive charges must have been packed.

It read "Danger."

It took him a moment to realise that the ordinary, in this case, was extraordinary.

"Danger," he said.

They all looked at each other.

"Open it up," said Cleves. "Right now."

The sappers unpacked their cutting gear and set to work, photographers recording every surface before they cut it. They tried to follow the design logic of the craft, detaching rather than dividing units. Those units, meanwhile, were placed onto a blanket, labelled in such a way that the construction of the whole would remain obvious. It was dark before they made much of an impression at all.

The Chief Constable had been in quite a pickle as to what he should get his forces to do. A notice to watch out for and detain the pilot seemed to be in order, but what could be announced to the uniforms in the field that wouldn't give the game away? Apart from anything else, who—or what—were they searching for? In the end, Cleves called Five's D Branch and got them to send three units of Watchers, with the aim of securing all the roads leading from this place. The commanding officer at Lyneham arranged flyovers by C-130s with full camera packages, and GCHQ agreed to photograph the area in detail by satellite on an hour-by-hour basis.

If their quarry knew anything about its surroundings though, thought Cleves, and judging by the notice, there was every chance that it did, then it would be long gone.

Every notice they found was written in English. British English, if the spelling was anything to go by. There was a great hoo-hah in the early hours when a label was rushed to Cleves' attention. It was from an unused food package: a packet of biscuits. No price or content information. The manufacturers were based in Lincoln.

Cleves didn't know what to think.

It wasn't as if this was actually a British aircraft. There was simply no such beast as this. But it wasn't his alien brought to Earth. It was as if, he thought, his cover story was becoming true. Ostentation, they called it: when a tale becomes reality. A classical thing. Magic. An action of the gods.

A sharp action, he thought for a while in the early hours. A joke on an old man. That he would never get to see their faces, never get to rise above the darkness which had entered him. He didn't necessarily want an enemy to unite the world. He wanted something the world could look up to, something greater than itself... than himself. He supposed he wanted something to give him a sense that all he had done had meant anything. He was hoping, he suddenly realised, that something would lead him away from the shabby course he was currently following.

It must be a joke. He couldn't understand the wreck any other way. He had his car brought up to the field and sat in the back of it, catching moments of sleep and being woken with each new development. His dreams were fragments around the subject of English notices. Once he woke thinking that the thing must be German. No, Russian. No, ah, that was when they were. It felt like something transcendent, but it was from Lincoln where they made the biscuits.

There were rocket engines, separated out in the crash and lying in pieces further up the field, that Cleves' experts, gazing at the picture files on their distant laptops, were saying were more advanced in design than anything they'd seen before. There was some sort of super-coolant around the electronics, as the sappers had discovered to their peril. That was what the men of Lincoln used as a superconductor.

The computers weren't like anything anyone had ever seen: boxes full of extremely fine fibre-optic wiring, curled bunches of it, in that cold liquid once more. There was not, his people said, enough of it. They could not tell how it stored information. They certainly had no system that could download its secrets.

This was not a craft, the consensus went, that those present could have made. Cleves was certain that nobody on Earth could have made it. He didn't have a technical background, but he heard enough engineers saying that they didn't understand the root technologies involved in some of the systems, that they didn't actually know what they were looking at.

So he could not even have his bitterness at a failure, a fake. If this was a fake, then it was more brilliant than the real thing.

Therefore... There wasn't a moment of revelation, but a steadily building idea, selected and strengthened during dozens of little dreams.

He thought he knew where this British shining thing must come from. Or rather *when*.

When.

But the second thought *did* come as a sudden revelation.

If this craft was from when... if there was a pilot out there from that when... why, then he could *know*...

Cleves could know if he were doing the right thing.

But he kept that thought to himself.

The voice caught them all by surprise.

It was a shout, as one of the sappers took a blowtorch to pull a support strut from behind the cockpit. Everybody stopped. There was silence for a moment. Then the sapper tried again, and the noise was repeated.

Cleves had got out of his car and been wandering around the wreck, drinking coffee from the mess van that had arrived an hour before. He'd been starting to feel irritated and tired. The solid mess of the crash site reduced everything to mundanity. The Chief Constable had gone home to his bed, content to be at the end of a phone. The Watchers were now in place, the sweeps starting, but there was no word of a wandering spaceman.

He spilt his coffee at the shout. It was different to every other noise on the site. He walked swiftly over to the hull as the sapper tried again, and nodded as the sound was repeated. He held up a hand to stop the engineer trying a third time and then carefully knocked on the hull of the craft. *Knock-tiddly-knock-knock—*

Knock knock.

The sound had come back from inside.

The sappers all took a step backwards. Suddenly Cleves felt bonfire night in the air again, the magic of an early Christmas morning. Sorcery had brought presents in the dawn. He tapped again. The same response again.

There were all sorts of protocols for meeting intelligent life. Most of them boiled down to: stand still and let it eat you. Cleves was certain now that he could ignore them all. He bent close to the casing and said, loud and clear: "Hullo there! Are you all right?"

A muffled sound came back. A shout. Clearly in the negative.

Cleves turned to the sappers. "That's a call for help. Find another way in. Keep asking. I think you were about to cut into their life support."

"But sir, what if it's—?"

"I should have thought you would have recognised it, Major. That's a woman's voice."

They went under, in the end, theorising that life support systems wouldn't be placed in the belly of the craft. To do that required digging a pit underneath and then pumping the thing up on hydraulic jacks. That caused a few more yells from inside.

Cleves paced. There couldn't be that much space inside what remained of the craft. Were they dealing with a child? Human, of course. He was sure of that now. But what sort of human? Would it be something elfin, wizened, evolved? That was how H.G. Wells would have had it.

Wells was about the only science fiction writer he could bring himself to read. He had hardly thought, in his early career, that he would participate in the war to end all wars, that it would be a war fought not with missiles but with economics. That he would see dull peace towards the end of his life. And yet he had. And Wells seemed to have known that at some point all the wars would merge into one and humanity would be cleansed and freed by it, to go on to something better.

And that men like Cleves would be left to find trouble of their own.

It was ten in the morning by the time they found the panel, and Cleves was dreaming on his feet. He fixed his eyes on the panel as they unscrewed each of four holding screws, a little boy at an airshow, waiting for something to appear.

They pulled the panel out and something slid out with it. A loud cry made them all jump. They held the weight of it, then lowered it gently.

For a moment they were all horrified.

It was a head. A human head. The head of a young woman. It was connected to a sort of palette, equipment beneath it, on a metal collar.

It... she... opened her eyes. They all reacted. They were expecting a scream. Cleves found half a smile forming on his face, the horror fighting with the greatest wonder of his life.

"You'll have to forgive me," she said. "I look a bit of a monster at this time in the morning." And then her eyes rolled up and her mouth opened. And she was unconscious.

Seven: Chips and Chipshopness

Fran was not at home on Sunday morning. Her Mum said she wasn't expecting her until around lunchtime.

Alison said again that she was sure that there was nothing wrong. Which was, by now, an absolute lie.

She went to the NHS walk-in centre down near the station, and after a two-hour wait she very soberly and carefully explained to the doctor that she had something in her eye that she couldn't get rid of. She'd been anticipating this moment since she'd woken up and found it still there, kept herself going by repeating to herself that a solution would be found (forming a mental playlist of two with that line from *Cabaret*).

The doctor had taken a light and looked into her eyeball from all angles. He'd made her look up and up until the muscles around her eyes ached. He'd asked about scratches, which Alison wanted to be the cause, but he couldn't find any. He didn't ask about bright lights, so Alison asked him, but he said that he couldn't find retinal damage of any kind. Finally he prescribed an eyebath solution, and didn't ask her to come back and see him, or go see her own doctor, if that didn't work. Alison had waited at the door of the surgery for him to look up at her on the way out. He did, finally. "Goodbye," he said, as though that were the only thing he was missing.

She saw from the look on his face that he didn't have time to disbelieve her. That the lack of anything physical in her eye hadn't galvanised him, as it would a TV doctor, but had switched her off to him, had allowed her to drop through the cracks.

She wanted to say to him, "Help," but if he didn't want to search for the thing in her eye, he wasn't going to be up for talking about the thing with the golden face.

During that day, she hung around the house, trying to read, hoping for Fran to call. Once the phone rang. It was Marty. Still no word from Fran. Yes, he'd talked to Patrick about it. Patrick was wondering why Alison hadn't called him. Alison said that well, he hadn't called her either, and Marty had known well enough not to take that any further.

Why *hadn't* she called Patrick? Because she knew he'd never believe her story, would look for the *truth* underneath that fantasy. And that would be a horrid process.

She called Fran's parents three times, and watched the hours move between the calls. They started getting worried too. The last call was at eleven at night, and they were relieved, and not at all cross with Alison. Fran had called in. A friend of hers was sick. Which friend? They didn't know. She was going to be away from home for a few days.

They'd told Fran to call Alison, and she'd said she would.

Alison had gone to bed and tried to sleep.

The Monday work day was as usual. Alison didn't want to tell anyone about her eye. It didn't ache. The thing just got in the way of her vision, a station identification icon on the TV screen of her life. She was just trying to keep moving.

Her mind kept sorting over the pieces, knitting them together. The golden man. The thing in her eye. Fran screaming. The End of the World.

She checked through all her current bets and, this being Monday, reeled off a list of tempting new odds for this Saturday's Premiership matches. No thought needed. She took small pleasure in doing the job so well, so easily. How her odds had got it exactly right, or exactly wrong, that Saturday. How Ted had fleeced so many punters with her numbers. For a moment of pride, looking at her new felt-tip boards being put in the window, she forgot about the thing in her eye completely.

Then she stopped beside the End of the World board, and felt the weight of that on her neck and cut the odds again. The End of the World: 2000/1.

At lunchtime, Alison wandered into the city centre, to the point where Stall Street (an incline of Benetton-ness) met Cheap Street. She stopped beside a cart from which a young woman in a gypsy skirt was selling big candles that looked like blocks of cheese, with a sideline in tinkly bells. It was raining like it had rained all last night. The lunchtime crowds were sweating in their coats.

She felt so lost without Fran. Sleep hadn't helped. She felt Fran lying to her parents, her parents innocently passing that lie on to her. What friend of theirs would be ill that Alison wouldn't already know about? She'd gone through a list in her head. Alison hadn't many friends on her own. Most of them were people she'd met through Fran, or Patrick's crowd, who were mostly *rah* farmers. Fran didn't like many of those, and hadn't really got to know them, certainly not well enough to look after one of them. Fran adopted the sad and lonely... and yeah, that included Alison. There'd been a transvestite monk, quite a few artists from Walcot, the local dealer, who she'd actually introduced to Marty, despite his in-depth knowledge of everything cosmic. She also had a line in old ladies, who started talking to her at the Post Office, and with whom Fran exchanged actual phone numbers.

She went to a payphone and carefully called the right cross-section of these people. None of them had seen Fran since she'd got back from up north. Alison had kind of known that would be the case, but it was something to do. Whatever she was doing, Fran wasn't looking after a sick friend.

She walked away from the payphone, putting a hand over her eye. It was like there was a weight in there, like something was holding it down in her head. God, had something got inside it, right round the back? Maybe if she used up her savings, went private? Patrick would help with that.

No. Only Fran could tell her what this was, because whatever had done this to her had taken Fran. Something awful had happened on her working holiday, and that had been too much to tell. And now something had happened to her again, or still.

There was one more thing she could do, something that had had to wait until Monday for her to do it. She hadn't done it yet this morning because it scared her, but now there was nothing else left to try.

Alison didn't look at headlines because she hated the larger stories they forced on her. Whole tides of dominoes falling into line, that these days led down to the sea: the domino event horizon. The End of the World. But people were worse than headlines. Her life to this point had been about shutting out extraneous conversations, about not letting the stupid weight of offhand British thought intrude into her bedroom. Which was normal when you were fifteen, but at twenty-two it was a shit way to be.

So now she was going to do what she found it easy not to do. She was going to stand here, at the meeting point of the two busiest streets in the city, and listen. She was going to let herself come to all the conclusions she'd been avoiding. She was going to let all the information of Bath into her.

She would find something. Something about Fran or bears or golden men or eye complaints.

And more than that, she would have taken a look outside, would have opened up the windows in her head. It was a leap of faith. The last leap. She would find something that would tell her the world would go on, that she and Fran were both okay, that it had all been a stupid delusion.

She took a deep breath, planted her boots firmly on the pavement, dropped her defences and told it to come on.

"Dot, sort of she didn't do nothing wrong sort of thing. So why should she—?"

"Hidden booklet, mate! Broke the box. Spam! I'm gonna get another now. Do *not* let me get pissed like that—"

"Slowly but surely losing more and more autonomy to Brussels. And we say no more. No further. The vast majority of British people want nothing to do with the ECU—"

"He don't want to wash them on his own. He keeps asking me to be there. And I dunno why. I don't like to ask him why. He's their Dad, they, you know, they see him as their Dad."

"Need my car. Fine, give me a bus service. Fine, give me a park and ride. Then maybe... It's putting the stick before the horse, or whatever."

"*Big Issue*! You can't have bought this one, sir, it's hot off the press today. Thank you, sir."

Alison stood there with her eyes closed for a good five minutes. She felt the consequences of all the voices, felt where they were headed together.

It was as bad as she thought it had been. It was worse.

She wanted to scream at them. The scream got bigger and bigger inside her. Don't you see? *Can't* you fucking see? This way to the unfolding. The horror. That was all. She could just see the end in more detail. It would be like a PC seizing up. The options would get fewer and fewer. Stuff would start linking with stuff. Like iceberg thoughts. A logjam of ideas. And there'd be a few last moves. Desperate big gestures. Bombs and diseases and shit. Bowls of corruption, tipping out onto the world.

And then it would all seize up. No more movement. Only old thoughts, running around inside little horizons. Intelligence... actual thinking things... would stop. You'd get a kind of simulation of that, until the whole thing... knew that it didn't know any more. Realised that it had stopped.

She opened her eyes and the scream turned into a kind of high crack in her voice. Tears were streaming down her face. They made the redness of her eyes big. She could see the thing in her eye huge now. In Technicolor. Golden.

She saw the last thing as the ice slammed shut on the surface and they all drowned underneath in a second.

No Fran. No Alison. No golden men or bears or eyes. Just the End of the World.

The surface unfolded in an explosion, flew into the air like a white flower. And with the unfolding, there went human life.

Someone was talking to her. "Are you all right?" the voice was saying. It was trying to be more gentle than it was.

The woman in the shawl helped her to her feet.

"I can't find my friend," Alison said. "I don't know what's happened to her. I never will. I can't work it out. The End of the World. I can't stop it."

The woman laughed, nervously and caringly. From the wrong place inside her, again.

Alison stumbled off, rubbing her eyes, unable to clear them, up her own local familiar gradient of chipshopness.

There was no hope. She couldn't swallow that down. There was no hope unless a miracle fell out of the sky.

She was heading for the chip shop, she realised. She hadn't been going to do that, because she and Fran had had chips the other night.

She and Fran.

And suddenly Alison was sobbing out loud in the street as she walked, with everybody looking at her. "Something will come along," she said out loud, feeling the dark purposeless direction of the waterfall still inside her. "Something has to."

Leyton had spent the night walking. He'd explored the city at night, stood outside the big illuminated windows of bars, sat on a bench by the river in the early hours. He'd revisited some of the places he'd visited in his youth, the obvious shrines. He'd sung to himself to keep his spirits up. He'd fallen asleep standing under an archway where there was a pub, and had stayed like that for an hour or so until the dawn light had woken him up.

He had nothing inside him in the morning. He huddled inside his coat, the collar high up against the frosty air. He was walking around the polluted ancestor of the city where he'd been in love. The city still used money. He had none.

He stayed in the side roads as people started to fill the streets: firstly the cleaners, people who were actually employed to sweep the streets, and the postal workers. Then the shopworkers. Then, as the clock struck nine, the shops opened and people flooded into them.

Nobody pointed at him, or hailed the security forces. He got a few strange looks, but nobody *said* anything to him. They really were afraid, though he saw smiles and hullos and kisses. These things happened anyway. It was acting out of line these people feared, talking to the stranger, getting involved. Perhaps it was because of the beggars. There were a handful of them, sleeping in doorways, left there by the tyrant as a warning. If you have none of my money, this is what will happen to you. That was one of the few things from school history classes that stuck in the head of a small boy, the gaudy illustrations of the ragged wretches, the victims of a rough coin bearing the image of the tyrant, struck because the world community refused to set up environmental links with him.

He found such a coin in the crack between two pavement slabs and plucked it out. His first sight of the tyrant. A woman. Elizabeth, who had taken on the title of Queen. She'd been ruler at least since 1991, according to the issue date, which was a long time for such a warlord. If she was still current. The driver of the tractor had referred to a man, Leyton was certain. Perhaps this "Queen" had some wicked advisor.

He pocketed the coin. He was going to need that five "pence." Or he was going to find out, first hand, what this culture did to those with no money. Late last night he'd found a shop that had a sign on the door saying it would cash "cheques," the window of which was blacked out. He'd decided he'd visit that at some point and see if, as he suspected, they'd also buy whatever he had that could be sold. He had no experience in the business of money. He didn't know if these people would see their concept of value in his coat, his cap, his cufflinks or his belt. But the darkened windows spoke of secrecy at least.

So he had the first stage of a plan, but he dallied over carrying it out. Everything he had to sell was something that connected him to his old life. And he was cold and shivery and needed the coat. He wasn't sure if he could sell it for enough money to buy another one and also get other things, like food. Maybe the five pence would help. People took some value from every transaction in such systems, he knew from his history classes. The culture was one of endemic parasitism. The tyrant would take the most. He didn't see how he could do anything here but lose. But he had to keep walking. He'd promised that to Elsie.

So he stayed in the centre of the town, wandering between the people. He was surprised that there were flower sellers and people who made candles and wanted money for them. He found it hard to believe that under such a merciless régime people would use their money to get luxuries, but the shops were full of them. How could these folk be sure that they would always have enough money to feed themselves? They must be living in fear, running to keep ahead of the axe, all the time. Asking money for flowers and distractions... there was something sickening about the idea.

Around lunchtime, he felt his strength starting to leave him. He had to go to that blacked-out shop soon. Where was he going to sleep? He found that he wanted to eat. His last meal had been dinner on Borneo: mushroom soup, beefplant casserole and Borneo's own huge vegetables, with treacle pudding to follow. He'd just eaten it, talking to Stewart Magemwe all the while. He'd taken the giving and taking of food for granted.

He couldn't do this. Not on his own. This world was going to kill him.

No, he said to himself. Something would come along. Something had to.

A familiar smell reached him. There were memories like that all over the city. He didn't know which were worse, the ones that took him back to his time with Elsie, or the unfamiliar, usually dirty ones that reminded him of his distance from his home. Fish and chips. They were quite near the sea here. The cod had always been good. He wandered towards the source of the smell and found a chip shop down a narrow road in the shadow of the rheumatic hospital. Joy amongst misery, like everything else here.

If he asked for food, surely they couldn't just say no?

He walked stiffly past a couple of youngsters eating their chips on the pavement outside, braving the rain under an awning. He didn't want to march. He was a petitioner. He hadn't felt like this since he was a child. It was an awful feeling, a place he'd been put by these barbarians. He knew he deserved to have food. He wasn't fat. They wouldn't mock him here for having had too much, as the shopkeepers of his own time sometimes did to a customer who asked for more. Here it didn't matter what you were like at all. All that counted was how many coins and notes you possessed.

There was a queue: a big group of young men, scaffolders who'd been working on the decaying brown flank of the hospital, doing a job meant for machines. They looked happy enough, despite the rain. They gave Leyton heart. They were hanging around for the new chips, which the men and women behind the counter were just starting to shovel into... copies of newspapers! They still did that! Leyton wondered if this was some nostalgic or old-fashioned chip shop. A couple of the lads were already eating. He took advantage of a gap in the crowd and stepped up to the counter.

"Excuse me," he said to the woman. "Can I have cod and chips, please?"

"Right you are, love." She went to pluck a piece of fish from the cabinet.

"I ought to warn you, though. I don't have any money."

She stopped. "We only take cash. There's a cashpoint up the road."

"No, I mean... I don't have anything to... pay... you with. I'm hungry, you can see I'm very fit, and it looks like you make a very tasty bit of fish. Would you be so kind as to give me some?"

She just looked at him, with the most terrible expression on her face. A trapped look, like he was trying to play some tasteless practical joke on her at a time when she was supposed to be at her most dignified. She crossed her arms over her chest, almost a defence, like he'd abused her. "What?"

There was an awkward silence from the group of men. A stifled laugh.

"I don't have any—"

"I heard you, love. You want the *Big Issue*. You want to move across there, I've got customers to serve."

There was indeed someone behind him now. A young woman. She was more miserable than he was. She looked like she'd been crying.

But now she was staring at him.

He stared back. There was something *incredibly* familiar about her.

Alison stared at the man in the cap and coat.

She'd walked into the shop trying to rub the tears away from her eyes, angry that everyone would be looking at her and thinking she'd just been dumped by her boyfriend or something. She'd cleared her vision just as she'd stumbled inside the fogged-up glass of the shop. She'd blinked. And she'd found her eyes fastened on his silhouette. Her brain had raced ahead of her before her thoughts became words. Her tears had shut off in that moment, surprised out of sorrow.

It took a moment for her thoughts to catch up with her reactions. This man wore a real uniform she'd never seen before. There was nothing costumey about it. It was real. And deeply British. But new. Different. And therefore not real.

He asked for food, she realised she'd heard that as she walked in, in an accent that sounded like he owned a stately home. There was a sound in his voice that she'd never heard. He sounded like he was surprised by the world.

And then he'd turned and looked at her.

She was suddenly even more ashamed she'd been crying.

She got everything else about his face a moment later as he stared at her. And that turned her sobbing at the End of the World into a prelude to something, the hurt that led into something wonderful.

Faces, for Alison, were about times and places and classes. They spilt who someone was straight away. As she'd grown up with being able to read stuff, she'd started to be really scared by how boys' faces, their eyes especially, were always about sex, almost all the time. She still had dreams about violentboy faces now. She'd got used to them as she got older, realised that the intentions didn't translate, didn't animate the bodies, that she could walk round them and talk to other things in them, or just scare them off, or play that one thing in them against everything else. She could have been such a tart in the fifth form, if anyone had liked her. By the time she'd really got the hang of it, though, other things had scared her and her vamping became small, private, sometimes a party or a girls' night out thing. Fran had seen it and said, "Always the quiet ones."

She'd been to see the statues that lava had made of the Romans at Pompeii. The guide had said their faces were startlingly similar to our own, that they inspired empathy because of that. Which was bollocks. The faces of the Romans had meant so much to Alison that she had to close her eyes and go and stand in the corner of the bathroom with the water running, because they came from a different time and place, and brought with them a wave of unwanted ideas, springing up out of the space between them and her. There was so much that she had to swallow a lot of it whole before it gagged her. It had come startling out of her for weeks after, bursts of associations: conclusions and dreams and livid daydreams that had made her stop and raise her hands from her A level studies and wonder for a second if she was living in the right time and place. The way the Romans had looked at each other, they way they looked at the death that was about to hit them... the way even they had some End of the World in them. That had felt like a small hard pebble knotting her gut, even back then, when the End of the World was a childhood fear, a long distance away. This lot were expecting the good life. But they were looking fearfully at the future and now were afraid that the future was here. There had been a tiny slave girl, looking up at her master with only a question in her face: is it okay to die now? Alison had never seen that look of being owned on anybody who was living.

So Romans were different. She'd got a jolt of their world, an immunisation to it. She now never wanted to read or see anything about them again, because it might connect and connect and connect, and then she'd have to find someone who would listen to her talk and talk about Romans to let it all out, and be like a Rome groupie, and there just wasn't anyone like that around.

That was another one of the things that had made her what she was. And she knew every one of those things in detail, of course, and knew that she could take a holiday from any of them, but that whenever she wasn't thinking about these chippings and clippings at her mind, back the habits would come. Never go too far into anything. If one look at something can change everything... take a quarter look.

But now she was staring and staring into the face of the strangest living man she'd ever met. The man who'd arrived as the answer to all her questions.

Her first thought was that he was from the war, from Grandma's old photos. Young men who looked old, with slicked-back hair, standing as if nobody had ever been photographed before. They looked like puppets, confined in how they could move. There was an authority hanging over them, in the way their gaze either avoided the camera or went straight out and through it, talking to the family back home. She'd seen these men alive in old age, as great-uncles and family friends, and they were still the same: made up of rods for back, arms, failing legs. They had big bad teeth that didn't fit their mouths, and heads that had gone bald from all that tugging Brylcreem, and catchphrases and smells and trousers too short for their legs.

There was something of that about him. Not that his hair or his teeth were like that. His uniform fitted him.

That was the second thing. The violentboy face dream jolt. Come quickly, they're roasting Tom. The public school cut of the chin and the broken-in, cropped hair, and the flighty, wine-winking eyebrows. She was scared of him for a moment inside this moment. Smoky clubs, male spaces, hoarse laughter, I did this on the battlefield because I was allowed to and why don't they let us do it at home, eh? He came from a real military culture that she didn't know anything of, that was from a long way away.

But then she saw his eyes, and they connected those two things. They were the eyes of a penitent monk. He'd run to the door of the monastery, yelling for sanctuary. They hadn't let him in. The eyes had all the strength of the military bastard, but none of the morbid laughter. They weren't watery and lost like the eyes of those uncles. They were those eyes, but new. She understood the photos now. This man had been hunted at full speed with complete determination by those who were trying to kill him.

He had been spared by chance as friends around him fell, and in just falling, astonishingly, died.

That astonishment had piled on top of him. And he had held it. He held it like those uncles held it, only they'd got too old and too familiar to show it. He was afraid and brave and lost and still for a cause that he believed in like she'd seen no modern young man believe in anything.

He wasn't cruel. He was not a coward.

Alison hadn't met anyone for whom that was completely true, herself included.

He was appealing to her for help in just this one long look. But he had not surrendered an ounce of himself in doing so. He was also looking at her like she was something he'd lost and now found again. He had asked for food in a way she'd never heard before, but a way she now understood.

"Oh," she said.

Leyton looked up from the girl at the sound of a shout from somewhere behind them.

One of the construction workers had pulled a page of newspaper copy out from under his chips and was shaking it in the air, showing it to the others. He looked suddenly angry. The page was covered with photos, and the most absurd large type. A children's paper? "It's him!" the man was bellowing. "It's him!" He threw his chips to one of the others and stepped forward to Leyton, thrusting the paper into his face. "Is that you?" He stole a look at the paper again. "Are you Douglas Leyton?"

Leyton stared at the photograph that was shoved in his face. It was him, and his name was written underneath. How had they known? But no, how could they have photographed him? And he looked older, greying...

"Is it you?" The man pushed him in the chest, the paper crumpling in his hand.

Leyton felt something give.

He was hungry and these wretched ghouls had refused him food. He was a ghost in a city that would one day be the place of his lost love.

But he was an officer of the Fleet. Elsie had told him to keep on going. And he was damned if he was going to deny his name. He looked the man in the eye and saw naked rage there. And part of him was glad. "Yes," he said. "I'm Douglas Leyton."

"You fucker!" yelled the man, and threw himself at Leyton.

The young woman cried out and jumped out of the way. The weight of the man slammed Leyton into the wall of the shop.

Leyton didn't think much in the next thirty seconds.

He broke the man's grip with a punch to his thorax. Then he smashed upwards with the heels of his hands under his chin and sent him flying backwards.

The others leapt for him. He assumed the stance and sent the first one over with an uppercut, then grabbed the arm of his comrade and smashed him flying against the wall. The third one he grabbed around the neck as he charged at his stomach and directed the butt into the same wall. The fourth he leapt up to and smacked twice, once on each side of the head.

The fifth one wasn't up for it. He squirmed into the corner, holding up his hands.

Leyton stopped himself and turned to check on the fallen men.

"I'm calling the police!" the woman behind the counter was yelling. People were crowding to the window, gawping in at them.

He'd lost his temper. He had to go. Now! But the rush of hot blood after his fatigue had left him feeling dizzy. He fell against the counter, tried to push himself to his feet. The men were starting to move, starting to stumble upright themselves.

The girl swam into his field of view. She was clutching the page of newspaper copy, looking between it and him. "It *is* you," she said.

He had the chance to get a good look at her now. And suddenly it dawned on him. The impossible had happened. The very thing. He knew *exactly* who she was.

"My thoughts exactly," he said.

Alison had grabbed the newspaper from where it had fallen. It was yesterday's *Bath Chronicle*. The headline said: "Is this the man who murdered Tommy?"

The photo was of this guy. Every muscle in the face was the same. But at the same time it wasn't. The face in the paper was animated by the same old things she'd seen in the world all around. The same horrors. It wouldn't have made her pause for a moment had she seen it in the street.

He'd recognised her. But she knew they'd never met.

"What do they think I am?" he asked desperately as she helped him to his feet. "What is that photo?"

She took his hands in hers, because she wanted to touch him, and because she wanted to demonstrate to all these shitty End of the World people that she was absolutely on his side, and because she wasn't going to let him get away from her.

"I trust you," she said. "Now come on!"

And she hauled him off his feet and out of the shop.

Eight: Knowledge and Being

Jocelyn opened her eyes.

She was very, very worried. She had a gap in her records, which meant she'd been unconscious. And she hadn't been unconscious since she'd died. If she'd been dreaming... well, she was still here. Everything seemed to be still here.

The last thing she remembered was the moment before impact: the incoming radio transmissions, the wash of cultural information, as she'd expected, then that moment of doubt just before they'd hit... Oh, and then there had been a swimming in and out of consciousness, some words spoken... What had she said?

The doubt was still with her. This was different. She had not been briefed for this. She was going to have to make it up as she went along.

She was on top of a table in a white room. She looked down. She felt wet. The bottom of her neck was sitting in a medical tray, filled with blood.

She screamed.

A door opened and in ran a man in a white coat. "What's wrong?" he asked.

Jocelyn was embarrassed now by that scream. "My body," she murmured. "I seem to have mislaid it."

The man looked shocked.

Which made her laugh. "As you were, you duffer. I left it at home. If you must know, it's the blood. It took me by surprise. I'm not a vampire, you know."

"Oh, I'm so sorry, we thought it best..." The man in the white coat started to fuss, bringing another tray over from one of the low lab benches and pulling swabs out of little plastic packets.

The door opened again and another man entered the room. He was in his sixties, tall and gaunt, with just a fringe of receding white hair. He carried an old leather satchel over one shoulder. He looked at her for a long moment.

"Nice to meet you too, I'm sure," she said.

"Oh dear. Do excuse me." He carefully stepped into the centre of Jocelyn's field of view and bowed. "We haven't been properly introduced," he said. "Nor can we be. But who do I have the pleasure of addressing?"

"I'm Jocelyn."

"Jocelyn who?"

"If you must, Pembridge, but we rather leave that behind."

"When?"

"With one's body. You can't take it with you, you know."

"No rank?" The old man took a chair from a workbench and sat in it, a comfortable distance in front of her.

"Oh, I always find that sort of thing terribly dull."

"So do I. This is a ward in the hospital wing of RAF Lyneham, an air base in Wiltshire. It's been specially done up to take care of you."

"Good-oh."

"As you might imagine, we have many questions to ask you."

Jocelyn smiled and kept silent.

"For instance: do you come from a world orbiting another star?"

"Absolutely. Could you get me home by afternoon tea?"

"You're making fun of me."

"Only a little. You can take it, can't you, soldier?"

He smiled slowly. It was a nice smile. He didn't take the bait and tell her whether or not he was a soldier. "Some of the others, you see, were surprised that you were human."

"And you weren't?"

"Not at all. Not after inspecting your craft. I'm not even surprised that you're British."

"Gosh."

"What I am surprised about..." he shifted in his seat, as if only now getting to the nub of the problem, "is that you're evading my questions."

"This is obviously an interrogation. What else am I supposed to do?"

"I would call it a debriefing. I am British. You are British. How is it an interrogation?"

She kept silent again. She had absolutely nothing to go on, no idea who this man was, or what beliefs or political system he subscribed to.

"You," he continued, "have the sort of accent that people these days associate with old films. They assume that such films employed actors only from the upper classes. They laugh when such actors attempt middle class or lower middle class roles. They don't realise that such accents were once aspirational, that people really talked like that. That once we all wanted to be Trevor Howard. That accent is my accent. Or it was. I'm sure that I too have fallen prey to the estuary influence in the decades since the war."

She saw his eyes sparkling. She desperately wanted to ask him what year this was. But the fact that he'd just tempted her with that meant she shouldn't. "You're going a bit too fast for me, chap."

"Do forgive me. I'm trying to make you feel comfortable. Is your pilot human too?"

"Pilot? I thought it was just me."

"We found the ejector seat and the parachute. Does she have a body? Or is she somehow intangible?"

"Indeed she is."

He inclined his head slightly. "So we are looking for a man. A very tangible man. That is the first question you have wanted to answer."

Jocelyn could have spat at him. "Oh, please. I try and be helpful and that's what I get."

The man in the white coat lifted her and started to wipe the connectors at the base of her neck. Everything was locked down, Jocelyn confirmed with a surge of relief. The automatics must have cut in. He couldn't do any harm.

"So," she said to the old man, deciding to be blunt. "Who do you work for?"

"The civil service."

"Oh," she said. "What a coincidence."

"Really? What department are you with?"

"I'm head of planning."

He threw his head back and laughed. "Dear me. Are we going to get anything out of you apart from musical comedy?"

The scientist placed Jocelyn in a dry tray. "Thank you," she told him. Then she looked back to the old man with the exaggerated sweep of her eyes that one learnt when one was just a head. "I rather think that depends on you telling me some things. About where I am, what sort of society this is, and all of that."

"Don't you know?"

"Only what I hear on the radio."

"The thing is, that will require time. Clearance from—" He pointed upwards.

"God?"

"Worse. The PM's office."

"So there's a Prime Minister? For someone who doesn't want to give anything away you're letting a lot slip."

"Who said..." he got to his feet and slipped both hands behind his back, his eyes never leaving hers, "that *I* didn't want to give anything away?"

"You just did. Aren't they recording all this?"

"I have the authority to forestall all that. I thought it would make you feel more comfortable if we just chatted." He was lying.

"Why is it you want to know so much so quickly?"

He made a show of deciding to trust her. "Because we need to know if your wandering pilot is dangerous. Or if you're dangerous. Or if you represent something that is dangerous. Medically, strategically, or otherwise."

She decided to trust him. Just a little. "I can answer the first of those questions. My pilot is not dangerous at all, and probably in need more of medical help than of quarantine. When you find him, please don't hurt him."

"I'll give orders to that effect immediately. Would you care to give us a description so we can pick him up without a lot of fuss?"

Jocelyn pursed her lips. "I say, is there any chance of a spot of tea?"

The men looked at each other. The scientist seemed to want to ask a question but couldn't quite find the words.

"And some cake," Jocelyn added quickly. "If you have chocolate sponge, then I will start to regard today as being less than a total loss."

The old man patted the scientist on the shoulder. "Make that two slices, please."

In the shared kitchen of her flat, Alison spooned soup from a can into a saucepan and put it onto the heat.

She'd skipped the afternoon at work, which felt, for some reason, like she'd played truant from school. Not something she'd ever done.

She'd taken Douglas Leyton across the city, along the line of greatest hidingness. Nobody had paid any attention. The men in the chip shop had run out and looked in all directions, but must have decided on the wrong one. The police probably hadn't been called.

She'd taken him into her house, led him up the dark and smelly stairs, encouraged him to sit on her bed. He'd been reluctant. A lady's room, he'd said. If there was another bedroom, he'd be grateful... But there wasn't. He'd accepted that. She'd taken his boots and coat and cap and tie and placed them on the chair, on top of her things. She could see he thought the place was a mess, but he hadn't the knowledge to ask why... he didn't know what any place was.

He'd started asking questions, but, eager as she was to hear them and ask loads of her own, she'd told him to lie down, and put the duvet over him. He'd struggled only a little.

Then she'd gone to make the soup.

She realised, as she stirred it and poured it into bowls, that she was singing. That line from *Cabaret* again.

It sounded strong once more.

She took the soup through to him, closing the door of her room with one foot.

He was asleep, his mouth open, almost painfully, as if the hurt inside him was draining into the pillows. He had stubble, she noticed. In rest she could study him at greater length. Maybe she could get everything there was to get. He looked to be in his late thirties, but he had a haircut like he expected to walk in somewhere and be noticed. A Dad shirt. Him being in her bed felt weird, like when she'd shared a hotel room with her dad, just six months before he died, as it had turned out. If he'd brought his bathroom stuff with him there'd be pots of weird-smelling shit and aftershaves that only old ladies liked. This guy wouldn't wear Joop.

Or maybe he would. The edge of his mouth was smiling in sleep. Maybe he'd be up for anything. There was no way she was going to get everything about him. That was the unique thing. That was why he'd been shining like a beacon for her when she'd stumbled into him. He was a contradiction, two things in one.

And then it hit her: the reason why she had been so sure when she saw him that this man was the answer to her questions about Fran, her eye, the End of the World. Only now, in silence, had her brain got round to sorting out the details of it.

Coat. Cap. Real. From an authentic organisation. Only not from now. And not from the past. Therefore...

Therefore, no End of the World.

You're standing beside living proof of that.

She put down the soup on the bedside table for fear she would spill it.

He woke with a start and looked up at her. "Terribly bad form," he said. "We haven't even been introduced, and here I am in your... room." He saw the soup and took it, blowing on it and then quickly starting to spoon it into his mouth. "Thanks. I'm absolutely famished."

"So." She sat down on the edge of the bed, not wanting to take her eyes off him. "What year are you from?"

He stopped eating, his eyes darting all over her face.

She couldn't help but smile. Mainly because now he didn't even have to answer. There was going to be a future. All her fevery calculations had been wrong. They'd led her instead to this amazing point. It was too big to swallow, but here it was. Big future! She felt like dancing around the room. "It's obvious," she said. "Go on, just tell me!"

And for a moment she almost thought that he'd look at her like she was mad and start to make his excuses and go. But no. She'd lived all her life with this skill. She knew when she could depend on it.

He gave in and smiled, rubbed his hair, which was all over the place already. "All right, yes. I'm from the future."

"What year?"

"Twenty-one twenty-nine."

Alison laughed out loud to hear it.

"I should be glad I ran into you," he said.

"Absolutely."

"Because I expected the whole issue of establishing my identity to be rather more complicated than this."

"I'm very good with people. I understand things."

"Um-hm. But what if I was trying to con you?" he asked like he was toying with her, like he knew the answer to these questions.

"You didn't try to. I asked."

"I might be that chap in the paper."

"But you're not. You're too young, for a start."

He looked aside. "I saw the photo. He looks exactly like me. Perhaps a bit older, yes. And he has my name, and... he seems to have committed murder."

She felt like taking his hand, but there was something about his body language that said she couldn't. "Maybe he's your ancestor?"

"My ancestor! Of course!" He lowered himself back onto the pillows and let the bowl lie on his chest for a moment. "Thank God for you! There always have been a lot of Douglases. But still... that could cause a few problems, eh?"

There was something else, Alison realised now. Something in the way he was just avoiding her gaze. It was harder to read him than it would have been to read anyone from her own time. He had ingrained body language that was like nothing she'd ever dealt with. But yes. She'd seen it back at the chip shop.

When he first saw her, he looked at her as if he'd seen her before.

He was still looking at her like that now.

How could she work her way round to asking about that? "Mr Leyton..."

"Oh, no misters, please! Call me Leyton. Or Douglas. Or Squadron Leader if you want to be terribly formal."

"Why are you here?"

"Complete accident. We were in Earth orbit. We hit something. We crashed in Dorset. Only... here... in the past."

"We?"

"Myself and Jocelyn. My head." She watched him realise that she was boggling at that. "My co-pilot and navigator. The poor old thing. She couldn't have survived the crash."

He was so open apart from this one thing. It was a big thing, but he wanted to keep it to one side. It was like he respected her already. What he'd said in the chip shop. He *knew* her. "You were in a spaceship?"

"I was on leave."

"Oh God. You're fighting a war."

He paused for a moment before answering calmly, "Yes."

"Who against?"

"We call them..." He blinked, slowly, and shook his head. "This sounds like a dream now. Like a story I'm telling you. Are even you going to believe this?"

"I will. I do." Then a thought struck her. "Do you call them the Golden Men? Are they like... golden men?"

He raised an eyebrow. "No."

"Are there any aliens who are like golden men?"

"By 'aliens', do you mean foreigners?"

"No, I mean aliens, from space."

"Indeed. Foreigners. Intelligent people from other solar systems."

"Whatever. Are there golden men?"

"There's nothing that I'm aware of that looks anything like a human being. You lot are due to encounter the Sooms in about... fifteen years? And they're—" He extended his fingers in a little scuttle. "Like beachballs with legs."

Alison didn't know whether to be relieved or scared. Could she really have two miraculous things in her life and find that they had nothing to do with each other? "So who's the enemy?"

"We call them the Rods. The inhabitants of three planets orbiting the star Zeta Reticuli. They're grey rods. About this long." He held out his hands like he was measuring a fish. "They whizz around the place."

"Why are you fighting?"

"They tried to get some of our colonists addicted to this drug they'd specially brewed up to suit our biology. We took action to shut that down, they responded with their whole fleet. We reacted. They attacked Earth. They diverted comets and asteroids into encounter orbits. There were... considerable losses. This was decades ago, over a century. This war had been going on for ages before I was born. Earth and its environs have been peaceful for a long time now. It's become a war fought in space, and on the colonies."

She wanted to say she was sorry. But it seemed like such a tiny thing to say about such a big, distant story. She was silent for a moment and let him eat. "Do you lot time travel all the time? I mean, is it something you know how to do?"

He laughed into his soup, spluttering, and had to put it down. "Corks, no! Maybe it was a natural phenomenon. A random dreaming. We thought it was another ship..."

"What's a dreaming?"

"The way we navigate. The heads do it. Something to do with... they sort of imagine where we're going and... Listen, Alison, I'm just a combat pilot—"

Alison felt something inside her shiver. Like something had nearly got past her. She found the words in her head a moment before she realised the depth of her question. She'd got him. "How... do you know my name?"

He actually halted the spoon halfway to his mouth. It took him a whole beat to think of something. "I... read it somewhere. Over there." He nodded towards a pile of letters on her table.

She looked hard at him. She was nearly at the point where she could ask directly what the hell it was that he knew about her.

He looked back to his soup. "So why," he asked quickly, "did you want to know about golden men?"

So was she going to level with him when he wasn't being completely honest with her? She looked again at the cut of his brow, at the curl of his eyebrows. If there was ever going to be a time when she had to chance reaching out to another human being, this was it.

She took a deep breath. "It's a long story," she said. "It's about a friend of mine who's gone missing."

And she told him every single bit of it.

He listened in less astonishment than she expected, possibly because, in this era he wasn't used to, he didn't know what was surprising and what wasn't.

She started at her childhood, at her ability to divine things. At her fear of the End of the World. And she went all the way through to the drunkenness, the kitchen, the encounter with the golden man and the vanishing of Fran.

At the end of it all he sized her up for a moment. Then he took a deep breath and blew it out with a puff of his cheeks. "Phew. Well, I don't know what to make of all that golden man stuff. And this thing in your eye..." He moved his head, trying to get a look. "I've never heard anything like it."

She opened her mouth at the sheer hideousness of it. "You don't believe me!"

"Well, alcohol can do strange things."

She had to hold in the urge to throw him out onto the street. She was speechless with anger.

He finished his soup, oblivious. After a few moments he looked up. "You know, I'd like to know what they're saying about the crash. I've seen what passes for newspapers here, but what do you do for the real gen? Is it all...?" He waved his spoon in the air.

"All..." she managed to hiss. "What?"

"Jungle drums. Whispers. Rumours down the pub, all that."

"And why should it be like that?"

They looked at each other awkwardly. "I was under the impression... the political system you're living under. Well, I *think* I know how you'd feel about 'Queen Elizabeth', but I certainly wouldn't want to jump to conclusions, and it must be hard to make do in such circumstances, especially when your friend has gone missing, but—"

"Who have you been talking to?" She proceeded to give him a quick and rather sharp lecture on the politics and history of the early twenty-first century.

Leyton's jaw literally dropped, she was pleased to see. But as she went on, his expression changed to a sort of wary vertigo. He thought he'd put his finger on one thing about this world, but he didn't even have that now.

Which served him right.

"Oh the oaf!" he said, finally. "The decadent fool was talking about
an elected government like he was Robin blasted Hood! If I'd known, I'd
have exited the tractor forthwith and found a better lift!"

"So your knowledge of history is so crap that you don't remember the
Queen?"

"Erm... Well, I didn't really think that by now you still had... Do *you*
know who was on the throne a hundred and twenty-eight years ago?"

"Victoria."

"Oh bloody hell, even I know that one, that's just because she was
there for such a long time. Who was before her?"

Alison found that she had no idea. But who was this bastard to ask her
questions? "History is only about really famous people," she said.

"Indeed."

"Loads of stuff must happen in the gaps." She went to her sound
system, found Radio 5 and switched it on. "There's the news you wanted,"
she said. "I'm going to make myself some tea."

She managed not to slam the door behind her.

It took her only the length of time it took to boil the kettle to think of what
Fran would have said about Leyton, someone who was completely lost,
with her as his only help.

And he could help her. He was the only person who knew everything
about her. She had trusted him with everything.

It wasn't his fault that for some reason... for some *reason*—

The way he'd said "indeed"...

She made two cups of tea.

When she got back to the room, she found him sitting on the side of
the bed, his back straight as a ruler.

He was listening to a story about how the floods were down to global
warming. He looked suddenly pale and tired.

"Nothing about a spaceship," he said. "They've kept the lid on it."

He sounded so lost.

Alison put the cuppa into his hands. "Do they have beer where you
come from?" she asked.

She took the man from the future on a quick tour of Bath. They stood
outside the Abbey in the rain, just as it was getting dark. They watched the
floodlights come on.

She pointed out the carved angels crawling down Jacob's Ladder
head-first like Dracula, and he pointed to the Bishop on the left of the door
who'd had his head knocked off and had it recarved from out of his beard,
so now he had a tiny head compared with his companion.

"You've been here before," she said.

"Often. It's only the really old stuff that survives." He raised his hands to frame the front of the Abbey. "That's a scene directly from my... my youth."

His romance. His dating. His courtship, he'd say.

She stopped herself from asking her name.

"Apart from the ladders," he said. "And the chaps with wings. Recent addition?"

"I don't know."

They'd discussed how likely it was that they'd run into the same sort of circumstances as at the chip shop, and had decided that it was probably unlikely to happen again. Leyton was relieved that he was only hiding from yesterday's newspaper, rather than from his tyrant queen. He'd refused any sort of disguise, though he had left his cap and coat at the flat in favour of one of Alison's biggest jumpers, which fitted him awkwardly, but not ridiculously. His straight back looked a little odd in it, though. It was a garment designed for a slouch.

Working people were crowding into shelter by the bus stops, forming long queues in the neon lights. Cars moved in slow jams along the roads. Alison took Leyton to deliberately modern places: a kind of time tourism, she thought. She kept looking at him against the backgrounds, his silhouette against the frontage of Robin's Cinema, in the window of HMV, drinking a coffee from Starbucks. If anyone else had her talent they would have seen him from a mile off, screaming of otherness.

She took him to Linley's Racing, after it had closed up for the night, and pointed to her odds in the window. England to beat Pakistan in the Test series. 50/1. "Hey!" she said, struck by a sudden thought. "Who won that series? We could make a fortune!"

"Who won—? I have no idea! If I had my *Wisden* handy..."

"Can you even name the Captain?"

"Erm... Ramprakash?"

"Nasser Hussain."

"Oh come on, I was close! Only one out! This is all before my time."

"Duh."

"So what is...?" He gestured towards the window. "You work for a place where people make wagers... for money?"

He'd emphasised the "you." Like it was unbelievable she did that. Not morally, but... she felt like she was being compared to... to something she *should* be doing. She said something quick to cover the nervous jump in her voice. "Oh God, when do they stop doing that?"

"In the mists of time. Way back." His eyes kept fastened on his reflection in the glass, unreadable even for her. Passers-by moved them apart on the pavement for a moment, and when they came back together he was smiling. "Gaps, as you said. I still can't get the hang of this cash business. To make wagers for something other than a favour... to actually profit by them..." He shook his head. "What happens if I put ten shillings on the cricket and lose?"

"You have shillings? When did they come back?"

"We *had* shillings. When we had money. When did they *go*?"

She shook her head violently. What was going on here? "We take your money. That's what happens. So you don't have money?"

"Not for... not for a long time. I find it odd that you have."

"How do you do without it?"

He ran a hand back through his awkward hair. "The World Government shares out the resources. Everybody gets assigned a certain amount."

"Everyone? Individually?"

"By district."

"How big's a district?"

"Well, we're in the district of Wessex. From Bristol to Andover, up to about Cheltenham... I could show you on the map."

"Isn't it all a bit... frugal? How much soup do you get?"

"Soup, salad, whatever. There's more than enough to go round. Actually, there wasn't when Joey Bowker was President, because the man was incompetent. I remember the blackouts from when I was a tiddler. But he only made one term. Sorry, you won't know what I'm blathering about."

"What happens if you want to vote in someone who'll change the system?"

Leyton looked at her like she was a silly child. "You get the occasional lunatic, but they never make it past the district elections. What other system would work?"

Alison slowly raised her hands in a gesture which took in everything around her, from the people marching past in the rain to the distant rumble of the motorway that led its traffic into the centre of this Roman city.

She watched Leyton's expression change into a kind of polite deference.

"You said," he murmured, "something about beer?"

It was quiet this early at the Porter, and there wasn't likely to be anybody about who was still carrying yesterday's *Chronicle*. Leyton sipped his first pint of Bellringer and settled into his seat with a little sigh of relief. "Terrific," he said, and looked over at her with new warmth in his eyes. "You know, I owe you a great deal. My goose was about to be cooked until you came along."

"Just get your round in and we'll say no more about it."

"Get my—?"

"Pay for the next lot of drinks."

"Ah." He reached into his pocket and placed a five pence piece on the table. "Will that do?"

"Fuck," she laughed. "We should go to the Uni bar." She realised that he was looking at her in horror, but trying not to show it. "What?" He'd glanced over his shoulder as if he'd been scared that somebody would overhear. And now he was actually blushing. "Oh..." She laughed again. "Sorry. I'll try not to, okay? But I can't guarantee anything."

"No, no, I won't hear of it. If that's what you're used to. I shall just fucking get used to it, madam." That little twinkle hit the side of his eye again. "Quite something to use such language in the company of a lady. Chin chin." And he drained his pint.

Realising what he was doing, Alison threw hers back too and slammed the glass down a second before him. She wiped her mouth on the back of her hand. "Oh brave new world," she said, looking straight into his eyes. "That has such tarts in it. Oh stop!" He was blushing again. Wonderfully. "So," she said. "Are you going to help me save my friend from the Golden Men? Are you going to help me get this thing out of my eye?"

He looked ashamed for a moment, and she realised he'd seen the hurt he'd caused earlier. He just hadn't been in a hurry to talk about it: the complete reverse of Patrick's guilelessness. But this was nice. This wasn't hiding things—apart from the one big thing, of course, that he was hiding. And she thought she had a good idea what that was. "I'll help you..." he said carefully. "With whatever you need help with. It's the least I can do."

"Cheers." He still didn't believe her. For some very good reason that he wasn't telling her.

"I thought my mission here was to save my ship from the hands of the tyrant. But if this is an elected government..." He rubbed the bridge of his nose with his hands. "I suppose I'll have to get in touch with them anyway, work something out. Share my info with them."

"You've got a lot of faith in democracy."

"Well... yes." He looked at her with surprise. "Shouldn't I have?" He took it as a rhetorical question, not waiting for her to reply. "At any rate, until some greater purpose becomes evident, I'm your man."

She stood up. "I'll get them in. Same again?"

"Indeed."

Indeed. She walked to the bar, bouncing inside. Even if this guy wasn't taking her seriously about Fran, even if she was still missing, she was absolutely wrong about the End of the World. Which meant she might be blissfully wrong about Fran and the golden man too! If Leyton didn't know anything about them, and he knew the future, and all about her and everything—

Behind her, the door opened, letting in a blast of wind and rain.

"Oh," said Alison, without looking around. "Hi, Patrick."

The single most attractive thing about Patrick was his confidence. If he wanted something, he'd just go out and get it. Once he and Alison had been lying in bed with the TV on, and they'd just caught the end of the news. The weather, he'd said, there's no harm in the weather. And Alison had thought, okay, you can only predict the weather a few days ahead, can't you? That's what chaos theory says, and so she had watched. And she'd found herself thinking of the terrible winter that they were going to have. All that rain. It had rained ever since.

Seeing she was hurt because of what he'd done, Patrick had got out of bed, dressed, popped to the shop across the road and come back with a huge tub of ice cream. Which they'd shared. And that had, indeed, made her feel better.

He used money like it was something that extended the reach of his hand. She had stopped saying when she liked a top or something in a shop window because his response was to put his hand into his pocket.

Apart from when he had been trying to impress her, he placed his bets with some intelligence. But he had too much pride. Alison had stopped advising him after he won a couple of times on the horses thanks to her and then tired of the sport. It was hard to watch him lose, but Alison always thought she'd step in and stop him if he put too much on something that wasn't going to win.

He talked loudly in pubs, often about how crap hunt saboteurs were. He'd only been hunting once, and said he hated it, couldn't stand it when they caught the fox. But all of his friends down in the country did it, and Alison often thought he was straddling the fence just for her. He was very certain of his opinions, and not afraid to argue if someone drunk came up and challenged him, as they twice had in studenty pubs. He'd ended up buying everyone drinks and got them almost on his side by the end of the night. He'd decided he liked R.E.M. after hearing one single, and then bought all their CDs.

He was like a big warm blanket.

And often she wanted to be wrapped in him.

But oh God, not now.

Patrick came straight to Alison and kissed her. "There you are!" he said. "I left thousands of messages on your answerphone."

"Sorry."

"Why haven't you called me?"

"I didn't want to worry you."

"Worry me? That's sweet of you, delish, but this is the sort of thing

I'm here for. Marty said you sounded really down, and I was all sulky
that you hadn't called me, but I really should have been thinking of you,
and as soon as I thought that..." He visibly realised that Alison was with
someone, and looked over in the direction that she'd glanced. His big face
folded into a suspicious stare. "Who's he?"

"My secret lover."

Patrick flopped his arms by his side, exasperated. "I hate it when you
say things like that," he said.

But Alison's attention had left him. She was still looking at Leyton.
He had a very complicated look on his face. At first her spirits had leapt
in a very awful way at the thought that this complicated look might be
jealousy. But it wasn't. And she was surprised at her reaction, but later for
that.

She didn't know what Leyton's look meant. He was staring at Patrick
in bewilderment. Like he'd skipped a chapter somewhere.

The moment was broken by Marty coming in. He wasn't dressed for
the weather, as always. His combats were sopping and his long hair was
plastered down the back of his neck. "Hiya," he said, managing a smile.
"Fran about?"

Patrick slapped him around the shoulder. "No sign, old son. I'll get
these. You go and sit down with—"

"Leyton," said Alison, giving Marty a hug.

Leyton enthusiastically shook Marty's hand. "Glad to meet you," he
said, and really meant it.

Alison continued to look at him. This was so weird. Leyton was
grinning like a schoolboy at Marty, and glancing uneasily up at Patrick.
There was suddenly something... nervous about him. For the first time.
She had a sudden flash of him watching cricket, applauding at a good shot,
meeting the players...

That was it. Leyton looked like someone who'd gone backstage to
meet the band—which fitted with her idea about his big secret.

But that didn't quite fit with how he was reacting to Patrick.

Patrick brought the pints and sat down. He reached out to grab Leyton's
hand.

"Patrick Flint," said Leyton.

"Ah," said Patrick. "She's told you all about me."

But she hadn't.

Patrick, it turned out, had already done a preliminary run-through of
most of the places he'd met Fran, with some help over the phone from
Marty. He'd gone from door to door like it was a military operation. Marty
had wandered to a few more in the rain, and been greeted with weed and
tea wherever he went. "Nobody's seen her. Stevenson said he'd met her,
and I got all, like, cheers mate, but it turned out that was from before she'd

left. So..." He flopped in his seat and managed a sad smile. "This has got to hurt. She went out with you, and that's okay, but she didn't even call me."

Alison told them everything she knew, with the exception of the Golden Man and the eye thing. She saw Leyton look at her when he became aware of the omission, but apart from that he didn't contribute to the discussion at all. The look on his face was still that he was the only person who'd come to the party in costume. But, beside that, she kept noticing him stealing glances, at Marty and Patrick, as well as at her, like he was comparing all of them to photos.

"Well," said Marty finally, "she's... off doing her own stuff for a while."

"She's dumped you," said Patrick. "Sorry mate, but she is clearly bonking someone else. Why else would she tell us all some story?"

Alison didn't want Marty thinking that. "Bollocks. She might have met someone who needed help. If she was seeing someone else, she'd have told you about it, Marty, straight away."

Patrick snorted. "You and human nature, darling. You always believe the sweetest things. It'll be Scott, Marty. Fran's got his sort of tits. Up to here."

Sometimes Alison wondered if Patrick went out with the same person she looked at in the mirror. "Scott's gay."

"That's why she's adopted him. One of her lost causes. She likes someone she can mother."

Alison was about to ask him to stop making generalisations about someone who was her friend, actually, when Leyton raised his head to look directly at Patrick.

"I think Alison knows her friend, chum," he said.

"You'd think so, wouldn't you?" said Patrick, laughing. "But she's such a darling. Always thinks the best of people."

Leyton raised his glass. "To thinking the best of people, then."

"And who are you, exactly?" said Patrick.

Alison saw the calm appraisal going on in Leyton's eye. She saw the fire there ignite for a moment and then be damped down. "I'm the chap whose *round* it is," he said. He looked to her. "Could you—?"

Alison reached for her purse. "Sure."

But Patrick put his hand on hers. "If this guy's down on his luck I'll get them in. Rather than have him sponging off my girlfriend."

Leyton shook his head slowly. "No," he said.

"No what?"

Marty was looking between them, aghast. "Mate... Guys..."

"I'm a stranger here." Leyton got to his feet. "I don't know how this place works. I don't even know..." He looked around them for a moment.

Then he just shook his head and headed for the door.

Alison jumped up and ran after him.

"Hey!" Patrick shouted from behind her, suddenly bellowing. "If you go through that door—"

But she'd already done that.

Nine: When Cherubs Attack

"What," Alison said, catching up with Leyton as he marched away from the pub, "was all that about?"

"He's your boyfriend? Patrick?"

"Yes. What's wrong with that?"

"Nothing."

"Do you know the way back to my house?"

He stopped, realising in a wonderfully cartoonish way that he'd been marching along without thinking where he'd been marching to. "No," he said.

They were standing in front of the white bulk of the Abbey, illuminated from below. The rain was falling in little lighted droplets, like stars speeding through space. Alison wondered if he'd ever seen it like that.

She took a step closer to him, wanting him to look her in the eye. "What's wrong about me being with Patrick?"

"There's nothing... I wouldn't presume to... I'm sure he's a fine..." And then he stopped himself, and did look her in the eye, and now his voice was suddenly hard. "It's nothing personal."

"I'm famous, aren't I?"

"Alison..."

"I'm famous. In the future. And so are Marty and Patrick."

She'd got it. She was certain of it. He was staring right at her, his eyes admitting it. Then... he was staring past her.

His eyes had fastened on something past her shoulder, and all the uncertainty and anger had vanished from his face—which frightened her hugely.

She turned smoothly to find out what he was looking at.

Something was wrong. It took Alison a moment to realise what.

There was something moving on the face of the Abbey.

For a moment she thought it was a person. No, a child. She put a hand up to shield her eyes from some of the light that was blazing off the building. It was a strange mixture of shapes... maybe some piece of rubbish had caught there... no, there was a face. It was looking straight at her.

"What—?" she said. And in that instant, something connected in her mind. A golden face, looking straight at her. Only then it had been much closer.

In a flash, the thing scampered horizontally across the expanse of the Abbey and off into the darkness.

"Is that your Golden Man?" Leyton asked. He sounded utterly astonished.

"Come on!" she bellowed, and sprinted off after it.

The Reverend Brian Whatmore had a congregation of six for his Monday night Holy Communion, one of whom had been asleep.

Whatmore would have conducted Communion for just himself and the choir and helpers, had he got no audience at all. Indeed, on a couple of occasions in other churches he'd done just that. But he'd been hoping for a better congregation on this first service at the Abbey. He was a visiting preacher; his own parish was in Somerset. But there had been some illnesses here, so the Bishop's representative had asked him to step in for two weeks. He'd prepared what he thought was a great sermon. An hour ago he'd walked up to the lectern, found his notes and looked up at the few who sat faithfully in the back pews. The great space threatened to overwhelm the meagre audience.

He'd been to Bath many times, had spent many nights working in the homeless shelter near the station, at the bottom of the hill. Brian saw the city as a ladder, like the ladders on the front of the Abbey. You could walk up and down that central line of streets and go from absolute poverty to the discreet designer shops at the top of the town, from money for food to shops that hardly wanted to reveal themselves as shops at all. It was a mediaeval shape for a town, and he hated it: the apartheid of two different branches of W.H. Smith, two different Boots, with the tourist traps running in a band across the middle.

The city as a cross. That image had come to him in his dreams. As a burden, the image on the land of the central problem, the war which Christ had come to Earth to fight. You could live at the top of the town all your life, high up in one of those clifflike Georgian brownstones, without ever having to see what it all ran down to, the streets that hit the river, and downriver, where the tourist cruises didn't go, the wrecks of houses along the banks out of the city, the hills and caves where the squatters ended up.

The riches of the city attracted them. And the city placed them, sorted them, arranged them like a machine arranged things on a production line.

Brian had spent time in Chile, and Mexico, had studied Liberation Theology as practised in the cities there. The bishops he'd known had no use for displays of money like the interior of this Abbey. They would not make the chilling differentiation that a certain cleric of his acquaintance in Somerset had: "The *love* of money is the root of all evil."

Above all, when the Latin clerics of his acquaintance spoke, they had something to offer their people in this world. And so their people really listened. He could be as revolutionary as he liked to an audience in the Abbey, he thought as he stood at the end of the night, shaking the hand of the last of the voluntary helpers and letting them out into the rainy night. They'd nod along to it, agree it was all terrible, even help with the various useful and practical schemes to aid the homeless. There were good people in this city, and running the Abbey. They did their best. They meant it. When he said, "God is with us," a lot of the people here felt it in their guts, like he did.

But what he would never convince anyone here of was the truth that the Brazilian clerics lived with every day. That a Christian should be concerned with the *root* of the problem. His sermon had begun, "Let's start by thinking for a moment about the problems of those made unemployed in the manufacturing sector, and the problems faced by farmers following the foot and mouth epidemic."

He closed the door behind the final helper and stood there for a moment, thinking. He was tired. He really should go and change out of his robes, get a pint. But he felt awkward tonight, like something more was required of him.

And then, from outside, he heard a strange noise.

Fran had thought that by now *we* would have access to what the pilot was doing at all times, but *we* had swiftly discovered *we* did not. So one of *us* had gone on a scouting mission in Bath, and searched for him and Alison.

Fran might have helped, but now she wasn't sure where she was. She couldn't be separated from the *we* so easily now. Not after her confirmation. She knew there was somewhere where she was, and she was being her usual self. That mind was running. There was quite a lot of pain, though. So she was glad to be *we*, who didn't do pain.

When one of *us* found them, all of *us*, all of the Four, from their places and minds and accounts and systems around the world, became material. This was very dangerous. One bomb, and everything could be over. Alison and the pilot must be important. Fran saw Alison running after *us*, and imagined the movie for her too. A beautiful crane shot of her running.

But Fran preferred being the cinematographer to being where Alison was now.

Alison and Leyton ran across the square, past benches, into a narrow road where the buildings overhung. They managed to keep pace with the phantom as it leapt from building to building. Alison rubbed her eyes for a moment as she ran. She could see that Leyton was getting equally confused. The thing was moving like a searchlight, hopping from surface to surface, like an optical illusion—but they were where the projector for such an image would be. And it was still there after she rubbed her eyes, which only reminded her again of the thing in her eye. And then it looked back at her: that obvious human shape, that face!

They pursued it, running into a gap between the buildings. Alison looked around for the creature, but couldn't see it. They stood in a sort of municipal nowhere, at the back of a car park and a supermarket: cobbled, but surplus to requirements. No windows. No doorways. They stood there, panting.

She felt Leyton tense at the same moment she did. They'd been led here.

Something moved all around them.

Alison thought for a moment that she was dizzy from having run looking up at the buildings. She raised her hands to steady herself as the air fluttered and hazed around her.

Then something struck her, across the side of the head.

She fell sideways, against the wall. She bruised her arm. It hadn't been a hard slap. She'd been cuffed. Deliberately, not with full weight.

Something had hit Leyton too, she realised, but much harder—from where an assailant couldn't be, across the shoulder, sending him staggering forward, falling onto his palms.

He leapt back to his feet and reached down to help her. They folded, back to back, looking around—

And stared at the things that were attacking them.

They floated in the air all around them, in a circle connected, like little girls playing a skipping game. There were four of them, but parts of them were shared like streamers. They had golden faces, and bodies that were shadowed and angled in awkward ways, like the light they were under was not the same light as that which bathed Alison and Leyton. There were, Alison was sure, parts missing. She saw them like art, like an image—like they were in a film and she was not. Except they were staring at her with empty golden eyes and slitted mask mouths. Familiar eyes and mouths.

An extraordinary sound was coming from them. They were laughing: not the laughter of babies, but the full-throated laughter of the winning side. She felt a great envy of them. They were the representatives of a higher authority. She wasn't good enough for them. They made her feel fat.

One of them swung its head, like a series of frames of film switching over and over. It looked straight at her. Its mouth opened and from out of it slipped a tiny, thin blade, with an end that was clipped into the arrow of the end of a sword. This creature had a sword for a tongue!

"Hello again," said Alison, feeling like she was talking to Father Christmas. "What are you?"

She didn't really want to hear their voices. But they did not speak. Instead, the circle *shifted*, became smaller around them. They were surrounded.

"You know," Leyton said over his shoulder, "in all the stories about you, they never mentioned this lot."

"Which is why you didn't believe me when I told you about them?"

"Right."

"And I'm not supposed to be with Patrick, either?"

"Spot on." Their backs pushed closer together, muscle settling into muscle.

In an instant, the circle contracted.

Leyton yelled as it dived at him. He ducked and pulled Alison down.

She felt the blades sweep her hair.

They'd passed over her.

Leyton roared and lashed out with both arms and for a moment connected with something solid.

He rammed it against the wall. Alison was beside him a second later, wanting to touch these things—

The black and the gold shifted into air and were gone. Leyton's hands hit stone, but slower, cushioned.

The circle swept round. Poised.

"Now!" shouted Leyton.

He grabbed Alison's hand, dived aside and they ran, sprinting across into the square, their eyes fixed on the Abbey. There was nobody else around. In moments there'd be people, but the drift of them meant gaps. The creatures had taken advantage of that for the ambush.

Behind them, in the sky, she could feel the sweep of their... wings? No, they didn't have wings. They just flickered against your eyeballs like a fluttering film. God, she knew them. Indeed, she felt like she should be intimate with them, that for some reason she should be their friend. They seemed to assume she was, which was why they weren't hurting her. She knew them so well from storybooks, from nursery rhymes, only she couldn't pin down which ones. She'd always known of little assassins with swords for tongues, like they had always been behind the wallpaper, a thing pinned down in a cool schoolbook when those lines of light slanted across the classroom.

From the Latin.

They were hot on her neck.

She angled herself towards the door of the Abbey as Leyton dragged her, feeling the impact of every fast slam of her boots on the paving slabs. Thank Christ she wasn't in heels. She could see their target, a little light above the wooden side door of the Abbey.

She didn't know if that door was locked.

Something sliced at Leyton's back. A whisper. He nightmare-stumbled, pistoned himself up. Alison yanked his arm and he was upright again, still running.

They were going to make it. If there was anything to make. Why would the creatures not follow them in? They were just running for sanctuary.

The doorway opened. A square of light. A vicar with a beard was staring at them. Staring at the sky above them.

Alison was surprised, for a moment, that other people could see what was after them.

"Up the Fleet!" Leyton shouted.

They leapt for the door.

The vicar stood aside, throwing up his hands.

They fell headlong onto cold and muddy tiles.

Alison got to her feet and stared into the sky. The vicar was staring with her. His mouth was open. She could see his fillings.

The creatures were circling, slipping over each other in midair like a braid, glittering and hissing and sucking the air behind them into darkness. They weren't moving in. For some reason, sanctuary was real.

They were wonderful, like the trailer for the next *Star Wars*. They had about them the promise of newness. They were the most cutting-edge things in the world.

One of them whirled forward and spiralled in the air in front of the vicar, its golden face looking smoothly at him. He held up a hand, half a greeting, half to reach out and touch the being that floated in the darkness in front of him.

The creatures twisted into nothing and vanished with a whisper.

The vicar crossed himself. Then he slowly turned to Leyton and Alison. "What are they?" he asked.

"Christ knows," said Alison.

Leyton gave her a hard stare.

Fran was astonished by *us* stopping.

The Four vanished back into their different places and started to think hard.

She lost sight of Alison and had only the distant sights of what was happening with her own body to think about. She thought she was asleep. Her limbs were tired.

Why did *we* stop?

It was one of those rules, the answer came. Sanctuary. The rules were there because *we* had become so much part of the underlying theology. *We* were pictured inside the churches, but *we* couldn't enter them. Fran realised that *we* still felt hurt about that.

Inside the churches they said Lucifer was a *fallen* angel!

Now *we* were thinking about what to do, since Alison hasn't accepted her baptism. That was unique. *We* didn't know how she'd managed to do that. The next step would have to be confirmation.

Alison had never liked churches. Or vicars. That was down to her dad.

They both seemed to her to be excuses for things. She just about managed to keep the meaninglessness of life at arm's length. The whole religious thing was about giving yourself a distraction, only then, like an addict, you insisted the distraction was real, that it applied to everyone else, too. Her dad had tried to make her see, had once grabbed her by the shoulders and put his head to hers, willing the Holy Spirit into her.

That was the night she had told him to piss off, which had really hurt him. But he'd never tried that again. Thankfully, she'd told him she was sorry for that way before the end.

Churches also reminded her of the End of the World. They had it written in their windows and in their architecture: big things looking down on people and thinking: now? Or now? When, then? When do we drop the world down on top of the humans? When will they most deserve it? Getting past the millennium, she had thought some time in the nineties, would get her over this fear completely. But actually it had just become more real.

She found that she was shaking. She hadn't been chased since school. Her last experience of violence was from when she was a kid. A shiver went through her that jolted her body from top to bottom.

She watched Leyton bob before the altar.

She didn't want to be in a church now. Her feet were heavy with fear, and when she found that the shaking was becoming continuous, she sat down on a pew. The vicar had excused himself, gone to get tea. He'd had the look on his face of an enthusiast suddenly coming upon something that excited him. Oh God, was he going to think those were angels after them? Or demons, or something? He wasn't going to be much help if so.

Leyton sat down beside her, looking almost as shaken as she was. But, she saw, he had a weird expression on his face, a kind of certainty.

"What," she asked, trying to keep her voice from breaking, "are you thinking?"

He looked at her, startled. And, she was sure, he made something up. "I suppose it's what I'm used to. A solid enemy. Something coming after me. And I even got my hands on one of them. Just for a second. If I can thump it, then it's easier on me than if I can't. One can't actually take arms against a sea of troubles. But one can thump Cupid."

She wanted to ask what he was thinking again. What he'd decided. But there was time for that. He was boxes within boxes. She didn't want to make him open all of them at once. "Are they, you know, from space?"

"I don't know..." He rubbed his chin. "I've never seen anything like them."

She was silent for a moment. But then she couldn't help herself. "So I'm going to be famous?"

He groaned. "I can't say any more about that."

"And Patrick and I aren't supposed to be together?"

"You were, you have been, but not..." He stopped. "I suppose all stories

lose a bit in the telling. The details must have got confused. But you must
have kept this stuff with the Cupids completely hushed up!"

"I must have kept schtum about you as well then, right? Unless there's
someone like you in these stories."

"My God." He looked alarmed suddenly. "No. You're right. I'm not
mentioned either!"

"You can't keep me in the dark now. This is getting serious. Tell me
what I'm going to do."

Leyton sagged. "I know your story so well. The story of Alison
Parmeter. I know the stories better than I know about the history of sport
or the monarchy or politics. And so I know that, at the moment, it's rather
strange that you and Patrick are still together."

"Well, I have been thinking about..." She decided to let that trail off.
"Go on."

"But you never know with history. Maybe the books I read and the
films I saw—"

"There's a film?"

"Several."

"Oh."

"Maybe those things generalised, made the details more straightforward. Maybe some editor along the line just didn't believe all this stuff
about Golden Men and pilots from the future. If I interfere, if I actually tell
you, I might really send it all over the place."

Alison leant back on the pew. "Now I get it. The whole of history
could depend on what you say to me. Chaos theory and stuff. The littlest
things have the biggest consequences down the line."

"Absolutely."

They were silent for a minute. "Bollocks to that," she said. "Tell
me."

"I can't!"

"Maybe you're already part of the plan. Maybe you telling me what
I'm supposed to do makes me do it." A sudden thought struck her. "Unless
it's assassinating someone. It's not that, is it?"

"No, it's not that. Nothing like."

"And it's definitely nothing to do with the Golden Men?"

"You know more about them than I do."

"If you don't tell me, I'm going to spend the rest of my life second-
guessing myself. And I can do that better than anyone else. I'll be leaping
on every cause and chance that comes along. I'll never get any sleep. I'll
really mess up history. You'll get back to the future and find out you're
ruled by dinosaurs. You've done it now. You're going to have to tell."

He thought for a moment. Alison smelt the smell of him, which was
like musky woodsmoke. It was starting to make its presence felt in the wet

clothes of hers that he wore. It was a good smell. "All right," he said.

"Right!" The bloody vicar, of course, chose that moment to return, carrying cups of tea on a tray, which he placed carefully on the pew beside them. "Go on, drink it while it's hot. Lots of sugar. For the shock. I've got blankets in the vestry if you want them."

Still looking at Leyton, Alison picked up the hot mug and took a sip of the tea. It had, indeed, more sugar than she'd ever tasted in a cuppa. The heat and sweetness felt good.

"Oh," said the vicar. "I'm Brian. Brian Whatmore. I feel like I should call someone. Like the police. But what good would that be? Are you sure you don't know what those things were?"

"Absolutely positive, Padre," said Leyton. "I'm just glad they couldn't get in here."

"Yes, sanctuary." Whatmore stroked his beard. "I do not believe in demons. Or a personified devil or any of that rubbish. But what else can they have been?"

"Did you see its tongue?" said Alison. "What sort of creature has a sword for a tongue?"

Whatmore opened his mouth again. "My God," he said.

Whatmore turned the pages on the huge leather-bound Bible that sat atop the lectern and smoothed down the page.

"His head and his hair were white as white wool," he read aloud. "White as snow; his eyes were like a flame of fire, his feet were like burnished bronze, refined as in a furnace, and his voice was like the sound of many waters. In his right hand he held seven stars, and from his mouth came a sharp, two-edged sword, and his face was like the sun shining with full force."

"That's him," said Alison.

"Then that's Christ."

"He's changed a lot."

"Well, actually it's only generally taken to be Christ." Whatmore flipped over the pages, his eyes alight with interest. "It's a description of the being who visits John on the island of Patmos to reveal to him the Apocalypse. John describes him as: 'One like the Son of Man'. That's usually taken to be Son of Man in capitals, a synonym for Christ. But there aren't any capitals in the original Greek. And 'like the' is problematic. Some scholars have said that John was just saying this angel, or whatever, was basically human, like a son of man. This is my speciality, actually. I did my thesis on the symbolism and political message of Revelation. But as to what this all *means*..." He stepped back from the book and looked straight up. "I'm reeling with having seen it. And there was nothing... numinous about it. Those things looked like... real things. Beings. Animals. People. But they were doing the impossible. Vanishing. Moving like they weren't there. I feel like a witness. Oh Lord, I won't sleep for a week."

Alison chanced a look at Leyton. He was frowning, deeply puzzled. And that felt like really bad news.

"Where in John is this?" he asked.

"It's not in John," said Whatmore. "It's from the Book of Revelation."

"Is this the Apocrypha?"

The vicar looked puzzled. "No, this is the Bible. The Book of Revelation. The last book of the New Testament."

Leyton was looking like he'd been hit over the head. His tongue wet his lips. He seemed to be having trouble with the words. "The last book of the New Testament is Jude. And what's an 'angel'?"

"Oh fuck," said Alison.

Ten: And I Feel Fine

They sat in the lounge of the Old Green Tree, staring into space.

Whatmore was at the bar.

They'd got there just in time for last orders. As soon as Leyton had said what he'd said, Alison hadn't been able to stay in the Abbey any longer. They had waited until a gang of pissed students were going past and run out across the square to them, keeping to the crowded places until they got to a pub. Leyton had theorised that the Cupids wouldn't have lured them into a quiet spot if they'd felt able to attack in public. Whatmore had followed them, nearly walking on Alison's heels in an effort to stay close to Leyton. He hadn't changed out of his cassock and collar.

"Perhaps... it doesn't mean what it seems to mean," said Leyton. "Maybe the Bible got revised before my time. This 'Book of Revelation' got cut. Someone took a dislike to these 'angels' and chucked them."

"And these cuts were so effective that you've never heard someone saying 'you're my angel' or 'angels at twelve o'clock'? So all-encompassing that you've never received a Valentine card with Cherubs on it?"

"What are Cherubs?"

"A kind of angel. Fat little boys with bows and wings."

"We call those Cupids."

"So do we. But those are Roman, I think. What's your Old Testament like?" She tried to remember some of the things her dad had told her. "What guards the Tree in the Garden of Eden?"

"The Holy Spirit."

"Who tells the Virgin Mary she's pregnant?"

"Same again."

"What goes around Sodom and Gomorrah testing people?"

"Where?"

"Two cities where..." She saw that Leyton had never heard of them, and slumped. "It's all different."

"It doesn't mean that—"

"Yes, it does. You come from a future that doesn't belong to this past. Something's been changed. We don't get to where you're from from here. In this world, we have the Book of Revelation in the Bible. I get the feeling you lot *never* did. You're a religious man, you'd have known something about it, even if it was in the Apocrypha."

Leyton silently nodded. The look on his face was terrible.

But Alison had to go on. "In your history, you'd got rid of money by now, hadn't you?"

"I think that must be so."

"And I'm... I'm not going out with Patrick."

"At least you're still a religious person."

"I'm... what?"

"You're very much a believer."

"I'm very much *not*."

He rubbed his face with his hands. "But how can this have happened? How can history... change?"

"It's been changed as far back as whenever Revelation was written. Or at least when it got included in the Bible. Even before then, if you don't know about Sodom and Gomorrah. But you know what the worst thing of all is?"

"I think I do. For you." He was looking seriously at her.

"You were my dead cert on there being a future. On the End of the World not coming true. If you don't come from my future, all bets are off. And with these guys with swords for tongues showing up... when the last time anybody met one was to announce the Apocalypse... As I believe I said before: oh fuck."

Across the bar, a pair of eyes slipped over the top of the *Sporting Life*. They fixed on the man who had sat down with the girl. They looked from him to a mirror over the bar. And then back.

The newspaper started to shiver. It nearly dipped, but then it was raised again. The eyes watched the man move, watched his hands flex on the table, watched his gaze as it held the face of the girl beside him.

Douglas Leyton couldn't hear what the two of them were saying to each other, especially since they were talking in whispers, so he went back to his newspaper, determined not to be noticed. And then a word leapt across the bar and made his brain select it, made his attention focus on it.

"Leyton." The man had said it. He was taking a pint from a vicar.

As inconspicuously as he could, Douglas moved closer. His reactions had been good enough to stop him from looking up directly at the mention of his name.

"Douglas," the man added.

Douglas had to hold his paper tight to stop it shaking again.

"So," Whatmore asked, sitting down, "why don't you know your Bible?"

"I know *my* Bible." Leyton look his pint. "I just don't know *yours*."

"There's only one."

Alison waved her hand between the two men, wishing the vicar would stop asking questions and just be useful. "It's really complicated. And you wouldn't believe it."

"I believe that I saw something supernatural tonight. Why don't you try me with the rest?"

Alison looked at Leyton. Then they both looked back at the priest. "Perhaps in a bit," said Alison. "When we know you better. Right now, could you answer some questions for us?"

Douglas waited until the three of them were deep in conversation, then quietly got up from his seat. Putting other people between himself and their table at every moment, he made his way towards the door. He couldn't remember which parts of which disguise he was wearing tonight. But it probably wouldn't conceal his appearance from a man who looked exactly the same.

He stopped on the threshold and looked back. He desperately wanted to know who this man was who'd taken on his name and face. And at the same time he didn't want to know. But he was equally certain he didn't want them to be seen together.

There was a window from the pub across the way where you could watch the door of the Green Tree. Douglas went to go and sit in it.

Whatmore took a sip from his beer. "Right," he said. "Revelation is generally considered to have been written in one of two time periods, either fifty-four to sixty-eight AD, during the reign of Nero, or eighty-one to ninety-six, under Domitian. We know it was written by someone who called themselves Yohanan, the Jewish form of John, who lived on Patmos, in the Aegean, in exile. He's had a fight with a priestess of some sort on the mainland, whom he insults by calling Jezebel. And he thinks his name alone, with no indication of which John this is, will be enough to get his scrolls read by the seven churches he intends to send them to. That's all we know about him."

"Don't we know which John it is?" asked Alison. "Isn't it the one who wrote... you know, the Matthew, Mark, Luke and John one?"

"Erm, we don't know it was those apostles who wrote those gospels either. The first reference to them as the authors is from a couple of centuries after the fact. But yes, it could be that John. Though he'd be pretty old by that time. Or it might be someone who wanted to use the cachet of his name, like a lot of Jewish apocalyptic writers who took on the name of a particular prophet. Most people, though, think that because there's that little personal spat at the beginning, he is who he claims to be. Whoever that is."

"So this is..." Leyton was clearly choosing his words carefully, "this is a book of prophecy about the end of the world? Not very Biblical, is it?"

Whatmore laughed. "Absolutely! It was a judgement call whether it made it into the canon at all. And these days it's a bit of a damned book. The Catholics only keep a couple of passages from it on their four-year reading list. You don't hear it read in the Anglican Communion very much.

But you ask if it's a book of prophecy. Even that's complicated. Three different approaches—"

Alison couldn't help but smile at the man's enthusiasm as he set three empties on the table. He was so into this Biblical trainspotting stuff; how could anyone devote their life to this?

"The Preterist approach: yes, these are prophecies. But they've all come true already, mostly in the couple of centuries after the book was written."

Alison blinked. "I didn't know about that one."

"It's not very popular these days, but elements of it are still present in mainstream Catholic theology. Then there's the political approach: it's all just coded language about the Roman Empire, about things which are happening then and there. Nero is the Great Beast, etc. But you should see the work it takes to get Nero to translate into 666 in Jewish numerology. It's not a neat trick by any means. That's all pretty mainstream. Finally, there's the futurist approach. These are prophecies which are yet to come true. It's all going to happen, the Four Horsemen, the Seven Seals, everything. One single line gives you the rapture, the salvation of the élite, the whole direction of the American Fundamentalist movement. Now that, if you ask me, Mr Leyton, is not very Biblical."

"But now we've seen the creature with the pointy tongue—"Alison began.

"What have you done to have angels attack you?" Whatmore spread his hands wide. "Apart from not being aware of the concept of angels?"

Leyton and Alison looked at each other again. "What indeed?" said Leyton.

Whatmore was feeling increasingly frustrated about what these two astonishing people weren't telling him. But he was very wary of anger. To him, anger was something reserved for the real battles: to save lives, to protect the poor. Those who used anger in their everyday lives were misled by the comfort relative wealth offered into thinking that their small conflicts were important enough to rage and rant over. They were, in short, led into evil.

So he took a deep breath and began a lecture on angels. "They're probably older than Judaism, early insertions into the stories which became the Old Testament. Cherubs, or Cherubim, are very high-ranking in the scheme of things, actually." He wanted to ask, again and again, who the man was. He wanted to ask until they told him. He was certain that here was a Christian who had grown up without certain Biblical concepts in his life. With bits missing. A Christian from... another world. "Not that I believe in angels. They feature in the New Testament in an entirely different way. The word there, in Greek, is 'angelus', which just means 'messenger', as opposed to the Hebrew of the Old Testament, where they're clearly all these strange creatures. These days the only people who are really into angels as Biblical are the ones who write books claiming they've got one hanging about and looking down on them, and that's just your old-fashioned paganism with the serial numbers filed off, eh? Listen, you and I, we were, well, we seem to have been brought together for a reason, and—"

"What?" He'd said something to upset the girl. She was glaring at him. "You're saying that we're on a mission from God? Bollocks!"

"Alison!" The man was angry with her. He had a kind of old-fashioned respect for the clergy that Whatmore had last seen in South America.

"No, no." Whatmore put a hand on his arm to calm him down. "I can't say what this is about any more than you can. But if I can help... I'd really like to."

The girl's glare faded a little. She didn't say anything.

"Look." He grabbed a beer mat and a pen and wrote down his address, phone number and e-mail address. "Keep in touch. Especially if you see any more of those things."

The man asked the girl to give him her number in return and, thank goodness, she did. The call from the bar came, time, gentlemen, please. They were going to go their separate ways. It looked like the girl was eager to do that, like she and the man were going to have some urgent, complex discussion that he would not be privy to.

As they left the bar, the man looked seriously at Whatmore. His glance communicated that there was more to say between them also.

Whatmore relaxed. This was not going to be struck from his hands.

He went back to the Abbey, thinking he ought to change and go home. He'd been loaned one of the church flats in the Abbey Courtyard for the duration of his stay. The Abbey was dark and the moonlight shone through the windows. It was a nursery space.

Whatmore walked into the centre of it and got down on his knees. He raised his palms to the ceiling. He couldn't help but laugh as he asked God his question. "What are you up to?"

Douglas got up from his seat by the window as Leyton and the girl passed his pub.

He went to the door, waited a moment for people to come between them, then slipped out into the night behind the couple. He'd been trained in trailing people. One of the rules was not to stare at the back of their heads. They always seemed, somehow, to notice. But Douglas couldn't help but look closely at the man in front of him. The shoulders were Douglas's, but held upright, like he'd had that walk beaten into him. The swing of his arms was something Douglas did when he wasn't trying to move unobtrusively. When Douglas had had hair, he was sure it had been like that. His excursions into his own brain had cut out the easy ways to whole sections of his memory. That didn't matter. Who he was wasn't based on his memories, or his choices. His reading had made him certain of that.

The ghost headed across town, over the broad main street, where it was easy for Douglas to keep track of him in the chucking-out-time crowds of people. The lights and the rain concealed him. It was always easier to follow someone in the rain. They looked down into themselves and assumed everyone else was doing that too. But this man wasn't looking down into himself. He was walking as if he wanted the world to see him. Except, Douglas noted, that he always stayed close to other groups of people.

As soon as they left the pub, Alison had said, "Right. Tell me about how I'm famous." She didn't feel as light-hearted as that. The shock of the attack had shaded right into the shock of finding that Leyton was from a different future, of the End of the World being back on. And the alcohol had made her think of where they were again, of how she was sure that the golden men had done something terrible to Fran. And to her eye.

But she could feel the tension and despair radiating off Leyton, though he kept his back straight and his head up. He was her last hope for the future, and she was going to take care of him. She also didn't want him to get at her for yelling at that mad vicar.

"You're just trying to take my mind off things."

"No, I just want to know how I'm famous."

"You may not become famous now. You're not supposed to be going out with Patrick this late. I don't even understand why there is a you. Don't tiny things have big effects? If things have been altered as far back as Biblical times, why are there even individual people who are the same in this world as in mine? Why is there a Nasser Hussain? Why was he ever England captain, if everything has changed?"

His voice was getting a little high-pitched. Carefully she took his arm. He didn't stop her. "Maybe the world is like a book. It's all written. Solid. If you change one bit of it, it's not like sticking your toe in the river. Everything doesn't flow and change and do chaos stuff around it. You edit one bit, you make the rest of the story fit the change, you don't alter the bits that you don't have to."

"Well, that's what my world feels like, rather. Like a story in a book. Like everything I stand for, the war I fought, who I am—" He stopped, calmed himself. "Terribly sorry. But I feel like it's all gone. Replaced by... this."

"We'll get you back to your future."

"What if it's not there any more to get back to?"

"It could be. Maybe you can go back to the first draft. Or maybe we can find the Golden Men again. Find Fran. Find out what they've done. Change it back."

That strange look on his face again. He changed the subject, just a little. "You think they've done this?"

She shrugged. "Dunno." She gave his arm a squeeze. "So. Famous. Tell me how I did it in the last version."

And so, looking up at the sky every now and then to make sure they weren't going to be attacked, Leyton began.

The man and the girl turned right, into the darker streets leading up to the Job Centre, past the little post office where Douglas still collected his dole cheque. There were fewer people here, but still the couple found them and stayed with them. It was almost as if they wanted to be followed. Douglas found himself considering an assault, a mugging, to seize the information in the man's wallet. But he could only do that under orders. His contact wouldn't take well to him doing that randomly, to him becoming a criminal. He was an upright citizen, he reminded himself. He had killed the boy only when he had no other option. When it was clear they had the wrong child, that the blackmail attempt was not on, his masters had achieved their ends in that case in a more subtle way. The landowner in question had been bought off. He wasn't quite sure why he was following these two. He knew where they were going anyway.

He had been feeling strange all night, dreamy. But he still had his principles, the rules by which he lived his life, the boundaries that kept him inside the world of other people. Perhaps something had got into the skull puncture after all.

The man and the woman headed onto the Upper Bristol Road, down past the newsagents, where once there had been a petrol station. They stopped in front of a row of road-blackened houses. Of course. He waited while she found a key and let them in.

Douglas stepped back into the shadows. He waited until they were definitely not going to come out again, and then went to the door. Six doorbells. He took out his pocketbook and made a careful note of the road, the house number and the names beside the bells. He was sure he could remember, but he wanted a permanent record in case he didn't. He wanted a piece of paper that he could eat or throw away.

Still unsatisfied, he turned back towards town. He glanced over his shoulder every now and then, hoping the man would re-emerge. He was missing something. He'd go back to one of his pubs that encouraged after-hours drinking and carouse and pretend to be someone else. Yes, that plan was quite solid in his mind, he found. He was going to be a military man this evening. He straightened up and threw back his shoulders and walked with the proud, easy-to-follow gait of his quarry. He would be younger, as the man with his name was younger. He would meet lots of people as Major Douglas Leyton.

Halfway down the street, his left hand took the piece of paper from his pocket and dropped it into a bin. He didn't notice it go. It didn't matter. He'd find he knew the address in the morning.

Cleves was woken at midnight. He had been given one of the officers' quarters at the air base. The adjutant switched on his bedside lamp and waited as he reached for his glasses.

He had set up protocols for which news was important enough to have him woken. Finding the pilot; any illness or alarm involving Jocelyn; anything interesting that was turned up in the continuing examination of the wreck, which was now proceeding in one of the hangars.

The adjutant clearly didn't know what the envelope he carried contained. Cleves put on his reading glasses, took a sip of water from the glass beside his bed and opened it. The man waited for return orders.

The envelope contained a photograph of a battered identity card, retrieved, so the note said, from somewhere inside the electronics of the downed craft. There was a photo on the card, and a name. Squadron Leader Douglas Leyton.

The face of the alien. Very human. Very British.

With a very familiar name.

Cleves thought for a moment. He placed the photo back in the envelope and resealed it, then he handed it to the waiting RAF man. "That goes to the Chief Constable. Eyes only. And have a secretary sent in here, please."

The secretary arrived, bleary from her bed, ten minutes later. During that time, Cleves had pulled on his trousers under his pyjama jacket. He dictated a series of memos and had them e-mailed to the various concerned departments from her laptop while he waited. Douglas Leyton: a name attached to a rather distasteful mistake of one of his underlings—a mistake inside a potentially disgraceful adventure, now appearing inside a hope. He felt as if his finger was poised on the chess piece he had just moved, about to let go, but he felt his opponent's eyes on him, waiting for him to do so.

Who was the opponent? Was there one? Or was this all what it appeared to be, a visit from the future?

A visit from the future. That was even less possible than a visitor from space. He had briefed the Prime Minister before he'd fallen asleep, with only that frustrating possibility to offer him. Jocelyn had been talking merrily to his men and to himself for hours of running audio and video tape. But she had not said a single thing, despite the presence of expert listeners, that had told Cleves anything about anything.

Which meant she had everything to hide. And a vast ability to hide it.

He shaved and dressed

Cleves called Cotton, got him out of bed, checked the list of dogs on his private payroll. He got a photo of the man's face sent to his own laptop, on the privacy cipher. He looked at it once, was sure, and then deleted it using the eraser.

The family resemblance was unmistakable.

He shut off the laptop and got to his feet.

Then he had to sit down again. He felt terribly threatened.

First, the craft landed at the centre of his most shameful secret.

Then the pilot of the future turned out to be from the same family... have the same name even... as the lowest mongrel employed by that secret.

No. There were coincidences. But this could not be one of them.

He mentally plucked the chess piece off the board. He would keep his clock running.

He had an opponent.

He did not know who it could be. Perhaps it was this pilot himself: the Douglas Leyton of the future.

He called his driver and asked him to wait beside the staff building.

Before he left, he had to see Jocelyn. He could no longer afford to be gentle with her.

She hadn't been asleep. She didn't appear to need it. She'd been chatting to the nightshift doctor. The lights were low in the makeshift laboratory. She raised her eyebrows when she saw Cleves. "Hullo, chap. What brings you here this late?"

"Douglas Leyton," he said.

"Pleased to meet you," she replied. But she'd reacted to the name.

"I've told you everything you wanted to know about our world. Our *time*. So why are you still concealing things from me?"

She thought about that for a moment. "Because I don't know if I can trust you with the truth. With the bare truth, with a truth that you'd understand, or with the truth as I'd like it to be. With any of them."

He felt a pang of fellow feeling for a moment. But he killed it. "Ah," he said. "That old one. What is truth?"

"Can't answer that for you now, can I?"

He sat down. "If you knew why I wanted to know the things I want to know, then you would tell me."

"And that's surely what every interrogator thinks."

"Jocelyn... if I may call you that..." Cleves was aware of the recording apparatus installed in this room. He felt badly about lying to her about that.

He indicated to the doctor that he could go, and waited until the man had left. "I am an old man. I began in this job during a time of which you may be aware from your history lessons. We call it the Cold War, though I don't know if that terminology has persisted."

"Do go on."

"Who I was was formed by the idea of two opposing power blocks: us and them. The Western World and the Soviets. The capitalists and the Communists. Every day I did something to make sure our side would not fall to theirs. Then, as I grew older, that situation fell apart and my duty became focused on many other matters." He wetted his lips at the words, thinking of how he'd actually lost sight of his duty, had given it up. He could taste rice paper. "What I wish to know is..." How could he phrase this in a manner which would not give his game away to all the people, up to the Prime Minister himself, who would see and hear these tapes? "Has all my loyalty been to any end? Is there peace and prosperity for Britain in the future?"

She thought for a long time. She was almost panicking, trying to keep even that from him. What did she know that he didn't?

"I'm truly sorry," she said. "I'm thinking about the safety of that future. I don't know how much I can tell you."

He had to find a way to let her say the very simple thing he needed to hear. "We could talk about the weather," he said. "What's it like in the time you're from?"

Her eyes narrowed. She'd seen through his question. Or maybe she was just going to dead bat everything. Go on, he urged her silently. That's the whole thing. Just tell me that it's temperate, and moderate, and British!

She didn't say anything.

He felt himself growing angry. "We can make many deductions just from your craft," he said. "It's armed for war, so war must still be possible. War in space. War against aliens? That would do so much to help peace now, to unite the world. And from the insignia, there is still a Britain. But has it changed? What sort of political organisation is there?" He suddenly found that he was shouting. "We *need* the answers to these questions!"

She closed her eyes as well, as if she knew what was coming.

He called for the doctor to come back in. He pointed him at Jocelyn. "Go to B," he told him.

The doctor went to the cupboard to prepare the syringe.

Jocelyn opened her eyes and glared at Cleves. "Don't make me dream," she said.

"I could say the same to you," he said. And then he left.

Eleven: The Trailer

For your consideration.

Alison.

A film directed by Hohiti Kenton.

Alison sits by the window, her brow furrowed in concentration, her guitar in her hands. She keeps trying to put the same sequence of chords together. But it's not working. "I can read everything," she says. "But I can't read this. Lord, help me find the reason."

Alison walking with Fran, through the spires of Bath. It's a holiday and the streets are lined with World Flags, the Earth bright blue against a black background. "I need some *reason* to do it."

"You've bally well got time. Your job at the factory takes up, what, three days a week?"

"But gosh, Fran, who cares if I've got these tunes in my head?"

"We all want to hear them."

"Why is it important that they come out?"

"Because—" Fran stops and turns to face her seriously, her golden hair blowing in the wind. "You have your God. And you have your work. And if that's not enough then you have to add the something that's missing. Otherwise nothing we do matters. One day, Ally, you're jolly well going to die."

Alison sits by the window, her brow furrowed in concentration, her guitar in her hands. She keeps trying to put the same sequence of chords together. But it's not working.

Patrick throws his head back, laughing. "Fran said what?"

They're lying in bed together, her head on his chest. The guitar lies abandoned in one corner of the room.

"I'm going to die," she whispers. "And I won't have *done* anything."

"You can *do* something to help me get elected."

"And I won't have *said* anything."

"You'll have said I love you," he replies, tenderly. "Many times. What else is there to say?"

Close on her. Anguished.

She throws the guitar down and walks out of the room. The music swells.

Another town. Explosions. People running, screaming. They're mown down by rebels wearing a crown insignia on their armbands. Alison watches from where she hides in a doorway.

Alison walks along a deserted road. Victorious rebels strut past, going the other way. One of them sees her and throws a coin for the beggar. They walk on, guffawing.

Alison picks up the coin and stares at it. She holds it in her fist. With a great effort, she crushes it into her palm. We see the blood on her fingers.

We see Alison running from fighting, a series of quick cuts. The battle of Hull, as seen from intimate angles. She's seen kissing a man goodbye, hiding with children in a cellar, and feverishly writing, with charcoal on the back of currency notes.

We see her in a church, on her knees, her palms raised to the ceiling. She has a smile on her face. She's getting there, she can almost see it now.

A long swing out from the darkness of an audience in an auditorium to Alison, on a stage, starting to sing. It's "Nothing Will Come From Nothing." One of her most famous, a defiant, passionate song.

As she sings, she starts to cry. And in her tears we see reflections of Fran, Marty, and of Patrick. And of a wavering, faltering scene...

Alison sits at home, in old age, still writing, humming something in her head, trying to write it down.

There's a knock on the window.

She looks up. Something fearful waits outside. But she's almost accepting of it.

We freeze on the image of her eyes, afraid but wise.

The audience knows what happens next.

For your consideration.

Alison.

Released on March 31st. Worldwide dates below.

Alison put the cup of tea into Leyton's hands. "I don't even know how to read music," she said.

"Did you ever think about learning?" He leant back against the side of her bed.

"Think? I don't know." She sat beside him. "Maybe when I was younger. And all that religious stuff. When do I get that?"

"You always had it."

"I'm a real failure compared to all that."

"Rot! You're still the same person. I can see all sorts of things about you that make you you. And well, you know... you're my hero."

She looked at him for a long time. He was smiling, but his smile was sad. "I hope I still get the chance. If we find Fran... Can you sing me one of my songs?"

"No." He looked away. "I can't sing."

"This other me. Does she have my... can she read things?"

"She was always said to be incredibly sharp. That's a line from the movie, actually, that she could read anything. She must have said something to that effect at some point. That's why I've been so careful not to... well, not to give anything away."

She knew, of course, exactly what he meant. "Leyton, do you know... Do you know how I died?"

He took a deep breath. He'd been expecting the question. "Yes."

"Will you tell me?"

"No."

"But now it might not come true."

"And in many ways that's worse. You'd always be looking over your shoulder. And you'd never know."

"But is it terrible?"

He put his hands over his face, but he did it in a pantomime way. "I won't give you any clues. Nothing to think about at all."

She was absurdly pleased that he hadn't lied to her. "Yeah," she said. "You're right. Thank you for that."

He lowered his hands, his face deliberately creased in the deepest, darkest frown. He managed to keep it as he sipped his tea again.

"I'm glad I was your hero," she said finally. Then she got to her feet. "Well, bed... We both need sleep... If those things don't come for us."

"I could keep watch."

"What good would that do? If they come, they come. But this building is full of people. If they don't like being seen... You need your sleep more than I do, anyway."

"Then we'll both sleep."

"Okay."

"You go and change in the bathroom. I'll take some blankets and curl up in the corner. Cosier than barracks. Warmer, too."

She stopped for a moment, looking down at him. He had nice hands.

She took her night T-shirt from under the pillow. "You make it sound so simple," she said.

Twelve: I've Never Found What It's Worth

The doctor injected Jocelyn in her neck. They must have made some deductions from all those careful notes that they'd been taking, for instance, that she had a miniature circulation in her head, a tiny pulse. And thank God for that, because otherwise they might have injected their filthy stuff right through her skull.

She tried hard to fight it, and to some degree she could, because she knew everything she was, and she had a mission. She didn't know how she could do anything to take it any further at the moment, but she would not take a step backwards.

And she was damned if she was going to tell them anything.

So she stared at the doctor as he was injecting her. "This may kill me," she told him. "If you're a doctor, how do you stand on that?"

"They pay my wages," he said, in a way Jocelyn had never heard before. He was sounding apologetic for something he was doing deliberately, and not blaming it on his superior officers, as Jocelyn had sometimes heard the military doing, but on his own need for money.

She wanted to bellow at him, about how stupid he was. But that would let out an emotion she needed to keep inside to fight. She felt the burn of the needlemark on her neck. "What is it?" she asked. "What have you put in me?"

"It's called Check," he said. Still that crawling in his voice. "It won't harm you."

"Oh, you know that, do you?"

"It just... loosens you up. Makes you say everything that's on your mind. You'll babble and you'll wake up with a hangover. There'll be someone in here in a minute, and I'll have to leave. It takes effect in about half an hour."

"I will not submit to this. What sort of democracy is this?"

"I don't make the rules." He headed for the door. "A hangover. That's all."

"If," she said, "you're lucky."

She'd felt the universe turning about her, starting just then. She was orienting herself, coming out of a dream. And then into one again. And then out—*where am I?* And then in again.

Without going. Firing blanks.

A man entered and sat down before her. She laughed. They had recording devices fitted in this room at all times. He was just here to prompt her, to nudge for particular answers in her babbling.

But babbling wasn't what she was worried about.

Dreaming was what heads called the transition between one place in spacetime and another, because that was what it felt like.

That slang term had been taken up by non-heads, pilots and their superiors, and had come to mean the whole process of such travel. A dreaming, for instance, was the visual sign that a ship was about to appear in space.

But only heads knew what these words really meant.

It was because heads didn't have their bodies any more. In a living human, there was a cluster of neurons in the stomach. That created "gut feeling," the huge importance of which was obvious only when it was no longer there.

For a head, the stomach neurons had been replaced by quantum computers, and through them, the universe itself. Living humans compared brain to gut. Heads compared brain to universe.

What would normally have been the process governing walking, reaching for something, leaping up, became the process of interstellar travel. That was why it got called dreaming, because the sensation was like the false movements one thinks one is making in dreams.

It was also called dreaming because thought got in the way. One doesn't think too hard about walking. Or about taking a ship from Earth orbit to the moons of Jupiter. You made your decisions before you went. The computer helped with that, laying out all the possible locations for the ship to be. The virtual locations in other universes always felt wrong. People who weren't heads always asked: why not select them? But that would just be wrong. Like walking upwards.

The heads had a religion of their own, which they spoke only to each other about, and only every now and then. It was a religion without texts. It was just what one automatically fell into believing when one took a ship through spacetime.

When you came out the other side you thanked the Lord and the Lady. Two things, each inside the other. The Lord observed the Lady. Perhaps every head had different ideas about what the Lord and Lady were. Jocelyn rather equated Lord with brain, Lady with gut/universe. When you disappeared from one place and time and appeared in another, the obvious thing, born of human experience, was to think you passed *through* something in the time which that journey took. (You always arrived later rather than earlier, and that was also one of those obvious things that nobody understood.) What you passed through Jocelyn had always thought of as the territory of the Lord and Lady, who were perhaps the same thing seen from two different angles. The universe, the presence of that *emotional territory*, that *underlying ideology*, was their pattern. It was the working out of a conscious design.

Heads didn't talk to the living about this because they wouldn't understand, and they would create something askew out of it, something offensive.

The important thing about all of this right now was that heads didn't dream like living people did. They dreamed only to travel. For a head, to travel was to dream.

And now she was being made to dream without any way to travel.

"What are you thinking?" asked the man. He had a plain, bland voice.

Jocelyn watched as his arms started to flail. She felt her brain looking for the powers that it had been detached from. Dreaming without comparison. He leaned forward, started to stand up on his seat. She tried not to let her mind start ramming against the universe. She couldn't stop it. She was trying to select. Her jaw locked.

The man was standing on his seat, his arms spiralling. "What's happening to me?" he was shouting.

Gravity. She felt herself trying to pull the universe open, to find the alternatives that would let her step out and step in. "Get out!" she managed to bellow.

The man fell back through the air and hit the far wall. He rolled up it.

Jocelyn felt the bench she was propped on giving way. She was a little up the incline. She held the universe inside her. She'd never given birth. God, this must be how it felt! She mustn't let it out! It would rip... It would tear... It would haemorrhage. She mustn't let it out!

The bench fell. The tray she stood in flew into the air. She and the bench were falling towards the man, who was crawling out of the way, closing his eyes so he could move—

She hit the wall.

The wall smacked the side of her skull.

Unconsciousness hit.

Which saved the universe.

She had a map slammed into her brain. She was a map.

All will be well, my child. See.

And she saw the map. The multistructure of the universe had collapsed to fit inside her head, all of the positions, put on top of each other.

Infinite/bounded/infinite. The choices made and the unmakeable choices. All fixed together.

It was the most beautiful thing she had ever seen. She had never seen it in the dreaming.

Because she had never dreamed of being in the whole universe at once before.

"My God," she said out loud.

Leyton dreamed of the world that contained all the worlds. He saw maps, one on top of another, each one replacing the next. New versions. The rewriting of maps.

He couldn't hold it in his own head. He had a body to run and a gut to compare himself to.

He dreamt that he and Jocelyn were flying together again. That they had a mission. The mission wasn't over. The mission was like nothing he'd ever imagined.

He woke suddenly. It took him a moment to realise that he was in the warm darkness of Alison's flat, on the floor at the end of her bed.

Damn it! He hadn't meant even to go to sleep! He'd just put his head down to pretend until she'd gone under. He was still clothed under the duvet.

He raised his head to look at her.

She was thrashing on her pillows, knotting her sheets around her. She froze for a moment in a muscular clench, her teeth bared.

He got to his feet, half wanting to wake her from her nightmare. But that would mean involving her more than she was involved.

The Golden Men had been after *him*. They had declared themselves to be his enemies. They had attacked him and carefully elbowed her aside. The matter of her friend must be a sideshow for them, something he and they would battle out between them.

He had only half made this decision when they retired. He had been going to go immediately back to the Abbey, do what he so desperately wanted to do, and then decide on his next move. Whatever it was, it would be one that did not put Alison Parmeter in danger, both for her sake, and for the sake of the Alison that she might one day still become.

She moved smoothly again, and for a moment he thought she had woken. She turned to look at him. With just her left eye open.

It gazed carefully at him for a moment, reflecting the shards of a streetlight through the gap in the curtains.

He looked back at it.

But it couldn't hold on. It was like she made a great effort and slammed it shut. The eye clamped closed and Alison turned again. She started to thrash in her sleep once more.

Something was thrashing inside Leyton too: the thing that had made his decision for him. He had dreamed... he felt that Jocelyn was alive. He didn't know how. It was as if she'd just taken him through a dreaming, that curious sense of being back to back with your head. That intimacy that was never talked of. It had come back to him.

The digital clock on the bedside said two in the morning.

Swaying on his feet, he picked up his coat and cap, as quietly as he could, and buckled his belt. He felt his chin. He hadn't shaved for two days.

She would have to excuse him the loan of the sweater. He didn't feel like going out there in just his flight-shirt and coat. He would have liked to leave a note, but he'd be writing in the dark and he didn't know what he'd say. He hoped she would know he was grateful.

He went to the door, steadied himself for a moment and looked back at the sleeping girl. She was as beautiful as she'd been portrayed in every film of her, as her voice sounded on all the recordings.

She muttered something in sleep. A song. A little catch of a high note in her voice. Leyton held his breath. Was this the Alison from his world manifesting herself in this less blessed Alison? Was he going to hear her sing after all?

"When I go..." the words were blurted, forced out, but clear for all that, "I'm going like Elsie."

Leyton stared at her. He waited to hear more. But nothing else came. Alison turned over and started snoring, off into deeper sleep.

"That's just it," he whispered, hoping and not hoping that some part of her could hear him. "You do."

Then he opened the door and set off into the night.

Thirteen: Station to Station

Pilate uttered the proclamation, freed Jesus the rebel, the son of Abbas, and sentenced Jesus the false Messiah, the son of Joseph, to death. Then he washed his hands, in public, as any Roman would do after sacrifice had been made. The crowd didn't understand the gesture, but Judas, in the clothes of a beggar, did. Pilate would see the future in these entrails. We are Judas, for this dream. We see things from his point of view.

Jesus lifted the olive wood cross onto his back, and the crowd laughed and called out jokes for Him to respond to. Not all of them, of course. There were followers of both Him and the freed Jesus Barabbas there, though the political prisoner had been spirited off into hiding. There were scuffles and shouts from the crowd, and the auxiliaries moved in to break them up. Jesus found the right balance and, groaning at the exertion, staggered away along the stony track. It led from the gate into the city to the quarry where the crucifixions were carried out. It would lead His body to the city dump, where the corpses of such sinners were left for the birds. He still wore His fake crown, but they had given Him back His own clothes. Judas had hoped for eye contact, but there was none.

He fell after only a hundred paces. Judas kept up with the crowd on his heels, driven by his own need to see, by the force of history being written around him. Or rewritten. He had to see this through to the end. He watched as, goaded by the crowd and urged on by the crucifixion team of four auxiliaries, the Son heaved the cross up onto His shoulders again and staggered on.

Judas didn't know if the old woman who tried to grab the crown from Jesus' head was His mother, as some of the crowd around him were already beginning to say. She was with Mary, the prostitute, and the few of the crowd who knew anything of the Son of Man's life had whispered that name, and the names had perhaps got confused. But she was weeping like a mother, trying, with grabs, as she was pulled back by the crowd, to take the filthy thing off the Son's head, to give Him back a little of His dignity. She wailed as she did it, ripping her shawl in her hands, as if those hands had a life of their own and grabbed and pleaded according to her heart. Jesus was smiling hard at her, trying to shove everything into that smile, trying to remove the pain from it, looking back as He walked on. Yes, Judas knew now, that had been His mother. For at who else, even as Jesus loved them all, would He look like that?

Judas knew Simon too, the father of Alexander and Rufus, who had been on the edge of the disciples. The group themselves had been together in the crowd, but had become separated. Some had already elected to go into hiding, Judas was certain. The crowd, not finding them, or finding their way blocked by the staunch little pockets of Barabbites and followers of Christ, had caught Simon at the edge and dragged him into the centre. They accused him of the things his sons had got involved with, and shoved him to help carry the cross. Jesus let him, smoothing a touch on His robe. It's safer for you here than in there. And it was, for the few strides he took with Jesus. Then the auxiliaries caught up and pushed Simon back into the crowd. The stack of the cross thudded into the ground and Jesus resumed hauling it and Judas saw Simon hustled away by friendly hands.

Judas did not know the name of the woman who took off her shawl and rushed forward, shoving it into Jesus' hands, and then, when His fingers could not take it, wiping His brow with it herself. The look on her face was that of one of the new followers, those who had come looking for Jesus in the last few days, eager and unschooled. She was pulled back in as they all were, shouting proudly, holding onto the shawl and flapping it in the air. So she had the image of it, Judas thought, but not the word. The cloth she held, she felt, had gained in value.

He fell again a few paces later, a great fall right onto His face, the weight of the cross slamming onto His spine and pressing Him into the ground. He got to his feet with the aid of members of the crowd who burst out to help Him and were fought back. He had small stones forced into His skin now, and mud caked right down the front of His clothes. Judas wanted to help, but knew that he couldn't. Even if he'd been freed from his own burden, he had to watch Christ shoulder His.

Women shouted to Him along the path. Even now they wanted Him to cure them, or were cursing Him, or sometimes a strange mixture of the two. You who think you can do everything: do something for me! We're afraid of you, afraid of the future! Unless you can soothe us. Then we'll be your friends and followers! There was this, and there was ritual wailing. They disgusted Judas. He'd always known what the mob was like. He was one of them. But the way they loved and tore apart at the same time, with no breath of thought between the two inclinations... It made him weak to think of what his place was going to be now he was back in their ranks again. He was surprised when Jesus took a deep breath, stopped for a moment, and spoke to them. "Daughters of Jerusalem," He said. The sound of His voice still made Judas want to cry. "Don't weep for me. This is for the best.

Weep for your own children, who will live in this world when I'm with My Father. Those who did this to Me can do this to them. And if they do this when the wood is green..." His voice became hard, not with anger, Judas thought, but with determination, "what will they do when it is dry?"

He fell again almost immediately. The words had taken it out of Him. They'd caused shouts through the crowd. Echoes. And already they were being misheard, mistranslated, misunderstood. "He has prophesied!" cried out a man beside Judas. "He has spoken of the end!" Judas nearly spat on his shoes. He'd seen that look. The Son was speaking of what was to happen in a few moments. Of his imminent victory over the Roman Empire. Over all empires. What he was doing now was a defence, a fortification against the future. He had no prophecy, because all prophecy was to be resolved in Him. Except that prophecy which simply said that the Kingdom would come, with all life in tune with the will of His Father, that the world would be saved.

The four auxiliaries caught up with Him as He neared the little dip and rise at the top of the hill and they took the cross from Him and stripped the remaining clothes off Him, as was the custom. Now Jesus looked truly dishonourable, emaciated as any other beggar, His ribs protruding, His arms thin sticks. His balls, Judas noted, were shrivelled, bruised, like they'd beaten Him specifically there. There were bruises all along His torso too. Jesus managed a high laugh as they did this, as if the irony of their being so afraid of Him had occurred to Him. There was something of a struggle for the garments, Judas noted, as always. They had been ascribed value too. Rather than fight in sight of the people, the auxiliaries quickly drew stones from each other's hands, and took the clothes according to that.

They took the cross from Him, and one auxiliary stood beside Him, hand on his gladius, ready to attack should Jesus leap to His feet and run. Judas could imagine Him, sprinting back the way He'd come, with the crowd after Him. He'd go and hide in the city, or be dragged into safety by the disciples. They'd be full of plans then. Let's get you up the coast. Let's get you to Rome! This was a world that would never be, because there were not many worlds each made out of stories or different happenings. Judas understood that, as he understood everything else. There was only one world, written and rewritten. And the most mighty hand was Christ's, because He was rewriting this world in His own blood, with His fingerbone for a pen and his nail for a nib. They crucified Him quickly, in the end, forcing Him to lie across the wood and hammering the nails into His palms. He squealed as the first nail bit. But he managed to hold His tongue for the second, as if He'd understood the pain now He'd felt it once. Then they nailed His feet to the sides of the olive stack, so His legs opened as if He was giving birth. As the cross was raised in the usual fashion, with the team leader's foot at the base, Jesus let out a long howl, the pitch of which changed with the angle of His body. The weight was taken by His arms, and the crowd hushed at the tiny sounds of ripping muscle. Blood slopped, but did not gush, from the wounds. Someone from the crowd brought a sign that said "The King of the Jews', and it was nailed to the cross. He barely seemed to notice it, His eyes fixed on the pain. Judas knew that crucifixions lasted six or seven hours, sometimes. The two men who had been hung to the left and right of Him had already started to yell and cry out for mercy that wouldn't be theirs until the early hours. He didn't think that Jesus would last that long.

And this part of the dream is different. It's in a different film stock, an intervention in the text by a different writer. We lose the point of view of Judas. This is the centre of the dream, Alison.

Jesus looked at the crowd. In place. Yes. He had made himself do it. He had nothing left to do now. Only die.

He looked above the crowd. There stood an angel. One of the unclean things. One of the four. It was the one called Abaddon. Jesus found his lips forming into a smile, despite the shuddering pain and the fear of death which infested his body. The angel was a man made of gold. Of course. The one he had encountered in the desert, that had insisted he call it Satan, had offered to sell him food. A sale not for money, because Jesus himself carefully carried none, but for some unspecified debt to be carried over to the future. Jesus had ignored the clenchings of his stomach and had walked away, though he kept seeing the creature in the corner of his eye as he went. The form it had taken then had been that of an encamped trader with his goods on a mat in front of his tent. But Jesus didn't believe in seeing the forms of things. It had said then that it was the Adversary, and had said it in a boasting, gleeful way, as if the Son of Man should have heard of it, somehow. Or perhaps as if it intended to make the name heard.

Jesus had heard that tone before in the boasts of adolescent boys, in his own boasts, when he was a youth going about in Nazareth. He had said he would change the world, that mighty nations would fall before him. He had picked up a wooden gladius his father had made him and had fought with Simeon, the son of his neighbour. Simeon had pretended to fall down dead the moment the wood touched him, and Jesus had screamed, certain he had killed him. He had endured the laughter of the other boys for days.

But something in him then had been sure that he *could* do that. That his touch might kill. He had had the arrogance and absolute ability of any young man, but alongside it he had had the feeling that such inner rage and desire should be contained, managed like a bull was managed in a pen.

As he passed his thirtieth year, he had started to see that rage as if from a distance. It whispered to him in the evenings when he was tired in the workshop, and in the mornings, when he washed his face. That'll show them, it said. You can get even. Pull this trick, make your influence felt here. If you're strong in the face of your competitors, you can outbid them, gain more of the trade, gain the respect of your peers. His family had no respect. There were still those who laughed at his bastardry, even though Joseph had married his mother quite swiftly, and there were many of those laughing who'd been in similar situations. That was what the thing inside your stomach and loins said, at the deep points of the day: you will feel better when you have triumphed. In that thirtieth year, he had started to disagree, to find that he could hear the voice, and say to it, as he'd said to the merchant in the desert: "You're not me."

He'd found that he wanted to say that more and more, until one day he'd laid down his tools and gone to his mother and father and said that he was going away for a while, and had wandered out into the world. They had given him supplies and people to call on for aid, and had asked him not to go. But he had gone anyway. He had left all the money and provisions with a friend, to be returned to his parents the next day.

He had to be free of those things. He hadn't known why then. He had discovered why very swiftly. He had started to talk to people on the highways, and in talking to them, he learned more, even as he started to teach. He found he had things to say that felt as if he had never learnt them. He did not find them from watching the way the birds flew or the river flowed, but from his reading of

what had always been inside him and inside the world. He
felt the bitterness and competition and guilt leave him.

He was given coins by the people who passed, the
furtively superstitious. They thought feeding a Holy Man
would gain them some advantage. "Only love can set you
free," he had started to say to them, pursuing them to give
them their money back, and instead trying to have them
give him some food or water. They didn't want to talk,
obviously, but giving back the money often made them
listen to him. He had started to say, "Give unto Caesar
what is Caesar's," about coins then, too. He wanted it
to be repeated, for people to understand that the Empire
had no power in those stamped icons unless the subject
people wished it upon themselves. It had served as a good
answer when they had tried to have him arrested too early,
by having him asked about taxation, about whether he
wanted his followers to overthrow the Romans, about the
piffling details.

He had realised, quite soon, that he needed a framework
for his big new thoughts. That containing, understanding
and taming the beast inside him was not enough. That
path led him to his studies, to the baths and the healings,
and then the deliberate trek to go and find John so the
great process about which the fate of the world depended
could begin.

So it could take him here.

His memories could not deflect him from the pain
now.

But he could consider now. There were no choices
left to be made. Nothing was left to write that had been
written. It was nearly done.

He had become aware, only during this last year of his
ministry, of being followed. The Roman Empire followed
him, obviously. There were their spies, and there was
Judas, poor loving Judas, whom he had once grabbed by
the hands and whirled around and around until they had
both fallen, making the rest of the disciples laugh and say
concerned things at once. Judas seemed to understand, in
a way that none of the others did, that words, even the
Scriptures, contained their opposites within themselves,
that everything could be read one way or another, that
words, in the end, were not to be trusted. The only thing
that one could lean on was love, love of oneself and the

Lord and the unselfish love of others. Judas knew that betrayal could be contained within the words of love, but that the action could be contained again within love itself. Simple and most complicated, Judas.

So Judas had his mission, as Jesus did. And that was the plan of his Father. Jesus had given Judas something from his Father to allow him to do it. Something he didn't quite understand. The ability to read what was written. It was good that Judas had a mission, after that, because if he had not divined it for himself his questions would have made him rot on the vine. Judas would have seen, as he did, the thing that followed them, even as it was contained within the Roman Empire.

The thing that followed them was the crowd that loved and the crowd that bayed for blood, the same crowd.

The thing that followed was the snake in the guts and cock of a young man, set free. The dog that killed chickens and did not eat. The two-sided coin. It was a hatred of oneself and therefore a desire to make oneself somehow better.

So it trailed the disciples enviously. It tried to give them money. Jesus had allowed the others to keep some of it to make certain details happen, after much thought. That was giving this hidden Empire a small victory, but that victory would not matter at all in the arrival of his Father's kingdom in the hearts of men. It would be a fortress of sand washed away by the tide. You couldn't live absolutely one way in the heart of another life. The coming of his Father's kingdom would clean everything, and all the coins would be given to children for them to use as things to throw and pile and hide in their fists in street games, all to be left in the dust at the end of the day.

Jesus found that he was smiling again at the thought of children with so many toys.

But the thing had trailed the disciples physically too. They had read in the Scriptures about angels, creatures like the monsters and giants of old, stories to entertain or thrill or fulfil, to make the point that that was all over now. The book would be closed and thrown away. Jesus doubted that his Father kept beasts.

But then they had started to see them. When Jesus had suddenly found that he could give Lazarus his life

back, had taken was what written and ripped it in two and
bellowed the rewriting of it to the sky, because his Father
was the Lord of life and death... there had been the angel,
the fiery golden creature, sitting between them and the
sun.

John had seen it best. He had come to Jesus that
evening and had described its every detail. He had said
that it was not in time, that it had not moved according to
the wind around it, that the shadows on it were not those
cast by the hour of the day. John saw things like that all
the time. But what he saw was true, despite, or because of,
the demons in him. John had tamed his demons as Jesus
had tamed his beast. They were both afraid of what the
watching angel had been. But Jesus had said, "There is no
beast or angel or demon or army that is greater than my
Father, and we are his children, and he will protect us as
his will is read."

He had not quite known, as he had carefully said the
words, exactly what they meant, only that he loved his
Father, and John, and all the people. And that the idea of
Lazarus eating with his family that evening and telling
everyone that the world was free and saved, telling and
telling and telling, excited Him more than anything.

He had expected these *angels* to interfere with his
passage up this hill today. He had been surprised when
they did not.

"Who are you?" asked the golden man now.

"I am Jesus Barjoseph. And I am my Father's son."

"But who are you?"

Jesus fought down, even now, especially now, the
beast inside him. He had wanted to bellow that he was
the adversary of the angels, that he had won. But such a
shout would have been a victory for them inside a victory
for him. So he made himself say gently, as he felt another
muscle tug and slowly tear in his arm, "I'm the light of the
world." Which he said meaning he was part of the light, in
favour of the light.

"So am I," said the angel. It had got between him and
the sun. In some ways the shadow was welcome. The heat
had made his throat roar with hurt.

"You're nothing to do with my Father."

"We have put ourselves within the idea of you and he.
It is our Kingdom that will come. On the back of you."

And Jesus saw what the golden man really looked like.

He was a statue in one of the Roman buildings, one of their gods who were not God. He had empty eyes, and the proud cheeks and jaw of dangerous male youth.

And Jesus realised that it was true, that the thing which had made the crowds grab for his garments, had made the woman called Veronica clutch her veil... it was sitting here in the sky before him. He had been a lamb, not for sacrifice, but for... consumption. Consumption by the dogs.

He had been fooled into a cross.

The pain of the realisation made him open his mouth wide, trying to gain the air and the muscles to scream. He could not. The beast rose in him, protesting, now it was free, about the pain and the unfairness and the uselessness of where he was now.

"Father!" he cried. Or perhaps the cry was a whimper. The beast inside made one's whimpers into bellows in memory. "Why have you put me here? Why have you left me?"

The golden man in the sky started to laugh. He turned his body in the air like a bird of augury. His armoured skin glittered like the sunlight on shields.

And a stream of golden piss arced through the air from him, splattering down Jesus' naked chest and filling his mouth with the taste of vinegar.

Jesus coughed at the stench of it.

He could not be in a lower place than this. All his dreams lost. His mission a prostitute's lure, a lamp to tempt the unwary. He was a horse stolen by an unfamiliar rider, and he was left fatherless. The words on the wooden sign were smudged by the piss.

He could not be in a lower place than this.

He understood completely the pain of separation. His cause had been everything to him, and it was gone, taken from him before his life had been. He understood how this thing had come upon the people now, how they had been victims of it. They are separated from the hands that make their garments. They can feel no thanks to them, for they do not know them; they paid them in coins and substituted this token for their love: someone else's face for free exchange. He had made things and been paid for them, but he had also known the joy of making things for people he knew.

He had been going to give the people he knew, which was all people, this thing he had made, this life he had designed for a sacrifice. He had been going to give them it, but...

But now he saw it. He bared his teeth at the angel in another smile.

But it had been incomplete. This life, this gift had been incomplete.

Until now.

Until that moment when he had understood, and understood for his Father, the need and the distance, the flaw that made people what they were.

This sacrifice would mend that flaw. Not now. But in the end. And the end would be all that there was. Because there was only one book. Written and rewritten. And he was the brush that would write in his Father's hand. And the angels had not been in the book, and would not be in the book, but were only there now, not his Father's beasts but, like Jesus and Judas, his instrument, but unlike them, unwitting.

He met the blank gaze of the statue in the sky. He dared to love it. For its purpose, though it didn't know it, was as divine as everything else was.

"We are the future," it said. "We will give them their Apocalypse. We will let them know their world has an end, and provide it for them in the manner they have wished for."

"I am the Apocalypse," Jesus told it. "I am the Revelation. After me, there is no more need for endings, because I have completed every prophecy and finished the book. My Father's kingdom will come. The world will be saved from evil. After me, there is no more prophecy to fulfil. After me they will be free." He managed to keep his eyes locked defiantly on the angel as the centurion approached to check his condition. The man had the look on his face of a believer. A seed at the heart of the Empire. One thing in another. And the thing at the heart of all things would be, and always had been, this moment, not the fantasies of the invader in the sky. Delighting in the imminence of his accomplishment, in the certain knowledge that what he was about to do would make

all whole again, would bring the angels into his Father's
plan, and not the other way round, Jesus threw back his
head and laughed.

And the film stock alters again, the hand writing the book changes back
to that of the original author. The dream is fought back into the original
point of view as the chemical stream in the brain where that poured from,
whatever pore or membrane that was, is shut off, and another takes its
place. We resume being Judas.

Both dreams are good dreams. But they are fenced in and surrounded
by nightmares.

Judas had stayed even as the crowd began to dwindle. After Jesus had
suddenly cried out for His Father, there were many there who had expected
Eli to arrive in a flaming chariot. Jesus had been muttering and spluttering,
the sweat covering His body. It was fearsome to watch, like a gladiatorial
contest. Then Jesus cried out again, "It is done!" And Judas knew it was
over. His body slumped and suddenly lengthened, His knees sagged, all
fight gone from the muscles, which now just wished to tear. Judas felt the
first real grief then, hitting him about the face. He wished to die, but he
knew he had to live. The crowd swooned and rolled, and some of them fell
onto their knees and faces. These were the believers and the new believers.
Some of them cried out that they could see the Kingdom. The Temple
as the world. The dead and the living all as one. The saints moving in
Jerusalem. Judas thought it, and knew it, but could not see it. He was the
word on the page, not the reader.

He watched from a distance as they wound the sheet around the body.
Mary the prostitute was there, and Jesus' mother. Mary seemed to have
found her that day. The whole thing was done under the eye of Joseph,
one of Simon Peter's friends, the merchant who'd made his fortune in
Arimathaea. He had always asked the disciples if they wanted money, a
house, servants, because he wanted to keep them like songbirds, pleased
at the words Jesus said to him. Helooked driven, like he was swatting
away the flies to getthis done. He looked like he had a horse on his back.
Or across.

Judas stood on a low hill near the tomb on the edge of Joseph's lands. The
tomb was of a Roman design, with all due Jewish ceremony, except that
it had been cut from rock and instead of a masonry door, there was only a
large boulder. It had been rounded so that it could roll, though only a team
of men could have done that. All very pastoral, like the friezes Judas had
seen in the palace, where painted skies made rooms look higher. Last night

Joseph's servants had rolled the stone, and the body of Jesus, wrapped in a linen sheet, had been taken in and placed where Joseph had planned to have himself interred, or so he said. In front of the tomb, a waiting crowd of people had already gathered, sitting and reading Scripture. Amongst them moved the non-Jewish merchants, Greeks, mostly, selling them food and water. In three days, the crucified God would leap from that stone, Judas knew, and show himself to the world, and connect the thread that bound heaven and earth. His own mission, his own existence, however, remained incomplete. He was not sure what he would do next. But Judas knew he had to do something, for why else had he been saved against all expectation? He smiled to himself, surprised by himself as only the things surrounding Jesus in the last few days had ever surprised him before. He might as well ask: why had everyone been saved?

Alison woke up and sat straight up, clutching her left eye. She could feel her heart hammering in her chest.

The dream. She'd had the dream again. Her body hated having it now. Her mind hurt at having had it. A religious dream. The terrible weight of it, like something sitting in her guts and making her sleep. An End of the World dream!

She must have been woken up. A sudden noise.

Across the way, she could see the shape of Leyton, asleep at the bottom of her bed. That both reassured and scared her, for some reason. One thing in another.

The light in the room changed.

Alison jumped out of bed, expecting Leyton to be moving too.

It scared her horribly when he wasn't. She knew immediately that he wasn't there.

That wasn't unique. Every now and then in life a detail had slipped by her, especially when her dream had disturbed her so, but why now—?

The Golden Man materialised out of her head.

That was how it felt, as if he slipped, like a tension headache, from out of the back of her eyes.

He changed all the shadows in the room, hanging there, looking down at her. His face was a golden mask, impassive. He was the Cherub that had attacked Leyton and the man that had hurt her eye. He was laughing, that mocking, arrogant laugh the Cherubs had had.

"What do you want?" she yelled.

"We want what we have," he replied. His voice was deep and strong. Very male. "We want the world. But now we want the pilot."

"He's not here."

The Golden Man turned and surveyed the room. "No. But he'll be back. Also, we want what we should have. You."

"Me?" She suddenly felt sick in her stomach.

"There are only so many eyes for us to give. They were once devices, way back in their evolution. They are limited. The process of fitting them is in two stages. One is a gift, the other an acceptance."

"I don't accept!"

The angel laughed again. "This is why we don't have rules," he said.

He raised his hand.

Alison covered her eyes.

But the blast of light went straight through them and slammed her head against the wall.

Fourteen: The Place Where all the Maps Meet

Whatmore woke afraid. There had been a noise. He thought for a moment that the golden things had got into the flat. He'd locked the door and bolted it, and had made sure all the windows were secure. He was certain of his faith, but what exactly made a place a sanctuary? He'd prayed, adding, after his usual list of those to remember, a plea to be up to this huge new situation that confronted him. He'd hoped to be able to wake up in the morning and get a fresh perspective on the whole thing, stop it from feeling so like a dream.

But here it was, in the middle of the night... actually, in the early hours of the morning, back to haunt him before he could get the sanity of dawn in his head.

The noise came again. It was someone ringing his doorbell, quite gently but insistently. Oh. Someone had woken up in a gutter somewhere and realised they hadn't enough cash for the night shelter.

He doubted the monsters would bother to knock.

Sighing, Whatmore climbed out of bed, threw his dressing gown on over his pyjamas and plodded down the stairs. He hoped the bell hadn't woken up any of the other tenants.

He made himself open the door slowly and calmly.

It was the man who called himself Leyton.

"Reverend," he said. "I'm sorry it's so late."

The vicar suddenly found himself very awake. "Come in," he said.

Leyton had walked quickly and stealthily through the streets back to the Abbey. He was expecting an attack at any moment, but none came. Perhaps the creatures didn't have any sort of supernatural intelligence, but relied instead on everyday surveillance. It was good to know they weren't vulnerable all night and day. There were a surprising number of people still about, people who came out of after-hours pubs, people who were slouched in shop doorways in sleeping bags, people who seemed to have business in the night, who walked quickly with briefcases. Their footsteps all echoed across the cobbles of the big empty spaces.

He went round the shining bulk of the Abbey into the churchyard and found the address Whatmore had given them.

The vicar looked pleased to see him. He let Leyton up into the little flat and made him a cup of tea.

"I'm sorry it's so late," Leyton began, lowering himself into a chair. "But there's... something I need to do."

"I know," said Whatmore. He sat down himself. "I know that look.

You want to take Communion."

"Good of you not to tell me to come back in the morning."

"Where you're concerned," said the priest, "I think we all have to make exceptions."

They went to the Abbey. Whatmore, who had thrown on his robes, unlocked the little side door. Leyton, feeling relief already, helped him assemble the wine and the wafers and the silverware. Whatmore said a brief blessing over them and they said the Creed together. Then Whatmore took one wafer and offered the other to Leyton. "The body of Christ," he said.

Leyton took the wafer in his mouth.

The vicar took a mouthful of the wine, and then offered him the cup. "The blood of Christ," he said.

Leyton swallowed the wine.

It wasn't as good as going through the whole service, but it was still a welcome warmth. He felt held together once more, standing on his own two feet... well, kneeling... for the first time since he'd got here.

"Let us pray together," said Whatmore. He got down on his knees beside Leyton and spread his palms upward.

Leyton bowed his head, hands together.

Whatmore led them through the Lord's Prayer, then a call for support and protection, and then a number of small interventions of his own.

Leyton found that he couldn't concentrate. He must be more shaken up than he'd thought. The words of the prayers were just so many syllables. He concentrated, as had been his habit when distracted in the past, on the meaning of each word, letting it roll around his thoughts as he'd sample a wine on his palate.

Normally, he would feel a great sense of presence at this point, the sensation of being listened to, of communication with the divine. But now there was only... He felt like he was giving a lecture, and the only audience was himself.

"God is with us," said Whatmore, resuming the service.

But Leyton could only frown. It didn't feel as if He was.

The taste in his thoughts was of himself, and the taste in his mouth was only of wine.

Afterwards, they sat in the pews and had some brandy.

"I couldn't feel Him here," Leyton said.

"I'm so sorry." Whatmore took Leyton's hands. And then, as if sensing the flyer's discomfort, let go of them again. "The Holy Spirit feels all around to me, at the moment. Every step I'm taking... well, no, that way lies madness."

"How does it feel when you pray?"

"Brilliant. One shares one's thoughts and hopes with God."

"I'm used to... Well, rather more than that."

Whatmore stared at him. For a moment he looked afraid. "Who are you?" he said.

"I'm just a pilot. A Squadron Leader."

"But where do you come from? Tell me everything."

So Leyton did.

Douglas was asleep, until a noise informed him that he was not alone.

He leapt up. His hand went to the pruning knife that he kept under his pillow and put it between the target and himself before his eyes opened.

It was an old man. He was looking down his nose at Douglas, his eyes sparkling in the light from the window. "Good morning, Douglas Leyton," he said. "Restoration."

"Restoration," said Douglas thankfully, replacing the knife. "Who are you?"

"Have you recently asked," the man replied, "that question of yourself?"

Whatmore sat nodding while Leyton told him the details, blowing through the gap between his palms every now and then to ward off the chill. Leyton realised that the priest must be a lot colder than he was, without a coat, and offered him his, but the vicar would have none of it.

"That is extraordinary," he said at the end. "So there exists this... gap, this change between your world and ours. I try and keep up with physics, theologians do these days. Isn't this just to be expected? When you travel in time, you end up in... I don't know, what would it be called, a parallel universe? But when you go back, you go back to your original one? Or something?"

Leyton couldn't help smiling. "That's my level of understanding too, Padre."

"Completely useless, then?"

"Check."

"But what interests me is, you say you feel more distant from God here?"

"It's as if you're exactly that: further from Him."

"I don't feel that."

"With respect, Padre, you don't know the difference."

"So we have Revelation, Sodom and Gomorrah and angels. You have a closer connection to the Lord. My God." Whatmore got to his feet and took a few paces from Leyton. "That's a Gnostic idea, you know."

"What is?"

"That this is hell."

Douglas had made the old man tea, which he had accepted, but was not drinking. They were sitting on opposite sides of Douglas's tiny kitchen table. Douglas felt the man sizing him up. He had to break the silence, he realised after he'd said, "What's your role within Restoration?"

"That's not a question an intelligence officer would ask."

"I'm not an intelligence officer. If you're a journalist, if you stumbled on that codeword—"

"I'm not a journalist. And no. I know you're not an intelligence officer. You are one of the dogs. Do you know they call you that? One of the handymen that Alec Cotton runs. Cotton will have told you his name. That is my credential. He isn't an intelligence officer either."

"Are you the boss?"

"Treat me as if I am." The old man looked as if he'd had a sudden thought. He got up, went to the single flap of curtain that covered the window and lifted it. He made a slow pass across his chest with his hand. Outside, a light amongst lights twinkled.

Douglas' stomach clenched of its own accord. "What do you want?"

"To meet you." The old man returned to the table. "To check a resemblance. And indeed, it's there. Very strongly. You are, perhaps, twenty years older than our man. And I am told you are the closest thing that exists, in this day and age, to a master of disguise."

"You want me to impersonate someone?"

"I wondered for a moment, when I saw you, if you had already done so. Under your own name, for some reason. When you can no longer use that name even to purchase your lodgings. I thought for an instant that I might be being toyed with. But no, that really cannot be. That would be slightly more ridiculous than the truth."

Whatmore walked with Leyton to the door of the Abbey. Leyton had made the man promise to go to Alison and explain why he'd gone, to give her any help she needed in her mission to find her friend. Whatmore had wanted to know everything about Leyton's future. The details filled his eyes with wonder. He had asked, time and again, about money, and how provision was made to recompense people for their services, and couldn't believe that the wealth of the Earth was put in a pot and doled out as it was asked for, with no obligations but the force of society. "I want to live in your future," he said.

"Reverend, so do I."

"Don't worry. I'll do everything I can to aid Alison."

"I may well be back to help," said Leyton. "But it's obvious that these creatures are something to do with me. I have to find Jocelyn. If she *is* alive. Maybe she'll know more about what's going on. Perhaps if she and

I can get back to our future, then all your troubles will vanish."

"Keep in touch won't you?" Whatmore reached into his pocket and gave Leyton the money he'd taken from the safe, the sum of the last few collections held at the Abbey. "This is for your mission."

Leyton smiled. "Mission?"

"You are in God's hands, Squadron Leader, I hope you return to your state of grace."

Leyton thanked the man for the money, made a note of the sum and promised to return it if he could. Then he left.

Whatmore watched the figure recede into the night. He crossed himself. "Protect him, Lord," he said. "Protect your servant as he does your work."

Fifteen: The Merchandise

Morning

Alison stumbled to her feet holding her eye. She headed into the bathroom.

It didn't look like there was anything wrong with her eye.

She stared into the mirror, trying to see anything in it.

She could still see the thing in her field of vision. Only now she didn't care so much. Why did she think it should hurt?

She had to go to work. She'd missed yesterday afternoon, which was really shit; if she did that too much she'd get the sack.

Her dreams last night: nightmares. Biblical stuff again. And she'd dreamed about the Golden Men. Good to be awake, get them flushed out of her system.

She went to work a different way that morning. The thoughts of what she had to do now were repeating in her head. Find Fran. Find the Golden Men. The bears. The End of the World is back on. Should be going to be famous.

Or... not. She stopped for a moment.

It felt like shitty, complicated dreamstuff. It felt like Leyton hadn't been there in the duvet at the end of the bed, like he was part of a dream too. She'd once, during those early weeks of the relationship when Patrick had stayed over often, woken up, found him not there, gone to the door of the bathroom and started chatting to him through it, only to realise after a few minutes that he hadn't stayed that night. Leyton was like that, a shape she'd made from a dream. She had to think back and remember what had happened last night to make him more real. She should have talked to him this morning, to remind her of where they were.

She went up to the top of Milsom Street. She was going to walk all the way down the city, from top to bottom. It just felt like fun on this wet morning.

Fun. The End of the World wasn't bothering her that much, then. God, where was it, after all? Everybody was getting on with stuff.

She bought a copy of the *Big Issue* from the man in the bobble hat who sold them outside Waterstones. He kept up a fantastic patter. They exchanged a couple of jokes. He deserved his pound. She wondered how the other two beggars further down the pavements could bear to look the *Big Issue* guy in the eye. They just sat under blankets, beside the cashpoints.

145

That was so stupid. It wasn't as if you got change from cashpoints.

She stopped again two steps away from the *Big Issue* seller.

Fun. Why was it fun? Because... She hadn't read anything from the *Big Issue* seller or the other beggars. She looked back at him. He'd walked out into the middle of the street and was starting to call again, swinging his arms to make a bigger spectacle of himself.

She couldn't work out anything about him.

There was his green woollen hat... just a hat. The knack of doing that was somewhere in the back of her head, not doing it.

She'd lost it.

She'd lost the ability to read stuff. She'd lost her curse!

Slowly, expecting it to come back any moment, she made her way down the street. Maybe this was why she'd taken this route this morning: to see the wood for the trees. To see things clearly for the first time in her life. It was as if someone had switched off a really loud piece of music. Hence calm. Hence rational. Hence fun.

After a few minutes, she started to notice all sorts of things.

She'd always dreamed that if she lost her ability, people would suddenly become complex mysteries to her, enigmas full of potential and teasing possibility. But it turned out that they were just as easy to read, it was just that they didn't come with as much baggage. The beggars were beggars. There was an old lady. There was an office worker. They were all just what they were. And lots of people were the same as each other.

A few hundred yards down the street it occurred to her that this was a bit like waking up after having been drunk the previous night. You'd done and thought all sorts of stuff that didn't feel like you. The state she'd been in must have been so weird. Because this felt... normal. This felt like what she *should* be used to, this state she'd never experienced before in her life. It was like the absence of pain instead of pain. You missed the luxury of it really quickly. She was almost scared that she'd forget the feeling of this difference, get really used to it before she could enjoy it.

This was why she had been afraid of the End of the World. She'd just looked too deeply into things. She'd been afraid of all kinds of weird shit. But all that had gone in the light of this new day. A huge history of business and development stretched back to create this street, from when the Romans had taken a British hamlet, found the hot springs and made the city a centre of tourism. There was no reason at all why it should stop now. She'd just been pulling everything apart. That way lay madness.

She put her tongue out to taste the rain. There was the tiniest hint of iron in there. Humanity's work, written into the rain. You could see the things people had done from orbit. The lights that covered the continents at night. The fleets of fishing boats. The straight lines of roads that crossed the deserts, sending produce north to south. You'd be able to see Bath too:

a little clump of living lights nestling in the hills. It was all so alive! So free and full of good stuff! It wasn't going to come to an end, no matter what happened.

She turned on the spot, taking in everything of the city around her at her own pace, not having it thrust itself into her eyes. It was a big, lovely system. The beggars contributed as much, in their way, as the office workers did. They asked, by their very existence, for voluntary and charitable groups, like the *Big Issue*, to evolve to help them, thus creating jobs. It all worked out. And it would keep on doing it.

As she passed Starbucks, she got a little flash of things connecting and it worried her for a second. But it was just a chain of associations, the sort of thing she'd heard about from other people. Starbucks... *Austin Powers*... Dr Evil. It stopped there. No cascade of meaning. No horrible endless stuff. She went in and got an Eggnog Mocha. She'd seen it advertised outside.

She took a sip of the sweet, hot drink. It felt great.

She increased her speed past the pastry shop. Didn't want to push it too far. She went into W.H. Smith, didn't know what she wanted, and came out again.

She popped round the corner into the smaller newsagent and bought a packet of cigarettes. Marlboro Lights. And some matches.

She'd always fancied one. The girls at school had laughed at her because she wouldn't do it. She'd been terrified of cancer and lung disease and all that. But now she was free from fear. She'd look really good with a cigarette. It suited the shop. She must have associated the taste with the taste of the air she was going to be breathing all day, wanted the tastes to be the same... Couldn't follow that thought any further. Oh, who gave a fuck what she'd done? She didn't have to think any more.

The lower stretch of the town started to repeat shops that she'd already passed higher up. There were two Boots, one with Edwardian details, one without. There were two big newsagents, the Smith's and a John Menzies, and she thought she remembered that one owned the other. The top one had big gleaming sheet windows and sat beside Waterstone's and the Pasta Italia. The bottom one was in a precinct, and was with the fifty-pence bookshop and the key and shoe repair shop. You could live entirely in the top of the city of Bath or in the bottom. There was no division between the two. It wasn't like apartheid or anything, which had been evil. This was just useful for people wearing heels.

She stopped outside Linley's Racing and fumbled open the packet of fags. She took the matches and awkwardly struck one, started the end of the cigarette burning. She could already see Ted inside, a fag in his mouth, working away on the boards.

She put the other end of the cigarette in her mouth and sucked air in through it. She expected to cough and splutter like in a sitcom. This wasn't for the taste, after all, this was a look she was going to work up in the next week or so.

The taste shocked her and made her smile. The hot, sweet, fragrant air was the most beautiful thing she had ever tasted. She knew that a cigarette meant all sorts of things, a huge pile of meaning. But now she didn't have to swallow all that to enjoy it. She took a long suck from the sky and knocked on the door of her place of work.

During the day, someone tried to put a bet on the month the Queen Mother would die, which was sick and wrong. Alison was very glad when Ted adopted a haughty, proud tone and told the man that Linley's would not put odds on anything of that sort. They didn't do death. Too depressing. And bad for the shop's reputation. Alison had a sudden revelation as she puffed on her eighth cigarette of the morning: that was how it worked. Everybody worked together, looking out for each other. The feelings of everybody else stopped Ted from doing anything shit. The feelings of everybody else would save the beggars and keep the world going.

She was astonished to see the odds she'd given on the End of the World. They should be hugely against, to encourage more of the kind of stupid sod who made bets they couldn't win on. She put them up to ten thousand to one against.

Ted got her to set odds on the rain stopping tomorrow. Taking a figure off the top of her head she said two to one on. Ted looked at her oddly for a second, and she couldn't quite understand what he was thinking. Which made her laugh with sheer joy. But then he nodded and went to a board and put it up as an actual bet.

Which made Alison pause.

Now that she'd lost her depression/insight, she was no longer hugely qualified to do this job!

She got scared for a while and went into the back, reading through the racing papers. She still knew how to set odds, of course. She'd learnt the business when she'd been able to learn stuff really fast. She made her usual notes on the form of today's horses, checking against the form book. But she no longer had the instinct for it. She took a quick tour of all her long-shot bets and found that her first reaction to all of them was how bloody unlikely it was that any of them would happen.

Except maybe the discovery of intelligent alien life. Maybe that was what the Golden Men were.

No, of course not. They were *so* here. They were classical gods, designed like the city was. Except they didn't have a crap end and a rich end. They had a burning end and an intelligent end, like a cigarette. They looked just like men. How could they be aliens? And the whole idea of aliens was stupid, anyway.

Could she put a bet on that, though? In case the Golden Men were suddenly going to walk in to Downing Street and announce something? Ted didn't approve of his staff betting in his own shop. But she could call one of the big national chains. Or get someone else to do it, Patrick maybe. They knew who she was. She didn't want to chop the odds for Ted or get a news story going.

She'd think about that.

But the problem remained: she was no longer sensitive to the chances of anything happening. She had swapped insight for fun. What the fuck. She would make it up as she went along, like everybody else did.

At lunch she went to the Orange Grove pantry and stood in the rain in front of the window looking at the sandwiches.

Everything had mayonnaise, even the salads. She could ask for none, but if she went in, she'd be tempted. She turned and looked at her profile in reflection. She was so bloody fat. She lit up again and turned away, shaking her head.

No lunch. No dinner either.

That afternoon she asked Ted for a raise. She thought she might as well, since her performance was going to decline radically. Squeeze a bit extra out of him before he realised and sacked her.

God, when? She used to just know things like that.

Ted had thought about it for a moment, looking at her like he looked at one of his odds boards. Then he nodded. "How much?"

Why hadn't she done this way back? She asked for three times her current salary.

To her amazement, he said yes.

She watched the clock all the afternoon, willing the time to go by. She was thinking about Patrick. Why had she walked out of that door when he'd said not to? He was lovely. And he could keep her comfortable for the rest of her life. She wasn't comfortable now. She had a crap flat, and it was rented, and she just hadn't been taking care of herself. She'd call him from home; it'd look desperate to call him this soon after walking out. Maybe he'd come back. Or maybe now she'd pushed him too far.

She nearly decided to call one of the big bookmaking chains, because if she was worth this to Ted, then what would she be worth to them? But she decided to do it from home. No record of the call. She'd pop home tomorrow lunchtime and do that.

She had her coat on at five and was ready by the door.

"Don't hang about if you've got somewhere to go," said Ted, with a smile.

She smiled back. Thinking that now she did: she was free, and she could go anywhere.

And then, brilliant thing on brilliant thing, the door opened and in came Patrick, with Marty behind him. He had his arms spread wide, as if he'd never threatened anything about her going. In that moment, Alison knew she owned him.

She threw herself into his arms, grinning up into his face, and let him, amazed, sweep her around. "I love you," she said. "I'm sorry."

"I'm sorry too."

They kissed, everything forgotten, and she was going to keep that going quite a long time. But Marty stepped up to them, and people in the shop were looking. "We've found them," he said. "We've found the Bears."

Alison was quite irritated to have Marty walking with them to Patrick's car. She wanted to go somewhere private with Patrick and have sex with him. She wanted to bind him to her. She wanted to have sex and have it be just fun and love and not the huge dark maze of shit that it had always used to be.

But Patrick was as keen as Marty was on finding Fran. And, okay, she ought to be keen too. It was just that now she wasn't mad any more, nothing too bad could have happened to Fran. She wondered if she should tell these two that she'd found the Bears herself? But no. Things like that didn't happen. They'd never believe her. And the way the golden things had flipped across the buildings... like they were lights or reflections or something. It had taken the vicar to make them actually believe they were real, and he was one of these trendy vicars who believed in everything, and probably had mystical experiences on every street corner and spoke in tongues all the time.

God, she'd been so brainwashed! She'd done it herself, just by thinking too much.

But now she said, "Bears, okay, where do we go?" because she wanted to make Patrick happy and she wanted them both to think she was a good person and concerned about her friend. Which meant she was, if they thought it.

"It's like when I heard about Special K," Marty began. "Ketamine. You're drinking and you hear the word from across the way, and you ask about it, gently like, and only if you're in the right company. Then you find someone who knows what they're talking about, and after a bit, a friend of a friend gets you where you want to go, and you meet someone who's actually got some. Big let-down that was. Wanted to meet the archetypal beings who govern our unconscious, yeah? Just a bunch of Pacmans." He made scissoring motions across his eyes. "Gobble gobble gobble. Anyway, so I spent all today going round to see mates who do stuff, and using this word of yours, 'Bears'. And nobody got it, and I thought this must be you dreaming. But then I went over to Bristol on the train, and there the story's totally different! I didn't even have to ask. This black guy in a bar down on the docks was handing out fliers for a club and it said 'On the Bearpath'. So I don't ask what that is, I just laugh and say, 'Bearpath, is it?' and he nods like everybody knows. So I ask the people I know I can ask, like Janey, 'cos she's always kind to me, and she tells me that she knows loads of people who've seen Bears, but she's never seen one herself. And she points out people who now say they have, but haven't. And I tell her I'm going back to Bath, and is this just a Bristol thing, and she tells me about Phil."

"Phil?"

"Phil's a dealer. Not my sort of shit, but I know him, he hangs around in the Three Cornered Hat. He can get you to the Bears, Janey says. She's seen him with the crowd who do this stuff."

"So that's where we're going," said Patrick. "To meet Phil and see if Fran's off with the Bears."

"Oh," said Alison, buttoning her collar against the rain. "Great."

Patrick had parked his car on a double yellow line on one of the nearly vertical streets above the Porter. The car only took two people normally, so Marty lay in the small space reserved for luggage as Patrick took them on a fast drive around the one-way system, parking illegally again on a similar incline beside the Three Cornered Hat.

Alison helped Marty out. The pub was busy already, full of people for whom five o'clock was just a number, the sound of a DJ calling through the rain from the top floor. The crowd that hung out here wore black woolly jumpers with holes in. Alison hadn't been able to do arty or cool; her talent had pulled everything apart, including, anytime she looked in the mirror while wearing anything that conveyed a complicated message, her.

But now she could, she thought on the step. Now she could do anything.

Patrick's money, of course, let him go anywhere. Now she would be at his side.

The Three C had the most serious anti-drugs policy Alison had ever experienced at a pub. On one of her few excursions here, she had actually been searched on her way in. Getting caught would not only lead to prosecution, someone had said that night, but, far worse, a life ban. Those who lived by the Three C died by the Three C.

They made their way to a corner table and sat down while Marty went off to get the beers in and talk to a particular barman. There was a big screen up, silently showing a shopping channel in a wan, daytime way. Big men in black jeans with T-shirts over pot bellies chuntered to each other through their beards. "Oh ah?" There was a laugh from across the way. "Oh ah!"

Alison felt restless. She wasn't dressed for this. She looked like someone who wasn't good at smart casual. She looked like a teenager. The girls in here had big make-up and wore fetish, and they had tattoos.

She really wanted a tattoo. Of what? Of something she stood for.

Christ, what would that be now? Freedom. The broken link. The woman who was never going to dream of bloody Judas again.

Patrick squeezed her forearm, pointed to a couple of Goths at the bar and laughed secretly at them. She laughed too. She'd be content to be with him. Wife, soon, maybe. She'd never met his parents. Never mind the tattoo, then.

She reached in her purse, pulled out a fag and lit up.

Patrick stared at her. "Since when—?"

She blew smoke in his face. "Am I being a bad girl?"

He looked complicated, in some way which she didn't get. Ha ha! "Err... no."

"In the movies, people only smoke if they're evil. In the real world everyone does it. Even doctors."

"I don't."

"Maybe you could start?"

He laughed. "Full of surprises."

"I am now."

Marty came back with three drinks, behind him a loose-limbed thin-faced boy in a long black coat. He had a big grin on his face. "Ah ha! I'm Phil. You're Patrick and Alison, and this is Marty, and you all know that." He pointed to a stool. "Sit? Ta." He had a deep Somerset accent, the kind, Alison thought, that it was weird to find on someone this young. Like he was a farmboy, or... but that was as far as thoughts like that could take her now. He looked around them all, sizing them up, and his gaze finally fastened on Alison. "I'm interested in what you'd like," he said.

"Hey!" said Patrick, in a laughing way that wouldn't convince anyone. "Easy, tiger!"

"What do you mean?" asked Alison.

"What do you want?" He waited, and then sighed, emphasising his words with a little indicative movement of his head. "What do you want me to *get* for you?"

"Coke, to start with," said Alison. She only knew it was true as the words were out of her mouth.

"Now we're talking," said Phil. "Very you."

Alison hadn't ever wanted it before. She could imagine making her deductions like lightning with a speeded-up soundtrack of Wagner in the background. But now... "Yeah," she said.

"Anyway," said Marty. He flashed a look at her as if they were acting together and he was glad she'd just pulled that move off. "We also wanted to see some Bears."

Phil started to laugh. "Everyone does now. It's moving over from Bristol. That's always how it goes. Manchester, London, Bristol, Bath." He drew a zigzag in the air. "The news moves before the supply. So you know what you're talking about, right?"

"I've met them," said Alison. She suddenly believed this stuff again. It meant more, coming from the mouth of a dealer.

"Yeah? So why don't you know how to meet them again?"

"I lost the person I met them with."

Phil nodded slowly, rubbing the streak of hair on his chin. "It happens. It happens. All right. It'll cost you fifty each. I take you to the party on the Bearpath tonight, at the right time. You make your own introductions. Not everyone there knows me, okay?"

"You won't be hanging about, then?" asked Marty.

"No," said Phil. "Too close for me. I saw one and whoosh!" He whizzed his hand back over his head. "Never again."

"How did he look at you?" asked Alison.

Phil peered at her, like that was a weird question. She looked to Patrick and Marty, and they were bemused too. Maybe it was. "Like he knew my dad," said Phil, finally. "I thought he was going to ruffle my hair."

Patrick put his hand in his pocket and pulled out three fifties, which he put on the table, keeping his finger on them. "So just what are these Bears?"

Phil didn't reach for the notes. He looked back to Alison. "You sure he's with you?"

Patrick let go of the notes with a snort and Phil took them.

"Always a pleasure," he said. "Be in here tonight at nine. Gives us an hour to get there. See you." And he headed for the door.

"You should have asked about Fran," said Patrick.

"Couldn't risk it," said Marty. "That was good stuff there, Alison. He trusted you. Your magic whatsit again."

Alison managed not to smile. Phil had trusted her out of something else. "It's six already," she said. "We might as well stay. I'll get them in, I'm rich today."

They had some beer.

Alison thought about calling home, calling Leyton. It was weird: she felt as if he wasn't really there. She knew he was, but it was like she wasn't the one concerned about Fran any more. Now Leyton wasn't all these millions of associations and connections, what could he be? She felt like she was putting up a friend of her parents or something; if he came out, she'd have to buy him drinks all night. Even Marty paid sometimes. Even if he was a crusty. Leyton was... she couldn't believe she'd picked him up in the fish shop. He'd just attached himself to her, and he'd told her all this stuff... and none of it made any sense.

She was kind of frightened to go home, actually.

She was going to see the Bears who'd attacked him, she reminded herself. They were real. So what he was saying must be real. Mustn't it? He had said she was going to be famous. That had been good. But then it had turned out she wasn't going to be. And the Bible was different where he came from.

What a nutter. No, there were all these reasons why—

There was no because. Some things didn't need because. She stared into her glass, sucking on her cigarette. The black pool looked back up into her. It was like beer. It was like when she'd really been into *Inspector Morse*—hey, she could watch that again now, and she wouldn't get the endings!—and it had been sponsored by Beamish stout. And she'd just started drinking Beamish. Fran had noticed, back then, and asked why. And Alison couldn't answer her. There are statistics about these things. The tiniest things change people's minds, so tiny that you couldn't imagine that any single person, if asked, would say they didn't vote for him because of his tie, or they bought that car because of the music, or they drank what they drank because just the words appeared at the start of their favourite TV programme... but they did. Because if you stepped back from it, you could see that pattern, that shape made by all those individuals. And none of them had any becauses.

Inspector Morse didn't even drink Beamish.

So she had no need for because for any of this. She was just being a real girl again. She was being human and bloody living for once, for the first time! And she wanted to meet a Bear because she wanted to meet one, and Fran would just be there when she did, and the mystery would be over and solved and they would be in the final ad break.

She pulled Patrick's head to hers and drunkenly snogged him, slipping her tongue against his. She didn't know what he wanted any more, why he wanted to find Fran again. Not knowing was great.

Phil arrived, to everyone's surprise, as the hands on the big shadow clock across the bar moved to nine. The place had filled up. He was in a fleece. He'd shaved. He was looking perky. "Made a day of it, then? Good plan. Let's go."

On the way to the door, he slipped a tiny envelope into Alison's pocket and tapped the side of his nose.

She grinned hugely back at him.

Phil led them across town, through the rainy darkness, up Walcot, along the big unforgiving façades of the large houses, past the antique shops.

Alison realised that, once upon a time, she would have got a sense of doggishness here. Of professional dog-walkers and wet halls and thick mats. She'd gone in exactly the wrong direction that night when she'd been searching. She hadn't thought of richness. And that was obvious now, that those kids they'd met might have been wealthy.

Phil stopped at a narrow alleyway between two buildings: an old gap. He looked up and around at the buildings. There were lights on in several high windows across the road, where a wall held up a little crumbling stretch of park above the A4. Above them there stood one of the Georgian façades, still one house, not made into apartments. Cars moved past in the rain.

There was a chipshop far across the way. Nobody stood outside it.

"Okay," said Phil. "Down here. We knock on the door, then we walk right in like we own the place." He led the way down the alley. They were between two Georgian buildings. The brown had streaked into black in this unseen slice of Bath. Up high to the left there was a thin bathroom window which glowed orange, and by that they could see. The rain splattered down on them.

Halfway along the alley, down a couple of mossy steps to the left, there was a wooden door, set into a serious masonry frame. Phil grabbed the doorknob and held it for a moment, waiting until they caught up. "Right," he said. "Be knowledgeable."

They nodded.

He knocked twice. Two big solid waps.

The door opened. A serious black kid stood there in a football shirt that said *Atari* on the front, like they were the team and not the sponsor. He didn't say anything, just looked at them.

Phil spread his arms wide. And stood there.

Suddenly, Patrick stepped forward. "How much?" he said.

"That will be ten pounds," said the man.

"Four please," said Patrick, handing over the cash.

The man opened the door and motioned for them to come quickly through.

Alison flashed Patrick the most deeply loving smile she had. He bobbed his head in return.

The door led into a dark corridor that smelt musty. They were relics of wine cellars, kept under the street so that deliveries could be made down entrances by the side of the road. The various produce merchants would have stepped inside to deliver their goods, would have met only servants.

When she'd foolishly been considering buying rather than renting, Alison had been taken on tours of several one-bed-roomed flats that were little more than cells attached to such cellars.

The man shouldered his way past them and led them to another door. From behind this one came the sound of muted conversation and music. White light shone under it.

He opened the door and they went inside.

It was a kitchen.

It was full of people, kids, mostly. Drinks in their hands. Smoke in the air. From the other side of the room, standing beside an empty dog basket, a boy with blond hair and padded shoulders turned to meet Alison's gaze. Chris. He smiled. "Hi," he said. "Welcome back."

If she'd still had her abilities, it would have been so much worse.

She remembered.

She had fallen against that huge old wooden door she was looking at now, laughing. There was a skateboard propped up in one corner, a wheel missing. That belonged to Chris. She had put a finger on one of the wheels and spun it while they were waiting. There was the big window, blackness and rain behind it. The exact angle. She was sure that at a similar time tonight the moon would be at a similar height, the height she remembered, beaming in through that big kitchen window.

She could see it all now. Something in her was letting her see it all.

It all flashed against her eyes, fast, from the inside. It laid itself upon this party of people in a kitchen standing around, bright colours on wan ones.

At the pub, there had been Chris and the girl Emmeline, whom Chris had known from school. They were too close to go out. And there was Al, the dark-haired one with the big teeth and the breezy, bouncy look, and Sophie, who he was shagging. Chris and Emmeline had kind of engaged with Alison and Fran in a drug-flirty way. We know something you don't know, are you worthy of knowing it? Alison had glimpsed that look waiting outside bathrooms at parties, when two people had come out at once and they hadn't been interested in sex in there like normal people. Mark, who she'd gone out with for two weeks at Uni, had once done too much of that and white wine and e at the same time and she'd taken him home shaking, and she'd had to talk to him all night, and walk him up and down to stop his legs cramping up, and had rubbed and rubbed his arms.

She hadn't got angry at him for it. She was glad now. It was kind of like an industrial accident. Part of the process, when you decided to get involved in the process. It could have happened to anybody. It could have happened to her. But not tonight. She was older and wiser now. An adult knows where the boundaries are.

Emmeline had started saying to Chris things like how she and Fran looked like they could understand the philosophy. Maybe Fran more than Alison.

Chris had disagreed: hippie skirts and those things in Fran's hair. Not good. Who did she stand up for? What did she believe in?

Fran hadn't been able to answer. So Alison had answered instead. She'd said that Fran believed in some sort of divinity, a power that looked after everyone.

Fran had looked complicated at her, like that wasn't quite it any more.

Chris had drained his pint, his eyes darting to Emmeline, who grinned back at him. They were laughing at Fran. "There's a power," he said. "We've met it. Maybe you have too."

"Let me ask you a question," said Al. He'd looked at the others. "Which one of the questions?"

"The DVDS," said Sophie.

"If you had the money, would you replace your favourite videos... you know, movies... with DVDs?"

Fran had just stared at him.

"Answer the question," said Chris.

"I wouldn't," Alison had said. "I don't have the money."

"But if you did."

"I don't."

"But if you did."

Alison had gone to the toilet. She'd been very pissed. By the time she'd got back to the table, Fran and Chris had entered into an earnest conversation and were repeating themselves a bit, like pissed people did.

"He's going to show us," Fran had said. "He says we can see the Bears."

There was something dull in her voice. Distant. Mechanical.

And they'd left the pub.

Chris's parents were property developers, and this was their second home. The parents were at the flat in London. Alison had stumbled into the kitchen and fended off a huge Labrador, which leapt up at her. Chris shoved it off and kicked it into the lounge, shut the door on it. It was a house of polished wood and paintings and brass things and rugs.

Chris slammed a bottle of Pernod and six shot glasses onto the table. "Run out of absinthe," he said. "We wait. We drink. We're on the Bearpath. I'll put some music on." He went to a portable CD player perched on top of the fridge and started the Eminem record.

They sat down and started to drink the Pernod. Alison hated it and said so.

"You try anything for long enough, you get to like it," Chris said. "How the fuck do any of us get drunk? 'Cos it tastes like shit, let's remember that. Wine. Beer. You drink cider when you're a kid 'cos it tastes a bit less like shit."

"This man," said Al, pointing to the stereo. "He's the only one who speaks the truth. It's all bullshit, man. It's rank." He had stretched the word like a West Indian. "The world we got is shite, and he says so."

"So what's the philosophy?" Fran had trouble saying the word. "Is that it?"

"It's that they've got it wrong," said Sophie.

"Who's they?"

"Everybody. We're not free. And we ought to be."

"Free?" asked Fran.

"You can't say the stuff you want to say," said Chris. "There's no free speech."

"Everyone's politically correct," said Al. "You can't say nigger... You're my niggers, it's the word they use about themselves. So why not? They can say it and we can't."

"We," said Emmeline, "are an oppressed minority."

"So you're very right wing?" Alison had thought that Fran would be bristling by now. Should be.

"No! We're not into politics."

Alison laughed. "Politics is into you."

"We're not into party politics. The parties don't work together enough."

"So that's the Third Way. Very Blairite."

"Blairite?!" Emmeline snorted and so did the others.

"Don't laugh at me!" said Alison.

"You can't say cunt," said Al.

Fran put a hand to her brow. "So you want to be able to say cunt?"

"We want to be free," said Chris.

"You need gold to be free, bitch," added Al.

"Don't call me that."

"It's just another word for woman."

"You know," said Emmeline, "like bitch, like a strong woman."

Bitch reminded Alison: she'd been following the talk back and forth with her head, not registering anything. She needed to wash her hands. The dog. The fall onto the pavement. Her hands stank and hurt, and had little bits of grit in the skin.

She went to the sink.

She remembered the water on her hands, the taste of Pernod on her mouth. The gleaming taps, the big sink. She remembered the touch of

Chris's hands on her arms. The whispered command to look around.

The lighting in the room had changed, she remembered.

She'd looked around.

The Golden Man had floated through the big window, a sun eclipsing the moon. His body was bright gold against the black, apart from the bits that were blacker. They were like the dark bits of the moon, glowing with some difficult light of their own. He was proportioned like a statue, the shadows of great, smooth muscles. Empty golden mask eyes. Hair that was swept back into one golden shape.

"It's the one called Michael," Chris had whispered.

The Golden Man had touched down on the black-and-white chequered tiles like Peter Pan. Not all his limbs were there. They varied as Alison moved her head from side to side. She'd like to say, a part of her brain remembered the thought, that she'd sobered up in that instant. But she hadn't. She'd gazed at the vision without knowing what it meant, and had started to laugh, in fear and wonder.

Fran, though, had understood.

Fran had understood. The size of that meant complicated things for Alison now. She couldn't get her head around it.

Alison had looked sideways at her. Fran was backing towards the door, her hands reaching behind her for it. She started to scream, sudden, strong little shouts. Alarm calls. Help me.

Alison was about to do it. Of course she was.

She saw something in Fran's eyes, in the memory now. That had been her ability talking, back then. Fran recognised this creature. She'd known it was coming. They'd met before. But it was like something from her nightmares appearing in real life.

What stopped Alison going to her was that Chris and Emmeline and Sophie did. She thought, pissed as she was, that they were going to help her.

But they grabbed Fran by the arms and shoulders and started pushing her forwards, her feet on her heels slipping off the tiles, towards the Golden Man.

Alison would have helped there.

But the Golden Man suddenly moved again, and all her attention shot back to him.

He moved towards her.

His hands were reaching out. That's one small step for woman, she thought. She held her palms up, ready to hit cosmic high fives with the starman.

He went straight between her arms and at her head.

Bits of him missed her.

She was face to face with him. And then the fear hit her. And that's why she'd remembered this bit only.

His hands appeared in front of her face: minstrel glove hands, a conjuror's shift to make a dove. You're my wife now.

There had been a light. A flash.

Something slammed into her eye.

She stumbled back. Fell over. Her hands leapt out, looking for something to grab. She hit the cupboards and slid down them.

That reminded her of something. She didn't know what.

She had put her hand to her eye. She had no pain now, but for a moment there had been tremendous pain. The pain of being penetrated.

They had stood looking down at her, in awe. She felt they wanted to touch her, but were afraid.

They weren't all looking down at her. Al was out of the circle. Behind them. He was feeding Fran to the Golden Man.

There were screams. Fran's screams.

Alison had found her shoulders fastened to the floor by her own body. A part of her didn't care. She started to laugh again.

The screams stopped, replaced by a sort of sigh.

Chris had leant over her. "Where do you live? Can you remember your address?"

Alison had nodded.

She hadn't seen where Fran had gone. Neither she nor the Golden Man were in the kitchen as she was helped to her feet. She looked about for them violently, stretching her head on her shoulders. It felt like later.

The kids must have called a taxi. She remembered sitting on a stool, time not happening. She was aware that her eye hurt.

They put her in the taxi. No, Sophie had sat with her. She said happy, encouraging things to Alison every now and then. Like she was afraid she'd tell on them? Like she was testing her loyalty? No, like she was joyful for a fellow convert. Like they were pregnant together.

Sophie had helped her into her house, sorted her keys out. Got her up the stairs, opened the door. She remembered the big, light, familiar space of her hall.

And then Sophie was gone. She could remember stumbling forwards. Part of her had been bellowing inside, screaming silently about Fran. Where was Fran? What had happened to Fran? But that part had been kept silent, reined in, imprisoned. It had seeped out of the cracks only hours later. Only after sleep.

And by then it had been too late.

She looked slowly up at the crowd of kids, realising that she'd spent seconds staring at the ground, blinking fast. She was aware of Patrick and Phil and Marty behind her.

Chris stepped forward, with Emmeline and Al and Sophie beside him.

As one, they began to clap.

The applause caught on. It echoed around the room.

Alison found herself inclining her head to accept the applause.

She reached into her pocket. "Excuse me," she said. "I need the toilet."

She found it without knowing she knew where it was. An accident, damn it, not a skill thing. Patrick and Marty and Phil, if he was still there, were probably getting drinks at the party and joining in.

She emptied the contents of the envelope onto the toilet seat. Fine white powder. No, a bit chunky. She didn't know how to do this. She'd seen people before and after, not during. She didn't even know why she had to put it on the seat. A movie thing. She'd seen it done like this in movies.

And why was she doing this?

Because this was the most secret, fantastic, centre-of-things party she had ever been to. And she wanted to be right for it. She'd been wrong before, but the Golden Man had accepted her anyway. He'd taken her head in his hands. Despite fucking Fran and her fucking screaming.

She got the feeling there was still something *wrong* about her. She ought to be different, completely accepted. Something about her was blocking her becoming the complete and utter ruler of her world. Coke would help with that.

There was a knock on the door. "Who is it?" she called.

"It's Chris," said the voice. "Not yet. Wait until it's time."

"Oh," said Alison. She awkwardly smoothed the coke back into the envelope, trying to get every bit of it off the toilet seat. "Right."

Chris was waiting for her outside, a glass of Pernod in both hands. Patrick was behind him, glaring.

Alison winked at Patrick and took one of the glasses of Pernod. She looked Chris deep in the eyes and they threw their glasses back together.

"I never thought you'd come back here," he said. "I thought you were further down the Bearpath now."

"I might be," she giggled. "It's brilliant! I don't understand!"

Patrick took her forcibly by the arm. "We're looking for Fran," he whispered.

"Fran? Your mate?" Chris stepped up to him, his eyes big. "She'll be here later. When the Bear arrives."

He moved back into the kitchen. Patrick glared at Alison again. "What were you doing in there?"

"Nothing," she said. "Unfortunately."

And she snogged him until he snogged her back and led him after the blond boy again.

Everybody was waiting. Phil was chatting to everyone. His contact wasn't there, so he was trying to be everybody's mate, hoping that nobody would ask what he was doing there. Marty stood still, tense, not even bothering to nod along to all the noise of conversation or the music. That looked better, Alison thought. Like he really was part of this lot. She saw that a lot of them were holding themselves tensely. The alcohol wasn't kicking in. This wasn't the party, this was the pre-party bit. If she'd still had her skills, she'd have made all sorts of fictional shit out of this.

She levered Patrick over to where Emmeline and Al were and introduced them all. Al introduced his mate Frank, the guy on the door, who'd now been replaced by someone else. They only let in people who knew. And they hadn't told anyone. The whisper was out. This house was on the Bearpath.

Chris looked at his watch. "Time we started," he said. "I think everyone's here who's going to be here. What have you brought?"

People started looking in their pockets, pulling out money, drugs, all sorts of shit. Phil saw what was happening and produced another envelope. Marty walked over, stood beside Alison and Patrick. Chris glanced over at the three of them and shook his head, with a smile that said that they were all okay. They didn't have to do this.

"You're further down the Bearpath," Patrick whispered to Alison. "What does that mean?"

"I don't know."

Emmeline had been gone for a few moments. Now she reappeared. "Okay," she called. "Come on through."

She led them down a plush hallway and under an arch made of wood that looked like it had once been part of a sailing ship, into a huge lounge where a log fire crackled away. The air smelt of air freshener. Weirdly, the television was on, with the sound down, showing the news: pyres of cattle being burnt, the foot and mouth epidemic, individual animal bodies being hoisted into the air like mad puppets and dumped onto the growing heap. The night behind the pyre was brown with the lit smoke, the brown of slops.

"I found it," said Emmeline, "and thought it kind of worked."

"Form a circle," said Chris.

"If you want," added Al. "We're all free."

The crowd of kids did so. Sophie looked at the clock and hurried things along, encouraging them to stand shoulder to shoulder, their hands out in front of them. "We need to summon him now. We need to offer him what he needs."

Chris held out his hands, like he was cupping breasts. "This is the payment," he said. "We are the élite. We are free."

His three mates joined in, and the circle did too. Alison listened to herself repeating the words, but came to no conclusions. They repeated them again and again, with no pause, until they were breathless.

Then they all stopped at once. Alison looked across and saw that Chris had raised his finger to stop them. He took some money from his pocket and handed it to Emmeline beside him. She gave him something back, Alison couldn't see what. Suddenly, everyone was buying stuff from everyone else, one to one. Phil handed out a small packet and got one note back and looked angry for a moment. Then he subsided. This was a ritual transaction, not a genuine one.

Nobody swapped anything with Alison. Or Marty or Patrick.

Everyone had some drugs now. Phil unwrapped the thing in his hand. "Everyone take it now," he said. "This is the attractor."

Alison recognised coke, speed, and what she thought was probably heroin. Patrick and Marty looked awkward. Patrick was against anything illegal; Marty didn't like amphetamines and, as far as Alison knew, he had never touched heroin.

But this wasn't being demanded of them. They were protected by her presence. What they did was up to her.

Alison saw Chris looking at her expectantly. It was being demanded of *her*.

She took the envelope from her pocket. She didn't know how to cut this stuff, or even if she had to. But she desperately wanted to be part of things.

"Now hang on—" said Patrick.

"Hush." She tapped the powder into her hand and raised it to her nose. She was aware of Patrick looking at her, but come on. How sad did he want them to look?

The whole circle was looking at her. Waiting for her, she realised.

She closed her eyes, put her nose to the coke and took a sniff. A long sniff. All of it. Every single little bit of it.

Ow! Fuck! Uhh!

She opened her eyes again, jolting. And everyone else was snorting. All of them! Fucking because of her! She was only their fucking leader!

"I'm their leader!" she shouted. "Your leader!"

"You're further along!" shouted Chris back, wiping his nose. "Call him, Alison! Call the Bear!"

She felt Patrick stiffening next to her, like he was ready to run. Marty was staring at her, his mouth open like a complete nobody, as if he couldn't believe she'd do that. "Stop fucking staring," she told him. She turned back to the room. "I want to call him!"

"Then call him!" That was Sophie.

She took a huge, brilliant breath into her lungs.

She felt the shape of her throat change.

It burst out of her before she expected it to come.

A long, ululating cry. An airburst noise. It shaped the air in the room. It was his name. Michael.

The pattern was bigger than her, but was made of her. It reflected her. It made her big. She was coke. She was the brand of coke. It was her dream. This was where she wanted to be. The process that had brought the stuff from some plant somewhere into her body was a sign that there was something bigger than the law. Something bigger than all of them.

She was finally part of something. She was finally free.

Feel the passion!

A door behind her opened.

She turned, holding herself tall. The sound was still hanging in the air, blasting around the heads of these kids that worshipped her, knocking Patrick and fucking Marty on their stupid heels, making them totter.

She realised that her mouth was open. It made the name. "Fran."

It was Fran.

We were pleased. But also puzzled. Alison had been confirmed. She was now acting like *one of us*. But Fran couldn't find her in *we*. She had been looking forward to that.

Also, *we* hadn't expected her to come and join in with the idiots who were starting to flock to *us* now. *We* were looking forward to more and more of them arriving, of course. Because that would help spread the pool of baptised and confirmed initiates, and help save the future, and it was fun. But it was a side issue. The real work had been done with Alison, and now all *we* needed was the pilot. He was the important thing.

Fran was aware that she was a little cold. It was really good to see Alison again. It was good to let her body say what *we* thought.

I'm one of the rulers of the world now. Or at least my Michael is.

So why did it feel bad when she thought that?

Fran was naked. She looked dull about the eyes, like she hadn't eaten for a couple of days. Her hair was unwashed, up at angles. She had an odd smile on her face.

A strange light came with her. All the shadows shifted in the room.

Everyone gasped and screamed and yelped and started to cry in anticipation.

Alison looked eagerly into her friend's face. They were sharing this! They were together in this! Yes!

Fran fell to her hands and knees and buried her head in the carpet in supplication.

Behind her, in what looked like a library, stood the Golden Man called Michael.

The light was his light. The change in illumination he brought with him, like he was on stage in his own theatre.

"The Bear!" whispered Chris.

They all fell to their knees, except Alison.

The light of the Golden Man swept around Fran. She made a long shadow in it.

She looked back over her shoulder.

The Golden Man stepped up to her.

Alison wasn't sure if she saw his golden dick. There was a mix of shadows and light behind Fran. But there was no mistaking the movement. He stepped up behind her and laid shadow hands on her back and hair.

He shifted to an odd angle, a different angle.

And he thrust into her.

Alison jerked her head back as she heard the cry.

Fran was yelling with each thrust. She sounded like she was in pain.

Fran was being buggered by the Golden Man.

The cry came from beside her. It was Marty. He was clutching his head. He was staring, his eyes bloodshot, at what was being played out in front of him.

Fran was swinging her head, grunting, co-operating. The Golden Man was impassive, statuelike, hard. He moved only as much as he had to.

Marty ran at him.

Patrick made to go too, but Alison grabbed him, loved him, tripped him and threw him onto the floor with herself on top of him.

Marty slammed the knife into Michael's chest. It entered to the hilt, just by his left armpit. Michael screamed. Fran screamed. Alison felt like she should scream. Michael staggered back, turning. He took the knife with him. Marty was yelling obscenities at him. Michael stopped for a moment. Alison watched. Was he going to fall? But then he steadied himself. He rippled away into the air. The knife fell to the ground.

Then he was suddenly in front of Fran, whole again. He'd rolled through the air in one smooth transition.

Marty nearly ran into him.

Michael waved his fingers in a wheel.

Suddenly he held a long golden spear in both his hands. A line of gold.

With one practised movement he stepped towards Marty and struck out.

The spear shot straight through Marty. It went over their heads.

Everyone cried out. It imbedded itself in the wall. The shaft had struck through Marty's stomach. His rainbow woollen jumper suddenly bloomed red.

Alison clenched her fist. Yes! About time!

The Golden Man gestured again. The spear flew back into his hands.

Marty started to fall forward, staggering, his eyes pleading around the room, his mouth starting to form words.

The Golden Man shoved it back into him.

And, in a blur, getting increasingly faster, again and again.

Alison watched while she held Patrick down, her neck stretched at an angle. She saw Marty dissolve into a mass of blood.

It started to stain the room, a mist that settled onto the wallpaper, coated the windows, pooled beneath him. And all without him falling or crying out. There was fur in the air, too, a flutter of wool and cotton shards. His body became a focus, a grey space at the centre of the red motion. It got smaller and smaller. It became a cluster of small things. There was no point where just his face was left. No last look. Who he was was lost at some uncertain time, despite the fact that Alison was staring into the whirlwind, was just managing to raise a hand to smooth his blood away from her eyes.

She felt no pain. No fear. She just felt the presence of her body, and exultation that she was now one of the people who *did* stuff like this! There was a light covering of something like water on her face and hands, the down of what felt like feathers settling on top of it and the air thick with the dust of what must have been bone. She was breathing him in. She coughed on him.

The small bundle of what remained fell to the floor.

The Golden Man swung his spear back into a rest posture and paused. He looked at Alison with the same no expression in his eyes. He stepped over to the offal, picked it up, weighed it in his hand. He walked over to Fran and, oddly, handed it to her. Fran sank back on her heels and took it in both hands like a gift, grinning happily at it.

The Golden Man held up his palm. It was fingerpaint-red with blood.

He walked through the circle of kids. It parted for him. The pattern still sang in the air. He walked the pattern.

He went over to a stretch of lounge wall that had been shaded from the red by an Ikea cabinet. He reached out a cultivated finger, like God's. And there he wrote, "This is the price."

He turned to look at Alison again. She started to laugh.

He swung his spear in her direction and walked over to her. Fran watched. She had started to smear Marty's blood down her cheeks, red on white.

The Golden Man took Alison's hair in one of his big hands. He helped her to her feet.

He looked down into her eye, his golden surface reflecting her. She was bouncing inside, the beat of her heart thumping and thumping. She was one with the gods! She was one with the universe! And it was a secret! A secret from all those wankers who thought they ran things. The people in this room ran things now. And people in rooms like this everywhere. The kids on the Bearpath. She could see the pattern, reflected in the being's eye, in her own eye. The pattern fitted over the world and defined it and contained it.

These creatures were exactly the summit and the epitome of everything she and her mates and everyone who had ever lived needed.

They weren't aliens. They were us. They were humanity made gold. Humanity that had won. They were the ultimate winners.

She let Patrick get to his feet. He was shaking. He had a whiteness in his face, like all the blood had shrunk down inside him. His mouth was opening, trying to form words. He was staring at the place where Marty had been.

Fran rose also, at the beckoning of the Golden Man. She walked over to Alison and hugged her. A welcoming hug. Alison held onto her.

"I'm in love," whispered Fran. "Isn't he wonderful? Aren't they wonderful? Isn't time going to be wonderful now?" It was her voice, but her voice made better. She used to have a kind of pitiful laugh in that sound, a sighing at the world, like she was having to fight all the time. Now she knew what she should be, and she was powerful being it.

"I'm glad for you," said Alison.

"You... bastards!" Patrick had found his voice.

"You killed Marty!" finished Chris, and everyone laughed. Except the Golden Man. He was too cool to laugh. Alison even saw Phil laughing along, though he looked frightened.

Patrick took a step backwards. "You... I'm going to... You can't kill everyone!"

The Golden Man turned and looked at Fran.

She nodded quickly, listening to him. "Chris," she said, "bring the laptop."

Alison felt a sudden pang of jealousy. Fran got to hear the voice in her head. The pristine, mint-condition voice. The newest thing on Earth.

Hadn't Alison herself heard it once? If she was the queen here, why didn't she get to hear it now?

Chris ran from the room and came back a moment later with a laptop. He sat it down on a little bloodstained coffee table between the Golden Man and Patrick. It was already on, displaying charts and tables. Financial information, Alison realised.

Michael took a step towards Patrick. He cried out and stepped back.

"Michael doesn't want to hurt you," said Fran. "We only want to help. We've been helping since before history, Patrick. That's what we travelled back in time to do. Michael wanted to show you what a human life is worth. For instance, here there will be a cleaning bill, for the carpets and the windows and the furniture. There will be bribes for everyone from the cleaners to the police. The cleaners and the police and anyone else who gets into the loop will prosper. They will make more profit. They will have children, and attach them to profit too. The human race will go on and on, all those lives made bigger and better because of one death. Life comes from death. That is what he says."

"That's ridiculous!" Patrick shouted. "Alison, tell them that's ridiculous!"

"Hmm," said Alison.

"You can't talk about someone's life like that! Like it's just worth that!"

"It's worth less than twenty pounds, he says, in terms of what's in the body. The death of Marty made a big profit."

"It's worth more than that!" Patrick was screaming now. "It's worth more than that!"

"Look at this screen," said Fran. And at once the display on the laptop changed.

Alison stepped beside Patrick to look. It was an online banking screen, a series of accounts, with Patrick's name at the top.

"My bank account," said Patrick. "How did you—?"

"We are these things," said Fran. "We are money. Interfacing with world banking systems is easy for us. We are a product of those systems, only from many years in the future. Now let's see how much Marty was worth. How much money will it take to buy your silence?"

Patrick was silent again, his eyes open in horror. "There's no way," he whispered. "You can't—"

"The whole message of the Bears," said Fran, "is that we *can*. All of us. This is to be a miracle. They can give everything. But they don't, because we have to learn to do it for ourselves. But the sacrifice of Marty, the item you brought to the party, has earned you everything. Name his price."

"I will not!" yelled Patrick.

The figures on the screen rolled. "One million," said Fran.

"I will not—" He turned away.

The figures rolled again. "Ten million," said Fran.

Patrick was silent.

"Fifty million," said Fran.

Alison watched Patrick carefully. She was sure that, when she'd been the victim of her curse, she could have worked out all kinds of ground-in shit about what she would have thought he was thinking. Sheer paranoia. Now he was just an equation being worked out. Everyone could see the end of it. There was no mystery about Patrick deciding one thing or another. History had already made the decision. The only intriguing bit was wondering when he was going to crash and take the money.

"One hundred million," said Fran.

"One hundred million?" said Patrick. He was slowly shaking his head back and forth to himself, no longer acknowledging the presence of anyone else in the room. "I don't believe you. Where do you get that kind of money?"

"We *are* that kind of money," said Fran. She fell to her knees again and threw her head back. The words burst out of her as the Golden Man stood over her, unmoving, thinking it all down into her. "We are an intelligence formed from the interactions between four human currencies in the far future. Human minds were interfaced with these currencies; experts plugged into the currency management systems through devices in their eyes. At the moment an exchange of these currencies was established across the solar system, with minds connected to the process, the pattern became conscious in the world. The bodies of the human managers became accessories to the larger minds. Because—?" Fran stopped and looked up at the Golden Man.

He raised his hand and licked across his palm. His sword tongue sliced. He held up the wound. Red blood dripped from it.

The kids leapt forward to drink from the blood, but he closed his palm.

"It is harder than that," said Fran. "This was just a sign that we are us, but we are not from now. These currencies have not yet been conceived. The Bears are from our future. We love us. We love you, Patrick. We can give you a sacrament. We can give you one hundred million pounds, or any sum, in exchange for your sacrifice. Is one hundred million pounds enough?"

Patrick had an unreadable look on his face now, a neutral look, like a man who'd had a door slammed in his face, but hadn't yet reacted. "No," he said.

The figures whirled again. "Five hundred then?"

"Do you want a girlfriend?" Emmeline called out. Everyone laughed.

Alison knew she should have felt jealous about that, but she wasn't. She looked across to the Golden Man. Michael. He had his hand on Fran's hair again. But she knew he loved her too. He would take care of her. She didn't need Patrick.

Patrick didn't say anything. He wasn't trying to make eye contact with her any more.

He just nodded.

"Five hundred million pounds," said Fran proudly. "You have to answer out loud. Is that the price? The price of your friend's life? We can keep going higher. Until you can say it."

"Yes!" Patrick shouted. "Yes! That's the price!"

Without looking at Alison, he ran at the circle of kids. They parted for him. He scrambled to the door and was gone.

The door to the lounge, and the front door of the house, didn't even slam. They just flapped, until a moment later the wind and the rain slammed the front door by themselves.

Alison sighed. The soft old thing. Maybe she'd go and find him later. He was very rich now. What he did was going to be interesting. Or maybe not. She had access to the pure stuff now, after all.

She saw Phil staring after where Patrick had gone. Then his eyes flicked quickly back to the others. They were filled with need now, like he'd seen what he'd aspired to all his life, and didn't want anything more than to be part of this.

The Golden Man turned back to the circle and moved to join it.

They all watched in anticipation.

Fran took Alison's hand. She looked into her eyes. Alison saw something there, the sign in Fran's left eye. They were sisters now: sisters of fashion and power.

Michael walked up to Chris and put his hand to his golden mouth. He took from his mouth something tiny. Alison looked closely. It was... a scroll. A tiny one. Like from some Biblical dolls' house. He put it in Chris's hand.

"Take the scroll," said Fran. "It's the next stage. Between where you are and where Alison and I are."

Chris put the scroll in his mouth. He bit into it, a little nervously. Then he began chewing eagerly. He had a dye of red in his blond hair now. He looked almost golden too. His mouth began to bleed. Light burst through his head.

It was the baptism, the same light that had taken her.

The Golden Man gave scrolls to Emmeline and Sophie, and they consumed them straight away.

He turned away from Al.

"Nothing for you yet," said Fran. "You need to want it some more. Our communion is want. You have to want for us to satisfy your need."

It looked for a moment like Al was going to object. But Sophie gave him a serious look and he didn't speak.

Alison frowned. She felt a pang again. How was it that Fran could hear the Golden Man speak inside, but she couldn't?

"The pattern is turning," said Fran. "We will come to visit you again. Bring more. But not many more. Only a few will be granted access. Only a few of them will take steps along the path. Only a few of them will be with us. Only a few of them will be like us. This is one place in time amongst many. Come with me, Alison."

He walked towards the door through which he'd come in. Fran followed. Alison followed her. The last person she saw as she left was Phil. He looked satisfied, fed, gone on this path.

She could feel the eyes of the others on her back, envious, wanting. She was the business! She was at the heart of the power of the universe! Marching in slow motion. Chords and trumpets ringing.

The Golden Man waited for a moment and Fran closed the doors behind them. The cry that she'd emitted cut off as the doors met.

They were alone in the library with him.

And then they were just alone.

He hadn't even looked at them. He'd just ceased to be there.

"We have to stay here for a bit," Fran whispered, heading for the drinks cabinet. Her nakedness suddenly looked weird. She plopped the mass of bloody entrails into a bowls trophy and put the lid on it. "Until Chris sees them all out. It's a bit of a magic trick. Can I get you anything?"

"Christ yes," said Alison.

The call was something that came from the origins of the Golden Men. The eye was the link. The tongue was the physical interface. The cry was the noise of information being exchanged at high speed, modulated through a human brain, and therefore let out through a human voice.

We loved big spectacles. Demonstrations of power made the hearts in the human bodies of the Four pound with excitement. Hormones rushed through their frames.

The rush was worth everything. Fran wouldn't have chosen to be the victim used for the rush of being in power and on top. But *we*, who she was part of, got to enjoy the rush too as she was in pain. Her pain contributed to *our* excitement.

We rule the world.

And then Fran was alone with Alison. She was acting like she was *one of us*. *Our* sacrifice of Marty pleased her, just like it pleased Fran. So now Fran wanted her words to be *our* words.

Alison couldn't sit down. She paced back and forth, throwing back whiskies, until the noises from outside died down. Fran produced some towels from under a chair and started to wipe the bloodstains from her body, as best she could. "I get so messy," she said.

"They've done this before?"

"No. Just... well, you know." She gave a little giggly smile. "Messy."

Alison didn't know. But she smiled back. "Right."

"I heard from Mick and Jules. In the caves. They've had problems. Decided to block everything up again. I think they have..." She tapped her own eye. "I'm sure it's all for the best. People shouldn't discover things they're not meant to know."

"Um-hm."

"I'm in hell," said Fran, her teeth still wide. "I hate who they've made me. Please kill me."

"Yeah, right!" laughed Alison.

And Fran laughed too.

Chris came back in, with Emmeline and Sophie and Al, after half an hour. "Christ, some of them wanted to talk," he said.

Fran had dressed now, in a black trouser suit which looked made-to-measure. There was still a rosiness about her face.

"So when do we see them again?" asked Alison. "The Bears, I mean?"

"Whenever you want," said Chris. "You can see them better than we can." He tapped the left side of his head. "You're the lucky ones."

"We are that," said Alison. She staggered suddenly, and had to put out a hand for Fran to hold her up. Her nose hurt. She wanted to go on somewhere and talk and talk, but she also wanted to fall over. "I'd better get home," she said. A sudden flash of a smile. "It's been emotional."

She gave Fran a hug. "Stay in touch this time," said Fran.

"I will," promised Alison.

Chris showed her to the door. Alison looked back and saw Fran sit down, her hands in her lap, waiting, her eyes already dreaming of the next time she'd see her lover again.

And that was that. The quest done. Funny how the biggest things in your life could turn into the smallest, just like that. Fran was back. The box was closed.

The door closed on Chris's smile.

And Alison walked off into the night, heading for home along the familiar streets of Bath.

There were other people out and about in the city that night that didn't belong to it, but Alison didn't notice them. She headed up past the Paragon and the Porter, making for home. They moved around her, becoming kissing couples on street corners, and office workers coming home from deep overtime, and the homeless in the rain. If she had still had her gift, she would have seen all of them, and become aware that tonight she was the thing at the centre of the maze.

They saw she was heading in the direction of her house. But, professionally, they didn't take that for granted. They moved to follow.

She was thinking about how to get ahead in this new world she'd found. Patrick had been bloody lucky. He always was. He had the money now. But this demanded more than money. This was about prestige, about a big now, about surfing the zeitgeist. She would have to dress better. She'd have to look into the business of shopping and find exactly the right wardrobe. She would have to find the right magazines to tell her how. The thought of going home was hard for her now. The place was such a mess. If anybody saw! If one of the Golden Men walked through the wall now and saw, she'd be out of the loop. And there was Leyton, too. He couldn't stay. He was a lunatic off the streets. She had to get him out as soon as possible. Maybe when she got back he'd just be gone, wandered off. That'd suit her.

So Fran had a thing in her eye too. So she got to talk with the Bears in her head and Alison got... just the distant feeling of it. Maybe something had gone wrong with hers. Should she ask about it, or would that look bad? Maybe she should just bring it up with Fran in conversation. But would Fran help? Or would she realise that she was doing better than Alison and say she'd talk to the Bears about it, but never would? Stupid thought. Fran was her friend. She'd searched for her so long, and now she'd found her. She and Patrick and Marty had found her, and they'd all been changed in just the right way as a result. So she ought to trust Fran. They were bonded by the Bears. By the future.

She was on the Upper Bristol Road now, going past the pubs just emptying out. She was on a stretch of pavement that led straight to her flat—she needed to move to a better place, get another raise to do that— and she was distantly aware that some of the pubgoers were walking in her direction too, past the ex-petrol station. The rain was beating down hard now. She huddled in her coat, wanting her bed.

She walked straight into the vicar.

He staggered back, and caught her before she fell. "Hey!" he said. "There you are!"

She didn't want to see him. "Hi," she said.

"I came to find you. But you weren't about, so I went and had a pint. Listen, your mate's got a message for you—"

"What?" She ran her hand back through her hair. The guys from the pub were coming up behind them.

"He said—" He looked up suddenly.

She turned round. There were three guys who'd been about to pass them. Heavy metal guys, like you got in the two pubs down this road. They had stomachs and black T-shirts and they laughed a lot. These three didn't look as fat as usual.

But they'd stopped, as if they were waiting for something. Now they were kind of hanging around, forming a little circle in the rain, laughing at something. A moment ago it had looked like they wanted to talk to them.

"Yes?" Whatmore called to them. "Sorry, is there something I can do?" He sounded a little afraid, as if they were about to mug them. But what muggers behaved like that?

"Don't worry about us, mate!" one of them called in a deep Somerset burr. "Just trying to get this fucking ciggie to light."

Whatmore turned back to Alison. "Spare a cup of tea for a vicar?" he asked.

Alison didn't really want to let him in, but she reached in her pocket for the key. "I'm really tired," she said.

"That's all right," said Whatmore. "I'm—"

And he grabbed Alison's arm and wrenched her off down the little street beside her house.

She screamed.

Behind them, the three men broke into a sprint.

She saw them do that, saw the look on the vicar's face, and ran with him, away from them.

The bridge was in front of them: dark metal against the trading estate behind her house, against the glowing cloud rain sky.

There was thunder. No, a gunshot! A silenced one! Right next to her ear! It had spattered off the side of the bridge!

"Halt!" shouted a voice.

They were shooting at her!

"Come on!" bellowed Whatmore. He dragged her round a corner, down a muddy slope by the riverbank. She slipped and slid and had to stop herself yelling again.

They crashed through some bushes, onto a cycle path, through some more vegetation.

There were shouts from behind them now, and shouts from ahead. And complicated whistles. There were sounds from all directions. They were right in the middle of them.

They came to a bare anglers' patch on the riverbank with a high gap in the bushes above and foliage to either side. Whatmore pointed at the river. He slipped down onto his bottom and sat on the concrete, his legs dangling into the water. He'd almost slid, so as not to make a sound.

Alison stared at him.

He motioned urgently to her.

She sat down beside him, not believing she was doing this. He slipped down to his waist into the water. She did too. The cold hit her like a blow up the front of her stomach, but she still had the coke in her. It kept her silent, kept her teeth together. She wanted to swim hard or hit something. She glared at Whatmore.

He grabbed her head and moved it to the surface of the water.

She wanted to fight him, but she saw the shadow moving above out of the corner of her eye. She and her eye were on the same side here, she realised. It was odd, even with the coke, to feel her whole self together again.

Whatmore slipped right under the water and held her.

She went too. A big breath.

Bursts of air from her nose. Mud underneath. Infinite cold. Darkness on her eyes.

Something powerful and skilled grabbed her and pushed her down and along.

They slid through the water. With the current, she realised. Downriver. All this rain. She imagined branches and leaves and plastic containers swept with them. They were with fertiliser, and chemical spills, and all the foot and mouth bacteria from the hot long breaths of pigs, washed down out of the city.

They waited in that long breath. After a while she felt him kick his legs and dared to kick hers too. She kicked and kicked and kicked.

They burst out of the water on the low concrete blocks of a weir, somewhere in Twerton, and staggered to their feet.

They were at the edge of another industrial estate. Cars were passing across the way; they were still beside the Upper Bristol Road.

Whatmore grabbed her hand and crashed his way across the weir. He climbed out, dragging her after him. The cold was entering them now, even worse out of the water. The wind was painful straight on, and merciful when it turned away.

Whatmore flagged down a taxi with its light on and hauled her into the back beside him.

"The Abbey Churchyard," he said. "Quickly. We've had an accident."

Alison stared up at the bulk of the Abbey in front of her. Whatmore had run to his house and was unlocking the door. It was completely silent here. There was just the low rumble of the distant motorway and the occasional cry of a bird or sound of a car from the street over the way.

Or was that silence just in her?

Whatmore got the door open, his shivering hands fumbling with the keys. He'd said in the taxi that he'd been in South America, that he knew when men with guns were after someone, having seen it happen a few times. He'd shaken his head when she'd asked if he'd ever had to hide like that before. He'd just followed the spirit, he said. Been determined that now *they* were here, in his own country, *they* weren't going to catch them.

Alison had been uncomfortable about *they*. Whatmore didn't know where she'd been that evening, that she'd seen *they* and they were... They were *us*. But Whatmore hadn't noticed. He was galvanised, his face alive with intent. "You go in, up to the top floor," he said now, thrusting the keys into her hands. "I've got a petrol heater in the Abbey, I'm just going to go and get it."

He headed off across the square. Alison looked at the key in her hand and back to the running man in black.

He was going to go into that thing. That fearful big thing from her childhood. The thing that had swallowed her dad.

She was startled that she was afraid of it. She could do anything, couldn't she?

She wanted to make sure.

She followed him.

She felt the cold even more as she trotted up behind Whatmore. He was at the side door of the Abbey, using another huge bunch of keys to open it.

She still didn't want to be near him. Or did.

He looked at her almost angrily. "Go and get in the warm!"

But she couldn't. She stared at him mutely. He seemed to realise that she wasn't going to move.

"I won't be a second," he said, and ducked inside.

She went to the door he'd gone through.

She could feel the shape of the floodlit building above her and square against her. She could feel it beyond what it was, like it was a big brand, one of her zeitgeist things. Something she wanted to eat or drink.

Only this wasn't fashionable. This brand was dead, and not in the usual way of being ignored, sinking to the bottom, shuffled off because you were the only person left buying it. She remembered that from her old life, a kind of rough Scottish bread that Fran had found in the supermarket which vanished after six weeks because only the two of them were buying it.

This was like an aggressively dead brand.

She looked up the great white wall above her and saw Christ, hanging there on the cross. The cross was the brand. That was what was aggressively dead. Deliberately dead. Dead like the hormones in that man's body. Dead like his sex and male anger died. Dead like the opposite of how much the Golden Man was alive dead.

The Golden Man had looked inside her and found the big stuff and freed it.

That man on the cross brand had looked inside himself and found the big stuff and killed it.

She made to run into the Abbey.

She couldn't.

She couldn't like she couldn't go into a bar and order a cider and black. Or a Babycham, without irony.

She couldn't find the self-mockery inside herself to cross that threshold.

Whatmore came out again, carrying the heater. He was about to lock up when he looked at her, obviously puzzled that she was still there.

Alison was aware that she was crying now. Or rather, that just her right eye was.

"Take me inside," she said.

"What?"

"Take me inside the church."

"What do you mean, take you?"

"Take me by the arm, drag me in."

Whatmore looked surprised for a moment, but then he put his arm through hers, steadied her shivering form and aimed them towards the door. "Ready?" he said. "One, two—three!" And he marched at the door.

She tried to go with him. But as the mouth of the unfashion opened, she freaked out. Her limbs thrashed out. She threw herself wildly aside. He couldn't stop her from falling, staggered back himself.

She lay there on the paving slabs. She was sobbing inside, but it was only coming from one eye. She was aware again of the thing in her eye. She thought she'd got used to it. She was locked out! She was a locked-out thing! When her new life should have bought her the key to everything! It wasn't fair! She'd been promised everything, and this was the only thing she wanted!

The whole thing she wanted. She wanted her dad. She wanted her dad! She'd wanted to be a child again, and the Golden Man had given her that: the confidence of being a kid, conqueror of the world. But this last holding-out pattern included inside it Mum and Dad and warmth and childhood and all the stuff that she wanted but now couldn't have. She'd given one childhood for another.

They would wipe out this pattern. They'd stamp on it, make it pay! They'd reduce the Abbey to rubble and rip Whatmore's head off and fuck his spine down the hole!

But she knew that would do no good. She'd seen that on the cross brand. The pattern of the Abbey, the pattern that excluded her... so that puny, stupid, vulnerable things could have sanctuary from *her*... it didn't care about death. If she stamped the Abbey flat, its pattern would remain.

That was a thought that came from her, whatever *her* was. The Bears, the angels, were written into this Abbey too, into the luxurious carvings, into the gold and glass. The Abbey was their prop, as everything else was. The Abbey was a square on the Game of Life board, the justification for weddings and funerals and births; the distraction from the depression that might otherwise make these cattle take their own lives.

The Bears had won, long ago. They'd *won*. They'd taken the Son and crucified him. His church was their bitch now. How much more could they win?

The rain fell on her head.

The rain was going to claim the world.

George W. Bush, two weeks into his presidency, had decided, the other day, that carbon dioxide was not a pollutant, reversing the manifesto pledge on which he'd been elected.

Good for him. He was free to do that. The American public could vote him out if they disagreed with that. They were free to do as they wished.

In a school assembly, Alison remembered hearing about Noah. God had promised that the world would never be flooded again. He'd promised.

Stupid child thing. She'd been tiny. Where had that memory come from?

Sanctuary from *her*.

She got to her feet. She saw Whatmore approaching, his arms open, wanting to help her.

She was so cold inside, as if something right at the centre was frozen.

Before he could touch her, she turned and ran.

It wasn't quite as cold on the eastern side of the river, under Pulteney Bridge. The bulk of the shops above cut out the wind. The river rushed by, over the weir, boxes and trees and cartons carried along by the size of it, bashed along in the dark.

The 'bab shop on the Grand Parade above was dark now. There was the occasional noise of a car or a milk float.

Alison huddled under the bridge with two of the homeless, asleep in the inlets in the stone. She imagined them in the caves up on the hill, on the rise from where she and Fran had seen the city. She knew them only by the sighs and the coughs and the mumblings in sleep.

There were facilities for them. There was no need for anyone to sleep rough.

She hadn't even got a coat.

Down this side of the river, up from the weir, the tour boats were moored. Above her, in the bridge, were shops and cafés and a puppet theatre. And under it there was this, like certain of the Georgian buildings, built as fronts on older, shabbier dwellings.

But you can't blame buildings. You can't blame a city for what's in it.

She thought she must be mad. She wondered where it had started. Was it when she'd first seen the Golden Man? When she'd first *thought* she'd seen him? Or was it when she'd accepted Leyton's story of who he was?

No. That was letting herself off. That was what half of her wanted. What did *half of her* mean? How could she have desires that she was not in control of? How could there be things she wanted that were not her? Made that way. The Bears had made her that way. They'd made the city. They'd made everything.

In the west. Elsewhere, maybe... But how did she know about elsewhere except through the west?

Little stitches of thoughts. Back and forth, like she was pacing a path in her head. A pattern. The cold, she realised, helped. She was seeking cold like, when she'd been depressed, she'd seek certain kinds of food, not just chocolate, but whatever stuff had what her brain needed in it. Fish. Fresh bread. Clear water. Oh Christ, they were in the food too. She was seeking cold like a pregnant woman sought cravings for her baby.

Cold did something. Cold switched something off.

The Golden Men could never infest the poor.

Cold would switch her off.

But what was the point of that? Where was the good sacrifice in that?

She realised that she was saying these words aloud, like the words of a song.

She didn't want to wake the sleepers. She got up from where she was squatting and headed off along the bank of the river.

There was a maze here, a round Celtic maze, built for tourists, a shape, so the plaque said, found etched in tombs. At the centre was an embossed carving of Sulis, the British god known only by his Roman name. He was a staring head with a mass of octopus hair. The spring of life—the spring that, in the seventies, they'd found had an amoebic parasite in it that made people mad. They'd had to dig and dig for a new source, right down underneath the city, to find pure water.

The maze didn't have hedges, like the big, square one at Longleat. It was laid out on the ground as paths of stone with grass between them, so you could just give up if you wanted to and walk off it. The paths shone in the low light of the Parade Hotel above. Alison had read somewhere that Celtic mazes weren't puzzles, that they led you round and round to the centre of whatever ritual construction they were found in. They were the pretty way, not the land of hard decisions. You got there anyway.

This one, though, was a puzzle, or had been made into one. She started to walk around it. She was probably suffering from hypothermia now, or frostbite at least. The cold had got so into her that she couldn't imagine warmth. If the police came down here to ask her what she was doing, she should go with them, be warmed up back at the station in front of a carbon-dioxide-emitting, snuggling gas fire.

She chose a path. It was a dead end. She turned back.

She'd evaded Whatmore so easily, despite his running after her. She'd gone round corners.

At college, Angus, who was in her class, had made a joke, what do you call a dog with wings, Linda McCartney. And that had been just after she died, only Angus hadn't been thinking about that, he might not even have known that she had, and of course that would have made all the difference. And Alison had yelled at him and called him a sexist and had walked out, and she'd heard the laughter right behind her, and she'd felt awful at what was inside her. She'd felt awful to be such a prig, to not have a sense of humour. She'd wanted to go right back in and explain, and say please don't hurt my feelings like that. Fran would understand. Fran had always understood, and had just said, the bastard. But she'd heard Fran laugh at stuff like that. She'd laughed at stuff like that. Not unwillingly, not just to fit in, but because she'd found it funny.

The one time Alison didn't laugh, she'd felt shit.

She walked in a long loop round the circumference of the maze, not liking any of the ways in. There'd been a time when she could have walked this on sight.

Angus had put a photo of her up on the "Am I Hot or Not?" website the next day. It was a web page where people voted on how attractive people were. She hadn't known what to say. She didn't let on that someone had shown it to her. She watched the score on the site change. After four days, she was averaging two out of ten.

She voted for herself. She gave herself a ten and felt proud.

And Fran had said well done for loving yourself.

Angus collected comics and she'd read some of Marty's and for a while she thought that she'd quite like to read some of them on a regular basis too. But then Angus had brought in the pride of his collection, a number one of some superhero book that had been *slabbed*, dipped in plastic and sealed for ever: turned into a stone that kept its value, that you couldn't read any more.

She wondered how much Angus loved himself for that.

Like love of self or others or God or anything was possible in this world. *They* defined love. The Golden Men. *She* defined love. *She* was *they*.

She chose a new path, turned left and right and found herself at the centre of the maze. She stared down at Sulis. His big empty meaningless town planning symbolic eyes gazed back up at her like the Golden Man's.

She was cold enough now. She could just about see it. Within the next few minutes, her core body temperature was going to get so low that she'd die. She was starting to die now. Her brain was working in a cold way, in the way of Antarctic explorers walking on and on through the white.

The chemicals, or electronics, or magic or whatever had stopped working.

She was cold enough to know that this was the hub, the moment.

Her eyes couldn't stop staring now. They were drying out with the cold. She couldn't cry or blink. The world had set into this one view. She reached up and put her hand to her left eye. It was a little warmer than the rest of her. The skin at the top of her cheek was inflamed. The brow above the eye was tight. The ridge of her nose felt like she had a black eye.

She had failed to save her friend tonight. She had watched Marty killed. She had seen Patrick take money for that.

These were the facts. Still, they seemed to have no weight.

She started to shiver violently. Her body was trying to die now.

She pushed her palm flat against her eye. The little golden icon bulged, grew green in the darkness.

She opened her palm again, made her fingers into a spear.

She was cold enough. She was. This was what it would take. Someone had to be strong. Someone had to stop it.

She took a deep breath and yelled at the world.

She shoved her fingers into her eye.

The pain was huge. Even in the cold. But she was better than the pain.

The top two fingers suddenly slipped behind the eyeball. Her vision wasn't vision now, it was full of red. She had to close her other eye. She could hear the blood bellowing in her ears.

The eyeball didn't burst. It popped out into her hand. She could feel all the way round it. It sat in the palm of her hand. She could feel the chicken sinew length of something trailing from it, connected to the inside of her head like a piece of greens caught in her teeth. Tethered hard.

There was warmth splashing from the socket now, down her front. Not as much as she'd thought.

She clasped the eyeball hard in her left palm. It still wouldn't burst. She realised giddily that the centre of the maze was getting covered in blood. The face of Sulis was red.

Oh God. Oh God.

She had to. No going back now.

She held the eye hard.

She threw her arm out sideways.

The string snapped.

The shock made her scream. She fell to her knees because her body couldn't stand and cope with the pain at the same time. She threw up, or something came from her mouth.

She couldn't see!

She pistoned herself to her feet.

She staggered towards the river. Must not fall in. Not now.

She clenched her fist round the eye. It was solid. It wouldn't burst.

She threw her arm back. She made her other eye open so she could see. She stretched her muscle. And then, before the reflex could make her close her other eye, she threw it as hard as she could.

It flew into the sky above the river, catching the light. It trailed bloody nerves.

It landed in the river and was swept away.

A duck flapped off the weir in shock and flew away.

Alison fell again. She started to laugh. She could feel it all coming back to her. The burden of it. She felt herself starting to read the river, where all the things in it came from. The destruction the weather was working upstream. What the river meant, what the flood of it meant.

What she meant. What the thing in her eye and the Golden Man and the terrible things that had happened to Fran and Marty and Patrick *meant*.

And that Patrick and she now had to be *over*.

"My God," she whispered, as the kaleidoscope burst into her brain again. "We've been invaded."

She used her key to get into Linley's Racing. She'd waited ten minutes because she'd seen a police car pass and realised in a moment that it would be back the same way while she was still in the shop.

She knew now that Leyton had gone.

She had used part of her shirt to bind her eye socket. It had instantly become sopping red and wet. She was going to need medical attention very soon. She was in great pain, pain that was starting to insist that it was the only thing she should be paying attention to. She was still cold to her bones. Maybe that was helping with the pain.

She switched on all the heating as soon as she was inside. She didn't switch on the lights.

Something about the cold had inhibited whatever they'd put into her eye.

How had they done that? They were in charge. They weren't an invading force. They strutted like the place was theirs, so they could do what they liked, give out their "favours" as they saw fit.

They'd been at Sodom and Gomorrah. They'd been there for the Bible. But they were new here and now. They'd arrived back in the past, and stayed.

She didn't want to think about what they were doing to Fran. The same thing they'd done to her, but Fran couldn't fight it. She didn't have Alison's gift. That, and the cold, had made the difference. Being who she was had led her to the cold.

She went to the cash register. Ted was going to be an innocent victim of all this. She opened the machine up and took all the paper money. A few hundred. She could have made that in an afternoon if she'd come in to bet against Ted rather than work for him. She'd made him much more than that.

On the way out of the shop, she thought about Patrick. That had been the worst, what they'd done to him. They'd violated and colonised Fran. They'd murdered Marty. But they'd twisted something inside Patrick and left him conscious of it.

She saw the look on his face before he'd left and something became solid inside her.

She went back into Linley's Racing, understood what the combination to open the safe was, and opened it. She took six thousand pounds or so, and headed out once more.

She saw the board with the odds on the End of the World written on it. She went to it and changed the odds. To 2/1 on.

The world was going to end or change absolutely. And she was working for Ted Linley still, whether he'd understand that or not. She was working for everyone.

She was going to bet against those odds.

Sixteen: Kyoto

They smashed down the door of Alison Parmeter's flat and marched in. Cleves waited for a moment, and then followed. The man Leyton came with him.

Cleves had in the back of his mind, always, a book that he would never write. His autobiography, the history of what he'd done to shape the twentieth century. Or perhaps someone else would write it of him, long hence, when his papers were declared accessible by the public. And they would thus, of course, miss the central fact of his life at the moment. His project that would not be in any of his papers. Or perhaps they would not. Perhaps he would be infamous. He had stopped even thinking of it as a real book, and used it as a sort of yardstick of truth. What would be said of him, as against what he did.

In this history that would never be written, he would say that he hated Douglas Leyton, couldn't bear to be in the same room as him. The man was a vicious killer. He'd murdered a child. In reality, Cleves knew that and still found him harmless: the odd angle at which the wig sat on his head, when you knew it was a wig; the continual twitching and sudden changes of subject. Leyton was like a clown, like a child's toy. It was impossible to be afraid of him, and Cleves only hated what he feared.

Just as well. For now that he had satisfied himself as to the existence and age of this Douglas Leyton, Cleves knew that he had to protect him from all possible harm.

He had asked Leyton, as a matter of crossing the Ts, if he had ever had an identity card, if he'd ever been a Squadron Leader?

The words "squadron leader" had galvanised the odd, thin man in the bed. He had got dressed in front of Cleves, finding a particular wig on a polystyrene bust at his bedside. His head was shaved bald, Cleves noted, covered in scars and patches. They looked like they were being continually replaced. The bedroom had been neat, ordered, everything square with everything else. The sheets were freshly laundered.

"I know where you can find Squadron Leader Douglas Leyton," he'd said.

Cleves had stared at him. "Really?" he'd said. "How?"

"Coincidence," said Leyton. "I'm pleased with the work I've been doing for our country, Mr—" And he'd held out his hand to Cleves. "Can't quite place you."

Cleves had not shaken the hand. "Take me to him," he'd said.

He'd brought a unit of Watchers with him. He'd already switched to one of their unremarkable cars to visit Leyton's house. Leyton had slid into the back with him and had directed the driver through the streets, round an extraordinary one-way system.

They'd come to a halt a few hundred yards down the road from a blackened row of houses. Leyton gave a specific address. Cleves activated his laptop and checked the electoral register. "Alison Parmeter," he said.

Leyton nodded. "That's her," he said. "Alison Parmeter. He's with her."

So Cleves had set the Watchers to watch, and had had the car parked quietly around the corner while they did so. He swiftly heard that there was nobody in the flat at the moment. They would wait until there was.

He faced the prospect of light conversation with Leyton evenly. He had been confined with many just as bad.

"So, how's the plan going?" the man asked. "Restoration,I mean."

Cleves almost laughed. Leyton was so lacking in even the most basic intelligence tact. He had been hired, according to his handler, Cotton, because he had wormed his way to the heart of almost every community in this city, including a couple in which Cleves and his godforsaken colleagues in Restoration were very interested. Leyton was a member in good standing, under various names, of the Countryside Alliance, the Freedom Party, the local Tories, even one of the hunts. He was a very effective natural agent. A chameleon. Despite the scandal over the death of the boy, which had, for a moment, threatened the existence of Restoration, there were two big advantages to employing Leyton: he was utterly blackmailable, and nobody would ever believe what he said.

Cleves had hit the button that raised a soundproof barrier between them and the driver. He had turned to look at Leyton, sizing him up. "It's going very well," he said.

"I've put together a large group of people," said Leyton, eagerly. "A number of them under my personal leadership. They don't know they're working for you."

"Neither do you."

"No, I don't." He'd said it like it was a given, not a bow to Cleves' authority. "So what does this Douglas Leyton have to do with this stuff?"

"Nothing," Cleves had said. "Apparently. That's the problem."

Now the men threw aside a bundled duvet at the end of the bed. "Not boyfriend and girlfriend, then," Cleves said.

"Not yet," said Leyton. "They looked pretty close."

Cleves was still angry with the leader of the Watchers for having let the woman get past them. The encounter with the vicar had seemed, from what the man said, genuinely random. And yet the clergyman had sprinted away. But Cleves did not believe in showing subordinates his anger.

"Search this place," he said. "Mr Leyton, let us go and find some vicars."

Cleves got the names and addresses of all the Bath clergy off his laptop. They found several photos, including one that a Watcher identified straight away. The vicar was bearded, young, a stern look in his eyes. Cleves thought he recognised the look from some of the dogs. There's a look you get when you've been shot at. He had always been grateful that he had never acquired that look.

The man, Whatmore, lodged in the Abbey Churchyard. It was a bracing night for a walk. It would wake Cleves up. He arranged for a handful of the Watchers to follow him at a distance, so he could talk more with Leyton.

What he was going to do required a dog rather than an accredited member of the Security Service. Leyton would serve as well as any—from his record, maybe rather better. And Cleves was certain he would not get hurt in dealing with a vicar, even one with a speedy pair of heels. He would probably have fled his abode, anyhow. They would find him by means of the proper authorities in due time.

Their footsteps were loud on the empty streets. Dawn was turning the sky to the east a stormy shade of negative blue.

"So," said Leyton. That eagerness to converse again. "What's the next step with Restoration?"

Cleves was beginning to tire of the word. The man's accent was all over the place, like he'd lost his natural speaking voice as Cleves had lost his handwriting. All he could write now were small, precise capitals, the result of having to write completely understandable notes at speed. He wished that Leyton's voice had gone that way. "It's progressing," he said.

"It's just that, with it not being an official op, I can see that it might not get the funding."

Cleves stopped walking.

They were standing outside Sally Lunn's Café, which claimed on a sign to be the oldest house in Bath. The bakery attached was already lit up, and calls and pop music came from inside. Cleves looked carefully at Leyton. The man wasn't being snide. He looked like he was sharing that detail as if it was something they obviously both knew. He was wondering now why Cleves was shocked.

Cleves didn't know what to do. "Whatever gives you that idea?" he said.

"Well, it's obvious, isn't it? How is it in the national interest to run a petrol depot blockade?"

"We are infiltrating those that *do* run—"

"Infiltration to the level of executive decision making. We could set up a blockade tomorrow. So we're going to, aren't we?"

"No, Mr Leyton." Cleves wondered if the man had realised that Cleves would allow no harm to come to him. He was obviously an ancestor of the Douglas Leyton that was still at large. He had no issue as yet. And it wasn't just the genetics. The name had been passed down also.

If this Douglas Leyton died now, the pilot from the future might very well vanish. And perhaps that would mean that wonderful ship with all its technological secrets waiting to be unlocked, and Jocelyn, the answer to so many questions, would vanish too.

And he still did not know why the Douglas Leyton of the future had come back to something conceptually so near to his ancestor. On his secret mission. Perhaps his aim was to meet or communicate with that ancestor, in which case it was also an idea to have that ancestor alive and handy.

He affected a powerful, offhand laugh. "That would be wrong."

"And if it's not the government who wants this done, then it's someone else. Which is why I wonder if we're going to get the ordinance we'll need."

Cleves thought for a moment, pretending to sniff the smell of new bread on the air. "Mr Leyton," he said finally. "If you were currently working for someone other than Her Majesty's government, would you care?"

"No," said Leyton. "Not at all."

"That's good then." Cleves took in a deep breath and headed once more for the Abbey. "Now come along."

Whatmore had gone looking for Alison for as long as he could before the cold had got into his bones. He'd even dared to go back to her street, stepping carefully and watching for strangers. At this early hour, thankfully, they stood out a mile. He saw a couple of people walking in and out of what he took to be her house, coming and going from cars.

At least she hadn't gone back there.

Finally, when it was clear he wouldn't find her, he went home. He put his heaters on to full and had a hot shower, sure that his core body temperature had dropped to something unsafe. Then he had several cups of hot tea.

He knew what was going to happen in the next couple of hours. He thought about calling the bishop, or one of his seniors at the Abbey. But what good would that do?

He knelt at the end of his bed, wrapped in a blanket, closed his eyes and opened his hands up to the sky. He went through his usual list of prayers, and then asked for guidance. There God was. Leyton may have said that, for him, the divine was a long way off in this world, and that in his it was closer, but Whatmore was used to what he had. He knew what God was, and what s/he wasn't. God was a place of immense power and forgiveness in his head. A thought that made him smile. "Forgive us our sins," he whispered to himself, in the prayer that Christ had taught, "as we forgive those that sin against us." The vast strength of that idea never ceased to amaze him. That there was a power that only wanted you to be kind, and would therefore be kind to you in return.

He needed strength at this moment. But this moment was what he had been waiting for all his life.

He almost smiled at the sound of the door downstairs being kicked open.

He'd confronted the Great Beast before, inside himself, where it was the anger that came when you felt wronged, the anger that wanted to lash out at those who'd hurt you. In life, the Beast was the policemen and the soldiers who'd become part of the corporate apparatus in parts of South America and Africa. Where civilisation had ended, and the only free voices were those in pulpits.

The mark of the beast was the corporate logo.

His thoughts flew as he heard the feet on the stairs. He recalled taking his two small cousins to the *Rocky and Bullwinkle* movie in a tiny cinema in Winchester. It was a fun children's picture, until the cartoon heroes went "into cyberspace," where corporate logos flashed by, each there for no reason other than to imprint themselves on the youngsters' minds. He'd nearly walked out, but he'd decided that that would upset the kids. So he'd let the beast win that one. He didn't even know how to begin a conversation with them about it outside. How could children, who were made to love patterns, be told that some patterns were the mark of evil?

"One day's work for one day's pay." That was what the Horseman popularly called Famine said before the opening of the Sixth Seal. The opening of the Seventh Seal wasn't the moment of doom, but the moment when everything was over, when God's quiet descended. The public didn't get that.

"One day's work for one day's pay." Meaning, that people would be paid only enough to live on for one day. No savings. No provision for a family. An apocalyptic scenario at the time it was written. And now most people were worse off than that, in debt.

Money is the root of all evil.

His thoughts stopped at that as the footsteps came to a halt in the room, right behind him.

He was proud that he'd used those meanderings to stay put. To not rise and confront them.

"Reverend Whatmore?" It was an old man's voice.

Whatmore got to his feet. There were two of them, the old man and... It was Leyton. Older, yes, but the same man. He'd changed the colour of his hair and eyebrows, and... what was it? He was wearing coloured contact lenses. But the build, the face, they were just the same.

Suddenly, Whatmore understood. "Oh," he said. "I see."

"What do you see?" Leyton stepped towards him.

Whatmore wished desperately that he could get through to the end of this. "It's you," he said.

"Ah." The old man went to the door and closed it. "No, my associate is not who you think he is. Assuming that you think he's your friend, and haven't just seen him in the newspaper."

"That's a very old photo," said Leyton. "And it caused me a lot of grief."

Whatmore didn't answer the old man's trick question.

The old man came back to him. He looked as if he had all the time in the world. "We're here to ask you about the whereabouts of Douglas Leyton," he said.

"That," said Whatmore, "seems like the definition of a foolish question."

"And we'd also like you to share anything you may know about him, or his girlfriend."

Whatmore stayed silent on that subject. "You have no legal right to do this," he said.

"Indeed!" laughed the old man. "Would you want to live in a country where we did?" He pulled up a chair and sat down. "My friend here is armed."

The younger man produced a curved knife from inside his jacket. "I've used this on children," he said, his voice suddenly changing. Now he sounded almost compassionate. "I know how. It's very quick."

"But it doesn't have to be," the old man interrupted. "We have drugs at our disposal that will make you tell us everything. The after-effects are unpleasant, far more so than those of a beating. I have some men waiting outside to take you to a place where we will have the freedom to administer them to you."

Whatmore went to the window and glanced outside. There they were, hanging around, looking meaningless in the light of the new day. He turned back to these people who were somehow in his house and looked between them. "Are you two singing from the same hymn sheet?"

Leyton hit him in the stomach.

He fell to his knees. Leyton yanked him back to his feet before his stomach had started to fully feel the pain.

"I don't know where either of them are," Whatmore gasped. And he didn't. But now he knew something far worse, something he'd realised that the old man hadn't. That he had to keep secret for the sake of everyone. But he knew the old man was telling the truth when he said there were chemicals that wouldn't allow him that silence.

"I believe that," said the old man. "If you had hidden her, you would have hidden yourself."

"Why do you want to find them?"

"Because only Douglas Leyton can answer my questions. About the future."

Leyton hit him on the crook of his shoulder. It hurt like hell. He fell again, and this time Leyton left him where he was.

He wondered what sort of questions this old man had about the future. He was certain he could tell him the answers. And it wouldn't be so bad to do that. He thought of Leyton's wonderful future: humanity set free; the fruits of the world handed out evenly to all, because there was, as there had been for centuries, enough to go around. But the key to all that was his other secret. This man, whoever he was, was the enemy of that future, the epitome of the past that Leyton's people had left behind. Perhaps the differences, the things that made this world hell instead of heaven, were down to old men like him. And perhaps, with him, he had brought the ultimate product of those differences. The ultimate despair. Or the ultimate salvation. Whatmore couldn't see the pattern. He had to have faith.

It was just as well that he did.

He had no despair in him, because although he walked in the valley of death, although he lived there, he feared no evil.

"Hell," he said, as if he was beginning to answer the man's questions, "isn't very canonical. There aren't many Biblical references. I'm wondering if that's something that got added too. Added in words... and added in fact."

"What do you mean?" The old man had taken a notebook out and was writing down what he said in tiny capitals.

"I mean," said Whatmore, "that I have only one thing left to say to you. And that is—"

Leyton reached down for him.

Cleves closed that part of his mind that would make his face twitch and wince to the sight of violence, as he had on many previous occasions. Leyton's instincts were the same as his own: that the subject should not be allowed to say what he desperately wanted to say. That way, when it finally burst out of him, it would bring so much more with it.

Leyton knocked the man around the room, cuffing him with the lightness that this stage of the interrogation required.

But then something insane happened.

The vicar leapt at Leyton. He grabbed the man's arm.

For a moment, Cleves saw the nightmare scenario: the vicar plunging the knife into Leyton's chest.

He leapt to his feet. "No!" he shouted.

But the blow had not fallen that way.

Leyton's knife yanked up into Whatmore's chest.

Blood appeared in the vicar's mouth.

Whatmore was glad he'd kept the secret. "I did this for you," he whispered to his killer, beneath Cleves' hearing. "To keep you safe."

The expression on Leyton's face told Whatmore all he wanted to know.

"What is it you wanted to say just now?" Leyton asked. He was holding the knife in, waiting.

Whatmore made sure he said the words. "Only love can set you free."

Leyton nodded. He understood.

He pulled the knife out.

Love roared into Whatmore's head.

The vicar's body fell to the floor.

Cleves got to his feet. "You killed him!" he whispered. "You killed a man of the cloth!"

Leyton looked at him. He had a gleam in his eyes. For a moment, Cleves thought he would kill him too. But then he just slipped the knife back into its sheath under his arm. "Did I?" he said. "I forget."

And then he headed out of the room.

Cleves thought about all the calls he was going to have to make.

Then he followed him.

Dawn came up over the body.

An hour later, Cleves was in his car again, heading back to where he'd come from.

He'd made the calls. He had called in Restoration dogs to clean the flat and remove the traces and set up some vagrant to take the blame if need be. He had not dared to use any official muscle, not with everyone at the highest level aware that he was in Bath that night.

It might not hold for ever. Someone might talk, compare notes. The Watchers might realise, if the dogs did not move fast enough and a murder rather than missing person story appeared in the press, that they had been watching the right address on the right night. Several of them had heard him declare his intention to see a priest.

If this happened, his plan, and his life, would fall apart.

The dog Leyton had vanished into the morning. Cleves, unable to chide him, had just asked him to take care, and he had nodded. The search for the man from the future and the girl would continue. But he, Cleves decided, would not be directly part of it. He would put distance between himself and the death.

He was listening now to the tapes they'd made of Jocelyn being interviewed under the influence of the drug. He'd heard all about the terrible effects on the room of her intoxication, the injured man. This was powerful magic: either a defence mechanism or a side-effect of, as she put it, making her dream. As a result, he'd ordered that she be taken to a specialist facility in London. No point in stretching the RAF's facilities any further, or putting their people in danger.

The drug had finally done what it was supposed to, following the drama. Jocelyn babbled, as they always did. Cleves listened to every detail without fast forwarding, as he always did.

They'd asked her about the future. They'd given her the list of questions he'd prepared. She answered only those.

She talked of a Communist paradise.

It was a world, she said, where everyone was given equal shares. She was a real apparatchik. They were, of course, at war.

But was this as a result of some sort of collapse? Was she overstating the quality of life as a zealot would?

Perhaps rather than spare the ancestral Douglas Leyton, he should have him killed.

The thin, very British voice took Cleves back to his younger days, when he had romanced girls who had sounded just like that. Who were as enthusiastic as that.

The car passed a convoy of military vehicles, on their way to kill infected cattle.

And Cleves was asleep.

Seventeen: The Three Men I Admire Most

It was evening. It was still raining. The pilot from the future stood on the gate and looked at the empty field. There had been enough empty fields on the way here, but he was fairly sure that this was where he'd crashed the *Crimson Dragon*. Only a few days ago, but now there was no sign. The field had been ploughed; the linseed had been harvested before its time—or, more likely, taken away and burnt. All traces of the crash had been erased.

He'd been right, in a way, when he'd first come here. This place was ruled by a dictator. Not a person, but a currency. He'd used most of what the priest had given him to get here, by trains that were late, cancelled, non-existent, full of rubbish, full of angry people. Then he'd hitched lifts, and met people who either desperately wanted him to come to the countryside, or to keep away from their farms. He'd worn his cap and coat proudly. He didn't think that there would be much risk of anyone taking him for this murderer, his ancestor who'd stolen his name. And indeed, nobody seemed to associate him with anything in any newspaper they were reading.

In his own time, his own universe, these would all be crops and animals designed before birth to not be prey to disease and devastation. His people, and yes, he was romanticising them already, had been the stewards of nature, had intervened and had kept on intervening to take responsibility for the damage they'd already done, and make it right again. He got the feeling from the people he'd talked to on the way here that they half-blamed the current primitive attempts at genetic science for what had happened.

So, where was he to go from here? If he was a new Dante, exploring the Inferno, then at least he had a goal. He wasn't quite sure what he'd expected to find here, but some clue, perhaps, something that would lead him to Jocelyn. He knew, from his dream, that she was still alive. If he could talk to her, maybe they could find some way to get home. And perhaps getting home would change things for all these people for the better.

No use shirking here, then. Elsie's voice again. He often used her voice to represent something in himself... what was best in himself. He had to get down into that field and start looking. They'd have left some sign of where they were going. Then the local people: someone would have talked down at the pub.

He leapt off the gate where he stood, ready to tramp on into the mud, but then a shout came from the stile on the other side of the field. A young woman was standing there, waving to him.

"Hey!" she called. "You took your time!"

She looked like she was wearing an eyepatch.

Leyton opened his mouth in surprise, and found that he was smiling. He went to her at a run.

Alison hopped off the stile and met Leyton, and hugged him.

They held onto each other for a moment. He was different, she realised. He'd seen something of the country on his way here. He'd understood new things.

After a moment, he realised he was hugging her, and drew back. He was going to ask about the eyepatch. She put a finger to his lips. "I have a secondhand car," she said. "Which I bought from the dodgiest dealer I could find, in the quietest possible way."

"What?"

"I'm on the run. Like you are. Now come on, I have food."

She put her arm through his, ignoring the way he started at that, and led him off to the road nearby.

They looked at maps while they ate in the car. It was getting dark outside.

"I think they would have taken Jocelyn here." Alison pointed to an RAF base on her Ordnance Survey map, sweeping away the crumbs with her other hand.

"How did you know I was looking for—?"

Alison looked at him. He shut up. "There are four RAF bases nearby, but this one is the one where all the experimental stuff gets done. All the hush-hush stuff. They already have the security there, and it's nearby."

"Why did you come after me?"

"Because I've met the Golden Men again." She told him about her encounter with the Bears. "I think they were trying to follow what you were doing using that thing in my eye. Only I was kind of fighting it."

He looked almost tearful at the story. Not that his face got anywhere near tears.

"Dear me, old girl," he said finally. "You have been in the wars."

"It *was* all rather dreary," she said, taking the piss.

"That's why I went, you know. So you wouldn't be in danger."

"I got that. Pity you were so completely wrong." She regretted being so sharp with him as soon as she said it. She'd spent over a day anticipating this moment. It was as if she'd been saving the pain inside her for him. But his stoicism was infectious. She couldn't break down in front of him. So she didn't. "I bought sleeping bags as well," she said. "Only let's get somewhere more out of the way."

She pulled on her seat belt and started up the car.

After a moment, she realised that he was staring at the process, fascinated.

"Or do you want to drive?" she asked.

They drove into the wilderness, the wipers knocking the rain back and forth. Alison had gone back to not wanting to hear the news, so they didn't have the radio on. She was feeling sensitive to the world, even more so now, almost complicit in what had become of it. She shared all the details with Leyton, in little bits. All the ways in which she'd gone over to the enemy, mentally and physically. Her willingness to disbelieve him, to betray him. He nodded and listened, and perked up as she came out with each new detail, letting the silences between them stretch out.

"You're very good at this," she said.

"I've done it many times," he said. "Debriefings. You know. First the technical stuff, then how it really was. Usually over a couple of brandies in the mess."

"Ever done it yourself?"

"I daresay. Also many times."

"I thought you were all stiff upper lip?"

He laughed. "Where does that saying come from?"

"I don't know. People like you."

"And what sort of people is that?"

"People... men... who keep it all inside. Who're so repressed that they can't talk about their emotions. That's what the expression means."

"Ah." He was silent again for a while.

"Well, don't just shut up! That's exactly what I mean! Tell me what you're thinking!"

"I was thinking that you must have suffered a great deal."

"Because I'm taking it out on you."

"Right."

"I'm only taking it out on you because you're the problem! Men like you! Men who won't—"

"I don't think I'm *repressed* at all, if that means what I think it means." His voice had grown a touch louder. "I think it's part of what being a man... what being a *person*, means, to be in charge of what's going on up top. To take responsibility for how you feel. Not to let the bad stuff out."

"And then you don't know yourself—"

"I know myself!" That was a bellow.

She stopped the car quickly. They were in a dark lane, somewhere in south Dorset, a muddy corner of nowhere. She ripped the seatbelt from her shoulder and turned to face him. "If you did—"

"I know what's in here! I don't let it out! I have seen friends die! I have seen my wife die! I have seen my entire future die—!"

"Your wife?"

He stopped, his jaw set hard. He was visibly in control. But only just. Then he unbuckled himself, awkwardly, opened the car door, and made to walk off.

She got out after him. The rain was battering down on the car, spraying back into her face. "Where are you going?" she shouted after him.

He didn't answer. He kept walking into the darkness.

Well done, Alison.

She locked the car and ran after him.

She grabbed his shoulder.

He turned at speed, and again she was sure he was going to lash out.

But he didn't.

"I'm sorry," she said.

He nodded. He didn't want to make eye contact with her. He was already aware, she saw, of how stupid he looked.

"You are in control of what you do. I know that."

He managed to look at her. "That's what I was doing, taking it away, getting it out of your way. Before..." He was lost for words again. The rain had plastered his hair to his forehead. "A chap has to be in charge of his own... what do you call it?"

"Testosterone?"

"Yes."

"You don't have that word?"

"Of course we do. I'm a pilot. I don't remember medical jargon."

Alison saw a whole world in those words. "I won't ask about your wife again," she said.

"No, of course you can. Foolish of me. You've suffered just as much. More. You've been in combat. You've lost... you've been wounded. You've been in the hands of the enemy. I'm angry at them, old girl. I really am. It's not you. It's not me. It's just that—"

"I know." And she did.

She led him back to the car.

She took it out of his hands. She kissed him as soon as he'd closed the door.

For a moment, he kissed her back. Then he pulled back. But she didn't stop.

And he gave in.

They lay under his coat in the back seat, listening to the rain on the roof of the car.

He looked like a child now. His whole face had relaxed. He had worried, while she was undressing him, about "certain items," and about her reputation. She had assured him that there was no need for such items, and that as a wanted criminal her reputation couldn't get much worse.

Finally he had lost all the things holding him back.

He'd started to apologise afterwards. She'd hushed him and reassured him. She took off her eyepatch and showed him the dressing underneath. He looked straight at it. He could deal with that better than he could sex. She told him about the private doctor she'd gone to. The work she'd done on it herself by instinct, reading herself. She'd never done that before. It had helped, she told him, that she seemed to be full of anaesthetic. The pain, the doctor had told her, should have knocked her out.

He reached out and stroked around the socket, his fingers touching her black eye. He told her that she was still beautiful.

There was a silence in which they both wanted to say they loved each other, but both for the wrong reasons.

So Alison decided to talk about the reasons. "You know what scares me?" she said.

"The End of the World."

"Yeah. But exactly, right now... I think the difference between your world and mine is important."

"Absolutely!"

"I don't think I'd read the End of the World in everything if we were in your future. I think you lot sorted it when you got rid of money. I think that capitalism can't react fast enough to save the world from this..." She gestured to the rain outside the window. "I think by the time global warming gets obvious, and the multinationals and the governments they influence start reacting, it'll be too late. It *is* too late. Because this is what's written now. It's written over what was once written."

"You're so romantic, dear."

"Take me seriously, Leyton. Please."

"Could you call me Douglas?"

"No."

"I do take you seriously. But this will not persist." He got up onto one elbow and looked down at her, the coat slipping from round his once wounded, pink-fleshed shoulder. "We'll get hold of Jocelyn, work out where it all went wrong. Work out a way to put it back. We'll save your friend from the hell she's in by shutting down hell."

Alison smiled for him. She didn't see how that was going to be possible. They were, after all, going to have to discover a way to travel in time to do that, since Leyton had done it by accident. But Leyton was right: if anyone would know, his "head" would. And he was pretty convinced she was still alive. It was a tiny hope, but it was all they had. And she wanted to smile for him. "So, now that you've dishonoured me and my family—" She saw him start to react. "Joke! Joke! God, I'll have to stop poking you like that."

He swallowed. "Well—"

She laughed. "Can I ask you about—?"

"Her name was Elsie. We met—"

"Erm, no. Later for that. If you want to. I was going to ask..." And she needed to be holding him when she asked this. She put her forehead to his. "Leyton. This might be important. You're going to have to tell me how I'm supposed to die."

He thought for a long moment. Then he sighed. "All right."

She settled in his arms.

"You have both eyes in my world. You never lose the left one."

"Don't try and reassure me that this can't happen. Just tell me."

"All right. This is the end of the story, the last thing that happens in one of the films. In some of the others, they go on a bit and talk about what happens to Patrick afterwards and..."

"Marty. Yes. There's another difference. The Golden Men seem to like making differences."

"I prefer the film that's just called *Alison*. The one directed by Hohiti Kenton."

"For you this must be like shagging Madonna."

"Your contemporary. That's my next trip."

"In your dreams."

"The movie was made only a few years... afterwards. Before I was born. Kenton's a director I greatly admire. He gives the whole story a kind of... caring distance. Like he'd like to get involved, but has to set the thing in motion and just observe what happens."

"I have no idea what you're on about. How do you get a picture made without money? Do people pay to see it?"

"You go to the central film stock and equipment library, show them your certificates of proficiency in film-making, and off you go. And people certainly do not pay to see it."

"Just asking."

"Anyhow, this is how the picture goes. Alison... you, I mean... she's been through all these terrible times in her life, been caught up, rather deliberately, in all these conflicts, and she's always managed to reflect the mood of the world in her work. Everyone loves her. She becomes the most popular star in the world. By the end, all right, she's not the latest thing amongst the younger folk—"

"How old am I? When it... happens?"

"Thirty-eight."

That made her inhale suddenly. Only another eighteen years. And she'd never done these big famous things. But she handled it. "Right."

"But she's still one of the classic artists, someone whose work demands respect. The world is united. We're about to reach out into space... That's rather an irony. The audience knows that that's how we run into the Rods, and a whole new conflict, and the end of your story rather merges into that."

Had there been a little flicker of difficulty with "merges"? It was hard to tell. Leyton was one of the few people who knew that she did what she did, so he had the best poker face. She let it pass. "So. Details."

"She's settled in one place, in one of the little country villages on the edge of London. The popular image of her is that she's a bit melancholy. Her work at that point is full of bittersweet nostalgia—"

"You sound like a cover blurb. You're a real fan, aren't you?"

He ignored her, caught up in the passion. "But never regret. She does an interview every now and then. Once in a while she appears at a party."

"So I don't keep a string of young lovers?"

"There's nobody. Everybody wants her to settle down and be happy, but she never does."

"Sorry."

"Adds to the mystique, though. She's devoted her life to God, people say."

"Yeah, right!"

"Anyway, although the world's basically united under one government, in this historical period, there are still areas where the people have opted out of the system. Religious communities. Islands where people with specific beliefs have got together. The world has diplomatic relations with most of them. They don't generally take more than their share of resources, anyway."

"You'd have had had wars with the places that did."

"We did. We won."

"So these are the groups of loonies that don't have anything the world wants, so you're not arguing the toss about being selfish with them?"

"Spot on."

"We're going to have to compare histories. You know, like we've got Revelation, you haven't. But we've both got Madonna. I'd love to see where the two histories diverge bigtime."

"Indeed. But—"

"I know. Don't let me deflect it. Go on."

"Not many of these enclaves are capitalists. That doesn't seem to work for them on such a small scale—"

"I thought you didn't know much about history?"

He pursed his lips. "Only the bits about you."

"Ah."

"But there are capitalist, or would-be capitalist, organisations at large at this point. Some political pressure groups. The Market Party, for

instance, were non-violent. They claimed that the then current situation
was an extreme fluctuation in the market, and that it'd eventually right
itself. They got a few candidates elected to the assemblies, in Germany,
mostly. They're still going in my time. Never in sight of actual power,
poor old things. But there were more extreme factions. The MDB, for
instance... I don't know what that stood for, something in French... they
bombed things from time to time. Food depots, grain storage centres, fuel
cell manufacturing plants. They'd take hostages. They demanded that their
prisoners be set free, that certain areas be allowed to develop their work
token and exchange systems into credit and debt systems. Nobody took
much notice. Perhaps they should have done. They're gone by my time,
anyhow. There's no pro-capitalist terrorism when I come from. The Rods
saw to that.

"Anyhow, on September the third 2019, the MDB entered your
estate—"

Alison knew she was just putting off hearing the end, but she couldn't
help it. "My estate? How do I get that when there's no money?"

"People who love your work give up a small part of their land
allowance to you. There are various charitable ventures on the same land
which I won't trouble you with. And, of course, with the population under
control, people have a bit more land in general than you're used to."

"Hmm. Go on."

"They made their way through your minimal security systems and
took you hostage. They set the place up for a siege. They were demanding,
and this is rather a bitter irony, that you be given ownership of your work
in a financial, rather than creative sense. That you should earn something
from every sale."

"Well—" She saw that he looked hurt. "How terrible. Go on."

"You, of course, disagreed with them. They said that was because you
were a victim of false consciousness, that you'd been programmed to think
that way by the life you'd led."

"Oh bloody hell."

"Indeed. Well, a lot of people volunteered to take your place. The
gardens of the estate filled with news crews and police, ambulances, and
the security forces, such as they were back then. Negotiations began.
But it became obvious, after a few days, that these people had prepared
themselves to die for their cause. You sang to them, famously. But none
of the recording devices caught it. We only know the title because one of
the terrorists referred to it in conversation. You seem to have composed it
during the siege."

"What's it called?"

"It's, err, well..."

"What?"

"It's called 'On the Path of my God.'"

"Shit. This really is a different me. Do they shoot me on the spot?"

"No. Eventually, it becomes clear that there's a limit to how far this lot are prepared to negotiate. They cut off communications. The cameras that have been sent stealthily into the house see you getting... well, they treat you harshly. They want you to make a statement in favour of their cause. They want you to just say the words. You won't. So... they injure you. And they take certain liberties."

"I really hope this lot get killed."

"It's decided that the security forces can't wait any longer. Patrick and Marty are with them. They volunteer to go in with the—"

"No they bloody don't!"

"No, actually, there is a lot of doubt about that. That might be artistic licence on the part of Hohiti Kenton's sources. But he kept it in."

"So they burst in—"

"And the terrorists are waiting for that. A lot of the rescuers are killed. Not Patrick or Marty. And all the terrorists die. But before they can get to him, their leader..."

"Say it."

"He shoots you."

"Where?"

"Alison—"

"Tell me."

"In the stomach and chest."

"So it's not quick?"

He paused for a long moment, and she knew it wasn't. That it was actually bloody awful and complicated. And she found that now she knew all that she wanted to know.

She laid her head on the crook of his shoulder. "Okay. So. Those different histories..."

They had that conversation about divergences. They talked about their histories all they could, and found many points where the Golden Men must have written out a detail of Leyton's to replace it with a bit of Alison's.

There were bits and bobs all over the place in the early stuff: a lot of things from the Bible, limited by what Alison could remember. It was as if the Golden Men had appeared at certain points and made changes here and there—often just because they didn't like something. "Sodom and Gomorrah," she said, "were supposed to be wicked cities full of wicked people shagging each other. When I was little, I kind of got the impression they were all supposed to be gay."

"The Golden Men probably don't like that either."

"Do you lot have—?"

"Some of the best military men and women I've known."

"Okay, so with Sodom and Gomorrah, the angels objected to the men of the city wanting to 'know' them, which kind of makes sense now I've met them, because they're so gonna want to be on top. They sent Lot, who was good, on his way, then blew up the cities, and that turned his wife into salt."

"Your Old Testament!" laughed Leyton.

"So what if these cities were some sort of basic commune?" asked Alison. "Maybe they were starting out that way. I'm sure they existed in your world too, only you haven't heard about them because to you lot they're just cities from Biblical times. We only know the names because they got destroyed. Maybe the Bears really freak when they encounter something anti-cash like that. Even when they know they've changed our history completely, they're not taking any chances on something new springing up."

"Which suggests they don't really know what they're doing," ventured Leyton. "You don't know the lie of the land, you let loose with everything you've blasted well got at the first poor blighter you see, just in case there's a squadron behind him."

"Good point."

"Well I thought so, old thing."

But apart from islands of change like that, mostly their histories tallied. Alison was quite surprised that Leyton's Europe had fought and won a Second World War against Nazi Germany. It was in the immediate aftermath that everything changed.

"Of course, with the victory came the spoils," said Leyton, as if quoting from some half-remembered textbook. "The allied forces of Britain and Russia made huge technological advances in the aftermath of war, applying the military technology of the final days to civilian applications. On the death of Stalin, relations grew warmer between Attlee and their new chap, Khrushchev. A Socialist alliance was born. Britain gave the USSR the Enigma coding machine and the atom bomb. The Soviets gave Britain vast manpower and natural resources. The Empire was revived under the Socialist Rule of Nations. Over the decades, the countries living inside that system grew closer and closer, and that was the basis upon which world government came about."

"But what about the other countries?"

"We were just so much more advanced than they were. There was some initial attempt at a balance of power, but the moon landing, according to the history books, rather put paid to that. The People's Empire Ship *Churchill*: Vanatchka, Hughes, Crofton, Chingkho. I used to have the flag on my wall when I was a boy."

"And that was that for nation states?"

"I suppose it's a lot more complicated than that, but that's what the history boils down to."

"So why should the aftermath of the Second World War be such a big deal for the Golden Men?"

He could only shrug.

There was so much they didn't know. She snuggled more closely into Leyton's shoulder. "Do you want to sleep?"

"Yes."

"Then let's."

Alison dreamed of good things that night, which made her aware, somehow, of what had happened to her and what she'd seen. The shock of losing the eye was still echoing in her head.

That and she felt shivery, cold where warmth wouldn't reach, sweating.

She woke Leyton up in the early hours and started to cry on him, big, racking sobs. He smoothed her hair.

In the morning they dressed, and she made sure he wasn't going to go all formal on her by grabbing him as he got into his trousers and jerking him off until he got into it.

And that wasted another hour and a bit.

They finally set off when it was more than first light—not that the rain let the light in much.

Heading for the airbase, they turned onto a major road. They were talking about the crash, how it had gone.

"Jocelyn said something really odd," Leyton was saying. "Just before we hit. She said 'see you at the Fitzroy Hotel.'"

It was all Alison could do not to do a U-turn there and then. She turned off the road at the next exit and sent the car back the way they had come. "For someone who's really intelligent," she said, "you can be so stupid."

Eighteen: Many Mansions

Humans called the star Zeta Reticuli. The Rods knew this, and were amazed by it. Zeta, so far down in their list of brightness and importance. To them it was the Star. And they were the Free People.

Their original home was the fifth world out from the Star, Earth, as they called it. They knew that the humans called their home planet that too. So did many races. The two planets they actually inhabited in the System were New Earth and Brilliant Afterlife, both closer to the Star. The first name had been decided on by the conglomerate that owned it. The second was a traditional name that had been kept because of its romantic imagery. Earth had been abandoned, but was now being reclaimed by brave prospectors and maverick developers, who had invested lengths of themselves in reinvigorating the world.

The Rods had been alarmed when they had first encountered the humans, many lifetimes ago. They were sorry for the first astronauts they met, who were cheerful, willing to communicate, intelligent, and brought with them their "heads," a recognisable unit of exchange that could have formed the basis of a wonderful new cultural relationship.

However, the astronauts were clearly in servitude to a fearsome dictatorship, a united species government that allowed them very little in the way of personal freedom. There was much that individual Rod authorities wanted to investigate about them and their home planet: the idea of "seasons," for example, that conditions on that world changed cyclically. Their hivelike governmental system was clearly a product of these changes, a social response to the fear of a swiftly changing environment.

Rod entrepreneurs had immediately set out for the nearest human colonies, ready to trade and to exchange culture and knowledge with these interesting new folk. Both species knew some of the same other cultures at the edge of their mutual empires. These species talked fearfully of the differences between the two races, but the Rods had a policy of approaching new cultures with a length of body ready to give, an obvious interest in mutual economic advantage that tended to bowl first contacts over with the generosity of the terms involved. The motivation was, largely, gold. The humans had a vast supply of the Colliding Neutron Star Stuff, their homeworld having been blessed with being in the vicinity of a cloud of neutron ash during its formation. And they, of course, did not value it anywhere near its true worth.

The expeditions had, of course, been armed. They'd never expected to have to use these weapons to protect their interests, but the humans turned out, either out of fear of their central authority or zealous belief in their system, to be fiercely defensive of their trading rights. They would not allow several of the Free Folk's products to even touch down on their colony worlds. This was clearly against all universal laws of free trade. So the Rods convened their arc and sent three liege armies to protect their investments. The humans responded with vast and sudden aggression.

And so began the Great War. The Rods had been losing, for many lifetimes now. Morale on Brilliant Afterlife remained good, but everyone knew that certain individuals were preparing to take their families offworld and head for the distant colonies. The arc, of course, had dedicated itself to fighting to the last. They would remain in their bow across the sky of the capital, locked body to body, until enemy fire rended them apart. And then the arc would be recreated, body by body, in the actual brilliant afterlife, and the links would remain unbroken. They had given lengths of themselves all their lives. Now they would give lengths of themselves in defence of their freedom against the hive invader.

There were reports of atrocities from colony worlds where the humans advanced. They had a fanatical zeal that the free-thinking Rods could not match. The Rods could only pray to God to protect them. "Sai, who gave all of himself without profit, and was expelled from the arc, and died and then rose again, his body complete, defend us from the atheist who would destroy us. Hear your people in their hour of need." They would say this and other such prayers as they saw their families die and their homesteads burnt. They had not believed for a very long time, many of them, but God's name was heard more often in these dark days than it had been for ages before.

And then it seemed God did hear them.

He sent help in a strange form: the form of the enemy.

The Golden Humans appeared on Marketday, in the circle beneath the arc. They looked exactly like the hive creatures, except they were coloured like the Neutron Star Stuff, which the arc initially took to be the mocking warpaint of élite forces, rather than the declaration of wealth it actually turned out to be. They caused mass panic. The biggest weapons were directed against them immediately.

But then, at speed, their wings a blur of excitement, Rods came forward to speak for them. The Golden Humans had contacted these Free Folk in advance, had been talking to them and arranging things. There were four of them. These were not humans, but something new. The bombardment ceased. The Golden Humans were invited to address the arc. They exchanged body for body, as only civilised species could, the quantities of gold on their skins delighting the arc.

They were time travellers, which shocked the arc. The leading Rod technological companies had never found any experimental avenues that suggested such flight was possible. The Golden Humans said that they sailed through a single wound in the body of spacetime, which was a proof of an old prophecy, some said. The Golden Humans offered proof of a future that was the salvation of the Rods. At some point in the future of the humans, as they abandoned their homeworld to the natural processes of global warming, as all industrial species did, they created a great trading system of stock exchange across their star system. Individual humans... at this point in the future, they must have actually achieved individuality... had linked themselves to this system to trade with greater speed and accuracy. This delighted the arc. The humans of the future had accepted the benefits of universal culture, were just people like them!

But better news was to come. These future humans had, over a time period called by humans centuries, changed with the systems they had merged with. They inherited their communion with the systems through their families, as it became easier to breed the links into the genes than to attach them to the newly born. The humans did this aware all the time of what they were doing to their species. The features of their merged progeny changed from their original pattern. They grew, initially in their physical selves, probes for interaction with other computers, which took the place of organs originally used for eating. But then there was a greater surprise for them: they discovered the Koew.

The ripple of relief that that news brought the arc spread swiftly to all the worlds of the Rod at the speed of dimensional bodylinks. The great loss of the humans was that they knew nothing of the Koew, the property of consciousness that all large systems of exchange had. The Koew was God manifest in the world, so Rods of many star cycles ago had believed, until the first scientific and philosophical investigations had proved that the Koew was a real, innate principle of the act of exchange. Two or more systems (three was the first certainty of Koew, two had a lesser or virtual form that was still the subject of much debate) exchanging information always achieved some form of consciousness. When the exchange was a competitive one, propelled by an evolutionary process such as the maturation of a global or larger economy, then true Koew was achieved remarkably quickly. The humans had turned their back on Koew, and thus on all spirituality, not even recognising that the principle existed.

But these Golden Humans from the future had embraced the Koew. They had recognised its consciousness, communicated with it, worshipped it, become one with it. They understood that victory was a matter of seeing one thing inside another, of swapping body length for body length.

They told the arc that there was one history. They were the only hope. Time travel could alter the future, but they had seen the map of the changes and thought they were part of that map. They had sent this party of four into the past, firstly to the Rods, to write the first line of what they knew had already been written, or chimed, as the Rods would have put it themselves.

The Rods measured the existence of the spacetime rift above their world with their instruments and saw that it was a fixed part of the universe, a thread that wound in and out of spacetime. It had been and always would be there at certain points and times. If it was an instrument of revolution, it was one that had always been present.

The Golden Men, responding to such questions, declared that their existence, though certain, was dependent upon them going back to the home of their species, their Earth, and changing it, far back in time. They wanted to change it to the world which they had sprung from, rather than the world it was now, which had produced the Rods' enemies. The arc asked where they had come from, then, if this world that would create them had yet to be created itself. The Golden Humans said, through their intermediaries, that they had memories of their own existences, could access the history of their folk, were convinced that they had come from such a future. The arc put to them that perhaps they had simply been born out of the wound in the body of spacetime. The Golden Humans maintained that this was not so. The arc felt sorry for them. It was as if some of them were thinking already, though they were too scared to express it, that they were dreams, figments of the imagination of spacetime, born out of the wound in its body. They were losing their faith, and had to create themselves anew to regain it.

The arc decided to help them. They gave the Golden Humans all the intelligence they had about the humans, their worlds, their history and the undiscovered Koew that surely existed, waiting to be born as the first seed of the Golden Humans, inside the human systems.

Then the Golden Men left to make that journey back to the home of their possible ancestors. They aimed, they said, to divert the passage of one human ship through the wound in the body of spacetime, from the time to which it had gone originally to the time they saw it should go on the maps they had compiled. That one alteration, they said, would be enough to ensure their creation. They entered the world once more.

And the universe changed.

And changed.

And changed.

And changed.

And that kept on, as music. A pattern within a pattern. The changes were surprises that made the music not obvious, but art.

And the Rods could only recognise that distantly.

And the changes were like the chiming of something bigger being *written*.

Nineteen: History Happens at the Fitzroy Hotel

Alison knew for sure one thing: when you're looking for someone, and the last thing they've said to you is that they'll see you in a certain place, it's probably a good idea to go there.

There were three Fitzroy Hotels in London. Two of them were huge. Those, Ally reasoned, wouldn't be much use to whatever security service had Jocelyn. They wouldn't be up to running a large hotel, and wouldn't want to liaise with an organisation big enough to do so. One of them was small, however, one of a line of six similar establishments in a little square near Paddington Station. Leyton had asked to pop into the station, and had spent half an hour walking around, staring at the ceiling, disgusted by the "boring engines."

Then they'd gone to check out the hotel. Alison had done her best to disguise herself, dyeing her hair blonde in the sink at their B&B in Aylesbury, where they'd left the car in a longterm carpark. She'd encouraged Leyton to do the same. He'd bought a wig, cut his hair back to fit neatly under it, and had got some of those contact lenses that changed the colour of his eyes. He dressed himself in very plain jumper and trousers, stowing his coat, suit and cap away in his kitbag, which he then stuffed into a sports haversack he threw over one shoulder. The effect, Alison found, was startling. They checked each other out in the bedroom mirrors. "You're good at this," she told him.

Now they stood by the black-barked trees in the middle of the square, looking up at the Fitzroy Hotel. They were going to do this for two minutes, while eating sandwiches, then walk on.

"Why would they take Joss into a big city?" asked Leyton.

"They wouldn't take the remains of your ship to one," said Alison. "But Jocelyn's separate to that, right?"

"But look here, I don't even know what Jocelyn meant when she mentioned this place. How could she know anything about what would happen to her when we landed?"

Alison didn't know. Her brain was tugging at something, but she hadn't worked out what yet. It would come to her sideways, when she wasn't thinking about it. But she was certain about the obvious bit. "It's the last thing she said to you before you crashed. So it's important. If it was a shared joke, why don't you get it?"

"We'd only met a short time before."

Alison shook her head. It was nagging at her. "She was assigned to you specifically. And in the middle of a war, you two were encouraged to go off on a pleasure cruise."

"What's that got to do with anything?"

Alison could only shrug. "Listen, if she's not in there, I'll buy dinner, okay? Ready?"

They wandered off as if they had all the time in the world.

Beneath the Fitzroy Hotel, in the third of six levels of underground bunkers, Cleves sat thinking about the rain.

It wasn't just the rain, of course, that made him feel guilty. It was the fact that he'd started to pay attention to all the global monitors, to the state of the ice spur that was melting beyond any cyclic variation, that might switch off the Gulf Stream. To the disturbed migratory patterns of birds. To every little sign, only now he had committed himself to a course which meant he had to ignore those signs.

Months ago, when all this started, he had got a few of his environmental chaps in, on the pretext of talking about green terrorism. He had asked them what the chances for the planet were. They were all dismal about it. If the environment was a very chaotic system, he was told, then things could very suddenly take a turn for the worse. Gaia, the goddess of the world, could shake humans off with water, could flood the world as God had promised not to. Or a runaway greenhouse effect could take hold within hours. Nobody knew. Nobody could predict the weather more than five days ahead—they never had been able to. All those longterm forecasts of Cleves' youth had been old men not knowing a thing.

He had a twenty-four-hour watch put on Leyton. He had made sure that no one could approach him without Cleves' knowledge, and that he could not vanish from his hand.

Then he had come to London to see Jocelyn.

She had not told him, in her babblings, anything definitive about the climate of the future, or how that future's political culture had evolved from the here and now. All she would say was "it does not." Which meant revolution, somewhere along the line. But had that revolution been in response to anything he was part of? Was her pilot's mission into the past anything to do with him? Was it against Restoration? Jocelyn had been asked questions which touched on these matters, as much as Cleves could touch on them, given the people who would listen to the answers. And she had answered at length. But in those lengths she had created mazes of aside and confusion. She was the most determined and clever prisoner he had ever heard interrogated. And now the word from above was that Cleves was asking too much about the situation in the future, and not enough technical questions about the ship. There was to be a further chemical interrogation on that subject, with technicians present, when Jocelyn had recovered enough to survive it.

If she let slip that the nature of her mission was against Restoration, then Cleves would checkmate her instantly by having Leyton arrested and hung in his cell.

There was a knock on the door. He answered it, and they brought Jocelyn in. They placed her on a table in this specially prepared room. It was bare, padded with pillows and duvets from the hotel above. There were handholds roughly stapled to the walls.

She looked tired. There were dark pits under her eyes. "You don't deserve to know anything," she said.

"It was meant to be more gentle than that. The effects are usually very straightforward. It's designed to be painless."

"They came in covered in cushions and pillows and kept asking the same questions. Very droll, I thought. And thanks for bringing me here. Such comfortable décor. Why do you care so much?"

They were still being recorded. "It's a private matter. The wish of an old man. I simply wanted to know what the future is like. Whether I should be examining what I do more closely."

"Well, now you know, soldier. I told your goons all about the future."

"The workers' paradise."

"Depends on the worker, chum."

"How is that possible? How does it arise? Is it the Chinese?"

"Nothing doing. Should have asked that when I was doped."

"Tell me," he said suddenly, "does it matter what I do?"

She looked at him seriously for a moment, and he was sure that she gave him a serious answer. "I don't know. That's one of the reasons I wanted to keep schtum."

"Once we understand the technology of your craft, we can use it to create an advantage over any new Communist threat. Even the Chinese, if they come."

"Not without my help. The leap's too big and there's not enough left. I was in the crash in question, if you recall."

He got the feeling she was looking deeply into him, reading him like a book. "We shall see," he said. "If it matters what I do, then we shall see."

"You sound," she said finally, "like someone who's regretting going to one party, and wondering if he can still make it to the other."

"I'm rather surprised," said Cleves, "that anyone is still entertaining."

The telephone across the room rang. He went and picked it up. It was one of the security staff from upstairs. He found, as he listened to her, that he had started to smile.

How do you enter a small hotel without being noticed?

They'd sat in a nearby café and thought about that one. From the look of the front, you went straight into reception, and there was the shabby little reception desk, with one woman sitting behind it.

They could walk straight in, or they could try to burgle the place. Leyton had asked if maybe this wasn't a secret installation but perhaps just a hotel where Jocelyn was waiting for them, but Alison asked him how, assuming his hunch was right and she'd survived, a head might have made a sudden break for freedom?

So no, walking in the front door wasn't on.

They waited until it was dark. Then they walked around the back into the alley where the bins were. They'd checked it out earlier in the day: a kitchen door, the sound of a radio from inside it. The rain was spitting down and the rubbish smelled terrible.

Alison motioned to Leyton to shush. She listened carefully for a moment and held a finger up for each person in the kitchen. Three of them. The sound changed. A door opened somewhere inside. Two.

Alison saw that Leyton was looking around, aware of the tall buildings looking down on them, lights on in the high windows. They'd be seen at any moment.

She was going to follow the patterns of headness through this building at a run. He was going to follow her, and deal with whatever got in their way. They'd checked out various military shops, but there was no way they could get their hands on any serious kind of gun. Leyton wouldn't carry a knife. He'd settled on a heavy spanner from a car spares shop.

She clicked her fingers. One person now.

They ran in.

They walked straight through a kitchen that was nowhere near as busy as it should be. A chef near the radio stirred a pan, his back to them. He didn't turn.

Then they were in a service corridor: blue and green paint, like they couldn't help but paint it like an official building. Official building polish smell in the air too.

Down. They had to go down. Up here was comfort. Bare comfort. A safehouse. Alison marched, Leyton on her shoulder, tensed, ready to fight. The corridors were long and dark. Distant noises. Not many people here.

They came to a lift. There were two simple buttons, indicating up and down. Alison chose down.

They got in. Alison breathed in hard as the doors slid together, expecting someone to stop them. But they closed.

The lift started to move. Down one floor. Then two.

Then it stopped. Between floors.

They waited. Leyton reached inside his jacket for his spanner.

Alison put her hand on his arm. "No," she said.

She realised as she did it that that was why whoever was waiting for them had warned them. So she would make Leyton see sense. They had been watched and understood. They were inside their pattern now. This was their maze.

The lift lurched again, and they halted a few feet further down.

The doors opened.

An old man stood there. "Welcome," he said. "It's good to finally meet you both."

Behind him stood two younger men. They looked like they might have guns. One of them extended his hand towards Leyton, palm up.

Leyton gave him the spanner.

The man laughed.

They searched them anyway. One of the men patted all the way down Alison's legs, professionally, not lecherously. It almost felt worse. They took Leyton's bag.

The men satisfied themselves that they weren't armed, then motioned for them to go forward.

The old man got out of their way with another gracious gesture. He was staring hard at Leyton, a vast smile playing about his features, as if Leyton fulfilled all his dreams. Alison realised that this was who she was playing against. This was the man who'd dropped her in the river and made her cold.

But he had not sent the Golden Men after her, or he would not be looking surprised and wondering sidelong, anxious to ask Leyton all sorts of questions. The allies of the Bears had no doubt.

They went through a pair of big wooden doors and into corridors that held offices and conference rooms. There were still few people about. Most of the doors were locked. The place smelled like the nineteen sixties, wooden and mothballed.

There was no difference to the décor down here. Alison wondered at that for a moment, then she realised: she'd been expecting gleaming metal.

When the doctor came into her room, Alison became afraid.

They'd separated her from Leyton and locked her inside a small office space with four elderly chairs around a round wooden table. She could have smashed the glass on the door, but she was pretty sure she couldn't fit through the gap that would make. Besides, they'd catch her in seconds.

She'd fallen into one of the chairs and run both hands through her hair. She felt woozy. She wasn't as scared as she expected to be. She was still on her mission, to save the world from the Golden Men. From money. Loving going out with... shagging... whatever the word was... Leyton.

He'd have said *courting*.

But there was more than that. It was like... she had her mission, and she was inside the mission of this old man. But it felt like... Destiny. Like she was stepping to the tune of bigger things.

This had been coming on for days, only she hadn't stopped doing stuff, had had her mission to keep her going. It was the chemicals the Bears had put in her brain, she realised. Coming off it, she couldn't sleep now, couldn't concentrate. It felt like she was trying to do something hard, like a tough move in a video game, and kept failing. Kept failing. Sod it. Do something else. Have a cuppa. But her body wouldn't. She felt like scratching her arms off.

Her thoughts were interrupted by the noise of the door opening, and at the sight of the white-coated man, she realised abruptly that yes, she could still get scared. Her mission didn't protect her from that.

He locked the door behind him and put his hands up. "It's okay," he said. "Just a medical."

She sat down again. She found that she was shaking. "Don't inject me."

"I will, but only to take some blood. Okay?" He reached inside his bag.

Alison put her left hand on her right arm. "What choice do I have?" she said.

The medic took his blood sample, then took off her eyepatch and looked at the wound. He tutted at what he saw, and said that another injection, of antibiotics, was in order, and that he was amazed she was still on her feet. So he gave her that, and cleaned the wound, and provided a new dressing, a white one. He took the eyepatch away with him. She wasn't a pirate any more.

After he left, nothing happened for several hours. There was no window, the lighting was constant. They were underground. Alison thought about patterns within patterns, but she came to no conclusions. She felt looked down on. She felt the weight of the infections in her eye, and the antibiotics battling them, and all that was inside her scrabbling nerves and desire for... for what the Bears had. If she went back to them and asked them nicely, they could put something in her other eye, give her the jolt again. Put her back up amongst the people on top, instead of down here in hell, suffering.

She heard her thoughts and grabbed the wood of the chair with both hands.

Her suffering wasn't important. She was not going back to them. If she was wrong about the old man and one of them floated in here now, she would scream at it and tell it to piss off and make sure that it could not have her.

She was here to save Fran from hell, and all of humanity and history from it too. She was herself, she was not a label. She desired nothing. It was just her body that did.

It was warm down here, a bit too warm. She took off her jumper, put two chairs together and tried to sleep on them.

Suddenly, that worked.

Leyton had been taken to a secure room with no window. He had grinned at the camera he supposed to be in one corner, pulled off his pullover and made a pillow of it. He lay back confidently, hands behind his head, one leg over the other: a display of cocksureness that he didn't feel.

They had had no hope of pulling this off. He could see that now. He had allowed his faith in Alison's abilities to blind him to that. That, and his insane desire to do something to get out of this God-forsaken world. They were caught, in effect, as soon as they'd walked in.

He hoped they'd let him see Jocelyn. He'd known, ever since he'd shared that dream with her, that she was alive. When he'd asked the men who searched him about her, they'd just looked at each other. He'd laughed to himself. He was catching a bit of Alison's whatchermacalit. They'd have done something else if she was dead, or if they'd never heard of her. The look had said: "That weird head thing!" And maybe there'd been a trace of a smile there, like Jocelyn had been entertaining them.

He hoped that Alison was all right. He couldn't quite square things about how he felt concerning her. He'd gone too far for it not to be important. Much too far. It was what they did here, she'd assured him, and that was rather grand, really. But it was frightening. All these genies let out of the box in this hell. He wanted to take her back home and make an honest woman of her. In some way.

He'd been driving too fast, with his Elsie. They were negotiating the country roads from London down to the South Coast. The open-topped car. The freedom he'd found with her. The speed. The oncoming lorry. The frozen smile. The tree.

He'd known, when he'd wrenched himself out of the wreckage and had stumbled over to her, how it was going to go, with her being a service wife. Her body was flattened across the tree trunk, curved at an impossible angle.

But her head lolled, undamaged.

He'd checked for a pulse and found none.

He knew death. He knew that it had come and gone in an instant.

He'd gone to what remained of the car, hauled open the boot, desperate, urgent, and had fumbled with the buckles on his kit bag. He'd unbuttoned his holster and thrown it to the ground. He checked there was a round in the chamber of his automatic and slipped off the safety catch with fingers that were not yet fumbling, because he knew it was just minutes before they would be.

He had knelt beside her, in that woodland roadside. Behind him, distant, the lorry was burning, and that driver was dead. He had not cared. For that once, he had not cared. He could hear the cries of birds and animals, still alarmed, rushing away from the wreck, the natural world blooming with life and running from human death.

He had put the pistol to her temple, ready to do it. They would court-martial him. He didn't care.

He had not been able to change that cheek that he had grown so used to.

He could grow used to it again. Could ask, against all practice, for Elsie to be his head now. But he knew, better than anyone, the horror of that: the slow process of dissolution and unattachment. The emotional hooks that scarred. It wasn't like living with someone who'd lost the use of their body. He knew several couples who dealt with vast wounds and disablements. This was different. This was living with someone who had more abilities, not fewer. Heads didn't retire. They didn't want to. They lived to walk in the stars. When pilots went on leave, their heads didn't want to go with them and live the nightmare of being stuck in one place.

She was in the forces too. She would hate him if he denied her the last chance to serve.

They would drive no more together. Not in space. Not anywhere.

He heard the ambulance approaching. The satellites had spotted the crash.

He took his gun back to the trunk. Then he went back to Elsie and kissed her goodbye.

Then he had walked away.

He was back in his cell of a room now. He was not there. He was here. In a new life. With a new love. He made himself smile for the camera. He didn't quite feel up to a new love. He felt that Elsie wouldn't forgive him.

If he ever got back home, maybe he'd call and ask her.

He leapt to his feet and started his exercises. No point in falling into a complete funk. He had to be ready to get out of this place, to take Alison and Jocelyn with him. There would be a chance. There always was. And there would be the interrogation to deal with. These secret police that Alison had said had come after her. In her own bloody country! That was the trouble with capital. It gave people mixed loyalties, a shattered structure of grander and lesser allegiances.

He would tell them nothing, just for the hell of it, just to keep on being who he was. He would not ask them about Alison, because that would reveal that he cared about her, and thus put her in danger.

The door opened almost on cue. The old man came in. Alone. He closed the door after him. "Good evening, Squadron Leader," he said.

It had taken an effort of will for Cleves not to go to Leyton immediately. Prisoners should always be left to stew.

He made it to half an hour before he gave in.

Now he stared at the man from the future from close range, seeing the youth in him that his ancestor no longer possessed. He'd rid himself of his rather useless disguise. Cleves' men had taken the wig and contact lenses, along with the impressive dress uniform that Cleves had just retrieved from analysis. He had it in his hands now as he entered, a friendly gesture, giving the prisoner back his identity. Meaning that it could always be taken from him again.

Leyton straightened up as Cleves approached and rubbed his nose. "Evening, old chap. Who am I talking to?"

"Why do you need to know?"

"Question of whether I salute or not."

Cleves smiled again. "I have been saluted. But I have never sought it."

"Talk English, old chap."

Cleves raised an eyebrow. He wondered if he still could be plain. "You are a Communist. I have not met one of those face to face for many years."

"Communist?" Leyton laughed. "You've been looking at the history books. That was what... I don't know, the revolutionary Soviets called themselves? Before World War Two?"

"What would you prefer to be called?"

"What I am. Which is an officer of Her Majesty the President's World Spacefleet."

Cleves didn't want to stop to take out his pad. He was sure he would remember. "Those concepts don't fit together."

"Don't they? Amazing what you can do when you're all on the same side, isn't it?"

"What sort of 'Majesty' can a President possess?"

"Don't ask me. I voted for the other fellow."

Cleves handed him his uniform. Leyton took it passively, then began, surprisingly, to pull on the coat, leaving the cap stuffed in his pocket.

It was chilly in here, but not that chilly. This was a man who needed his symbols to preserve his sense of self. Cleves sat down at a distance from him.

"You are fighting a war—"

"Ah, so you have got Jocelyn somewhere about the place. What do you make of her?"

"Who are you fighting?"

"Why should I tell you?"

"I'm a representative of Her Majesty's government."

Leyton laughed and sat down on the chair opposite Cleves, straddling it. "Her Majesty's government in shackles. Led around by the needs of money. You have starving people on the street out there. Attend to them and then I'll talk to you."

"I saved their parents from death. I saved the world from destruction. Many times."

"You saved it for the Golden Men."

Cleves couldn't conceal the shock he felt. Those words. From the centre of who he was. From long ago. Nobody knew. He had never told. He mustn't reveal that to Leyton. Or to the cameras. "Who?"

"Your masters. They're running this game. Alison doesn't think so, but it looks to me like they're some sort of foreigner."

"Foreigner?"

"From another planet. You know."

"You mean aliens?"

"That's an ugly word. Still, they're an ugly crew. And they're pulling your strings." Leyton pointed at Cleves meaningfully. "You were invaded back before your history started. And they're still in control now."

Cleves took a few moments to absorb that. He threaded his fingers behind his back and wandered around the room. Leyton did not appear to be lying. In fact, he seemed eager to talk and talk, and tell the truth all the while.

And he had used that phrase: the Golden Men. "I am at the highest rank of government," he whispered. "And I have sought such creatures. I would know."

"They run the system, chap, not your government. They only intervene when they think things are heading the wrong way. Or for fun. They're not fond of me. You keep me locked up in here, and I daresay you'll get to meet one."

"I may do just that. To see if your story is true."

"You won't get much proof. One of them will walk through the wall and we'll go a couple of rounds, and that will be that for Mrs Leyton's boy."

"So when did you rid yourself of the control of these creatures? And why don't you think the Communists called themselves that *after* the war?" Cleves' thoughts were racing.

Leyton thought for a moment. "Tell me your bloody name," he said.

Cleves took a deep breath. There was something so British about this man, something so like what he himself had always stood for. And yet he represented what he had always fought.

There was something about his eyes...

He got up, went to the door and called to be let out.

In the adjacent room, a bored-looking officer sat watching the DAT recorder and CCTV cameras log the activity in Leyton's room. Without a word, Cleves switched everything off and took the key.

The man looked seriously at him. "An equipment fault, sir?"

"Go and have a cup of tea. I can't resume the interrogation until it's fixed now, can I?"

He had had such conversations before. The officers involved inevitably stiffened a little, aware that terrible violence was about to be done nearby. This one got to his feet and moved swiftly off down the corridor.

The key in his pocket, Cleves headed back to Leyton's room and made sure the door was locked behind him.

Leyton waited, his eyes ready. He'd probably come to much the same conclusion as the surveillance officer had. He looked surprised, though, that it was just the old man who had returned. He was no longer a physical threat on his own.

Cleves sat down again. "My name," he said, "is Frederick Cleves. I am the Chair of the Joint Intelligence Committee."

Leyton saluted. "Pleased to meet you, sir."

"I am currently, however, the servant of two masters. Large amounts of cash are being deposited in an account in my name, held at a Brazilian bank. Half of it is for the use of a cross-service operation I am currently running under the codename Restoration. This half is used to convince doubting section heads that they are chancing their necks on the nod from those on high. As Chair of the JIC, I have total authority to mount such black operations, and have done so on the verbal contract of the Prime Minister or Home Secretary of the day on many occasions. In my years as a junior Case Officer within the Security Service I have even been part of such operations conducted by previous JIC Chairs *against* the Prime Minister and Home Secretary of the day."

Leyton nodded. "No more than I'd expect of you lot."

"The other half of the money is for me. My payment. I have had some ethical difficulties with this."

"No doubt."

"When I am feeling particularly weak, I blame it on the dissolution of the Soviet Union. The fall of Communism. The resources of my security services had been redirected, were being, in a continual competition for budget and authority, turned towards organised crime. But the drug gangs were too small to interest me. I organised several Special Intelligence Committees, one for each supplier state and thus associated supply chain, and angled inter-agency co-operation into several good missions to plant agents within the South American cartel bases and support them once they were there."

"I don't understand a word of this."

"Good for you. And then... well, the druglords did not play back. They either fell to the snares or they did not. There was no exultation when they did. Another would just take their place, blindly, ignobly, like fighting a machine. It was like defeating a computer game. There was no crusade, no ideology involved. If cocaine was ever made legal, we would become the paramilitary arm of Customs and Excise.

"I dared express such thoughts at an inter-agency do held in Chatham. Everyone at my table agreed. We were all ideologues, had been committed to the downfall of everything that threatened Western Democracy. And now we had won, with China slowly turning into Disneyland, so we ought to retire. And die.

"The first letter arrived the next weekend. There was no betrayal offered to me, no agents' lives to be surrendered as currency as I came over the wall. I had simply to create and run a network for a particular purpose within the shores of Great Britain. I had done that before. And the nature of the organisation did not directly confront my duty. It would not, in fact, until the last possible moment—if it even came to that. Restoration was a perfectly legitimate mission to run agents at the highest levels of the various fuel protest movements—"

"I've heard about those," Leyton cut in. "And let me tell you, I have rarely heard anything so stupid."

"That is the nature of my job. I ate every letter on rice paper, and tasted squid ink on my tongue. If interested Ministers discovered the project, I could tell them every detail of the operation and they would have been pleased that I had, as always, acted in their interests without their knowledge.

"That would be until the point when the various double-blind dupes in my employ, thinking they were working for everyone from MI5 to the CIA, actually grabbed the country successfully by the bollocks and forced down the price of fuel. Which would mean forcing down the duty levied on it. Which would mean increased profits for the oil companies in a market that has been threatened longterm by green politics, creating a cultural imperative that would stand several elections, making governments afraid of green taxes, and delivering to my new masters a huge slice of panic buying before the shortages hit and relief buying afterwards."

"The politics of hell," said Leyton. "I'm getting about one word in three."

"So you have not travelled back in time to halt my plans?"

"Don't fool yourself."

Cleves leaned forward. "Restoration will give my children and grandchildren independent wealth in a world that I can no longer predict. I thought, in the first few weeks of planning, that I was hurting nobody, until I became aware, through following a detail in my old friend's letters, that similar operations were being planned consecutively all across the civilised world.

"That was when I started to worry about the rain, and investigate all the other little details. That was when it occurred to me that in shielding my descendants against the future, I might have helped to doom them. I got into this thinking that the great enemy of my youth, Communism, was dead, and so I could do what I wished. I discovered, through doing what I wished, that my enemy would rise again. I have sought to hurt no one. And in so doing I have killed a priest." Cleves felt a tremendous rush of relief at unburdening himself. He looked up at Leyton, wanting to hear his response.

"There. I have told you everything. Now what do you have to tell me? About the weather of the future, the results of my actions. And about the Golden Men."

Leyton was looking hard at him, though his eyes were still soft. "Nothing," he said.

"Nothing."

"What you do may or may not matter, old sport, because your present doesn't lead to my future. The Golden Men have seen to that. I've travelled in time. So, it seems, have they. They've changed everything. To enslave the world. It looks, sir, like your 'side' won this game a long time ago. If what you're doing is going to lead to vast pollution, the End of the World... well, you're just delivering the *coup de grâce*."

Cleves believed him. He took a card from his pocket, the original of the ID that the technicians had found in the wreck. He handed it to Leyton.

As his fingers touched it, the thing lit up inside, came alive with links and connections and possibilities. A piece of functioning future technology. "You see?" said Leyton. "It really is me."

Cleves took the card back from him.

Slowly, he got to his feet. He headed for the door.

He didn't even call farewell to Leyton. Or thanks.

He leaned on the door as they locked it behind him.

He gave the key to one of the officers. "You can switch the cameras back on," he said. "He's a tough one, all right."

He had known he'd been in the wrong for a long time. Why had he needed proof? Now he had to do something about it. He headed along the dull corridor back to his office, desperately trying to figure out what.

Leyton stared after the old man, puzzled. Then he sighed and resumed his exercises. "Any chance of some grub?" he called to the camera.

They woke Alison at some jetlag hour when her body couldn't tell what time it was supposed to be. It must be the early hours though. She was surprised to have been asleep. She felt even more like shit. A hand on her shoulder shook her. She opened her eye.

It was the old man. He was looking kindly at her. The doctor was with him.

She was somewhere else, she realised. She had something over her body.

She was in an operating theatre! She struggled to sit up.

They held her down. Then she realised where she was: just a long tube. She was lying on a medical bench at one end of it. A brain-scanning machine. A nurse was standing nearby.

There must have been something in that syringe besides antibiotics. "What is this, where—?"

"We have a whole hospital down here," the old man said. "For the use of those who used to come over to us. That was the function of this building in the old days. We keep it up to date." It sounded like he wondered why. "Alison, have you ever taken any illegal drugs?"

Alison almost laughed. She didn't see the point in lying. "Yeah."

"Cocaine?" asked the doctor.

"Just the once."

"Heroin? Methadone? Opiates of any kind?"

"No."

The doctor shook his head. "You've got the brain of an addict. The neuro-receptors in your orbital frontal cortex have suffered tremendous damage."

"The what?"

"They process learned behaviour patterns. They help us remember how we achieve specific goals. What patterns work. The neuro-receptors produce or respond to dopamine, which is pleasurable. It's released by the presence of heroin or various other drugs. But those drugs also destroy the receptors. So you get imprinted with the idea that taking the drugs equals pleasure, but stop being able to experience that pleasure."

"Isn't that hellish?" murmured the old man. "The pleasure of a job well done turned into meaningless pleasure at the cost of one's independence. You wonder... how the human race can have come upon such a thing by accident."

He was talking about Capitalism and Communism, Alison thought, trying to lead her into a conversation about it by getting her to make the obvious metaphorical comparison. She was frightened at the thought of brain damage. It was what the Golden Men had put in her eye that had done it. The ideal mechanism for their philosophy. But she wasn't about to tell him that, either.

"I've never taken heroin," she said.

"I believe you," he said. "Come on now, get up and put some clothes on."

Alison realised that she was wearing only a medical smock.

They gave her some bland underwear, trousers and a shirt. She dressed in the room she'd fallen asleep in.

The old man entered just after she'd finished changing. There must be cameras everywhere. The most frightening thing of all was that they hadn't asked her anything yet. She wanted to know what they'd done to Leyton, but she was damned if she was going to ask. Let them ask her. The sweat was still bursting out of her, making her cold. They'd offered her methadone. She'd said no.

"We're going to take you to see your friend," the old man said.

Alison nodded.

He put a hand on her shoulder.

She flinched at it.

"Please don't worry," he said. "Nobody's going to hurt you. You've been through a terrible ordeal."

Alison nodded again quickly and kept her gaze on the floor as they led her off down the corridor.

They unlocked another door, showed her inside and locked it behind her.

Leyton was standing in a bare room, a laboratory of some kind. There were pillows on the walls.

She carefully didn't run over and hold him. They mustn't know he was... valuable to her.

He grinned broadly at her. He didn't look hurt. "Hullo! How's tricks?"

"Could be worse." She mimicked him and moved closer to him, sharing that grin and the eye contact. He understood the situation.

The door opened again, and a man in a labcoat entered. He was carrying a medical tray. And on the tray—

Alison stared.

"Alison," said Leyton, "this is Jocelyn."

The man put the head onto a bench and silently withdrew. They heard the door lock behind him once more.

"Bloody hell," said the head on the tray. "It's Alison Parmeter."

Alison let her mouth open and then close of its own accord. The obvious response was, bloody hell, it's a head on a tray. But she only thought of that a few moments too late. Her brain was still getting used to the whole "no body" thing. The head was staring at her, obviously a little in awe of her.

"This," said the head, "is not what I was briefed for. Pleased to meet you, sister."

"Sister?" Alison's only other thought was that Jocelyn had a weird haircut, kind of an evolved forties look.

Jocelyn raised an eyebrow. "Well, you know how it is."

Alison felt a strange connection to this woman. She walked closer. She almost wanted to touch her, to show some physical affection. But that was impossible. She understood now why these people were regarded as dead. Jocelyn watched her as if she was waiting for her to come to some obvious conclusion.

And then Alison did.

It was the way Leyton had been so careful with what he said in front of her, not just because he knew about her abilities; but as if he had a professional relationship with those abilities. Every day. That hesitancy at the end of the story of her death. He hadn't finished it. He'd thought it would be too horrifying for her. Or maybe it was that taboo in operation again. "Oh," she said.

Twenty: The Missing Reel

June, 2024

"She must not be allowed to die!" The shout came from a sad-eyed old man, standing on the green banks by the hospital. The call was taken up by first a handful, and then thousands of the extras amassed at the real Salisbury Cottage Hospital. The exterior hadn't changed much in the last five years.

Hohiti Kenton checked in with each of his cameras in turn. They had only a day at the site, so he'd chosen to set up a pattern of cameras, all placed out of shot of each other, and do the crowd scenes in one go. The crowds were hard to control; they'd all taken the week off from their voluntary labour and were in a party mood.

He flicked between the monitors, looking at the details. "Bring it down," he said into his mike to four, knowing that his words would go straight to the actor's earpiece.

The original protestor's expression crumbled from anger to despair.

"She must not... she can't..."

Hohiti waited a moment more. "And cut," he said.

October, 2024

The studio set, months later, was a perfect reconstruction of the hospital interior. It even had ceilings, so Hohiti could shoot upwards, giving the scenes at the bedside an echoing quality. The original hospital was still in use. They hadn't even considered asking for permission to film there.

Records of exactly what had gone on in this place five years ago were nonexistent. Hohiti paced the set at dawn, before anyone else was around, wondering, as so many people had wondered before, exactly what the circumstances had been. Everything concerning this phase of Alison Parmeter's life was still cloaked in secrecy. He'd invented a character called Dr Lamb, who'd come up with, in secret, a new neural process designed to transplant heads from one body to another. The doctors attending Alison, in the script, try to give her a new body, and fail, and Lamb decides to risk trying to keep her head alive without the support of a body, to build, for the first time, a functioning system inside the head itself. Such a leap. There was some literature about the theory behind such a process, dating back to the last century. But nobody thought anyone had ever done it. But however unlikely it seemed, there had to have been someone like Lamb. And he had to have gone from theory to successful practice within two weeks. How else could Alison have survived?

She herself hadn't known. Or if she did, she had never said. All papers relating to the aftermath of the terrorist attack had been destroyed, so thoroughly that there had been endless conspiracy theories concerning the motives behind the assault and the results. Some said that President Cranbourne himself had arranged the attack to stir up anti-capitalist feeling, and had never expected it to result in the death of the star. He used secret military technology on Alison, and had all records of the incident wiped. He'd failed in his attempt to get re-elected shortly afterwards. There had been several novels and movies about the espionage angle. But Alison, in Hohiti's view, didn't come out of any of them well. She was just an object, the victim. In telling her life story, he wanted to clear away all that murk and give her a doctor who simply wanted to save her.

Never mind that Lamb perversely faded away, having done his work. If they played that, they'd have had to have had some hokey scene of him saying "no, no, let others take the credit," so they'd decided to have him vanish from the picture as soon as the operation was complete. They stayed with Alison as she adjusted to her new life as a head. The first head. They ended with her big announcement to the world, when she was revealed to be alive and well and broadcast a thank-you speech from the steps of her old home. The announcement was that, all her life, she had been able to read the world, to read whatever was put before her. She had previously put all of that gift into her work, the lyrics of her songs. But she would never sing again for the public. She had composed a religious piece during the siege, the one that the terrorists claimed she had sung to them. (They would do that shot through soundproof glass, these bastards gazing in awe at something the rest of the world would never have.) But nobody else would hear it. No copy of it would ever be found. Like so much else of Alison's later life, it would remain a mystery.

The final scene was a coda, of Alison, as a head, looking at the stars. That was designed to lead into the sequel.

Hohiti turned as he heard someone approaching. It was Russell DaCosta, the medical advisor. He had been called in today to brief the actors on the use of the machines. DaCosta had worked in head design. He was still bound by the Official Secrets Act, but he enjoyed having a vodka with Hohiti late at night and telling all he was allowed to tell. He had a secret smile about him that made the director think, at times, that there was some official blessing for this project coming from somewhere. But such things could never be admitted.

"How is your Dr Lamb today?" Russell asked, slapping Hohiti's shoulder.

"Still bloody not working. Why do you always ask the wrong

questions?"

"Not working? Alex? I thought he was fine—"

"Alex is fine. *He*'s working his arse off. He has to, because the character's not working. He's unreal. He can't exist." Hohiti put a hand to his brow. "Why do I keep putting this off? We've got to find a different way to do this. But we've gone for the hospital scenes. Maybe we could just marginalise him completely, cut from—"

Russell listened sympathetically to Hohiti's train of thought for a while as they wandered to the canteen. "I have read the books of those that were there," he said.

"You mean you were there yourself!"

"And they are all heavily censored. But they point to a person like Lamb."

"But where was he before? After? Why doesn't he appear in the literature of your speciality? What sort of science has no originator, no point of origin?"

"If I knew, I still could not tell you. But I say: go with Lamb. Play him up. Make him larger-than-life. The audience will know. They will say, ah, here is the start of the myth, here is a noble spot of mythologising, rather than all this grubby theorising."

Hohiti stopped and thought for a moment. Yes, that could be a way to go. He made eye contact with Russell, and frowned as a thought struck him. "Am I being *instructed* to do this?"

"Instructed? Who am I to instruct the great director? I am an advisor, and that is my advice. You enjoy this business of secrecy a bit too much, I think."

Hohiti shook his head and went to get his advisor a coffee.

That night, frustrated with the way the scene was going, Hohiti looked over the technical papers again. He'd prepared these with both *Alison* and the sequel, *Alison and the Stars*, in mind. He had some of Alison's music on in the background, as he often did. He had read, he thought, everything there was to read about her. He could teach a course on her. He loved her as only someone who studies someone who is gone can.

The process by which Alison, and the heads that followed her, read the details of the world was called Mirroring. Mirror neurons occurred in a region of the brain called F5, part of the premotor cortex. When you watched someone else performing a task, these neurons fired, as they also did if you were performing a mechanical task yourself. Mirror neurons were what allowed people to learn by watching, and to empathise with and understand other people's experiences and emotions. Hohiti remembered teaching his sister to drive a fuel cell lorry, how his feet had unconsciously stamped on nonexistent pedals in the passenger seat. That was mirroring at work. It was also linked to the origins of language, that feeling of wanting to *say something* when she'd got into the wrong gear, of itching to hit the pedals himself when she needed to brake. That was how people had first started talking to each other. Mirroring was also about "gut feeling." The F5 area didn't just compare the state of the rest of the brain to other people's actions. It compared it to reactions from the spinal column and from the "second brain," the cluster of neurons in the stomach lining. The human body always had its own second opinion, giving rise to all those notions of duality, of heart and head, of there being something more than just us.

Alison Parmeter had, through whatever process of nature, been born with an extremely large and complex F5 region in her brain. And once she'd become a head... Hohiti let the page drop from his hands. He was still amazed at the leap. It was like the divine touching the Earth. Without a gut or a spine to refer to, it was said that Alison immediately found something missing in her perceptions, that she described the sensation of loss so accurately that her scientist friends attached her to a quantum computer.

Instead of reading people or events, or, Hohiti smiled, the locations of fish and chip restaurants, Alison had found that, with her new connection, she could read the universe. And so she had the biggest idea in human history. All these were to be the first scenes of the sequel.

Not that any of them rang true.

Instead of referencing her gut, Alison had found a way to reference the state of all the possible realities that could be formed at any given moment. It was something, she said, that heads without bodies ought to be able to learn to do. Her abilities had been unusual in that she had developed them while having a body. Living heads with no body to respond to ought to be able to expand their F5 region, just as cabbies expanded the region of their brain that handled geography when they learnt "the Knowledge." There was something about that thought that had always astonished Hohiti, the idea that thinking about something changed one's brain so it could think about that something harder, that thought could change matter. But he was certain that was true. Unlike the whole matter of how Alison had supposedly taken humanity to the stars on her own. Which was nonsense.

The papers slipped from his hands. His head slumped forward. And he slept.

And dreamed.

The scenes of the new movie. The only thing he'd thought about for months.

They'd asked the World's Sweetheart if she wanted to take them into the universe. And she'd said: damn right. (Alison being taken into the ship.

People throwing petals to her on the steps.) They'd sent her up in an orbital spacecraft, the sort they'd used to ferry crews to the Station on their way to the Moonbase or to Mars. (Her face settling into peace as the capsule orbited the beautiful jewel of the world below.) She'd started relating unconsciously to the suggestions of her new quantum gut.

(The first fuzziness of the first dreaming about the hull. And then nothing where there had been a spacecraft. Cut to Proxima Centauri. The giant star. The tiny new star blazing into life in the bottom corner of the frame.)

She walked them to Proxima Centauri that day. They'd had only so much fuel for manoeuvring. They'd expected to go to Mercury. But everybody had been saying, so the story went, that she would take them to the stars, so she'd just gone there.

(The crew staring at the sights outside. Alison smiling. Are we there yet?)

So they'd taken as many photos as their film allowed, and recorded all their data, and had encouraged her to quite swiftly dream them home again. Her pilot, Major Anna Knight, had sent the data by radio beam; it was now on its way to Earth beforehand, in case they never made it home.

(The tension of the preparation for the return journey. Everyone keeping a smile on their faces. Much banter. Nobody talking about the possibilities of not getting home.)

When they did, Knight had apparently been quite surprised.

(Cut to the future.) After that, head after head, recruited from the dying, had gone into space. They all had the option of that or being allowed to die. Not one of them had taken it. There was, however, a personal horror to all this. Wives felt overjoyed that their husbands had come back from the edge of death, but then to have them without bodies, doing such demanding work, away almost all the time... It had become clear that this was too much to bear. (Alison, talking to other heads, realising that they were a class apart.) Heads swiftly came to be regarded as still being dead. They had gone beyond the veil, and though active, they stayed there, and their loved ones moved on.

(Adventures in space. Meeting the first foreigners, all the different beasts: creatures with the faces of leopards and wings on their backs, and many heads. A menagerie of things that would once have been terrifying. Befriending them. Alison's ship narrowly missing a Rod ship, the first encounter that was not quite a meeting, a presentiment of the current tense negotiations with these most worrying of foreigner races. Looking at the receding shape, making conclusions every second.)

And then autumn. The idea that heads had a finite life too, that the systems decayed like all systems did after the second birth. These days heads could live a human lifetime, longer even, but not then. Her second death, only two years after the first, had created a new tradition, resulting in a second funeral, new plaudits, a gravestone which became a place where all those who were searching for something arrived, in books and movies and in life.

And never the final music. Nobody ever found it or heard it. And some said it had been concealed by the same authorities that concealed how her second life, that had been the most important lived by a modern human, had come to be. Perhaps she had wanted it that way.

End credits. Music.

Hohiti woke up with a start, a hand on his shoulder.

It was Russell. He'd snuck into Hohiti's office and caught him with his papers on his lap, snoring. "So," he said. "Having slept on it, what do you think about Dr Lamb?"

Hohiti rubbed a hand back through his hair. "I suppose... we can't *know*. Not yet. We're going to have to make a leap of faith for something, a character that fills in the gaps of a historical personage, that represents someone, perhaps many people. At least it shows us where those gaps are. We'll invest in Lamb, with all our heart, and hope they buy it."

"Good," said Russell.

Twenty-One: God in the Machine

"Indeed," said Jocelyn.

They both looked at Leyton.

"What?" he said.

Jocelyn inclined her head to Alison, an odd little bob that was how it must be to nod without a body. "They'll have this room bugged, you know. That's why they've put us together."

"I don't know, the old man seemed..." Alison realised that if he was as nice as he seemed, she was giving him away now. "But does it matter? What can we do about anything now?"

"Come on, Joss," said Leyton, butting into their conversation. "If anyone knows a way out of this fix, you do."

Jocelyn raised her eyes towards a corner of the room where Alison gathered she'd spotted a camera. She'd kind of got the idea there was one there too, only it hadn't appeared to be very important. Her head was still reeling from the idea of what happened to her in Leyton's future, of how she became a head. She was going to have to ask Leyton how that happened. But not right now.

Looming things were looking down on her at this moment.

"You know," said Jocelyn, playing to the camera, "I hadn't any idea of how to do that until I was told they were bringing me here. To the Fitzroy Hotel."

"Yes," began Leyton. "How—?"

Jocelyn continued over him, "These chaps forced certain information out of me. The basics of what our future is like. And that was terribly dull of them—"

Alison saw the flash of anger in Leyton's eyes.

"But in doing that, they made me cut loose a bit, showed me a few stops on the cosmic grand tour. So they needn't feel guilty. All their sins against this one are forgiven. And as the result of all that, yes, now I rather think I do know a way out of this fix. Call it thinking on my feet." She glanced at Alison. "Darling, what have they done to your eye?"

Alison had been only half listening. Was it the cold turkey that was making her feel this, or was there something else? She'd been looking into the corners of the room. She was being observed, yes, obviously. But it felt like... Like this was an important bit, and important bits were watched by things beyond this room. The Golden Men? No. Something... something that was a pattern, something they were inside. All of them. It felt like her dad's horrible urgency. It smelled of church wood.

And now that thing was about to give itself away. It was in the wings.

It was going to make a surprise entrance. Stage left.

Oh, bugger. She wanted to ask the same question Leyton did, about how Jocelyn had known that she would end up in this building. But this feeling of immanence was stopping her. She got the feeling that she really didn't want to know.

She realised, a moment later, what Jocelyn had said to her.

"Show me, you poor thing."

Hesitantly, Alison reached for the dressing, and took it off. She knew what the wound looked like: she'd stared at it in the mirror enough when she'd had to clean it. A reddened, scabbed socket led to a deep mass of dark scabbing right at the back, further in than looked possible. There was nothing, she had realised, looking at it through the tears of her one good eye, between that barrier and what remained of her optic nerve. She could poke her fingers into her brain if she wanted to.

Jocelyn made a noise. For a moment, Alison thought she'd clucked in sympathy. But then she realised it wasn't a mouth noise.

"Pick me up, skipper," she said. "I want to get a closer look."

Leyton grabbed the head and lifted it up. There was something odd, Alison saw, in the stump of the neck: a white spur that had emerged from a tiny metal plate, flush against the metal that covered the base of the neck. Just where Jocelyn's spinal cord would have been.

The spur shot out. It was on the end of a thin line of optical wire. Alison could see lights playing inside it.

"So," said Jocelyn. "Shall we go?"

Leyton stared at her. "Joss, what is that?"

"Special equipment. Just in case. I got all the bells and whistles for this mission." She lowered her voice and looked Alison in the eye. "You can do this. We can travel in time. Brain to brain. Head to head."

Alison realised, a moment later, what was being asked of her, and felt her stomach heave.

There had been so much pain so far.

To take on so much pain again. She couldn't do it.

But she knew that only intellectually, she realised, like getting pregnant for the second time. Your body only remembered that this was a rollercoaster she'd been on before. This was why she had been born a woman, so she could handle such pain. Maybe this was why there *were* women and men.

No, she mustn't start thinking like that. She was going mad.

"Why me?" she said. And she meant it.

But she didn't wait. She grabbed the white spur, which felt like bone between her fingers. She saw that Leyton was about to say that she didn't have to do this if she didn't want to, that they'd find another way. He wasn't even sure what they were about to do, and still he was going to say that.

She didn't want his feelings for her to stop this.

She stuck her fingers into her eye socket and ripped the scar tissue away.

She remembered the pain as it hit her. She nearly threw up.

She took the plug of bone. And she shoved it into the socket.

Light shot into her head. She could see two things at once.

She heard the door crash open.

"Hang on," Jocelyn said to her. Then she said lots of other things in a moment. At once. On top of each other. And Alison's brain replied to every thing.

And then the light was in the room.

And they were on their way.

Alison understood all of this at a distance.

It was like being really pissed, and finding that a bit of your brain was looking at bus numbers and taxi ranks and getting you home without you being involved. Or seeing video of what you were saying when you were really caned, like Marty had done to her once. All this story that you're in, but you weren't there for that.

So this was a mixture of what she felt at the time and what she put together afterwards when it had stopped happening.

They got out of the room. The room was damaged as they left it; it sort of bloomed open. That hurt the people who were coming through the door.

They wrenched and twisted, and there must have been a lot of pain. The wrenching was because this was a rough version of how things were supposed to be. This was like a parachute. An emergency escape. Not pleasant.

She could feel Leyton still beside her. He was holding on to her body and Jocelyn's head. Those three physical bits were sliding along beside them. They couldn't think now. Thoughts were choices. If/thens. The dream that Jocelyn was stitching together was making all the choices, choices she was comparing at a speed so fast the answers came before the questions with the same facility inside Alison. The two of them together could do this.

They were looking for something familiar. The choice of a parachutist. You can't go to another country, just pick the softest place beneath you. Nearly a fictional parachutist dream. Not good. Jocelyn wrenched Alison away from that. She was unschooled. She had to work at this! They had the time sorted. They needed a place.

Alison knew her city, and so did Leyton, so Jocelyn fed on that.

They went into smoothness, into proper dreaming. There was the interstellar, the big human dream of the future.

Then they hit the rapids. The wound in spacetime. The thing that was supposed and not supposed to be here, but just was. It was deep red outside.

They went straight through it. They encountered things, visions, fragments of big dreams that Alison would find herself dwelling on for mornings afterwards. Dwelling on as in: had that thought been a dream or... what thought?

The four Golden Men were there. They were the inhabitants of this stretch of the river. They had been born here, Alison got the feeling. They didn't like to admit that. They were a human number. She and Leyton and Jocelyn were there as well. All just standing there, to be played.

So they got where they wanted to go as redefined by this tear in the world. There wasn't anywhere else to go to, at the moment. The rip was the defining place of how everything went, the omphalos, the centre of the wheel. It was off-centre. The beams across the wheel would make the world jerk along until it was righted.

Stupid thought.

Was that a dream?

What had she been thinking?

She could see something through her other eye again, the one that had been looking inside.

There was water as far as the eye could see.

Alison and Leyton stood on the side of a rainwashed black hill, holding Jocelyn. The wind cut into them. They must have appeared from nowhere, though Alison had no idea of how. Her boots were planted in the muddy grass like she'd just woken up standing there. They were a couple of yards from a shore of long reeds and mud.

There were islands in the water, chains of them, here and there, to the point where the eye lost them in the low cloud. Dark shapes loomed up from the water. The air tasted foul. Alison started to cough. It was like a syrup had settled on her tongue. Dirt. Smoke. She snorted it out of her nose. The water shimmered with rainbows. The daylight was diffuse above, the sun lost in layers of mist.

Alison reached up and took the link from her eye. The wound opened up and started bleeding again. She grabbed for her handkerchief, but Leyton was there with his, holding her upright. He'd put Jocelyn down in the tall wet grass. He took off his belt and started to bind the handkerchief to Alison's head.

"Well," said Jocelyn. "Here we are."

"Where?" asked Leyton. "Are we home?"

"It's certainly our year of departure, Skip. But not our future. It's the only future currently in existence, the future that arises from that past we just came from."

"What... what is this thing?" asked Alison, staring at the bloodstained probe in her hand.

Jocelyn made the noise again and the spur shot away on the end of its line, vanishing into the base of her neck once more. "It's an emergency mechanism," she said. "A head normally compares itself to the computers in its ship. But two of us can compare ourselves to each other."

"Two of us," said Alison. Her head was still reeling. She needed to have space to think about the idea she'd had just before they'd left. It was the biggest idea she'd ever encountered. She couldn't read it all at once. What Jocelyn was talking about paled beside it. "I'm going to be a head." That was the easy bit.

"After you die, yes." Jocelyn confirmed that coolly.

Alison pushed away from Leyton's explanations and stumbled off up the hill, her boots slipping in the mud. Her body hurt as well as her eye. She still felt feverish and shivery. It was the opiates in her brain. She was going to feel like this for a long time. She made her way, slipping and sliding, up to the brow of the hill. The wind was worse here; it got through the thin clothes the intelligence men had given her.

On the other side of the hill there was more water, more islands. Buildings sat, low and lowering, on some of them. A few were forested, the trees with sooty or silver bark, like metal filings standing upright on a rusty magnet. A chain of the islands stood in a rough circle. In the centre, three spires broke the waves, encrusted black and green. One of them was a church, the other the familiar peak of the Abbey, one of them a mast of some sort, a telephone thing, an ugly building she didn't recognise. The shapes of other buildings lay under the lake, making it dark under the rainbows.

"Bath," she said.

And then she fell unconscious.

Twenty-Two: John's Apocalypse

June, 95 AD

John sat on a rock, throwing stones into the Aegean. The sea was flat and blue today and reflected the sky. There was no breeze. He sat at the tip of the northern arc of the island with his back to the mountain, as far from the town as it was possible to be. He wore his priestly robes. He was gazing out at the circle of little islets that formed a ring in the water with Patmos itself, watching an eagle slide over the water.

Judas could see that he was deep in thought. He was probably thinking of Ephesus, wondering if he would ever get to see the city again. John was an old man. They both were. The authorities knew John had been one of the Twelve, that, together with Peter and James, Jesus' brother, he was the authority on Christianity. These three were the ones who'd seen the man Paul start the whole movement up again, to mobilise it when it looked like Christos worship would become a scattered cult like so many Judas had encountered, this despite the fact that John had violently disagreed with Paul's desire to let the non-Jews fully enter the church. That was *changing* things. John had always hated change. He didn't enjoy the speed of history like Judas did. Getting old hadn't helped with that.

But John's life, now he was eminent, had always been spared. They said he ranted, and was taken over by... well, they didn't want to call them demons. Judas was sure John knew, in his milder moments, that he could be fearsome when he was so inspired. Jesus had laughingly called him and his brother *Boanerges*, the sons of thunder, because their voices were loud and strident in defence of the cause. He'd made sure there was always laughter about that, as if he was uneasy with it. Judas had heard the Master raise his voice only twice.

Judas had been on the island of Patmos for a week. He had heard John had been exiled here. He did not get letters from the others who remained; how could he? But he heard the gossip in the churches he attended under his new name, so he had come to see that he was all right. He had so desperately wanted to approach John directly and tell him of his family, his two boys and the girl with the piercing eyes who could count the number of apples in the orchard while they were still on the bough. But no, he was dead to John now. He wasn't even sure the old man's frame would be able to stand the news of his "resurrection." James, his brother, hadn't been that much older, but he'd been in his grave for many years.

John had been causing trouble on the mainland. Women again, in the sense that he could never trust them. He had started a fight, by letter from Ephesus, and finally, on a trip to see the churches in old Pergamum, in person, with the priestess in charge of the church at Thyatira. As far as Judas could tell, the row was about whether women had to try harder than men to free themselves from sin if they were to enter the Kingdom. The priestess had replied to all John's letters with kindness, and finally demurred to John's wisdom, but had made the mistake of not finally and utterly submitting her will to that of the great man. She had never actually accepted his thesis. Judas remembered the Master having a conversation with John's own mother on the subject, and taking quite the opposite stance to the one that her son was taking now. But old John was allowed his rants. Or so everyone thought.

Perhaps the Governor of Asia had been paying close attention to the letters he received from Diocletian. The Emperor had discovered that a number of those plotting against him in the capital were Christians, and had put the world on an alert to watch for subversive activity from the sect. This was, as everyone who followed the news from Rome knew, so much bluster. It was designed entirely to cover the fact that Diocletian had used the charge of heresy against the Gods of Rome to lock up the conspirators who were about to put a knife in his ribs. But the Governor could hardly act like he knew that. He could hardly do nothing.

So when the legionaries of old Pergamum found a mad old man tearing the paint off the walls of Christ's church in Thyatira, and attempting vainly to throw its Priestess to the ground while encouraging the gathering crowd to assault her... well, that was the nearest he was going to get to something he could tell the Emperor. It must have been the toss of a die as to whether John or the Priestess got exiled, but Judas supposed John's leadership status decided it. The exile was for six months, and John had been allowed to take what belongings he could with him, and leave the rest in safe keeping. It was, in short, the lightest possible punishment. Nothing that would get the Christians... especially those from the Thyatirian church... sitting in the street outside the Governor's palace in Pergamum City.

Judas really didn't know why he'd come, except that he cared for John as one of the last of the twelve. The Apostle had been given lodgings and food by friends on the island. He was fine. And Judas had finally decided that, though this might be the last he saw of his old friend, he was not going to approach him and make his first and last attempt at reconciliation. He would have had more luck with Peter, but that would still be no luck at all.

Judas was going to turn away and head south to the town, to find a boat to take him back to the mainland, but then he heard a noise.

It was a young girl, the daughter of some fisherman. She couldn't have been more than fourteen. She was visibly with child. She was coming up the path towards them both: John on his rock and Judas in an olive grove a few feet away. Judas stepped back behind the trees. He would not have John noticing him by accident.

He saw John turn at the sound and stare, his brow furrowed, as the girl approached him. His eyes were fixed on her stomach. "Child," he said to her in Greek that still carried a Jewish accent after all these years, "are you married?"

And then the light changed.

Judas automatically stepped back behind the tree. It was like a new sun had come out on this brilliant day, like the Lord was suddenly with them. Judas' body, if not his mind, had learned to be afraid of such newness.

He peered carefully from behind the tree again. John was on his knees, his head bowed towards the girl—or rather, towards what stood above the girl.

An angel. He was robed, with a golden sash. His skin was blazing, afire, a new sun indeed. He was holding something in the fist of his left hand. From his mouth extended a tiny point of light. Judas stared at it. His tongue. The angel had a sword for a tongue. His face was passive, settled, like this wonder was the most natural, ordinary thing. The look reminded Judas of his Master, long ago. But the angel didn't have his Master's peaceful bearing, his easy gait. This was not the Lamb.

Judas chided himself for being so slow to throw himself to his knees. Was this his curse, to be cast out of the light, again and again? But it occurred to him, as he thought this, that his being cast out had been part of his Master's plan then, and perhaps this was why he was made this way, and that he would wait to worship as long as he damned well pleased if the end was his Lord's end.

So he was a witness that lived outside the light. Again. But for years now, he had known the light in himself, and needed no angel to show it to him.

Therefore he listened and watched and commissioned those things he saw to memory, trusting that he was there for a parallel purpose to John's.

The girl was speaking now, in a small voice that was gentle as the water on the shore. She was speaking for the angel. She said that he had a message for John, and new words for him to spread as far as he could. He was to be told the secret of the way this world would end, a new interpretation of the prophecies of Daniel.

Judas was shocked. His father had always said the world would end, and he had never believed it. It was one of those things, like the way the Law of Moses dealt with food, that the Master had said was secondary, something aside from the Kingdom. Himself, he had always assumed the Kingdom would arrive here, in the world, and that everyone would live like the Twelve had lived.

And that he would have a seat beside his Master at the table again.

The end of this world would not allow that. Judas swallowed the fear and the hurt. He *liked* the world. He was *of* it. He loved what the Master had been within it, not without it.

How soon? But the girl did not say. She was listing to John the churches he should first write to with the messages that would follow: all the largest seats of the Lord in Greece and Pergamum. He should use his authority to identify himself, and offer details of who he was, that those churches would believe that the revelation to follow was given with all his faith and was not written by someone else in his name.

"Those who believe must know," said the girl, "the whole world must come to know, that all things must end. That there will be an end to this world, when the accounting will be done, when the value of each man will be assessed, when those who deserve it will be rewarded and those who have to pay the price will do so. Let them live in fear and respect of this end."

Judas felt like grabbing a rock and running at the angel. Was this what he had heard at his Master's side? No. He had heard the promise of brotherhood, of eternal life. Was he here to stop this, to save John? Surely he would not be required to smash everything twice?

The girl asked John to rise and approach the angel. He did so. The angel opened its fist and offered the old man something.

John reached out and took it.

Judas strained to see what it was. A little scroll, so small that surely nothing of importance could be written on it?

"Eat," said the girl. "Understand what we have done to the world, to what has been, and what is to be. Let them know of the changes."

John didn't hesitate a moment. He grabbed the scroll and popped it into his mouth. He chewed quickly, painfully, swallowing it.

The girl and the angel watched him for a moment. Then he cried out and fell to the ground. He started to thrash, his robes sending up clouds of dust which rolled up over the angel in the gentle breeze, but didn't tarnish his golden skin.

"The whore!" he shouted. "The horses! My lord Apollyon, I see you on the horse! The sevens in the sevens in the sevens!"

Judas closed his eyes and made himself continue listening. He had not seen one of John's fitful possessions in decades. He found it as distressing now as he had then. He had always talked about sevens. They had been right about John at the time: he was not possessed by demons. But Judas felt, in his heart, and did not know what to do with the thought, that he certainly was now. Perhaps he always had been, across time, seen from another angle, ready for this angel that he called by that near-Roman name, Apollyon.

He didn't understand that thought that his nature had thrown into his head. He was taking in John's yells, the story of war and punishment and famine and debt that he was rutting at the world. The promise of punishment, the taking on of wrath. All this had been absent in the things Judas had thought he stood for. Even Paul, the eager reteller of a truth he had not entirely heard, had not talked of this, though he had let a little of his human anger into his new expressions of the good news. The Apostle shouted of the return of Nero, as the Romans had always whispered, but he seemed to mean that there would be many Neros, for he named many dictators, foes he shouted should be overthrown. "The Beast is the Beast!" he said. "Six hundred and sixty-six!"

That was a riddle of the kind the old men used to make on the steps of the Temple. One for the first letter, two for the second. "I love her who is 545," as the little boys would chant. Judas understood it immediately. *Therion*, the Greek for beast. If you said it in Hebrew, you got a love letter for 666.

Why did the angel want to include a simple trick like that in a prophecy?

As a snare, the answer came. A lure to set one thing against another. "545" could be any of the girls down the lane. "666" could be any leader, any fool.

John finally came to a halt, panting. He raised himself to a kneeling position again and thanked the angel for showing him this revelation. The girl thanked him in return. The angel fluttered, changed its shape to that of empty air and scrolled away.

John got to his feet, looking at the girl. "So," he said finally. "Whose child is it you bear?" Judas could see he wanted it to be the angel's, so he could regard her as without sin, a new Mary.

"That of a friend of my father," she said. "He has paid me to keep silent. But I could not be silent to the Apostle. My path is chosen by the angels. They will protect me and let me thrive." Then she turned on her heel, her message delivered, and walked off down the path.

John stood for a while, not wishing to follow her. He was halfway between disgust and awe. He did not know the flavour of his message, only that it suited him for it to go one way, being clothed as it was in the guise of the lust he hated, within himself, and without.

Judas knew all this from one look, as he knew everything.

John set off as fast as his old legs could carry him. He looked certain of the story he was going to tell now, certain that his faith had been proved: that he had seen a being that lived beside the Lord in heaven.

And Judas, watching, was not sure of anything, not sure of what he was going to do about the sights he had seen today. *Antichristos*, John had lurched. But Christ was in all of them. And so, it seemed, the Antichrist was now going to be. The Son of Man, and... the opposite. Two men at odds. But that should not be so. Because, surely, the Master would say, they're the same thing. We contain both. Christ and Antichrist are the same man, even split across time.

Judas could not make it make sense, even with his skills. He knew only that he would tell the story to his daughter with the sharp eyes and see what they could make of it together. He could not see his Master in any of this, except he knew that his Master triumphed through not being in any of this. Not in the dust an old man raised by his humping the world, anyway.

He waited until he would not encounter his old friend on the road. Then he headed for the harbour, wanting to get home like a man with a ghost at his back. Though he had several days' travel ahead of him, he would do them at speed.

Twenty-Three: Alison and the Flood

April, 2129, but different

Leyton, Jocelyn and Alison sat together on the shore, Alison's unconscious form wrapped in Leyton's coat. She looked so vulnerable with her eyes closed, he thought. Such a child. He would rather look at her than at the city. The old city of him and Elsie, flooded and empty. The springs, he supposed, would be bubbling up amidst the dark waters somewhere here, lost in the deluge. There were many new buildings he didn't recognise, glimpsed beneath the shifting, rainbowing waves. In the distance he could see shapes that would be Coombe Down, Oldfield Park, Pennsylvania... the shapes of a series of stepped buildings, with masts and perhaps washing and what looked like flags on top. Their own island was only a hundred yards across, a sandbank covered with seagrass, with a crumbling cliff. Leyton wondered which sloping field this had been. It was the oldest buildings that disturbed him, the spires that poked from the central basin. He could imagine the vault of the Abbey full of water, the fish that lived in there and the alien life that squirmed around the lectern.

It felt as if Whatmore was down there. As if, somehow, he and Elsie and Alison were all down there.

Alison murmured in her sleep, things he couldn't quite hear. Horses, she said, at one point. He hoped she dreamed of a green meadow somewhere. The rain spattered down on them. They could leave again, of course, once Alison had recovered, but where was there to go? His world had been wiped. Alison's past led to this future. He was relying on Jocelyn's absurd confidence. And she'd told him to save his questions until she'd worked something out.

"Ah-ha!" Jocelyn said.

He turned to look at her. "Figured it out, have you?"

"Rather. I've been checking my internal computer resources, trying to work out what the world is like with this level of flooding. There's some good news. There should be significant landmasses, Skipper. Still quite a lot of Europe. And there's a touch of Britain left too, northwards. Which is good. Because that's where we have to go."

"Do we? Why?"

Jocelyn managed a smile. "I've seen the map. The plan of how all space and time fits together. I don't remember everything, but I understood the shape of it. There are points where things get joined up. Up north from here is one of them. A place and time where a jump, through that rift, from one time and space to another is made. Or rather, it will be, in about a

241

week. I planned ahead for that, you see."

"A jump? How? There's some other way to get out of this world? Or do we just have to go north and then have you two jump us out again?"

"I don't know. Really. I assume something will crop up."

"So... this map included things that haven't happened yet?"

"Of course it did. It was a map of everything that's written, past, present and future, and all the ins and outs and rewritings."

"So we're going to go north, find whatever we have to find and do this hopping around in time whether we like it or not?"

"Not at all. It may be written, but I think we have to do the writing."

"But what if we do something else?"

"Then another spiral is added to this whole bloody mess. Another map is slapped onto the table across the last one. But I think there's something underlying all the maps, a greater structure. I have faith that it will all work out the way it's supposed to."

"Faith indeed, Joss. We're not even off this rock yet."

From across the water, there came the sound of a claxon. A dark shape was moving swiftly towards them, with the chug of an engine. A human shape appeared at its summit and started waving to them.

Leyton looked down at the head beside him.

She looked smugly back at him.

The owner of the craft was a stocky man in an oilskin who stared at Jocelyn open-mouthed.

Leyton told him something like the truth, that she was the beneficiary of new medical technology. He came round to the idea quite quickly, and showed little interest in how they came to be stranded on this rock, or what was wrong with Alison, taking them immediately to have been shipwrecked. He offered to save them, for a price. He was, it turned out, what he described as a free ferryman who was for hire. His trade normally consisted of running people between the North and South Islands, which roughly approximated to North Wales and the South Downs. There were a series of artificial platforms and larger islands around here where scattered communities still lived, and he'd been delivering packages to some of them. It was lucky he was passing.

Leyton glanced at Jocelyn. Luck had nothing to do with it.

He found it hard to haggle terms with the man. The ferryman didn't recognise Alison's currency, and seemed astounded that they didn't have "chips" in their hands, which would, apparently, provide some kind of credit. That, he appeared to think, made them into fugitives. He was finally, having weighed some in his hands, persuaded of the value of the metals contained within the coins. After a while, Leyton let Jocelyn do the bargaining. It was more than he could stomach, the thought that this child of the dirt would actually leave them there if they didn't give him something. He finally took ten of the weighty gold-coloured coins in exchange for passage. He helped Leyton lift Alison and Jocelyn onto his boat, which had a furled sail the ferryman said he had no idea how to use, and a small, chugging engine which he had switched off the very moment he didn't need it. Leyton wondered that he didn't ask for payment for the lifting.

They headed off across the water and the ferryman, having set their course, came back on deck to talk to them. Leyton asked after the major power structures, nations or groups in this part of the world. The man talked of gangs, some of whom were distantly allied with, or claimed the protection of, the "launch authorities," who you could pay to take you off-planet. There were still a few reasonably large settlements, but the ferryman stayed clear of those. Unless you had corporate protection, and big credit to buy lots of fuel, it was dangerous to go near. The only reason someone went to a city was to sell themselves into prostitution, to get food and lodging in return for sexual favours. There were no public security services, only private ones that you could hire for the duration. There were small wars everywhere. A map in the cabin kept him aware of the latest declarations of territory and conquest from the warlords, all of whom claimed to be the emperor of all Britain. He was running drugs and guns for at least five of them, he stated proudly, three of whom were at war with each other.

The situation reminded Leyton of the world he'd conjured up in his head to explain Alison's reality to himself when he'd first landed there. In his timeline, the pretenders had seized either large areas for weeks, or tiny "kingdoms" for a few years. It had taken all his capacity for fooling himself to believe that something as stable as Alison's Bath could have existed in the sporadic rebellions he'd read of in the latter years of the twentieth century. But this was chaos made real, every hand against another, Alison's terrible world made a hundred times worse.

The ferryman finally appreciated the mood of his passengers and retired to the wheelhouse. Alison had been given a bunk downstairs. Jocelyn had given the sailor directions to take them as far north as possible, to what the man vaguely referred to as the Great North. "Or previously," she said, "the Peak District."

Leyton stood holding onto the rail, looking out at the reflecting water as it grew dark. They were sailing into open sky, the clouds giving way behind them. Jocelyn had been strapped into a small net and left to hang from a hook on the wall of the cabin. It was the kind of free-floating experience heads preferred, and, she said, she didn't get seasick that way. They watched the sky darken, waiting to see stars they'd recognise as spacefarers did. Their eyes adjusted to the dark and they found their first one, too bright, low against the horizon.

"That's got to be a station," said Jocelyn.

"A touch not bright enough."

"Brighter than Venus, though. Wait a sec." She closed her eyes, accessing her internal maps. "It's Mars."

"Mars?" Leyton's eyes fixed on the glittering coin in the sky. Yes, it did have a reddish tinge. But around it... there was a halo. Like you could see around Earth from a distance. The shipyards, the elevators... "They're doing construction work." He called the ferryman onto the deck.

"That's Mars," he said. "Paradise. They're making it into new Earth. Those who can afford it have gone."

"And what's on this paradise?" asked Jocelyn.

"Big towns. Big roads. Companies that employ all, provide houses for all."

"And the Golden Men?" asked Leyton.

The ferryman frowned at him like he was mad. "What're you talking about?"

"I'm paying," said Leyton. "I can be as mad as I like."

The ferryman shrugged and headed back to his wheelhouse.

"They stay behind the scenes," said Jocelyn. "Even now they've got the human race to bugger up the world and have started work on the next one."

They were silent for a while, Leyton's gaze taking in the red light that reflected off the water and the shape of distant islands. "So," he said finally, "are you going to tell me?"

"Tell you what, Skip?"

"How you knew, before we crashed, that we would meet again at the Fitzroy Hotel?"

"Oh," said Jocelyn again.

Alison woke. She couldn't remember her dreams. Something about the ocean; somebody had been telling her something really important, that she had to tell to someone important again, and it was kind of like a storybook thing. But it wasn't there in the day. She'd forgotten so much.

She was going to be a head. After she was killed. She was brought back as a head. That was really important, so... the first head?

Shit. She didn't know how to think about that.

Not that it was going to happen now. Maybe. Possibly.

She concentrated on the here and now.

She was lying under a rough, scratchy blanket. It was dark. There was wood all around her. Movement. She reached out a hand and found that she was lying in a bunk with a wooden surround. Another bunk loomed over her.

She put a hand to her eye and found a clean dressing there. Leyton must have taken care of that. No pain at all. A sense of local numbing. Like Jocelyn had had some anaesthetics handy. Or maybe she just wasn't awake enough to feel it yet. She still felt desperate for something she didn't understand, like she was bashing her head against a wall. She couldn't work it out. The wood around her was creaking to a regular rhythm.

A ship. She was on a ship.

She let her head slip back onto the pillow. The air was better. There was salt. They were at sea. And she had obviously been looked after. So she was in no danger. Nothing to be done.

She tried to sleep again, and couldn't. She found that the sides of her mind kept sneaking around to plans to get back in touch with the Golden Men so that they could put their thing back in her eye, their control mechanism. She desperately wanted it, in exactly the way she'd wanted that particular toy for her birthday when she was six. In exactly the way that the right pair of shoes was supposed to make you feel better about anything in your life. In the way that chocolate stood in for sleep, or, as she'd always said to Fran, God, when you hadn't had enough of it.

But she knew she wasn't going to try and get in touch with them. She had had the strength to pull her eye out in defiance of them. She had seen what they'd done to Fran. She didn't know where that strength had come from.

So she was going to be awake and hurting. So she was going to think.

So she was going to think about the huge things that had come into her head before she and Jocelyn had got them out of the hotel. She didn't want to. She felt threatened by the thoughts that had accumulated around this stuff.

Like she'd said: Leyton's commanders had given him a brand new head, whom he'd never met before. She had equipment that he wasn't even aware existed, like she was on a special mission. They'd let him play about in orbit in the middle of wartime. Leyton had given her some of the flavour of the late days of the war, that there was no longer any threat inside the solar system, that they were pursuing a routed enemy, far off. But still, you don't let your pilots go on risky pleasure flights when they're on leave, do you? Or maybe you did. Maybe she was reading too much into this.

Still, Jocelyn had said she would meet Leyton at the Fitzroy Hotel. And she'd survived a crash that Leyton had assumed would kill her, without a scratch. And when they'd met she'd told Alison that this wasn't what she'd been briefed for. Which meant, if it wasn't just flippancy, and Jocelyn apparently valued accuracy in everything she said, that she'd been briefed for *something*. Before a pleasure cruise.

Alison didn't want to lie here and have this work itself out in her head. She wanted to be around people when she got there.

She hauled herself over the side of the bed, steadied herself against the rolling of the ship and stumbled towards the door.

She tottered out onto the deck and found that it was night. She made her way round the rail, staring at the stars and getting the cold and the sea spray in her face. The stars hadn't changed; she recognised the constellations. She saw Mars, and understood what it was immediately. The natural parallel to what things were like down here.

They probably had rain on Mars now. They'd learn to have too much of it.

She recognised the silhouette of Leyton near the bow. The cap and the coat. His voice was raised. He was trying to order Jocelyn to do something, and she was refusing to do it.

To do something. Or to tell something.

Alison stumbled up to them and grabbed Leyton's arm for support. He nearly reacted, in anger and surprise, nearly yelled at her too. But he didn't. His rage became concern in the shape of rage. Exasperation.

"Alison, you shouldn't be—"

"I'm here to be on your side. Jocelyn, you have to tell us."

Jocelyn raised an eyebrow. She obviously was starting to resent having another head around. "Why do I have to tell you?"

"Because I'm your commanding officer!" yelled Leyton.

"Because he told me how I was going to die," said Alison. "He trusted me with that. If not the bit about becoming a head."

Leyton only realised then. "Oh. I really just thought—"

She kissed him to stop the story right there, and turned to Jocelyn again. "He believes in letting his company know what they're in for. You can see what has to be done. And it's obviously horrible. But if there's reason enough to do it, we will. Please. Have faith in us."

Leyton looked sideways at her, as if he wasn't used to someone stepping into the middle of this relationship. "Well, Joss?" he said.

Jocelyn sighed theatrically. "Very well," she said. "On your own head be it, sir."

"You've never called me sir," snapped Leyton. "Don't start doing it now."

"I've wanted to," said Jocelyn. "Many times. But, you see, or I'm sure you won't, I never *did*."

"What are you talking about?"

"It's a long story. But we have time now. And, as the World's Sweetheart here has pointed out, I ought to trust you two with the gen. I knew there was something up when I was taken out of flight school several weeks early.

They said I was suited for special duties. But I quickly realised that these chaps in white coats knew all about me. They'd followed me all my life. And death. They knew every detail. Which comes as a shock to a prudent and diplomatic girl. They told me they had a special mission for me. I'd learnt how to take a ship through a Dreaming and that, I was shocked to realize, was all I needed to know about my chosen profession. Chosen, that is, as opposed to death in the wreck of my wedding limousine."

"I'm sorry," said Alison.

"So was I. Anyhow, these chaps took me to our London, to a building as drab as the one we left behind in old London town. To my horror, the President was waiting for me there."

"What?" Leyton looked startled. "Old Jackie?"

"Yes, and me with my hair in a state. Old Jackie told me that the mission I was going on was the most important one in the history of the human race. Lawks, I said. Had they got the right girl? They assured me they had. Indeed, they knew they had. They knew more about me than I'd forgotten. They told me that they'd had someone watching me from the day of my birth. They were waiting for me to pop up on my birthday, at the precise hospital. Where were you on my wedding day, I asked? Watching, they said. Um-hm, I said. So, anyhow, after we'd flirted awhile, they played me what they'd been waiting my whole life to play me. A black box spool. The flight recorder from the *Crimson Dragon*. A recording of our fateful flight, Squadron Leader."

Leyton looked astonished. And a little more than astonished. This, Alison realised, was really going to hurt him. She was just starting to be aware of the effect it was going to have on her as well, her brain jumping ahead to where it had wanted to go all this time. "But how?" he whispered. "How did they get that?"

"They never told me," said Jocelyn. "I did ask. But it was all need-to-know. They were quite upset that I needed to know as much as I did, if that's any comfort. I was asked to study everything on the tape. In detail. I had to learn everything I said in that cockpit, all my cues and lines. They drilled me over and over. I copied it word for word, even breath for breath, in rehearsal."

"You copied..." Leyton was on the verge of stammering. "Words that you were going to say?"

"They said that they didn't know what the consequences would be if I got it wrong. Somebody said that if I missed something, the universe might go bang."

"So," Alison murmured, her brain swirling, "no pressure."

She lost the conversation. She wandered away. Leyton didn't stop her. He was too transfixed by the rest of it.

She went to the rail and looked out at the water, feeling change inside.

Leyton felt betrayed. He wasn't sure by who, or how, yet. He felt like an animal trapped in a corner. Jocelyn was telling him all this quite calmly. But the words were hitting him like serious wounds. Nothing on the surface. Just words. But big impacts underneath. He could see the pain, waiting for him in the future. Poised above him. He wanted to find something to fight against. But there was nothing.

He saw Alison walk away, turning her head from him.

"They knew you were going to lose your last head, Skipper," Jocelyn continued. "They were waiting for it to happen. They knew just how it was going to go down. They showed me footage of it when it did. They made sure I knew all the details of that, too."

Leyton put a hand to his face. "Sorry you had to see that," he managed to whisper.

"Then they introduced me to you, as your new combat head. As soon as I got into the cockpit, I was following the script. The *Crimson Dragon* had been refitted with certain additions, known to me but not to you. It wouldn't have been much use in combat."

"Additions like what?"

"A lot of munitions space was taken up with extra systems to make sure that, no matter what kind of crash we had, I would survive. As it turned out, the emergency cabin came in pretty useful."

"But... there were no extra precautions for me."

"Let me get there. Our lift-off was monitored by just about every camera on the planet. And yet here's yours truly, under orders to act naturally, for the sake of the cosmos."

"So... they knew what was going to happen?"

"They thought so. We encountered the rift in spacetime as we were supposed to do. I said all my lines. We went through right on cue—"

"Your lines," said Alison from the rail, "included that bit about the Fitzroy Hotel." She still hadn't looked at them.

"Yes," said Jocelyn. "I didn't know what it meant when I heard it, or when I repeated it."

Leyton found he was wrestling with the concept and dashed it aside. "You're saying the Fleet knew what was going to happen to us?"

"What they *thought* was going to happen."

"And what was that? Exactly."

Jocelyn took a deep breath. "They thought that we were going to be sucked into the rift, and that the ship would be taken back in time to the year 1947—"

"Not Alison's time?"

"The *Crimson Dragon* originally... whatever that means... crashed in a field in Kent in May 1947. The whole thing was kept secret. Not hard to do, immediately post-war. And, sir... this is why I wanted to keep this from you..."

Leyton could almost hear it coming.

"You were killed in that crash."

Alison heard that distantly. She wanted to go to Leyton, but she couldn't.

The universe felt too big inside her head.

Her mind found the question again.

Jocelyn had learned her dialogue, the words she'd spoken in the cockpit... from the words she'd spoken in the cockpit. She had not thought those words at any point. She had not been the intelligence that devised them. Her unconscious hadn't blurted them out. She was not the author of those words.

The words had come from... outside time.

But amongst those words was an instruction, a deliberate clue. Jocelyn would see Leyton at the Fitzroy Hotel. She had said that without ever knowing what it meant, without understanding that it spoke of her future—the future into which she was not supposed to be heading.

Wasn't there something in physics about information not coming out of nowhere?

That had been where the sense of looming had come from, the feeling that things were looking down at her. Only, in the past, those things had always been frightening, controlling, dominating.

And now those things had set her free.

She closed her eyes again, letting it settle into her brain. This didn't mean she had to start going to church, did it?

She had to start dealing. She concentrated on the rain for a moment, then she made herself turn back to look at Leyton.

Her lover, who was dead, was leaning against the cabin of the ship, leaning with his whole body. It was a frightening physical expression. His right side had slumped, his arm dangling, like his mind couldn't deal with the actions of his body any more. His eyes were flicking like he was in a dream. He was trying to listen to what Jocelyn was describing now, how she, according to her briefing, had *originally* been plucked from the wreckage of the *Dragon* and briefed the authorities of 1947 about all that had happened.

That was why, as soon as she had realised they were in the wrong year, she had ejected Leyton from the ship, so that he could make a difference, so that he didn't have to die. That was also why she had tried to keep silent when interrogated by the old man. She hadn't been briefed to give up her secrets to him.

She was trying to make Leyton feel better. But nothing could do that now.

Alison went to him. She slipped her arms around him. She put all thoughts of a greater reality out of her head. "Hey," she said. "Wake up."

He bit his lip, and looked at her. "I'm not real," he said. "I'm not supposed to be here. As soon as we get things back to normal... I'll be dead."

"And so will I. In time."

He looked away from her. Then he gently disengaged himself from her and walked off, his eyes on the distance, until he was lost around the side of the cabin.

Twenty-Four: The Lamb in the Mud

Cleves watched the video footage, the blaze of light, the bulging of the lens, the shaking. The men half through the door who'd died from some kind of impact, their limbs and internal organs stretched out of shape, their brains pulverised.

He'd felt the tremor himself. For a moment he had been back in the 1970s, with nightmares of nuclear destruction making him think of flashes overhead and thunder in the bunkers. Now we are alone. The world above has gone.

He had run to find out what had happened.

He was held back by his officers. There was a man with a Geiger counter sweeping the corridor and doorway. After a moment, he nodded.

Cleves had stepped forward and through the doorway, over the three corpses. One man's arm had been elongated into a vast hand across the door and wall of the room. At the end of it was a spray of metal film, the deconstruction of his gun.

The floor had gained a pattern, a polish, of lines all heading to a central point. The lines were etched into the tiles. He knelt and put his fingers to them. Fine striations.

He had stood up and looked between his men and the blackened circle at the centre of the wheel.

The captives had been spirited away.

That had never happened before. That could not happen.

He was already replaying in his head all that they had said, the recordings that had been made. It was he, listening live, who had sent the men running to the room when he saw that spur emerge from the head.

Everything they had said was true.

He turned to one of his officers, a Restoration man. "Find Douglas Leyton," he said.

They told him that Leyton was still at home, that they still had every eye on him. Cleves returned to his office by the Thames, biding his time. Tomorrow was the day when Restoration was due to become operational. All his cut-outs were in place. Nobody could prove anything. The body of the vicar had been hidden. He fulfilled the normal duties of the JIC Chair, then he sat through a meeting of the Alien Incursion Special Intelligence Committee, the one he had been so proud of creating, and found that they had nothing of interest to say at all.

He had already briefed the Cabinet on what had happened this morning. At least they still had the remains of the spacecraft, but without Jocelyn's input, as she had said, that was just scrap metal.

But she had said something else. It kept repeating around his mind. "We can travel in time. Brain to brain. Head to head."

He kept thinking about that, and what Leyton had said. The Golden Men.

He had heard that phrase only once before. But it had been in exactly the right place.

It had been from the mouth of Oleg Gremyenko, a traitor from the KGB, just about the last to come over before the Gorbachev régime had started unravelling the power structure. Cleves had got the idea at the time that the man wouldn't have come over had the process of Glasnost not begun. Perhaps he was afraid that if things opened up, his past deeds would be redefined as crimes.

He had told Cleves an incredible tale of factions within the Politburo consorting with aliens. Golden Men, he had said. They brought riches. They offered them freely. He had beentelling this story ever since he had walked into the British Embassy in Moscow and thrown his gloves onto the table.

He had been brought to Cleves as part of a standing order concerning material such as this. Cleves' reputation allowed him this eccentricity. Those passing it to him tended to assume there must be something in it because of his interest. He credited it, rather than it discrediting him. At higher circles, the fact that in all his time reviewing such material he had never given any of it credence was what maintained his dignity.

He had found the concept of Golden Men laughable. Very Russian. When Russians saw flying saucers, they contained men in silver suits and robots with square heads. He had told Gremyenko that unless he had something more to offer him, something sane, he would deny him sanctuary in the West. He would throw him back.

The Russian had changed tack immediately, and had started spilling everything he had.

A few weeks later, the Berlin Wall had become history.

Cleves kept one ear on the conversation around the big table as he thought this. He did not allow his features to display the emotions he was feeling.

At five on the dot he wished the doorman a cheerful goodnight and moved out into the rain in the courtyard. He told his driver he fancied walking tonight, shrugged at the man's baffled expression and headed off into the murk.

He allowed himself to watch for Watchers, keeping his eyes on reflections and passers-by and crossing his tracks, quite naturally, several times, until his path was a complicated pattern on the city. Finally he was satisfied. He had completed that little performance for himself alone.

He entered a callbox and slipped a pound coin into the slot. He checked his notebook and found a number for Oleg Gremyenko's home in West Sussex.

A blank-voiced woman told him that Oleg had died, only last night.

Cleves offered his apologies, but not his name. He clickedoff the call and was about to put the phone back on the hook, but then he picked it up again.

He dialled the home of his old friend in Canada. He took a deep breath as he heard the ringing tone.

The rain beat down on the phonebox. It was an old-fashioned red one, kept that way for the tourists: a deliberate anachronism, the country as it had been. Efficiency sacrificed to history. Was he really going to do this?

Yes, he was.

The line clicked open and a familiar voice said hello.

"George," said Cleves. "It's me..." Another deep breath. "I don't think I'm on for your fantasy cricket league. Sorry to let you down."

"I..." The sound of a man not used to choosing his words carefully. Cleves had made sure that none of the codewords they used for Restoration were registered with the Echelon intelligent listening system, but they still had to be careful not to form chains of words that might set off any of that system's minor alarms. A minor, with Cleves' name attached, might become a major, might, at a long shot, find its way to a human operator. "Are you saying you've joined somebody else's league?"

"As if I'd do that."

"This is unacceptable. They'll have my head."

"Of course they won't. Don't fret."

Cleves could hear the panic rising in the man's voice. "We're only a day from the start of... of the season! Have you gone mad?"

Cleves almost laughed. "No," he said. "I think you'll find that I've become sane. Goodbye." And he hung up.

He quickly called his three central men on Restoration with the stand-down codes. They were all astonished.

But Cleves found that, inside himself, he was reconciled to his course of action.

He went home to Swanage and found that Julia and her family had popped over to visit. For once he left all his workin his study and spent the evening playing with little Augusta. She wanted to be a train, so he crawled across the carpet behind her, making train noises, and stopping when she decided they'd reached a station.

He only switched on his computer late, to check his e-mail. He expected something from George. Dark hints, threats even, which would mean nothing. They needed him. He was the Chairman of the JIC, for

God's sake. What could they do? He was half tempted to call the PM's Office and warn them about Restoration, say he'd got the lead from an informant. But no. He'd said he hadn't changed sides, and he wouldn't break his word to George. He was just out of the game.

The new file on his desktop caught his attention immediately. *Image*, it was called. He opened it.

It was a photograph of a six-year-old girl being raped by a man in a mask. He had never seen anything so repulsive.

He deleted it, then emptied the recycle bin, then used his security software to erase every sign that the file had ever been on his computer.

Then he stood up, shaking. They must have come in through the garden, before he'd even got back to his house. There were no security personnel, not these days. They had broken the security on his PC and planted that file.

No. No human hand could have done that. Not in that time.

Through the walls, Leyton had said. The Golden Men.

There might be other files. It would take days to search the disc and make sure.

The telephone on his desk rang.

He grabbed it before Sue could pick up the extension. "Yes?"

The voice was George's. "I've been on to my people," he said. He sounded distant, oddly dry and triumphant. "The season will proceed. Won't it?"

Cleves felt like his bladder was going to give way. "Yes," he said finally. "It will."

"I'm sorry, old chap."

"Are you?"

"I have one more message. Visit the central player. Tonight. And make sure he doesn't play. All right?"

"All right," said Frederick Cleves.

Twenty-Five: The Compass Rose

The ship headed north, passing great headlands in the night, peaks that rose out of the murk covered in lights and black shapes where no light shone at all.

Alison had returned to her bunk in the evening and had managed to sleep some more. She was aware that her body still wanted to betray her.

But now she had her mission.

The shape outside of space and time had spoken to her through the words it had put into Jocelyn's mouth. And she had decided, painfully, against who she had been, that if such a power existed, then she should serve it. The irony was that she'd found her new direction at the same moment that Leyton had lost his.

She woke in the night and realised that he hadn't come to her bed, so she went to find him. She had been wearing the same clothes, the clothes the old man had given her, for hours now, but it was too cold to undress, even under the rough bedclothes.

She went out onto the deck. Jocelyn was still hanging in her basket, looking out at the sea. "We're somewhere around Birmingham now," she said. "I'm told we should make landfall around dawn."

"Doesn't it get to you, not being able to sleep?" Alison was aware that she was shivering beyond the cold again. She must look so white.

"What choice do I have? He's on the other side, by the way. Go round the back."

Alison nodded to her and made her way round the square bulk of the cabin at the stern. She found Leyton still staring at the sea.

She went to him and hesitantly put an arm around him.

He looked down at her with a sad smile and hugged her back.

"How are you doing?"

"Never better. Bracing night on the pond."

"Leyton—"

"If they had just *asked*, Alison! That's what's been bothering me. It's as if they thought I might turn my nose up at it. Every time you take off you live with the idea that you might not come back. You give your life for your duty. And they thought that when it came to the crunch I'd pull up short of that. I'd have gladly ridden that rocket to prevent all this! I'd have understood my death. What greater privilege is there? But they... how dare they? How dare they, Alison?"

"It wouldn't have made any difference. You'd still have ended up here. And perhaps they thought it was kinder—"

"It was not!"

"And they weren't keen on Jocelyn knowing, either. But they were forced to tell her, because she had to brief the authorities when she got there. You and she were supposed to create your world, you realise? The crash is where your civilisation got its technological advances, the lead it needed to win the world over and put an end to capitalism. That's why the Golden Men changed where you ended up. Just that one rewrite was enough to change your world. Into mine. So it finally becomes this."

"I realise that. I may not be a head but I'm not completely dopey."

"Originally the powers-that-be in 1947 kept it all secret. Your society is built on a time paradox, and it doesn't know."

"And your society is built on enemy action, and it doesn't know."

"Leyton, something I've realised..." And she explained the vast conclusions she'd come to regarding the information from outside time.

Leyton nodded. He wasn't too surprised. "Yes," he said finally. "I hadn't thought about that, but... well, brother, we are treading where the saints have trod and all that."

"What does that mean?" She sounded more sharp with him than she wanted.

"I felt it when I was praying with the Padre. That God is... further off... from this world. And if He is, then He'd want someone to do something about it, and I suspect it's yours truly."

Alison hugged his arm again. "How can you take on board this huge thing just like that?"

"I am in the military. We're often told to take on grand schemes and make them work. Just us. And it makes sense of the other conclusion I'd come to."

"Which is?"

He took her by the shoulders and looked carefully at her. "Alison. Just so you know: if I get a chance to complete this mission, I'm going to do it. My superiors didn't give me the choice, but the Lord has. I don't intend to fail Him. I'm going to put things back to how they should be, and spare the world this bloody rain."

Alison held him for a long time. "Talking about God like that... like She's—"

"She!"

"Like *She's* in the room. I'm so not used to it."

"Well, you would have got used to it if we'd had time. If we'd had the chance to—"

She shut him up with her hand. "It's not just you. If you get the world back to what it should be, then I know exactly how and when I'm going to die. And I do it to give you lot... the power to come back here and do this. Oh God."

They held onto each other in the rain. The deck rolled beneath them.

She got the details out of him, little by little, of how she became a head. It was the plot of that movie. And finally, with the sea spray hiding his tears, he told her about Elsie.

"Would it be a sin," Alison asked at the end, "for you to come back down there with me and make love with me?"

"Well—"

Alison started dragging him. "We're doing Her a big favour," she said. "She owes us."

Leyton let himself be dragged.

He was very gentle with her during sex. She said that he treated her like the good china, and so then he was enjoyably rougher.

Afterwards, she lay on his chest and he talked to her softly, playing with her hair, highly and hugely romantic. That would have scared her, normally. He'd fallen so hard for her. But now they were the people of big romantic things. They were fucking on the way to destiny and death. She appreciated being loved during that.

He asked if there would be a time and place to marry her. He hoped there would be. She said sure, okay, absolutely, in the face of what they were doing that looked so impossible. He talked for a long time about how she was an innocent victim in all this, how he had a duty to protect her, and how he was sorry he'd failed in that duty...

Until she said "innocent my arse" and whispered explicit come-ons in his ear and he had to take her again.

They were woken by Jocelyn's calls from on deck.

"Well, *I* was up all night," she said as they arrived in their hurriedly pulled-on clothes.

A large landmass was rising out of the mist in front of them. It was sparred with rocky outcrops. It faded way back into the distance, and Alison could see the dawn lights of what must be towns back along its bulk. Ahead of them was a cluster of buildings with a tidal break that stretched out into the water. A rough road led uphill to a wooded summit where there were lights. There was detail under the waves, as if the break was built atop a deep history of buildings. As they got closer, Alison saw that the water was lapping just below the floors of a row of stilted metal shacks.

"This is Kidsgrove." The ferryman wandered into view, a coil of rope in his hands. "From here a convoy into the Peaks. If you really want." He pointed to one of the stilted huts. "Master Rees is boss. You pay him passage across his land."

"He's in that hut?" asked Leyton, pulling his cap down over his wayward hair.

The ferryman sighed at them. "His people," he said. And he threw the rope over one of the moorings at the end of the breakwater.

Kidsgrove turned out to be a very depressing place. Alison hadn't expected the population to be so big. The muddy streets were teeming with people: tradesmen with hoppers on their backs, selling food; kids in rags running about your knees, calling for anything you had to give them in an accent so deep Alison couldn't pick out individual words; all manner of beggars, a line of them along one side of one particular street, each with their own special pitch. One or two of them sat still, unmoving. They looked to be dead. A few of the people looked relatively well off. They wore thicker woollens, and plastic boots. Rows of houses were stepped up the side of a hill. They were upgraded versions of houses such as you'd see on any estate in Alison's own time. They were painted matt black, except one that was glaringly white, because, she gathered, something had *gone wrong*, and their roofs were red brick. The roads that led up and across the hill were familiar Tarmac, churned and potholed. The market and central shops sat in a big wound down the middle of the hill, with tracks leading to and from the houses above. The whole village was on a rise above the harbour, reached by the long gravel path up which they'd trod.

Rees's representatives in the customs house had shown surprisingly little interest in Jocelyn. They'd asked how much she was worth, in a dialect different to the one the ferryman and the street kids used. Jocelyn had started to answer indignantly, but they'd laughed. It was a joke. A power joke. Something the commoners passing through their hands weren't supposed to understand. They wanted to know why these visitors weren't chipped. Alison simply said they were fugitives, and the man with the highest authority—he had a green jacket with silver lace sewn into one shoulder—had nodded, pleased at their honesty, and said that passage into the Peaks would cost them fuel, metal, drugs or a blow job. He didn't seem excited by the prospect of the latter.

Leyton gave him about half of what remained of the coinage the vicar had given him. They still had quite a sum in notes, but what good was that going to be here?

Finally Master Rees's men had nodded and opened the door for them to be on their way up the hill. They never even found out who Rees was.

They made their way through the crowded streets to a shack that had a painted sign above it, declaring itself to be a Convoy Centre. They discovered that they were in luck as a convoy had assembled itself in the town over the last week and was due to set off today. To join it, they could pay fuel, metal, drugs or—

Leyton gave them some more coins.

They found a handcart at a vehicle dealer and used more of their precious metal to buy it. It contained all their possessions, plus Jocelyn, quite easily, and Leyton and Alison could take turns pulling it. When she said this, Alison expected Leyton to quibble and say that he'd do it on his own, but he just nodded. That was one of the things she liked about him, Alison decided: the way the world he came from kept producing surprises.

The convoy: people with horses, which were gazed at in awe and worried at by the kids; people in trucks, people on bicycles, even, assembled over the course of the morning around the edges of what could roughly be described as the market square, an open space slanted at an angle uphill that Alison thought had probably been a car park. The large low buildings behind it, which the street kids they talked to described as a "Rees Place," was probably the supermarket it had been attached to. Once upon a time.

The Convoy Officer earned his commission by going around the convoy, checking everyone's name against a list. Leyton gave a false name. Alison thought that was a bit extreme. There seemed to be only four Golden Men across the whole history and geography of Earth. When they weren't sent for, and they didn't have her eye to lead them to their target, they appeared to be in the dark about how to locate the fugitives. But then she saw a ratty look on the face of the traveller behind them, a ragged boy with a pony, and she changed her mind. The Golden Men produced a web of need wherever they went. And the biggest commodities, like their names, would find a way to their attention.

When he was satisfied that everyone was present, the Convoy Officer made an oft-used spinning motion with his hand in the air, and the leading petrol lorry set off at the funereal pace of the slowest members of the convoy.

They passed out of the gates of Kidsgrove and settled into a long slow climb into the misty heights. Alison looked back as she walked, glad of the woollens she'd bought, and saw the sea receding behind her. She looked across at Leyton. He was already smiling back at her.

There was, she thought, something to be said for having found a purpose. Even a fatal one.

It took them three days, at that pace, to reach the woods.

They stayed every night in a huge communal tent, with sentries chosen by lot taking guard outside in a shift system. Alison was grateful her lot never came up. Her body was wretched, not wanting food, subsisting on liquids, her mind urging her as she trudged along the muddied roads to find the Golden Men, to get the eye thing back. She needed it.

But she did not.

She and Leyton had initially been somewhat nervy about sharing a bed in sight of everyone else, but nobody gave a damn. Noisy shagging was the order of the night, interrupted by shouts to keep it down. In the end, they just cuddled. It occurred to Alison, stupidly, that she was running out of contraceptive pills. There would be a time, soon, when they couldn't have sex at all. She wondered what this messy future had instead, and shuddered. Where would they even get rubber?

Alison saw the moon on that first night, through gaps in the scudding clouds, when she went outside the tent to have a pee. There was just a slim crescent. The dark mass of the rest of it looked different. The light coming from it was of a different quality. Even the way the Earth reflected sunlight had changed. There was something glaring and glossy about that darkness. Alison didn't like it. Hell's moon, she thought as she headed back to the warm and dry of the tent.

Jocelyn's expression was firmly clenched one morning. She had, she said, been approached. She had declined. She was glad that they were due at their destination during the next day.

The treeline was a couple of miles to the west of the convoy's path. It was going on to Lancaster by a winding route, which, Alison thought, was going to take weeks. So Leyton, Alison and Jocelyn rather thankfully said their farewells and sent their handcart off down an overgrown side road.

What remained of the Peaks was fascinating. The vegetation had grown higher up the banks of what had been mountains, forming chains of long forested islands, with occasional plummets into river valleys below sea level, and expanses of high barren moorland.

The woods had returned to nature, but nature darkened by the air. Silver and black-barked trees with greyed leaves made silver moths and black birds that flapped between them. The grass was an artificial green, bright with chlorophyll, that greyed and died to ferns in the lightest shade. The forest floor was brown and black, slagged and industrial.

Alison was glad she hadn't grown up in this world. Her fear of the End would have been screaming at her every day. It was so close at hand. You could feel the pieces slowly locking, the water rising, the air getting harder and harder to breathe. The End, for this world, was two or three decades away.

Jocelyn led them, consulting her internal maps and compass.

"This is Grinlow Woods, near where Fran used to go on holiday," said Alison as they climbed a rocky outcrop and stood, breathless, overlooking a valley, the sides of which were covered in conifers. The sun, which looked bloated and parched, had emerged for the first time from behind the cover of sulphurous mist.

"We're nearly there," said Jocelyn.

"Ye gods and little fishes," said Leyton. "I've never been as glad to hear anything."

She led them down into the valley.

They found, after several hours of precise searching, a particular cave entrance that Jocelyn had in mind, along the bank of a wide and raging river. When they complained, Jocelyn told them that she was attempting to pin down a location she had only glimpsed for a moment in a mystical trance. Even with a head's intuitive feeling for maps and points of reference, to get it down to within a few hundred yards was—

"A miracle." Leyton said it just before Alison did.

They found an old building, half collapsed, near the entrance to the caves. It was gaudily painted, with images of stubby silver spaceships on the dirtied hoardings. They had been promoting the caves, whenever this dated from, as some kind of theme park, with rides and virtual reality equipment. Alison found a price quoted for taking home any piece of stalactite you could knock off. Slingshot stones provided, five for a fiver.

They used the remains of the kiosk to make rough torches, tearing up the shirt the old man had given Alison for the rags. Jocelyn had advised Leyton to exchange the last of their money for some fuel for just this purpose. Alison realised that she was betting on them getting out of this world, as she'd bet on them getting out of the Fitzroy Hotel. She was keen on those Long'uns now.

All is written. But they still had to write it.

They walked into the mouth of the cave as sunset approached, their torches blackening the dark ceiling even further. They sent a cloud of bats thundering and chirruping out into the evening. They'd probably stay out there, Leyton said. Up with the lark.

The long flat mouth of the cave gave way to a narrow passage, a single metal rail attached to the wall running back into the darkness. Alison realised, as they approached a group of decidedly phallic red stalagmites, that they weren't just in an associated cave system, but—

"This is Cocks Cave," she said. "Fran mentioned that. We're in Poole's Cavern, the cave she worked in."

"Coincidence?" said Leyton.

Alison and Jocelyn raised their eyebrows at him at once.

They continued past many of the features that Fran had described in her postcards. It made Alison feel very lonely. The poached eggs, the rail with one growing there... She could hear Fran's tone of voice in the letters, the tiny jokes, the caring closeness with her co-workers. And that had all been turned into this, where the brightness of the mineral deposits was dulled everywhere by the black scarring of human hands. Ceilings that should have been full of millennia-ancient stalactites were stubbled with their remains, whole fields of them shorn off for visitors to take home. Only the absence of humanity, in the last few decades, had allowed new things to grow here: fresh poached egg features, a new mottled spur atop the Swan.

But even there, the quality of the rock had changed. The minerals being filtered through the hill were different, the colours more intense: rainbow silvers and artificial golds. Their feet kicked over lumps of broken and discarded machinery, the remains of some half-hearted mining or mineral extraction attempt. The supply lines had stretched too long; the riches were slipping out of human hands. This place had become the sinkhole of ambition, the last nest of nature, slowly poisoned by industry, where the minerals were the biggest fingerprint of dead humanity. The cavern was once more full of broken metal.

They came to the source of the river and found that the walkway rail still just about ran alongside it, though they had to hop from outcrop to outcrop on a couple of occasions. The river was big and loud now, roaring and echoing down the caves. It had blurred the differences between the individual caves a little, but Alison still recognised their path. They passed the Mary Queen of Scots and moved into the sixth cavern, where Fran had often talked about working on the plan to open the seal on the mysterious Seventh Heaven.

The sixth cavern was full of dead machines. Their torches flickered around the mineral-covered contraptions: the remains of video games and what must have been virtual reality devices, all stripped of any worthwhile metal, with just the awkward skeletal bits and sheets of plastic left. These were all covered in lime deposits, the metals dissolving into thin strands of orange and yellow minerals that stretched from floor to ceiling.

"The obvious place for a theme park," said Alison.

"Twits," said Leyton.

It took a while for them to find where the entrance to Seventh Heaven would have been. Alison remembered Fran telling her that the chamber had been sealed again, which was such a shame, such an undoing. She'd been so happy about the possibility of opening it. It made Alison remember the old-fashioned, happy Fran, who seemed still to be real somewhere that Alison couldn't quite place. The world of her imagination, she realised after a moment. She'd kept the wish of her friend alive. Maybe there was some way to save her still. If only they could get back...

They finally located it when Alison remembered the Brain or, as the official guidebook had called it, the Sculpture, that the big lump of wet crystalline rock was supposed to sit right at the entrance to the new cave. It had a corner of its own here, which looked like it might once have been lit.

Behind it was a rockfall, an old pile of stones. It didn't look ancient, but like something some manager of this site had decided had been the best use of the space, to show off the Brain. It had the movements of mechanical scoops and diggers written into it. It obviously went some way back, though. It would take months out of their lives to move it by hand.

They all just stood there, lost.

The universe felt very real again, suddenly. Alison thought that maybe this was a test, and then that perhaps those recorded words of Jocelyn's had spun into time just from sudden random thought, from some God that woke and slept and cared nothing.

Or perhaps, the stronger voice that had held off her addiction said, this was just the latest trial on a very hard path.

Leyton took off his cap and coat and rolled up his shirtsleeves. "Right you are then," he said. "Where shall we start?"

Alison looked at him, not daring to be cynical, loving him.

And then Jocelyn said "oh" again. In that significant way of hers.

They both looked at her expectantly.

She had her eyes tight shut. Then she opened them and smiled. "Heavens," she said. "Would you two pick me up and step back from the rocks, please?"

They did so. Jocelyn told them to halt after about a hundred yards. "Hands over your ears," she said. Then, hanging from Leyton's elbow, she closed her eyes again. "Assume remote," she said. "Starboard manoeuvring engines. Firing."

Alison felt the concussion through her hands. It sent a sharp pain straight into her ears. But the most extraordinary thing was the fear and awe that went deep into her stomach. She imagined ancient cavemen singing in booming ceremonies, creating their gods through echoes and pressure waves such as this.

But that was just her thoughts. Her gut knew, more than if she had been struck with light in any cathedral, that she was in the presence of God.

The light broke through the rock wall in front of them. It sent individual boulders flying, down the slope that led away from them. It cracked some with heat and broke them. Finally a gout of fire broke the rock and blasted out to blacken and reflect on the cavern wall.

To reflect towards—

"Shutdown," said Jocelyn.

The fire vanished.

Alison's eye glowed green inside from the sudden lack of light. She thought of the angels, what they'd put in her eye, for a moment, and she was afraid, all of her, even the animal part that would welcome them back. But it was just nature. Just the brightness on her iris.

The heat was intense. Some of the rocks, down the tunnel, were glowing. The smell hit them in a wave of heated air and made them all cough, made the flame of their own torches flicker.

Leyton slowly took his hands away from his ears. "The smell!" he cried out. "That's motive fuel! Jocelyn, how—"

"I have no idea," said the head, looking smug. "I was highly surprised to feel the signal beacon."

Leyton led the way at a run to the gap in the rocks.

Alison was at his shoulder as he thrust his torch through the steaming gap.

A vast space had opened up in front of them: an echoing cathedral of stone. But it wasn't dark in there. Every untouched stalactite and brilliant formation was shining, illuminated.

By the lights of the *Crimson Dragon*.

Twenty-Six: Mayday

Leyton could hardly wait until the rocks were cool. He started grabbing at them and wincing, letting go, until he could get a hold long enough to haul them out of the way.

"I felt it there, the automatic response beacon," said Jocelyn. "So I switched on the lights, made sure the supports were anchored and fired the thrusters."

"But what's it doing here?" breathed Alison. She had had an image in her head of Leyton's ship all this time, but she had never imagined it looking like this: sleek, homely, perky even. It didn't say killing machine. It said Rule Britannia. And it still thought there was a difference. On the fuselage, beside the cockpit, which stood open, were painted the red, white and blue circles of the RAF, with an eagle in the centre. The eagle was grasping an olive branch. This was meant, thought Alison, to be a peacekeeping craft. Only a series of black rods painted by the cockpit indicated otherwise.

"And how can it be so perfect?" Leyton hauled away the last rock and heaved himself up into the gap. He grabbed Jocelyn and brought her through, then took Alison's hand and led her after.

The space was huge. It extended up into the echoing darkness. The *Crimson Dragon* was a tiny metal thing at the bottom of it. They could hear the river roaring into this space too, over somewhere to their right.

In truth, the ship wasn't "perfect." It too had been covered in mineral deposits, huge stalks of stalagmites forming along its back and wings, in the shadows. The rockets had knocked quite a few of those loose. There was also layer upon layer of guano. The air in the cavern was, perversely, quite dry. And the ship looked like it was built not to rust. It could have been here, Alison realised, for centuries.

Leyton went to the fuselage and touched it, his eyes shining in the white lights that beamed from the wings. Then he frowned. "Oh," he said. "This isn't right." He ran a finger along the black undersurface of the wings. "This is made of some different material. Heat resistant, but... rather old-fashioned." He knocked the hull in a couple of places. "It's been refitted. Rebuilt, almost."

Alison boggled. Her reading of the world couldn't read *this*. "But how did it get in here?"

"There's a head in there," said Jocelyn.

Startled, Leyton leapt up onto the foot notch by the cockpit and stared inside.

After he didn't turn around for a few moments, Alison hauled herself up beside him. "What?" she said. At the back of the cockpit sat a white, parched head, a man, a face with all the water sucked out of it by time. A transparent partition stood between it and the open cockpit, so the bats had never been inside.

Leyton slowly looked up at Alison. He looked like he'd been slapped round the face. "It's Hohiti Kenton," he said. "My favourite film director."

"Now that," said Alison, "is something you don't see every day."

Jocelyn inspected the controls and declared everything to be in order. The special equipment that, in the event of a crash, had allowed her to retreat at speed into an aft security cell was still intact, as was the flight recorder, and all the other secure fittings. Whoever had restored it had put back everything they had that was original, and replaced what they could like for like.

There were just a few things for which they didn't have quite the like.

Nervously they activated the rear compartment crash sensor and watched Hohiti Kenton's head vanish in a blur of motion. They levered the compartment open. There was nothing else in there.

It was when he was sitting in the pilot's seat that Leyton made the biggest discovery of all. His hand played over the edge of the cockpit. He shouted and withdrew it. There was the tiniest trace of a russet powder on his fingers. "Blood," he said.

They followed the faint trail using the *Crimson Dragon*'s sensors. It shone lights on the ground looking for a particular chemical signature, a procedure used in combat, Leyton said, to follow microscopic trails of debris from an injured enemy craft. After a few minutes of adjustment, the beams revealed a ragged trail that led off into the cavern, towards the rock wall.

"It's a very small trace," said Jocelyn. "The shapes of the molecules rather than the molecules themselves. This is hundreds of years old."

"Can we tell what blood type?" asked Leyton.

"Don't make me laugh, Skip."

Alison followed the trail across the floor until it got to the wall. It went up a slope of white mineral deposits, and... she cautiously looked up the narrow rock chimney. She thought she could feel the stirrings of air in the pipe, but there was no light up there. This, she thought, must be one of the exits to the surface that the bats used. There was just about room for a human being to get up there. She shivered at the thought of the passage, though, through bats and confined spaces. And what if it didn't remain this wide all the way to the top?

She showed Leyton the chimney. He frowned. "So this pilot, whoever it was, gets out of the cockpit, wounded, and staggers straight to this pipe and heads on out? Talk about purposeful!"

"Maybe he used the ship's sensors in some way? Worked out where he was going before he got out?"

"The needs of space combat are not those of being encased in rock," called Jocelyn from the cockpit. "He might have figured out that there was a space up there, but he wouldn't have been able to follow it in detail to the top."

"Who was it?" asked Leyton. "Who would have a film director as a navigator?"

Nobody wanted to hazard a guess.

They talked about the strangeness of all this, but they couldn't come to any conclusions. Hohiti Kenton had died in his bed, as far as Leyton was concerned. He'd read obituaries, accounts of the old man complaining that his life's work wasn't finished, that there was yet another film to be made about Alison Parmeter. He had, apparently, got quite obsessed with his two greatest triumphs towards the end.

"And this is how he gets to meet me," said Alison, putting her hand against the panel that separated her from the head.

They decided they should bury him, so they extracted him from the cockpit and dug, using pieces of metal from the sixth cavern, a pit in the shale and mud beside the river. It was, Alison realised, a courtesy. The animals down here would actually find the head quite quickly. But it was better, somehow, than staying in the cockpit of a ship. Besides, if Jocelyn was right, they were going to use the ship to get out of here, and there wouldn't be room to take Hohiti with them.

Leyton said a few words over the grave about Hohiti's achievements. It was good that he was such an enthusiast. He really meant what he said. After he'd finished, he looked to Alison.

Alison tried to remember the words. She felt awkward. "Is there any music?" she said. "You said you were listening to Vaughan Williams..."

Leyton went over to the cockpit and checked. He emerged a moment later, looking shocked. He held in his hand a small black cartridge. "Alison," he said. "This is yours."

"What? No it isn't."

Leyton turned the cartridge to show her the spine. Written there, in a rough, familiar hand, was the title. "On the Path of My God—Song—Alison Parmeter."

"Oh," she said. But then she frowned. That wasn't such a surprise. Not if she was so popular in the years Leyton came from. Though the title rang a bell. Leyton had said— "When did I write that?"

"That's just it, Alison," he said. "It's the missing song. The one that only your killers have ever heard."

Alison thought about that for a moment. Then she closed her eyes. "Okay," she said. "I can do this now. Then we'll play it. Okay?"

Leyton didn't say anything. He came to join her and Jocelyn by the grave.

Alison tried to remember some of the things that had been said over her when her dad had dragged her along to a church service. She couldn't get anywhere near the proper order of things. She didn't have to. She would just say the words that came into her heart. "God is with us," she said. She expected the others to say something in return, but they didn't. Wasn't there some response to that? She decided that she'd just go for the prayer that had been repeated over and over at school, the one that every child knew. "Our Father, who art in heaven..." She was pleased to hear Jocelyn and Leyton joining in, though they said "is" and not "art." "Hallowed be thy name. Thy Kingdom come. Thy will be done. In Earth as it is in heaven. Give us this day our daily bread. And forgive us our sins. As we forgive those that sin against us. For thine is the Kingdom, the power and the glory. For ever and ever. Amen." There was a pause. Alison opened her eyes. "Oh, and ashes to ashes, dust to dust..." She hadn't remembered anything from the funerals; she'd been yelling all the while. She felt like she'd missed so much, a huge part of who her father had been. Though he'd been maddened by it, and it wasn't a mad thing, really. It was a calm, big thing.

She put her hand in the mud and dropped a handful of it into the hole. "In the midst of death, we are in life."

Jocelyn coughed. She looked up.

"You got that the wrong way round," said Leyton. But they were both smiling at her.

Alison smiled back.

They gathered around the cockpit afterwards, Leyton having finished off the burial and patted the grave down as hard as he could.

"So this is the religious piece that I was supposed to have written while I was being held hostage?" said Alison.

"Right." Leyton's hands trembled as he slid the cartridge into the player. He pressed play.

It was a piano piece. Just her fingers on the keys. Alison thought about the movements her own hands would be making, at how she couldn't guess how to make those patterns now. She didn't even sound shaky, though she must be doing this while people with guns wandered past, or stopped to stare at her in unsought wonder.

It made her feel less than she should be.

Then she heard her voice. It took her a moment to get past the shock of how she sounded. There was always a distance when you heard yourself on tape, but normally it was to do with remembering saying the words and hearing them again from someone who seemed to have a different voice and a solid set of attitudes and emotions that weren't your own maze of indescribable contradictions. This wasn't like that. It was a voice that was hers, only older, not only with a separate persona, but a separate self that was saying new things. The force of the sensation made her stagger. She had to hold onto Leyton's shoulder. She looked at Jocelyn. This was a feeling that only the two of them had ever experienced: being outside yourself in time. Being a vessel, a witness, a messenger. She tried hard to memorise every single word. She knew she would listen to this many times, in the next few hours, to get every bit of it fixed in her mind.

The look on Jocelyn's face said she understood.

The song was about finding Patrick. About how who he was was the most important thing of all. It was a song to a lost love, but lost how? In the world this Alison lived in, Patrick had been lost to her through her own determination to pursue her talent as opposed to his self-interest, which in that world had expressed itself in a desire for power rather than wealth. So this was a song about missed opportunities.

Alison agreed with Leyton, now she heard. This Alison had an insight that made you feel she was speaking for all the ways the book was written and rewritten. The words made her cry. And several times a particular line spoke to her about the contents of her own mind. It told her that the faith that was there could remain. There was a verse about the Trinity, a concept that Alison always had, and still, found meaningless. Her future self had gone further down the road, explored even more. There were references to the Goddess, too. She hadn't given up the practices she'd shared with Fran, on those nights looking down on the city, beautiful, unflooded. She was still a contradiction when she'd recorded this, still working out the way the patterns clashed and merged with each other in the world. The song was a reflection, a meditation on those patterns. It wasn't a route map. Her future self had decided that, rather than send a simple message, the song, the art, was important. She wanted her younger self to feel, Alison immediately understood, her part in the journey. To understand that those who make the patterns write the world. That she had choices.

Leyton had turned away, his shoulders square. Alison put a hand on his shoulder and made him turn back. He looked bravely at her, openly weeping.

Which made her start again as she held him.

They played the song several times.

"So," she said, as the last echo of the piano faded. "That's the message. We have to find Patrick."

Twenty-Seven: Various Artists

Douglas Leyton had known they would be coming. He had become aware, before he realised it, of being watched. He had felt their presence in his life suddenly. The old man had been careful not to send anyone Douglas had met on the night they hunted the man with the square shoulders and his name. So he noticed them passing as he stopped to tie his bootlace, found them in the corner shop when he bought his paper, stood next to them in an entirely new pub that he'd picked.

Last weekend he had stood in a farm picket line. They had been waiting to have a shouting match with the representatives from the Ministry of Fisheries and Farming, to defend the healthy animals of the area from being slaughtered as a precaution against foot and mouth. He had been one of several Restoration members amongst them, all of them playing their roles, swapping information and maps, representing their various local groups, getting ready for the big event.

Leyton was playing a role always. He was holding on.

They had waited for those in power to come to the gates of the farm so that they could protest at them for the waiting cameras. They had a cute little lamb ready with the little boy who regarded it as his pet, to hold onto it while the vets dragged it away.

Of course, the vets, being sensible, had never come. They probably thought that the farm deserved the visitation of the disease, if that was their attitude. Douglas, who in this incarnation was called Gerald and had blond hair and a scar from a military past that he didn't talk about, had commiserated with his fellow country dwellers, and had had a few pints with them.

It had been a pleasure to play that role outside of his new role one last time.

He had made the decision to go tonight. He knew what he had to do. The time was right. Not too much running around. A straight run.

He waited until the early hours, with the lights off, going about his house, taking out those packages that he'd prepared for this eventuality, checking their contents. He forgot why they were there, exactly. He supposed that he had constructed a new identity so he could slip away from his life as an agent, should he choose to do so. He didn't know why he would ever choose that. It gave him a little thrill to affirm to his superiors his name and position in the world at regular intervals.

With his bag packed, he went to the bathroom and looked in the mirror, still with the light off. He was wearing a deep disguise, a mass of misdirections that at the same time looked like nobody.

He reached under the hair and pulled the plaster off the oldest trepanation scar.

A shiver of pure oxygen ran through him. All was clear. He would see them. His muscles would not fail him. He would kill and maim as suited this latest definition of who he was, in defence of who he actually was.

In the lounge, his mobile rang. A text message.

He'd picked it up and taken it before he'd thought that it might be dangerous to do so. A mark of his new confidence.

He recognised the number. It was Cotton.

The message said GO.

It meant that the protestors were already moving. The order had come down from the old man, or those who paid his bills. Odd that he'd had that urge to talk with him about that; very unlike him. Very unprofessional.

That was why the old man had put his Watchers on him: because he thought Douglas was able to betray him. Douglas had played his part since; he had put a little more work into the organisation.

But now they wouldn't need him. So GO, which had meant that he should head for Shepton Mallet and link up with a group heading for a Bristol refinery, now meant that he should go too. Away. Another new life. He had got the date exactly right.

It didn't feel right. Unfinished business, like all his lives were unfinished. Was that really the reason why Cleves had put a noose around his neck?

He knew the old man's name.

Of course he did.

He held the phone. What did his body want him to do?

He had never asked before. His impulses had deserted him. He was going to have to make a decision.

It was made for him. There was a soft thump from the bedroom.

He ran for the window before half of him had even heard the noise.

The pane shattered as it was supposed to, into big pieces. Stage glass. It had made the front room cold all winter. But it was there for the moment when it would be a prop.

He dropped onto the pavement, the shards clattering into the ground around him. He swept his arm from his eyes and into his jacket.

The first man round the corner got the knife in his neck and out.

He fell, and Douglas was running.

He felt the impact of the bullets by his feet. They were shooting for his body, silenced, so the noise that echoed down the street was like a sack hitting the ground. They were planning to put him down and then put one through his head.

He leapt over the wall and through the gap in the wire, into the industrial estate. His house stood at the end of the row on the council estate, next to

the wire, looking down over the city. He ran into cover and threw himself
flat, then crunched across the gravel on his elbows. He could see a way
out, from one piece of wasteland to the next, and then into the maze of
warehouses and office furniture showrooms and superstores.

He ran for it.

They didn't have big lights to bring to bear on him. Their vehicles
couldn't get through the gap. They knew he had no gun, so he heard a
couple of them come after him through the gap. But the wasteground
sloped downwards to the town, so they were silhouetted and he wasn't.
There were more shots, but way off. They could hear him, but not see
him.

He ran haphazardly, letting his feet bounce him from cover to cover.

Then he hit a pretty wooden fence at the edge of a carpet warehouse.
He vaulted it. He ran past the forecourt, sure they'd be sending their cars
speeding around the corners under the moon, looking for the way into the
estate, frantically consulting their GPS maps. He found the side passage,
the narrow walkway that led round the backways of all the buildings. It
was fenced high on both sides. He came to crossroads every so often.

He felt the breath heavy in his lungs. He was getting old.

His next life would be stationary, but he didn't feel like he was running
towards it.

He had had a plan. What had it been? It seemed to come and go, like
the moon through the clouds.

Was he choosing these pathways? Like he must have chosen the house
and the gap in the wire? Or were they choosing him?

He took two lefts one after the other, deliberately.

He ran straight into the man.

He fell, rolled, righted himself again, the knife ready to throw.

It was Cleves. He was alone. He looked shaken, frightened even.
Douglas was shocked. He didn't think this man could ever look that way.

"I found you!" he gasped. "Quickly! Before they get here!"

And without even thinking that Douglas might intend him harm, he
grabbed him by the arm and dragged him off towards the rear of one of
the warehouses.

"Tell me the truth," said Cleves. He had sent most of his Watchers to flush
Leyton out, seeing that he would have prepared this escape run. Then
he'd run ahead of the remainder, sent them the wrong way, claiming to
know the ground. He'd followed the map on his GPS handheld and saw
there was a place where he could see Leyton coming. He'd climbed a fire
escape, feeling the wrench in his aching old limbs, and looked down on
the maze of wire tunnels.

When he'd seen the running figure, he'd taken a moment to check his map again and jumped down, positioned himself in a place to step out.

He hadn't thought what his words would be. There had been no plan and no thought of danger, and that had worked. They had only moments.

He'd jemmied open the door of a garage and flung it closed behind them, wedging a concrete brick to it. Now they stood in an oily space with no lights. It felt like a room for an execution.

Douglas' hand went to his knife. He looked like a scared rat. He would do or say anything to get away. "What truth?" he said.

"The truth. About who you are. About what you're doing here."

"I am... who I am."

Cleves couldn't hold back any more. He stepped right up to Leyton, into the way of his knife. "You're him, aren't you? That's where you went. You could still travel in time. You're older, you've lived here a long time, but you're him. That's why I'm supposed to kill you, that's why I'm trying to save you."

"I'm who?"

"The man from the future. Squadron Leader Douglas Leyton. You're not just his ancestor. You *are* him!"

Leyton looked at the ground. "You're Frederick Cleves," he said. "I knew. I was going to do what I have to do. The priest I killed. He told me."

And with that Cleves knew. Leyton knew his name only because he had told him. Days ago in his life. Years ago in the life of this man. "Tell me what happened. How did you get here? What do I have to do?"

Leyton looked at the ground. "I did things to my head. To try and... It needs two heads. Not just head to gut."

"You were trying to be a head?"

"I wanted to get home. I knew I was going to... I knew who I was going to be." His watery eyes fixed on Cleves. "I knew who this Douglas Leyton person was. I'd read the newspapers. I'd been misidentified as him. I met him, briefly. That hasn't happened yet." He took out his knife, looking at it from all angles, as if contemplating how to take apart a carcass. "I was appalled at what was in front of me. I had taken on this weight deliberately, but... my strength failed me. I was weak. I started to tinker with my head, to try to fix something up, to learn what I could. To escape my burden. That sounds like a good story, doesn't it? 'Tinker' doesn't sound like me at all..."

His speech was wandering. Cleves stared at him. He might be the same man, but what good was finding him like this? He had only moments.

He reached into his pocket. He pulled out the identity card Leyton had left in the wreck. He grabbed Leyton's hand and slapped it onto his palm.

The card lit up in recognition.

Leyton stared at his own face, twenty years younger, glowing at him.

"What time is it?" he asked.

"Nearly four," said Cleves.

"Where is he?"

"Who?"

Leyton held up the card. "Me."

Cleves quickly wet his lips with his tongue. "He escaped with the head and the girl. I gather they fled through time."

"Then it's nearly over," said Leyton. "Oh Lord, it's nearly over. It can be. If I want it to be. I can go home. I can be something someone else wants me to be. Needs me to be. I can see the line. Got to the point. Finally. Jolly good thing too."

"I don't know what you're talking about. Please—"

Leyton slipped his knife back into his breast pocket. "I have so little time," he said. "You have to find me. You will find me. In about four hours. Keep the Golden Men anticipating. Tell them."

"How?"

"By telling whoever sent you after me. I'll be with Patrick Flint. A major news story."

"Who's Patrick Flint?"

"He's a billionaire. Now I have to go. Get a tank of petrol. While I still can." He made to go to the door.

Cleves got in his way for a moment. If he went... if he wasn't telling the truth... if none of this was true, and all that there was was rain and paperwork... the Watchers would be here in a moment.

Leyton looked at him.

Cleves stepped aside.

Leyton went to the door, hauled it up and ran out into the darkness and the rain, not looking right or left.

Cleves swiftly followed him. There were shouts from outside.

He closed the door behind him. He made sure there was no sign of it having been opened, nothing that would be spotted in the dark, anyway.

He carefully lay down on the ground and the rain fell into his face for a full minute before the Watchers found him.

Twenty-Eight: Terms and Conditions Apply

Patrick Flint was a very rich man.

He had booked himself into the Parade Hotel as soon as it happened, into the suite right at the top, which looked down on the weir from a great height. It had become his home. Now he stood in his new clothes by the window, watching the rain in the small hours of the morning. Dawn was starting to colour the storm clouds to the east. He was aware of his new high-performance car in the garage below. He had ordered champagne from the attentive all-night room service, and was drinking it very fast.

He had made massive donations to charity. He had done what he thought Alison would want him to do. He had not called her. He had made the *Big Issue* operation secure in this town for the next decade. His parents were already well-to-do, but he had made sure, through investments, that none of his family would ever have to worry. He had called Fran's parents too, and tried to find a way to give them money, but they were concerned only with the whereabouts of their daughter and had asked if Alison had managed to get hold of her, or if he had seen her. They were still where this dream had started, when all the rest of them had been grabbed... or mown down or flung about or something. Lucky bastards. He winced at that terrible guilty gut thought. They weren't lucky. Of course they weren't. They'd lost a daughter to torture. He'd been back to the house, stood across the street many times. He'd seen nobody there. He'd tried to remember the ceremony, to call the Bears himself, but he'd always stopped or "forgotten" how to do it. He didn't know what he'd say or do if they appeared. Fight them. But how? And wouldn't that be wrong? He'd taken their money.

He had lied to Fran's folks. He hadn't managed to find a way to bring his offer of cash for them into the conversation. He had put the phone down and taken a chair in this wonderful room and had smashed it into the carpet. Then he had called room service and asked for it to be removed. He had given the woman who came to do it a huge tip, and had rung down to the concierge and had had to actively persuade him that he should pay for a replacement chair.

If he couldn't do that for Fran, he didn't know how he could even begin with Marty's folks. They lived in Salford. They'd all gone up there once, ice skating. Marty had skated in a straight line, his arms held out to either side. Incapable, but no fear. He'd just guffawed until he fell.

There had been no police, no interview, nobody asking questions about Marty.

He could feel the silence through the window.

In the window, he could see the reflection of the noose that dangled from the light fitting. He'd hauled on it, checked the shape of the knot, made sure there was a clear leap from the bed now that the chair was gone.

He'd been to a solicitor today, and made arrangements for his huge, mad wealth to all go to places where it would do good. He was doing this very well. *Now*, he was doing things very well. But he could hear what those weird kids who hung out with the Golden Man would say about that. Great. The solicitor gets a bit. Profit is made everywhere. The charities employ people. They help people who are outside the system get back into it.

He would be a tiny wave in the ocean, a little ripple, pulled under. The one who'd been unable to fight the deluge. The one who'd given in.

The world was theirs. It had always been theirs. His last gestures were his hand going under. He'd left some of the cash to Alison and Fran. They'd either like that, with how they were now, or maybe they'd fight. If anyone was ever going to fight, it would be them.

He finished the champagne and turned.

He thought about undressing, but no. He didn't want the maid who found him to see his little belly. He'd look less frightening dressed, less strange. He had considered a note, too. But what would it say? Nothing that anyone would want to record, or believe.

He put down the glass.

He stood on the bed, reached for the noose and tugged on it again. The ceiling rose held.

Oh well.

He put the noose around his neck and pulled it tight. He backed up along the bed, feeling like a little boy: the springiness under his feet, *bounce bounce*. Back to his childhood, or fighting Alison with pillows.

Alison would miss him. He was being selfish.

No, she wouldn't. She was theirs now. Like he was. Well, no more.

"I'm sorry, Marty," he said.

He ran for the end of the bed, his arms flailing in panic.

He leapt. His eyes closed.

Impact. He felt the noose constrict suddenly at his neck.

He felt like his head was going to explode.

His eyes popped open.

He was hanging there, slowly rotating, his toes trying to reach the floor. His neck hadn't snapped. He clawed at the rope. He couldn't budge it.

The room was turning grey. He was going to die slowly. So... stupid!

It wouldn't be long until he passed out. He must. He must try!

The room stayed grey. A great hurt started pounding in his head.

He was trying to breathe. He should swing on the rope, hold it, use his muscles, get his feet onto the bed. His feet were bicycling, trying to save him. But he mustn't—he couldn't try and fail. He had to let go and die, no matter how.

He heard the door open and felt a wave of shame. They'd found him. It would look like something sexual. He wanted to say something, but couldn't. He kept on hanging, flailing, dying.

The man walked in front of him. It was Alison's friend, Leyton. How—?

He looked different. Older.

He took something from his coat. A knife. He was smiling at Patrick.

Ridiculously, Patrick started to panic that Leyton was going to kill him.

The man reached up, found the weak point in the noose and slipped the knife into it.

The rope whacked to the ceiling. Patrick hit the ground. The noose broke from his neck. His lungs sucked in a huge breath, which hurt like burning.

He stumbled, rolled to his knees, crawled.

When he slumped by the bed, he saw that Leyton had sat down against the wall and was looking at him, interested, playing with his knife. "Get yourself cleaned up," he said. "We have a mission."

Twenty-Nine: The Four Horsemen

The cave called Seventh Heaven contracted and sealed itself as the *Crimson Dragon* burst from it.

Alison was glad that this time she didn't see it departing. She was sitting in the passenger seat. Beside her was Leyton, at the controls, while Jocelyn navigated using her quantum computers. Alison's help was not needed this time.

They had waited a day before doing this, a day of silence and darkness as they conserved their energy and ran out of fuel for the torches. Jocelyn said that they were waiting because they had to. The maps she had seen showed that they didn't leave immediately, but waited for this time. Thus the rift they were following, the wound in the body of spacetime that they were lancing and creating, visited the caves only then, and only then could they decide to escape.

Alison had tried to pray. She didn't know how. It was just words she said inside, words she was used to saying as a child. But now they found the shape of something in the darkness of the cave. They described something. It was like a source of confidence and strength, not the product of the Golden Men's eye, but instead of it: a solid shine or hum of continuing, eternal *somethingness*. She'd missed it before because of all the noise. She understood why they called it radiance.

It was very simple. It told her only that everything would be okay. And it told her that at a level beneath words.

It troubled her that it could be an anaesthetic, or even a stimulant that made you an addict, like the eye drug had been. It had gravity. It pulled you towards it. It was the centre of the pattern. You could lose who you were to it. But Alison got the feeling it didn't want that. That it was just real. Many of the words on top of that were the sort of words the angels, the Golden Men, talked.

So she understood, but didn't accept; kept it at a distance from her while taking on the love. Like her and Leyton. They had each other for only so long, so they felt a space. But they had each other now, so they didn't. They'd made love on the last night, before Alison's vigil, having left Jocelyn on the other side of the ship.

Her future self had told them to go home and find Patrick. She had listened to the song so many times; the map agreed. So they left as dawn was coming up outside, before the bats returned.

Alison looked out of the ship's cockpit now into the dreaming. It was pure black out there, as it was for everyone except heads like Jocelyn. They could see the ship, the spear, falling through the red.

But suddenly, the view outside, even to Alison's eye, turned red.

The Golden Men had found them.

Outside the *Crimson Dragon*, swirls of gold turned into hands in the red, faces looming over them, crossing spears of their own. All four of them were here. They had in their hands the fire that had destroyed a city.

Perhaps this was the point they knew they could kill them. Or would kill them. Perhaps they had read the maps too.

Leyton looked up from his controls. "Four targets on the radar," he shouted. "I'm engaging them."

"Nobody's ever had a battle in a dreaming before, Skip," said Jocelyn. "We're making history."

"Nice choice of words," he murmured. His thumb flicked a button on the joystick and the ship bucked as something left it.

A moment later, four blooms appeared on the screens dotted around the cabin.

"They're still there," said Leyton after a second. "They got out of the way. How long before we're out of this?"

"As long as it takes!" called Jocelyn.

"Right-ho." Leyton grabbed the joystick and pulled it back. "Let's show these blighters what we can do."

The spear spun in the wound.

Christ was on the point of death. He was laughing at the angel that stood in the sky looking down at Him. "Now you see," He said, "it is as if one of your horsemen is Me. As if a quarter of your legion is Me. By which I mean in undoing God's work, you will always do it."

The Golden Man spoke. "We will only be born if we undo it. We are fighting to be created."

Jesus saw the wound in His side, blood and water pouring out. "You are born from My side," he told the angel. "So you are created. But you will not see you are part of My Father's plan until that plan is accomplished. So you will not enter the body again until the body is done. That pattern will be called sanctuary."

It was done as it had always been done. He had seen what was written, and had realised that He had to write it.

"It's done," He said, still smiling.

And He died.

In the dawn, across the British Isles in the early years of the twenty-first century, tiny history was happening. The repetition of it across the world made it bigger history.

Convoys of trucks met, their drivers exchanged greetings and made sure of their directions. They talked to police officers who stopped to ask what was happening. They'd expected something like this. They radioed it in. The pattern began to form.

A people's protest. A throwing down of coins. Good-natured men and women arrived with their mugs of tea and their placards outside the huge oil terminal on the Severn Estuary near Bristol. The silvery domes shone dull in the early light under the storms. They talked to security men and drivers, who all agreed, quickly and simply, that there was no point in trying to run this blockade to get petrol to the stations of the West Country. There had been no memo telling them to do that. Only an understanding, an implication, a suit wandering around the canteen having words. Even those words had been neutral, the subject of misunderstanding, one thing, but entirely another.

This protest was for the good of everyone.

And the rain poured down on them all.

Before the news organisations woke up, the dozen major oil refineries from Scotland to Essex had been cordoned off by what amounted to just a ribbon, a token. The ribbon pulled tight. The government was under pressure.

It happened everywhere there was any question of raising the price of fuel. It was a global force, a demand for lower prices for the little man, for free trade, against the great forces that were ranged against the individual.

The only protest against the rights of the individual would be by anarchists on May Day, who cared nothing for any cause, public safety, or property, and spoilt the holiday for thousands of people: a minority of thugs who sought only violence, who were a distraction from those who were using their rights to peacefully protest. Their actions cost the City millions every year.

Amongst this moved Restoration. They led the news agenda with examples of peaceful protest and police acceptance.

Cleves was following it all, theoretically in charge, so he gave orders every now and then through his arranged back doors from his car. He waited on a hill called Pennsylvania on the Bath to Bristol road, his laptop receiving and distributing information. He cared nothing at all for this. He was on the wrong side. At least he knew it. He was waiting for the moment when he could change.

His Watchers had found, and were following, the man called Patrick Flint. Beside him walked Leyton. They kept asking if they should move on Leyton, if the kill order was still on. Cleves told them to wait and see what they were up to. He had called his old friend George and told him that they were about to move in on Leyton. That it would happen any second.

He heard that Flint was intercepting news crews and, oddly, taking some of them off course from the protests. How he was doing that, he didn't know. Vast bribes, perhaps. Career-changing ones.

Not all of them went, of course.

Cleves touched the tiny handgun he had taken from his safe that morning, in the holster under his armpit. He had never worn it before. He found himself feeling it more and more.

April, 100 AD

Judas sat with his daughter with their backs to a tree, eating apples. He was an old man now. She was fifteen, the daughter of his third wife, a Jewish woman called Sarah who he could never convince of the Word—though he kept trying. They lived where the Law paid them no heed and nobody asked their business. His daughter had asked him today about the marks on his skin, and why he had ever been that despairing when the tales he told her were full of joy and hope. She could see, he was certain now, as well as he did. She could read the world, better than her brothers and sisters.

So they had walked in the orchard behind his farm at twilight and had talked about sadness.

She had suddenly asked him when the World would End.

"It won't," he said.

"But the Empire will split up. Everything will be chaos. It's obvious! The priests say the Christ will return then."

"He said only love will set you free. That there will be birth pangs. That the Kingdom will come."

"So why is the end sitting there, like a rock in our way? You told me about the Revelation to John."

Judas laughed, which annoyed her. "Rocks get moved. They roll away at the last moment. And the Revelation is certainly a rock. I've read some of the versions that have been sent around from the churches. What shit! No, what seems to be put there for the end is really there for the beginning."

"How do you know that?"

His old eyes looked into the distance and saw someone on the brow of the hill, at the end of the orchard. He was walking towards them: a light through the trees, as if he carried a lantern. "I don't know," he said. "Go and tell your mother we have a guest. A stranger. We must be ready to welcome him."

His daughter got up and looked down the meadow. "I don't see—"

"Everything that I do. But you will. Now go on."

She frowned and walked back towards the house.

Judas got to his feet and started to walk towards the man. A slow smile spread across his face.

For the first time in decades, he was surprised. He held his arms wide to respond to the greeting.

They found him lying there, the apple in his hand, spread out, hugging the earth.

When they rolled him over, they found the smile still on his face, and peace in his eyes.

Hohiti Kenton left the screening early. He wandered out into the gardens outside the preview theatre and watched the fuel-cell buggies with courting couples in them dancing against the moon.

He didn't want to be there for the cast and crew to applaud. He felt like a cheat. He hadn't completed it. He hadn't done what he'd set out to do. His false creator figure, Lamb, had appeared and then vanished, an obvious trick, a piece of art rather than someone in a story. And yet he'd already heard people in the crew talking about Lamb as if he were real, as if he'd actually come up with all the new techniques that had kept Alison's head alive, but been unwilling to take any credit for them.

He stopped himself, looking down from a little bridge over the River Fleet. Huge, healthy flowers grew on the banks, modified to soak up the pollutants of the street and feed on them. There were more of the sounds of courting coming from under the arch: laughter, murmured declarations of love. He shouldn't think that badly of the public. They weren't stupid. They'd take Lamb to be what he was, a gesture that there was a gap.

It was just that he shouldn't have made a movie with a gap.

He closed his eyes and prayed for a moment and felt the closeness of the Divine. The enlightened moment of History, in his case. He felt a little better, as he always did when he used the words of Marx. The idea of synthesis, of opposites coming together like waves, time and time again, until they produced a divine standing wave, was at the heart of who he was. He had dedicated the picture to History, and to Alison. The same thing.

He felt like he was listening to the lovers now. He blushed.

He went back along the bridge and decided to have drinks with his crew and conceal his anger over his unfinished portrait. It would be rude to do otherwise, and would send out a bad signal to the journalists present. He would claim illness. All would be settled in time. He just hoped that one day he would be able to know that truth for himself.

Leyton completed the loop, taking the *Crimson Dragon* over in a giddy spiral.

The four Golden Men roared after them.

Alison saw it. She saw Jocelyn reaching for the place where home and safety was.

The Golden Men threw their spears.

One swept through the silent engines.

One skewered the wing and sailed on through.

One missed.

And one hit the back of the cockpit.

The canopy shattered upwards.

Leyton rose in his straps. There was nothing to breathe.

The dream red rained down on them. In a moment it would engulf them.

"Jocelyn!" Alison screamed. "We have to get out of here now!"

And so they did.

The *Crimson Dragon* burst into existence high in the sky over the rainy land below.

Oxygen masks broke from the cockpit in front of them. Leyton grabbed the stick with his boots and put his on. Alison waved a hand to grab hers and slipped it over her face.

The wind hit seconds later. They were low. Her hair billowed up. The straps held her down. She was groggy. Jocelyn was smiling giddily at her, not needing to breathe, anchored down.

The air of home, even this high, even like this, tasted so sweet compared to the air of the future.

"Here we go!" yelled Leyton over the comms link. "That's home down there!"

"Home?" said Alison.

Leyton laughed. "Britain, anyhow. Whatever it is, it'll do."

He hit a control and a roar and a push sounded from beneath and behind them. They were coming in under power. Alison saw the landscape she'd grown up in spiralling giddily towards her. The West Country. They were heading for a long thin strip of land. An airfield. "A tiny one," called Jocelyn. "But the strip's long enough."

From behind them, there came an impossible noise: a vast discord, a clarion. Like the universe breaking.

The four Golden Men burst from space behind them in a shower of gold and fell at them, their voices keening in the increasing thickness of the air. The atmosphere buckled around them, licked them with fire, gave them steeds like waves breaking on the shore.

"Angels at twelve o'clock!" shouted Leyton.

"How tiresome of them," said Jocelyn.

The *Crimson Dragon* hurtled towards the green and grey far below.

The television cameras at the tiny airstrip in Dorset were already pointing up, watching Patrick, who stood at the top of the steps that led to the radio hut that was the tower.

He had paid three local roving news camera crews amounts of money that, should they wish, would allow them to retire. A couple of them were on their mobiles, hoping to keep their jobs even now, trying to fob off producers who were demanding they be elsewhere. Every petrol station on the way here had had a queue of cars that led back a mile, and this was just after breakfast on the first morning. He had done all this on the orders of Douglas Leyton, who was standing there with a curious and ever-growing crowd of locals who had seen something was going on, assumed it was to do with the protests and come to see.

They were looking up at him as if he were some sort of leader, Patrick realised. But it was actually Leyton, moving amongst them, talking to them calmly, being everyone he had ever been, that would be leading them. They started chants every now and then, about bringing down the government, about how the countryside would fight on.

Patrick had no cause beyond the one he'd been given.

He looked at the sky again, and then at his watch.

"Soon," he said into the microphone, and heard his voice, a second later, burst around the edges of the aerodrome from the speakers. "Soon you will see... what you came here to see."

The crowd shifted and started to boo and call out insults. For a moment Patrick thought they were angry at him, but then he saw that, through the gates, a number of official-looking cars were approaching. "Fight!" the crowd started chanting. "Fight!"

From the cars stepped ordinary men in suits. Behind them came an old man.

Patrick looked into the crowd. He couldn't see Leyton. He put a hand to his throat, feeling the rope burn beneath his high collar. He had to say something. "Who are you?" he called to the man.

The crowd had half approached, half fallen back from the cars. The old man walked up to them, took a couple of steps through them, as if looking for someone. The crowd started to repeat Patrick's question, in smaller, more complicated variations. The old man looked up to Patrick on the steps and called something out. He had to repeat it several times before Patrick heard it.

"I'm Frederick Cleves."

This caused a bit of a stir amongst the men who'd arrived with the old man.

"What do you want?"

Cleves opened his mouth, and for a moment Patrick thought he'd said something. But he hadn't. The crowd noise rose and fell as everyone tried· to hear and asked what they'd heard.

But then someone gasped.

Patrick looked up, because a section of the crowd was looking up.

The sun was in the wrong place. No, there were two suns, illuminating the lowest level of cloud, right overhead, and to the east.

A single boom like thunder hit the ground.

It broke through the clouds.

The crowd yelled.

A silver spacecraft was roaring down towards them, its wings blazing with the heat. The crowd swayed, panicking, starting to run, wanting to see. The old man stayed exactly where he was, and so did Patrick. No more running for him now.

The camera crews stayed, all their attention on the sky. "Are you getting this?" one reporter was shouting into her phone. "Are you getting this?"

He narrowed his eyes. Was it him, or did that ship have RAF roundcls on its wings? The cabin was a mess. And there were scars, blackened sections of fuselage.

He didn't have time to think anything else.

The craft shot overhead, a giant shadow with a giant noise.

It arced up into the air, turning, its silver wings shining.

And behind it, through the clouds, arrived something else.

They were gigantic. They turned the sky into a backdrop of red and gold. They were angels coming down to Earth. Monstrous angels.

There were four of them: Golden Men on frothing golden horses, their limbs one with the creatures in a slowly boiling image that twisted and turned against the sky.

They were getting closer. They were coming down.

The crowd started to bellow and scream like dying cattle.

The silver craft turned in the direction of thc Golden Men and light lanced from its wings. Missiles became lines of white in the air. Explosions buckled the vision, made the Golden Men writhe and scatter out of the way of the concussions.

Patrick fell to his knees. He could see, in the crowd, Douglas fighting his way through, heading for the airstrip, Cleves standing, staring, his face set hard against the screaming mass around him.

The camera crews were doing their best to train their equipment on the images above.

But then everything changed. The giant golden figures became light, falling shafts of light, like leaves twisting in a hard breeze down to Earth.

The craft was skidding against the sky, firing flame from its sides. It was slowing, angling down, heading in a long low pass towards the brown line of the runway.

"That's all we have!" called Jocelyn. "Told you it'd be useless in combat."

"So we'll meet them on the ground," said Leyton, hauling back on the stick to bring the nose up.

Alison watched the green field thundering up at them. All the people, running and screaming. She had to find Patrick in that lot, but she didn't know why.

The landing gear extended with a roar. Moments later they hit, rolled along, jets whining backwards. Then they started to slow.

She looked frantically upwards. Where had the Golden Men gone? Were they streaking down from above now, looming in for the kill?

The craft halted, a heat haze flickering the shape of it.

Half of the crowd was running towards it, half away.

The camera crews were sprinting for it, their gear activated, their images bouncing. Breath in microphones, reporters frantic to keep up.

The Golden Men slid into view between them and it.

The crowd skidded to a halt.

The pictures from this sight, Patrick realised, as he wandered numbly through the mass of calling and yelling and screaming people, would be the lead item on every immediate news service now, would wipe the fuel blockades off the front pages, would be the most important sight on Earth.

The Golden Men stood. They had spears. They were from another world. They looked ready to make a proclamation.

Then something scrambled from the blasted cockpit of what looked so like a British spacecraft. He stood up against the sky. The viewpoints focused in on him. He filled the frame.

He stood in his coat and his cap, one hand up to shield his eyes from the glare of the Golden Men. He was aware of the gaze of the cameras upon him. "Hey!" he called. "Give a fella a hand with these chumps?"

The Golden Men turned.

He leapt out and walked towards them. And now every eye in the world was on him, and what he was going to do.

"Who are you?" called a reporter from the crowd.

"Squadron Leader Douglas Leyton, World Spacefleet. I'm from your future."

Patrick blinked. That was Alison's mate. He looked back to the craft and saw a smaller figure climbing down from it. She dropped to the ground and ran, at an angle from the Golden Men, towards the crowd.

It was Alison! He started to push his way through to meet her.

Cleves stared at what was happening in front of him.

Leyton's words had galvanised one of the Golden Men. It flashed towards him, the spear ready to run him through.

Leyton swung his body and met its chin with a solid right hook.

The Golden Man was thrown off his feet.

The crowd cheered.

They instantly knew whose side they were on, Cleves realised, just from pictures. And the pictures would now be flashing around the world, getting into the eyes and minds of all humanity, giving them a future. Giving them hope.

"Open fire!" he yelled to his men. "Give him some cover!"

The officers ran forward and assumed firing stances. Tiny cracks started to sound across the field and one of the Golden Men staggered, knocked this way and that by the bullets, wounds blooming on his body.

Another of them fluttered at the crowd and most of it reeled back, but a few of them, strong young farmers who'd come here for a fight, leapt at it.

They grabbed its spear.

They were on top of it. Their anger had come bursting out of them. They were ripping it apart. The crowd roared and advanced.

They swept into where Leyton was dodging the spears of two Golden Men.

Cleves saw Douglas in the crowd. He was struggling in that direction.

He made after him.

He fell just as Douglas and Leyton collided.

He looked up and saw them staring at each other, just for a moment. He saw Leyton's face fall as he understood the man was him, that this was what he was going to be. Then the face rallied. The expression clenched down on pain and anger and came up with hope.

He grabbed the hand of his older self, whose face was accepting, remembering, filled with the pain of nostalgia. The handshake was full of purpose. Their eyes met.

A Golden Man surged through the crowd, ripping them to shreds in a blur of movement. He was like a tornado of flesh. He was bearing down straight at the two Leytons to make the final stab. To spear them and change the world.

Cleves stood up.

He leapt forward.

He found the tiny handgun under his arm.

He pulled it out. He threw himself at the blur of slicing motion in front of him.

The gun shoved up into it at an odd angle. He felt the wind of blood on his face. And something warm happened in his body below.

He pulled the trigger.

The tornado exploded into a thrashing shape, thrown aside at speed.
It hit the ground and was a Golden Man with a hole in his body.
Cleves looked down.
His eyes filled with blood before he could see.
He fell to the grass on his knees.
He never felt his head hit the ground.

Patrick grabbed Alison and swung her out of the way.
"You're you!" he was shouting. "You again! Sweetheart, I never thought I'd get to see you!"
But Alison turned her head to see that Leyton was okay.
He was, standing back from a crowd that were on top of a Golden Man now, screaming at it, wrenching at it, holding it down by their weight, snapping its spear into smaller and smaller pieces that were being scattered and seized upon. He was walking towards them, his hands in the air, starting to ask them to stop, to show mercy. His coat was covered in blood.
And there was a figure running for the ship, sprinting across the airstrip.
And one Golden Man was swirling after him.
"Leyton!" she yelled. "The last one! Stop him!"

Douglas now knew nothing but running.
He had seen what he used to be. He would have hated what he had become, only now he saw the purpose of what he had become and the uselessness of fighting against it, how fighting it had corrupted him.
But everything would be forgiven if he could only get to his ship.
He leapt for the ladder.
The Golden Man filled the air around him. The blade sliced the air by his head. Hands grabbed his shoulders, trying to lever him off.
The ground moved under them both.
The *Crimson Dragon* had leapt into the air, floated there on her rockets.
He stared at Jocelyn through the canopy. She raised an eyebrow at him.
Powerful hands seized the Golden Man from below, but the Golden Man held on.
Douglas hung on, his limbs stretching, caught between the two worlds.
Below him, he could see his younger self, doing as he remembered doing, running for the Golden Man. Leaping.
The weight of himself dragged on Douglas Leyton's legs for a moment.
Then it all fell away.

The *Crimson Dragon* burst upwards.

He clung onto the ladder. Then he swung a leg into the cockpit. Then both. Then he was sitting in his old seat. His hands found the joystick. Then let go again, accepting his fate. He turned to Jocelyn. He ripped off what remained of his disguises. "Hullo, Joss," he said.

"Long time no see," said Jocelyn. "Welcome back, Skipper."

The spacecraft fell from the sky.

Alison dragged Leyton from the mass of people who had thrown themselves at the last Golden Man. His eyes were fixed on the shining mass of the *Crimson Dragon* as it ascended, and then suddenly started to fall.

"No!" he shouted. "It should be me! It should—"

The rift blew them off their feet.

It was the first time Alison had seen it from outside. It was like a concentrated knot of the universe had suddenly come slicing into the world. It went across and down and through the ups and downs and acrosses at once.

The crowd bloomed into the air. The Golden Man went at their centre. They stretched into a plume of flesh as the shape of the ground beneath them bulged like it was giving birth. The Golden Man burst into the sky and vanished.

Alison felt a tug on her eyes. She held onto Leyton. She was aware of Patrick, somewhere behind her, shouting what sounded like prayers.

And then everything changed.

May, 1947

Douglas saw the little village speeding up at him: the fields of Kent.

"It's finished," he sighed. And he realised that he had been given a great blessing. This time, he had done his duty consciously. He had written something of his own.

"It's been an honour serving with you," said Jocelyn.

"Forgive us our sins," said Douglas Leyton. "As we forgive—"

Jocelyn vanished in a blur of motion into her secure compartment.

The land reared up at the cockpit.

The aircrew from the nearby airfield were there in a matter of minutes.

They found an almost complete example of an aircraft that looked far in advance of anything they'd ever seen, but the roundels on the wings said it was one of theirs. And the materials of the wings and the fuselage didn't look *that* far beyond what they were capable of.

They found the body of a pilot, crushed in the forward cockpit. The craft had landed on its nose.

They were horrified by what they found as the door on the rear compartment opened. "Find the flight recorder, chaps," said the woman, with an accent and a look that completely undermined her monstrous appearance.

The RAF boys asked her who the pilot had been. Why they'd crashed.

"He saved us all," she said.

Thirty: Imbolc

It was a summery sort of spring, and the sky was pure blue and empty of clouds, and Fran was up on Bathford Hill, watching Alison sing at her own wedding.

Fran was the Maid of Honour.

As she stood there, smiling, listening proudly, she remembered.

The history books told the basics, how Alison and Douglas Leyton and Patrick had all woken up, last autumn, with hundreds of other people, in a sunny green field in Dorset. They all knew something huge and wonderful had happened. But they had no idea what. They wandered about talking to each other. They realised that, beneath the memories of their regular lives, they all had strange, askew memories of another existence. A fuel-cell buggy slipped out of the blue overhead and landed and two World Security officers staggered out. They just wanted to talk to someone, to share the sudden impressions that had entered their minds.

They, like everyone else in the world now did, remembered the fears and tensions of living in a nation state, armed against other nations, where they had no guarantee of having enough food, where they had to compete with each other, and do things all their lives they didn't enjoy. They remembered using money. Those who had been in the field remembered Golden Men, and a silver ship.

Leyton, he'd since told Fran, was the only one who didn't have two lives in his head, which suited him, since he also had to put up with living in the wrong time. On that extraordinary morning, he'd just smiled at Alison and said he hoped she remembered who he was. And then he'd kissed her.

People came up to them and started asking, wasn't she Alison Parmeter? They were amazed. They started asking for autographs.

"This is my boyfriend," Alison had told them. And as she'd signed the first piece of paper, she'd whispered to him, "I'm going to have to learn how to play the piano."

The number of times they'd told Fran that.

That was the big change. The memories sank into the world. They made things different. Everyone had something to compare themselves to. They had the airy, joyful knowledge of who they were today, and the gut sensation of what they could have been, had things been terribly different.

"When they meet the Rods," Alison said to Fran as they staggered from inn to inn through the streets of Bath on one perfect October night, "they're going to treat them differently. They're not going to get into a war with them. They're going to understand how they feel."

"What are Rods?"

"Aliens. I mean Foreigners."

"Oh. Do you think that's what this has all been about?"

She thought about that for a long time. "That," she said, "and giving Leyton and me some time together."

That turned out to be the night, when she got home, that Leyton asked Alison to marry him.

Just before the landlord of the final inn had told them that they'd hit the Beer Limit and he couldn't give them any more, Alison had told Fran that Leyton was going to do that.

Alison had her own set of memories from this timeline, to go along with the memories she'd brought with her from Hell. She told Fran that she still felt it was that way round, for her, that Earthly reality felt like it was laid on top of her hellish original existence. That, along with her insight, was, Fran thought, what made Alison the artist she was.

Those memories went like this: Patrick had knocked on Alison's door that morning, asking her to come quickly, because there was something on the news about a spaceship landing in Dorset. He'd been trying to win her back, as he did every time he lost his latest girlfriend. The two of them had rushed down to the place where everything seemed to be happening by grabbing hold of one of the fuel-cell buggies that were racing to the scene.

After the Memories had burst into the world, and Alison had suddenly gained a lover in the form of Leyton, they'd come back to the city to find Fran straight away.

She was completely out of it. The Memories had hit her hard.

They found her at Marty's grave, sobbing her heart out.

It had been a cerebral haemorrhage. Fran had grieved, but at least, she had thought, it had been quick. Marty had worked so hard at his forest management, he'd just over-stretched himself, doing what he loved best. But now she had terrible memories of how he'd died in another way: a vision of him being ripped apart. In that vision, she laughed at his pain and did nothing to help.

Fran couldn't say that vision hadn't changed her. The Memories of Hell had changed lots of people. It was all for the better. It made the good things feel more precious. A couple of weeks later Alison and Fran took a portion of chips together and thought about having to pay for them, and Fran had burst out crying and thanked the Lord and Lady for where she was now.

She was glad that Alison was there. She held her, and for the first time she said it to her. "Thank you. For coming to rescue me."

So here they stood, at Imbolc. Fran had watched Alison and Leyton being handfasted by a priestess and married by a vicar, with Patrick and their other friends attending. Fran's mum and dad had stood in for Leyton's family. Patrick had a serious girlfriend with him. Alison and Leyton both said both sets of blessings, and the gathering, mostly, said both sets of prayers.

A few of those in the know had got nervous when Alison approached the piano. But after the first few notes they relaxed. Fran thought she had gained a kind of roughness, an honesty, an innocence.

She played and sang some old favourites, recorded by the handful of respectful journalists who wandered along, and then she began her first new composition, a religious song.

Below, Bath was shining in the sunshine.

A couple of days ago, Fran had been fretting about not being able to find a certain kind of lace for Alison's garter. Alison had said to her: "Fran, it's okay, these are only... patterns... details."

"But," Fran said, "God is in the details."

Fran had some dark in her now. And Alison had some light.

And then Fran had first smiled the smile that she wore again now. Alison had read that smile and knew.

In the end, however long that took, everything was going to be all right.

Epilogue: The Last Seven Unfoldings

September, 2019

They made love for the last time, that night at the villa. And they had prayed together. They had withdrawn from life for the last month or so, determined to enjoy their final weeks together, to gather all the things of their life into one place.

There had been no children, of course, though everyone expected them.

She sang to him afterwards, at the piano, remembering the words she had repeated over and over in her head and had secretly written down for years at a time, recopied and destroyed. But this was the first time that she'd recorded "On the Path of My God." He took the cartridge afterwards and put it in his pocket. He would take it with him when he left the house, so that it couldn't be found or damaged.

She understood what that tremor had been in her hands now: not fear of what was, but fear of what was to be, and relative inexperience, compared to the mighty instrumentalist she was supposed to be. The words comforted her, however, as they always had.

She kissed him for so long before he left, wondering how she could do this.

But they had to. It was this for the world. His sacrifice would be bigger.

He left by the back door, not wanting to encounter them as they moved up through the gardens.

Alison went to the big window and watched them come, tiny lights through the trees, trying to hide their presence.

She closed her eyes and prayed as she heard the side door being smashed in. "Thy Kingdom come," she said. "Thy will be done."

April, 2023

Hohiti Kenton waited for Douglas Leyton at the little restaurant, at the table beside the river where the pleasure boats would moor for lunch. He felt very nervous. Leyton had granted him the only interview he had given since Alison's second death. Since her first, even. He had agreed on the basis that he and the film director would spend a few days together, so that Leyton, as he put it, would "know who he was bally well talking to."

There he was! Hohiti leapt up as the man approached his table. He had not seen many recent photos. He was still straight-backed, square-shouldered. The garb of a priest suited him. He had been ordained only in the last month, having studied for Holy Orders ever since Alison's first death. He was the greatest mystery in Alison's life. Many people said he had been on the spacecraft that had brought the Memories to Earth. A handful said that he was the incarnation of Grace, or the Koew, as the Rods had it, with their whimsical belief system. They had recently exchanged some of their *body lengths*, who were now living the life of Earth and reporting home about it, for a precisely requested quantity of the Holy Spirit, or History, as Hohiti thought of it. Ironically.

Leyton's only public pronouncements had been to angrily deny that he was any sort of mystical being, which generally managed to finish off the rumours for another few years. He sat down opposite Hohiti and offered his hand, which the young man eagerly shook. He started to say this was an honour, Reverend—

Leyton silenced him with a gesture. "I very much doubt," he said, "that this film you want to make will ever be made now."

"But—"

"But you may be interested in this." He placed a cartridge on the table. It was labelled as the missing song, Hohiti realised, with a shock that caught him in the chest. "I can also answer all your questions about how Alison came to live her... second life. How the heads took us to meet our friends in the stars. I know who your 'Dr Lamb' really was."

"How do you know about my script?"

Leyton smiled sadly. "I've seen the movie," he said.

Hohiti's mouth slowly started to open.

He didn't understand what the noise from his right was.

Until the terrible weight and force hit him.

"I didn't know the accident would happen then, or how it would happen, old chap." Leyton was looking down at him now. "I just knew that it would be soon."

Hohiti was dead inside. He could not adjust to the idea of life as a head. His life had been saved from the aftermath of the speedboat wreck on Leyton's own recommendation. "You were right. I won't get to make my movie."

"You still could. The technology exists. And I would give you all my support. But which would you prefer, to make the movie or to know all the answers to your questions?"

"You know the answer to that. If I have to be like this."

"You don't. Not for very long."

September, 2019

Russell DaCosta brought the head into the operating theatre. Everyone turned to look. They were aware that they were being let in on one of the greatest secrets of the world government, a secret that had been kept for nearly three quarters of a century.

"Steady, chaps," said the old woman DaCosta had called Jocelyn. "Show me the patient."

The medics had been warned what to expect. Jocelyn was an ancient face on a metal collar. She had been an advisor to the King in 1947, and to World Presidents since there had been World Presidents. And now she was here to do something new. To create another like her.

They set her down on a prepared space beside Alison's body. They had cleaned the wounds and put her on a life support machine. But it was breathing for her. Brain activity was at a low that suggested she was approaching death, the pre-death dream that some said was one's preparation for the experience of God.

Jocelyn looked at Alison. She had waited so long for this sight.

She had known Alison and Leyton a little in their new lives. She had dined with them when they had had their audiences with the President. They had talked on the phone more. A gentle voice in the night.

But they had not been close. That was the burden they bore, the knowledge of time, bearing down upon them. The weekend Alison was due to die, Jocelyn didn't know how she could stand it. She isolated herself, cut off all communications.

But Leyton had finally arrived, his face a mask.

She had let him in, and when they were alone he had cried his heart out. This was not normal grief. He had been grieving for Alison with a quarter of himself since the day they were married, or before.

And now Jocelyn could do this last thing for Alison, and for herself. Because after this, she had just one more little thing to do before she could give herself up to history and die. She was quite looking forward to it. "All right," she said to her audience. "Let's start by looking at some technical specifications..."

June, 2023

The Reverend Douglas Leyton stood holding Hohiti under his arm in one of the hangars of the Spacefleet base at Boscombe Down. He had used all his favours, and Jocelyn's security clearance, to get here. He had said goodbye to her. He had disposed of the remainder of his and Alison's estate.

And so now they were looking at the *Crimson Dragon*, updated with the latest available technology since it had been reconstructed "as an exercise" in 1952.

He went to the cockpit and placed Hohiti in the navigator's seat. The man had not had time to learn what he had to learn to survive this journey. He knew that. He had been resolved to do this since Leyton had told him of Jocelyn's part in the creation of head technology, how Alison had achieved her second life. Leyton got in in front of him.

He had taken care that he was not dressed as a man of the cloth today, but he had brought the materials of his job with him. He took communion with Hohiti inside the cockpit, and blessed the ship. He made it an instrument of the Divine Will.

Then he started up the navigation controls and set the engines to take them up a little way. He checked the time. There were seconds left before the rift passed through this point in spacetime. He sent the ship into a gentle hover. Whatever killed Hohiti, he was certain it hadn't been the crash.

The wound hit them.

And it took them. And Hohiti tried to ride it.

April, 29 AD

Judas Iscariot stumbled through the gateway of an orchard. It was night, a deep, silent night that felt like the Earth itself was mourning.

He had the money in his pocket. He had declared, to anyone in the street that would listen, that he was going to buy land, that he was going to make his mark on the world, to take some of it back for himself against the harm it had done him.

He was very drunk.

He had set aside the coil of rope in the corner of the meadow, over near where the cows were watered, earlier in the day. He had planned for this. He had kept himself drunk in planning for it. He did not want his plans being turned into yet more service, yet further terrible deeds.

He felt desperately guilty, desperately, horribly sorry. He had kept saying that he would do this, had kept himself apart from the others as if he had already done it, and had not seen any of them or been close enough to them to hear their voices.

He had gone to see his Lord and Master crucified. He had watched that with the crowd, from a distance.

Could there be, horribly, something still for him to do?

No. There could not be. Only die.

He went to the tree, threw the rope around it, secured the knot, placed it about his neck, climbed the branch, readied himself to fall.

He had placed the silver in the trunk of the tree, for his wife to find when she read his note. He was going to leave the world without the thirty pieces. Without money. Of course—how else could you leave it? Fool Judas.

He was so sorry. He wished to find someone to forgive him. He needed to find peace inside himself again. And all those things seemed so distant.

So the only way to find forgiveness was to die.

But those who took their own lives would not be forgiven.

Or so they said. Had not his Master shown him that love made anything possible?

But how was this love?

And why did he deserve love? Because he had carried out his Master's last desire. And had so killed Him. He did not deserve love at all.

It did not matter. He would subject his body to that separation between two ideas. He would leave his flesh and be smashed between things. He'd just do it and see.

He wanted sleep. He wanted dreams. He didn't want to do, or even to watch.

He let go of the tree.

The noose snapped about his neck.

The rope above his head snapped.

He hit the ground face down in the mud.

And, as the power of the drink shot up into his head, he fell asleep.

The *Crimson Dragon* soared through the wound in the body of the universe.

The Golden Men followed the ship. They played about it like lightning. They attacked Leyton because it was all they knew to do, from their point of view, from the time at the end of this journey.

Leyton kept his eyes on the instruments. He could hear Hohiti shouting and praying fervently from behind him. He was being pulled into the dream, he yelled. He pressed the button and Alison's music flooded the ship. Hohiti fixed upon it, concentrated on it, on what he'd lived his life thinking he would never hear. Their passage became easier.

The Golden Men were sweeping around the ship, suddenly hitting it, knocking it from side to side, toying with it. This was the first time they had seen anything like it.

"Not long now!" he shouted.

The ship fell into the darkness of the cave called Seventh Heaven.

The year was 1980.

The lights illuminated every corner of the space where no human had yet walked.

The ship touched down. The lights dimmed.

Leyton opened the cockpit.

He could feel them all around him, and in his heavy heart, but he knew they could not touch the craft, nor disturb the rest of Hohiti Kenton.

Hohiti's face was peaceful in death. He had been pulled into the dream and had elected to stay there. He would never be part of this hell.

Leyton stood up in his seat, reached for the ladder.

A spear sliced the air, slit his hand. The blood ran down the side of the cockpit. "No," he told the Golden Man that was forming and reforming, caught in the sanctuary that existed around the craft, caught by its own desire to enter. "You don't get out for many years yet."

Repeating prayers to keep them at bay, he stepped down the ladder and looked across the chamber. He dreaded what was ahead of him. But he knew that he could do it. He had carefully left the cartridge of Alison's song in the *Crimson Dragon*, not just so his younger self could find it, but so he wouldn't have it to torment himself in the years to come.

He remembered his path.

He reached the narrow chimney of rock and looked back to the ship.

The Golden Men were circling it, trying to get in.

He took the last wine and the last communion wafer from his pocket and performed the service. He made the cave part of the body of Christ, as it always had been. As the universe was.

The Golden Men were trapped here now, just for a while, inside one sanctuary, outside another.

"And so you'll stay," he said, "until the seventh seal is breached."

He left them then, in their floating golden circle, thinking about how they were now part of the story they thought they had written.

He put his foot on the lowest spur of rock and started to climb.

Darkness. Exhaustion. Pain. Despair.

And then light.

He pushed through the roots of a tree, hauled himself up amongst the lime soil and the gravel. His skin and clothing had been torn.

It was a rain-sodden, misty night. The fog hung on the black trees. The moon was visible above only as a lighter path of cloud. Water that tasted of chemicals fell into his eyes. He could hear the rumble of a distant motorway.

Douglas Leyton stumbled upright.

He would try to hold onto his virtue and himself in hell. He would try not to be changed by it.

He started walking off into the mist, remembered only by the ghost of a woman who, far away, that night, was being born.

And loved only by God.

About the Author

Paul Cornell's previous SF novel was *Something More*. He's worked extensively in British television, and on *Doctor Who* in its many different forms (including the episodes "Father's Day" and "Human Nature" for the new series). He's the creator of future archaeologist Bernice Summerfield, who's celebrating fifteen years of existence in her own range of books and audio plays. He also writes for Marvel Comics, starting with the miniseries "Wisdom," and his collected *2000AD* comic strip "XTNCT" is available from Rebellion Books. He lives in Oxfordshire.